Accidental Evils

Steve Dimodica

ISBN: 1542418097
ISBN 13: 9781542418096
Library of Congress Control Number: 2017900374
CreateSpace Independent Publishing Platform
North Charleston, South Carolina

Of your philosophy you make no use, if you give place to Accidental Evils.
—William Shakespeare

Acknowledgments

I WOULD LIKE to thank several individuals for their assistance in the writing of this novel: CW, a warrior for many years in SF; David, a DIA quiet professional; and my content editor, Lauren Longenecker, for her diligence and insight.

Prologue

September 21, 1976
Washington, DC

THE LARGE WHITE Chevy pulled into the driveway in Bethesda, Maryland. A young couple stepped from the car and entered the house. Twenty minutes later, the couple exited the home accompanied by a mustached man in his midforties. Together, the three climbed into the Chevy, allowing the older man to slide into the driver's seat behind the steering wheel. He shifted the car into reverse and backed the vehicle from the driveway. They started their daily commute into the District of Columbia.

The three passengers, an older boss and a recently married couple, were coworkers. They passed the time discussing the day's pending business and the dreary Washington weather. None of them noticed the gray sedan that followed several hundred feet to the rear, trailing them from the moment they left the affluent suburb.

The driver guided the Chevy along River Road to Forty-Sixth Street, then to Massachusetts Avenue, and finally slowed as they turned into the traffic of Sheridan Circle. This section of Massachusetts Avenue, often referred to as Embassy Row, quietly housed several foreign missions and diplomatic residences. It was a tranquil part of the nation's capital.

Suddenly a crackling sound grated under the driver's seat, followed by a white flash. A huge explosion rocked the car. Windows shattered, and the chassis buckled as the Chevy's frame lifted into the air. The vehicle lurched sideways, careening wildly before smashing back to the road and plowing into the side of a small Volkswagen parked in front of the Irish embassy.

The force of the blast tore the mustached driver's body in half, severing his legs at the hip and catapulting the limbs twenty feet from the car.

The young husband in the rear seat crawled through the fractured back window, only to see his dazed wife stumble from the front passenger seat toward the sidewalk.

He rushed to the aid of his boss. The driver was still trapped in the car, barely alive, semiconscious and in shock, his torso shredded, his head rolling sideways as he mumbled incoherently.

The husband tried to pull the driver from the Chevy to no avail. Then he rushed back to his now-collapsed wife, who was bleeding heavily from her mouth. A doctor who had been driving in Sheridan Circle at the moment of the explosion stopped to attend to the young woman.

Slowly the gray sedan that had tailed the Chevy from Bethesda glided to a crawl. The occupants took a long appraising look at the carnage in the street and then quickly sped up and exited the circle.

Chapter I

June 8, 2006
Washington, DC

ISABEL SOTO FINLEY stood between her parents and watched as the first woman president of Chile laid a wreath on the monument.

A small crowd had gathered along the grass in Sheridan Circle to watch the ceremony. It all seemed a bit surreal to young Izzy, yet she knew it carried deep emotional meaning for her mother. She heard her mother, Constanza, draw a deep breath, but rather than look up, Izzy chose to squeeze her hand. This was a poignant moment and therefore deserved respect.

"Let us always remember," said President Michelle Bachelet, "the journey that we as the proud people of Chile have long endured for the sake of dignity and the adherence to democracy and human rights."

Isabel's father, Arthur, wrapped his arm protectively over his daughter's shoulder, pulling her close as Bachelet spoke.

The three listened in silence as several more dignitaries delivered stark memories of the horrific day thirty years earlier.

A few news reporters had gathered for the event, the first official visit to the nation's capital of the recently elected Bachelet.

At the far side of the gathering, almost unnoticed by the onlookers, a lone photographer snapped pictures with a telephoto lens. The focus of his attention was not the Chilean president or the memorial, but rather the people in attendance. He took a close-up of Izzy and her parents.

After twenty minutes of prayers and short eulogies, the crowd began to separate. A few individuals placed flowers on the sidewalk next to the stone base of the monument dedicated to Orlando Letelier and Ronnie Moffitt. Then Izzy and her parents stepped forward, and her mom laid a single lily gently near the plaque. The middle-aged woman cried openly, tears flowing, and mumbled a quiet prayer.

After a few moments, the three turned and walked back to their car.

Chapter 2

December 14, 2006
Gladwyne, Pennsylvania

THE OWNER OF the mansion, a man named Burdis, leaned back in his wheelchair and swung the mouthpiece on the portable oxygen tank to his lips. He took a shot of air before speaking. "What did you say your names were again?"

"I'm Mike," said the first man, hovering over Burdis in the large study. He pointed to his left. "He's John."

"Got it," said Burdis, manually propelling his wheelchair toward the sitting area. "Over here, you will be more comfortable."

The two visitors followed their host across the study.

"I've been expecting this day for some time," said Burdis.

Mike shrugged. "It's only been about six months. They wanted to let things settle."

Burdis nodded and motioned with his hand, indicating that Mike and John should make themselves comfortable. "So, take an event, any event," said Burdis, pausing to suck in a second breath of oxygen, "that is at its core inherently evil."

The two visitors exchanged a look before John nodded.

"Now add to that event," said the cripple, "the unexpected consequences—both direct and indirect—that follow." Burdis leaned forward and made a great effort to choose his words carefully. "Then watch as those consequences flow disjointedly out of control."

Their host started to spasm, his face turning purple, coughing as he fought to expunge the air from his lungs. It took him a moment to regain control.

"This is the story," said Burdis, finally able to finish his thought, "of that accidental evil."

Mike removed his suit coat, folded it neatly, and laid it across the back of his chair. He looked down at their host and spoke quietly. "Maybe we'd better start at the beginning."

Chapter 3

Cusco, Peru

CALIXTO LOZEN BOUNDED up the crumbling stone steps. It was a rocky trail, contouring along the mountainside, settled in mist and flanked by a thick Andean forest.

He led the group of eight, alert; his senses focused as the early morning sun jutted its first triumphal rays earthward, penetrating the thick clouds in a promise of light and warmth.

They hiked the famous Inca Trail, the fabled mountain path that joined the town of Cusco to Peru's most historic destination. Calixto moved easily, demonstrating a natural balance, a lightness of foot that suggested exceptional energy.

There were five tourists, two couples and Lozen. The arduous trek of seven days created tension, and the couples seemed to argue a lot; Calixto traveled alone, keeping to himself, always polite but engaging in little conversation. When he did speak, he demonstrated a fluency in both English and Spanish.

Behind Lozen, the Peruvian guide motioned to his two porters. They watched in appreciation as Calixto negotiated the difficult terrain. It was the Salkantay Trail, the longest and most difficult of the alternative Inca Trail choices. Yet Lozen seemed to glide along the rocky path day after day as one would stroll down a sandy beach.

The three Peruvians decided among themselves that the energy came from Calixto's legs. They were hard, chiseled limbs, the legs of an athlete, honed through years of exertion and training.

"Señor Calixto, por favor," said the guide, holding up a hand and pointing rearward toward the two couples.

Lozen nodded and stopped in place. Two minutes elapsed as the other hikers caught up before finally the guide motioned again. Calixto started forward.

He never complained. This attribute also struck the Peruvians as odd. Lozen's passport said the United States, but he didn't act or look like an American. In addition to his stoic demeanor, Calixto had unusual features. He was tall and thick through the neck and chest, with a strong upper body that tapered to a narrow waist. His smooth complexion covered high cheekbones that looked as if Lozen could go days without shaving. His jet-black hair was medium length, but he tugged it straight back into a very short ponytail.

At the top of the steps, the Peruvian guide pointed, and Calixto shifted to the left. He saw the break in the ground as the trail widened, and slowed his pace to squeeze between two stone walls and several crumbling pillars. He entered the final pass of Intipunku, the Sun Gate.

Lozen stopped. He adjusted his rucksack and took a sip of bottled water. The rising sun broke through the fog, and its golden rays burned off the last crusty cloud cover of the early morning. Then Calixto stepped forward and surveyed a huge, contoured, cascading plateau of layered stone edifices and hillside structures blending together in a mosaic of rhythm and organization. Calixto Lozen beheld his first magnificent view of the spectacular Lost City of the Incas, Machu Picchu.

A second later, his cell phone rang.

Chapter 4

December 14, 2006
Gladwyne, Pennsylvania

MIKE AND JOHN listened intently as Burdis began his story. Their faces were passive, their demeanor respectful. Mike stood and paced to a small side table, where he poured a glass of water for their host. Burdis took several sips before reaching for the mouthpiece. He took a shot of oxygen before speaking. "You have to place the actions in the context of the times. Historians are prone to sit in their ivory towers and dissect events with the clarity of hindsight."

Burdis grimaced before continuing.

"We were just out of Vietnam, and the red menace was in full bloom. Chiang Kai-shek had died a year earlier, and the opposition was bottled up on Taiwan. Mao had just died, and the PRC was in a power struggle. We had lost Asia."

Burdis squeezed his eyes shut and paused, as if the memories were painful. "Even more disconcerting, Brezhnev had consolidated his power in the Soviet Union," he said, "and the KGB under his guidance was demonstrating increasingly aggressive behavior."

John loosened his tie and inched closer as Burdis's volume started to fade. The oxygen-deprived voice became a whisper.

"Blame it on Kennedy," said Burdis, "the *revered* JFK. He blew the Bay of Pigs invasion years earlier when he canceled the air cover *just* as the anti-Castro troops stormed the beach. To this day, we face a communist stronghold ninety miles from our shores."

Mike helped their host drink some more water.

"Somewhat of a benign threat," John said quietly.

"Yes, *now*," replied Burdis, sitting forward in his wheelchair, "but then? Put it in context. The domino effect was working. The Reds were determined to spread their success in our hemisphere. They were going to turn all of South America against us."

Chapter 5

Cusco, Peru

CALIXTO ANSWERED HIS cell phone as he gazed down at the grandeur of Machu Picchu. "Your timing is impeccable," said Lozen.

"Are you sleeping?" asked Isabel Soto with a laugh.

"Hardly."

A touch of embarrassment crept into Izzy's voice. "Am I disturbing you? Are you alone?"

Cal glanced over his shoulder as the other hikers in his party caught up and passed through the Sun Gate. He heard their gasps as they first experienced the spectacular panorama.

"Not exactly," said Cal.

"I'm sorry; I'll call back."

"No, no," said Lozen quickly to his sister. "It's okay; it's not what you think. It's just other people."

Isabel seemed to relax over the phone.

"Izzy, I wish you could see what I'm looking at," said Calixto.

"Where are you?"

"Peru."

"Peru? Are you serious? You sound like you're here in Tucson."

Lozen laughed. "Well, trust me, I'm not, but there's not much interference up here. I'm pretty high up, and I'm looking down at the Lost City of Machu Picchu, carved out of the side of a mountain, and the sun is breaking through the mist from the east."

"Wow," said Isabel, releasing a wistful sigh over the cell phone. "Someday."

"Your time will come."

Suddenly, in a burst of inspiration, Izzy spoke excitedly over the phone. "I know; that's it!"

"What?"

"My senior thesis. I'll go to South America for my twenty-first birthday trip."

"To Peru?"

"And Chile," said Isabel, formulating the plan in her head as quickly as she spoke. "I'll need to do research on the Dirty War, all that stuff Mom spoke of."

Cal paused as he considered her statement, then he asked, "Have you discussed this with anyone?"

"Not yet, but it's a great idea. My dad wants me to do a scholarly paper, with thorough research, and I've been searching for a topic. This is perfect. What do you think?"

Calixto moved a little closer to the edge as the other hikers gathered for a view.

"Izzy, you are a woman now. I think you should think it through, and if it still feels right, then you should do it."

"It's part of our heritage, Cal. I think I should understand how Mom got here. How *we* got here."

"Life is short," said Calixto, "but if it's worth doing, then you need a plan."

"When are you coming home?"

"I'll be back in the states in about a week," said Lozen. "A couple of more days here in Peru, and then over to Bolivia to check out Lake Titicaca. We can talk then."

"Okay," said Isabel. "Love you."

The cell phone clicked off.

Chapter 6

THE TWO MEN sat bound and gagged in the dark warehouse. It was long after closing, and the docks in Buenos Aires were quiet.

Milling around the dirty cement floor were several other men, captors, smoking cigarettes and whispering in unintelligible conversations as they waited.

Finally, a side door at the far end of the warehouse opened, and the sharp echo of footsteps bounced off the rafters as several visitors entered the cavernous building. They paced toward the dimly lit corner.

A bull-like man stepped forward. He was medium height, in his late thirties, with a barrel chest and slicked black hair. He studied the two prisoners.

"Are these my entrepreneurs?" he asked.

"Sí, Santista," answered one of the captors.

The barrel-chested man leaned to his left and knelt over the closest prisoner. He placed his fingers under the man's chin and raised the face upward until they made eye contact. Then he gently pulled the gag from the prisoner's mouth. "Do you know who I am?"

"Sí," replied the prisoner nervously, "you are the santista."

"What is my name?" asked the barrel-chested man.

"Patsy, I mean *Pasquale* Bellocco."

The santista grunted and stroked his slick hair. Then he stood from the crouch. "Smart enough to know who I am, but stupid enough to steal from me."

11

He motioned, and the captors repositioned the gag over the prisoner's mouth. Then Patsy Bellocco walked toward a small electrician's table that stood off to the side. Bellocco surveyed the equipment for a minute and then reached forward and selected a cordless electric hammer drill with a long screw bit. He held the drill comfortably in one hand and depressed the trigger button several times. The six-inch screw bit whirred to life, spinning rapidly in a powerful circle.

Patsy turned, and with a flick of his hand, several captors grabbed the first prisoner. They spread-eagled him on the floor. Terrified, the prisoner began to squirm. He pleaded for mercy through the gag.

Bellocco ignored the prisoner and placed the pointed head of the screw bit directly over the center of the man's left knee. Then he paused and looked over his shoulder at the second prisoner before speaking. "Can you see okay?"

The second prisoner's glazed eyes and flushed face told the story.

"It's important," said Bellocco conversationally, "because you're next."

Then Patsy depressed the trigger button on the electric drill.

Chapter 7

Tucson, Arizona

Isabel entered the kitchen of her parents' home and reached into the refrigerator for a bottled water. "I just got off the phone with Cal. Did you know he was in South America?"

"No," said her mother, looking up at Izzy from the salad she was preparing. "But then, I rarely know where your brother is."

"He's in Peru," replied Isabel. She twisted the plastic cap off her water bottle.

Constanza Finley raised an eyebrow and gave her daughter a dubious look.

"I'm surprised he told you. All that hush-hush stuff. Cal rarely talks about where he is or what he's doing."

"He's not there for the army," said Izzy. She took a long drink of water. "He was hiking."

"In Peru?"

"Yes."

Constanza walked to the sink and washed her hands before responding. "Must be in the Andes." She thought for a moment. "Machu Picchu?"

"Exactly," said young Isabel in an excited tone. The daughter was clearly delighted over her mother's deductive skills. "How did you guess?"

"Not that difficult," replied Constanza. "It sounds like something your brother would do." She looked over at Izzy. "Who was he with?"

Isabel recapped the water bottle and set it on the counter before answering. "I think he was alone."

"That sounds like Cal too."

The daughter looked at her mother with a quizzical expression. "Do you think Cal will ever settle down?"

"I don't know," said Constanza. "That would be nice, but," she searched for the right words, "I think your brother is too independent. Women like security, and Cal has a wanderlust. He doesn't put down roots."

Izzy said, "Well, it sounds like fun. *I'm* going to go to South America. To Chile."

A sudden look of concern crossed her mother's face. She studied Isabel for a moment. Her daughter was an exceptionally attractive young lady, with raven-colored hair, violet eyes, and a healthy glow set against porcelain skin.

"What are you talking about?" asked Constanza.

"Chile," said Izzy. "You and Dad said that I could take a trip to a destination of my choice when I turned twenty-one. Well, I'll be twenty-one next month."

Constanza's expression turned very serious. "But why *Chile?*"

"Because I'm Chilean," answered Isabel.

"You're American."

"Of Chilean descent, and my middle name is Soto." Izzy looked confused at her mother's hesitation.

"So?" said Constanza.

"I need to understand my roots," replied Isabel.

"Now you're Alex Haley?"

Constanza was visibly disturbed at her daughter's decision. She shook her head, a stress line stretching across her temple. "I don't understand. Why *Chile?*"

Isabel shrugged. "Cal said that I should do it."

The mother's face turned red with anger. "When did he say that?"

"A little while ago," answered Izzy, "when we spoke. He said that I was a grown woman now, and that if I felt that strongly about something, then I should do it."

"You're still in college."

"Yes," replied Izzy, "but Cal feels that life is too short to have regrets." Isabel adopted a defiant posture.

"Damn," said Constanza as she threw down a kitchen towel and glared at her daughter. "Your brother is a grown man. He's a soldier for God's sake—a specially trained soldier. It's hardly the same thing."

Isabel rolled her eyes in mock exasperation. "Mom, don't you think you're overreacting?" She took her water bottle and paced from the kitchen.

For a moment, Constanza Finley reached up and wrapped her hands around her face. Then she took a deep breath as a tear crept into the corner of her eye.

Chapter 8

December 14, 2006
Gladwyne, Pennsylvania

MIKE AND JOHN stood in the far corner of the study and discussed the situation. Their host, Peter Burdis, had slumped back in his wheelchair and drifted off to sleep. This was the second time in an hour that Burdis had faded in the middle of his story. Clearly, the very act of breathing, and therefore living, was a challenge for the man.

"What do you think?" asked Mike. He took a moment to look across the expansive library, with its floor-to-ceiling bookcases.

"His mind is still razor-sharp," replied John. "Dates, times, names—all from thirty-plus years ago, and not a moment's hesitation." He shrugged before continuing. "But physically he's a wreck."

Suddenly Burdis seemed to pop awake. He sat forward in his wheelchair and motioned.

They crossed the study and sat again within feet of the mansion's owner. Burdis continued his narrative, picking up the story at precisely the point that he left off. The fifteen-minute interlude was ignored.

"So now we turn our attention to nineteen seventy, the presidential election in Chile. We support and finance Jorge Alessandri, a right-leaning former president. The Soviets do the same for Salvador Allende. In a three-way split, Allende receives one percent more votes than Alessandri. He did not have an absolute majority, mind you, which was required by the Chilean constitution."

Burdis coughed, and covered the spittle with his handkerchief before speaking again.

"But as fate would have it, the National Congress anointed Allende the new president. Richard Nixon went berserk. He was beside himself. The only thing he hated more than the Kennedys was the Communists."

Peter Burdis reached for his water glass, using the silence to rest his lungs. After a minute he continued.

"On September fourth of that year, Salvadore Allende became the democratically elected president of Chile, and the administration's worst fears were realized: an irreversible Marxist regime had taken power in South America."

"And these fears," asked Mike, "they were justified?"

"Absolutely," answered Burdis. "First, Allende nationalized all the banks. Then he privatized large industries. Finally he sped up land distribution and started spending money on social programs like a drunken sailor—housing, health care, education, and family assistance."

"And so the country of Chile fell into stagflation," said John, touching his tie in an absentminded fashion.

"Worse," said Burdis. "Per capita production dropped, and farm cultivation decreased. As exports fell, Chilean trade deficits ballooned. Inflation skyrocketed to one hundred and forty percent. Workers went on strike, and truckers blocked highways."

Burdis stopped talking as his face turned red with exhaustion and lack of air. He took a moment to use his oxygen mask.

"And then…" said Mike, prodding, leaning forward until he almost touched the wheelchair.

"And then," replied Burdis, patiently finishing the sentence for his visitors, "the coup de grâce. At the end of nineteen seventy one, Fidel Castro visited Chile and stayed for four weeks in Santiago, as a guest of Salvatore Allende."

Chapter 9

Tucson, Arizona

ARTHUR FINLEY, PROFESSOR of Humanities at the University of Arizona, entered his well-kept home in the quiet Tucson suburb. He set down his briefcase in the foyer and called out to his wife, "Connie, I'm home."

Arthur moved toward the sunken living room and poured himself a drink. This was one of Finley's daily rituals—the pleasure of a cool, well-made cocktail at the end of a long day. "Connie?" said Finley a second time, circling the first floor in search of his wife.

After a few minutes of wandering the split-level ranch, Arthur finally entered the screened porch. He saw his wife, Constanza, huddled in the corner of a wicker couch, her body wrapped in a tight ball, her knees tucked under her chin.

"Connie, is everything all right?"

Constanza looked up at her husband of twenty-two years, bleary eyed, deep lines of concern etched in her face. Clearly she had been crying.

"What's wrong?" asked Arthur Finley. He put his drink down on a side table and sat next to his wife.

"Izzy."

"Is she hurt?"

"Not yet," replied Constanza. She looked at her husband. "She wants to go to South America. To *Chile*."

"What? Since when?"

"Since she talked to Cal," said Constanza, letting out a deep sigh of frustration.

Arthur took a sip from his drink and held up his hand. "Connie, please, start at the beginning."

His wife took a few minutes to recount the conversation of earlier that day that took place between her and their daughter. Arthur Finley was a thoughtful man. He listened patiently to Constanza and digested both the content and the emotional context that it posed. Then he scratched his chin and swirled the ice cubes in his glass before speaking.

"I wouldn't worry. It sounds like a passing whim because she spoke to Cal."

Constanza shook her head. "Izzy reveres her brother," she said. "He can do no wrong."

Arthur grew pensive again, biting his lip in thought. "We did promise her a trip. But I'm sure that once she understands the many choices, she'll change her mind."

The tears started flowing, and Constanza whispered, "I don't think so. She was...resolute, almost defiant. Izzy has it in her head that she *needs* to go to *Chile*."

"That will change," said the husband confidently. "She's young. It was a brief conversation with her brother—nothing more. I'll pick up some colored brochures. Once she understands the possibilities, she'll be dreaming of Paris or Rome. Give it a few days."

Constanza shivered in the warm afternoon air. Her lips trembled as she spoke. "Our little girl wants to go to Chile."

Chapter 10

February 5, 1989
Tucson, Arizona

TWELVE-YEAR-OLD CALIXTO LOZEN knelt in the dirt and listened as his father spoke.

"You must *feel* the terrain, Gray Wolf," said the adult. "Every animal has tendencies, and the land will expose their movement. The ground will tell you a story."

The father tugged at his long straight hair and extended his right arm in a slow, sweeping motion to their front. Then he shifted the large hunting knife in his hands and pointed at the tracks in the sand.

"See here, Gray Wolf, the size of the footprint, the depth, the spread—it tells you things…are they male or female? What are they carrying?"

Calixto Lozen's father was Indian, a Native American, a tracker for hire raised in the wide expanse of the Arizona wilderness. Like all fathers, Naiche, as Cal's father was known, strove to teach his son the lessons of life. The only difference was that Naiche had a different set of skills.

"You must appear like the morning mist, Gray Wolf," said the father, "and then like a shiver in the air, be gone."

Cal nodded as his father used the blade of his knife to indicate the multiple footprints that covered the ground.

"Never move in a straight line," said Naiche. He slowly walked forward, leading his son, searching for snapped twigs, scuffed dirt, or hair snagged on a mesquite tree. These were *cutting signs*. The landscape was the book Naiche used to teach his son. He paused and pointed at the tracks on the ground. "We know there are four adults—two men and two women," said Naiche, studying the prints. He pointed. "Here, the tallest is over six feet tall; the shortest, five feet, four or five inches." The father surveyed the ground and grunted. "These match our lost hikers."

Calixto noted the depth of the prints and the differences in size and shape.

"They are moving slowly," said the father, "maybe two miles per hour at this point." He pointed to a smudge in one of the large prints. "This man is hurt; he is limping."

"How much farther?" asked Calixto.

"We are close, Gray Wolf," said Naiche. "They passed through here maybe an hour ago."

Calixto pointed toward a series of footprints that intersected the path at an odd angle. His father shook him off.

"Too dry; those prints are three days old," replied Naiche.

The sun was blazing at midday. Occasionally a hot, brisk wind blew from the south and swept dust over the footprints.

The father and son continued following the tracks for another twenty minutes. Naiche suddenly stopped, looked to his right, and held his outstretched arm at a thirty-degree angle. He smiled and winked at Calixto. "Voices. I think we found our lost hikers."

They traveled the last hundred meters in two minutes. Naiche and his son came to a shallow recess in the terrain, a small clearing, surrounded by mesquite trees, cactus, and wild shrubbery.

"No wonder the rescue helicopter couldn't see you," said Calixto's father in a loud voice.

There was a twinge of fear as the four city dwellers turned. Clearly they were surprised by the sudden appearance of the father and son.

"Are you here to help?" asked one of the women in a halting voice.

"That's the plan," said Naiche.

He moved toward the taller of the two men and quickly assessed his swollen ankle. It had fang marks and point tenderness. "Nausea? Vomiting?"

"Yes," answered the man, gritting his teeth in pain. He had a fever.

Calixto's father pulled a cell phone from his pocket, speed-dialed a number, and spoke quietly. Several times he looked at the terrain, then back at the sun, using his straightened arm to estimate an azimuth and a distance as he focused off to his right at a mountain range. Finally he nodded and hung up.

"Help should be here in about thirty minutes," said Naiche. "It looks like a spider bite, probably a brown recluse. Where are you all from?"

"Chicago," said the second woman.

Cal's father smirked as he spoke to the four young hikers in a quiet tone. "We could have a long discussion about wandering off into the desert for a nature walk, alone, without proper provisions and precautions...but it will hold for another time."

"Who are you?" asked the first woman.

"I am Naiche," answered the father. He pointed at Calixto. "And that is Gray Wolf, my son. We are Chiricahua, and today we are your saviors."

Chapter II

December 14, 2006
Gladwyne, Pennsylvania

MIKE AND JOHN had positioned Burdis in front of the large picture window, permitting their host to look out across his beautifully manicured lawn, resplendent with gardens, a trellis, and a large in-ground swimming pool.

He closed his eyes for a moment, basking in the warmth of a late morning sun. They gently swiveled their chairs to either side, leaning forward as Burdis spoke.

"The next year and a half saw us institute a full-court press. The CIA spent eight million dollars—a staggering sum back then—to create pressure on the regime. We exploited weakness, magnified obstacles, and funded right-wing paramilitary groups. We did everything we could to spread disinformation and fuel opposition to the Allende government. ITT, the corporation, was caught in a scandal bribing officials. Allende was planning to nationalize the Chilean telephone system, and ITT had spent countless dollars to publicly control seventy percent of the enterprise. They would soon lose their entire investment if it were nationalized."

"It sounds like things looked bleak," said John, nodding to spur Burdis on.

"Bleak and desperate," said their host. "The KGB and the Cuban Intelligence Directorate were everywhere."

Burdis broke into another coughing spasm, and he allowed Mike to clean the spittle from his lips. He took a sip of water before continuing.

"And then, on September eleventh of nineteen seventy-three, Augusto Pinochet led a coup d'état endorsed by the United States. He was the Chilean Army chief of staff. The heads of all the armed forces joined him in a military junta. The navy captured the coastal city of Valparaiso. The army closed the radio and television stations in Santiago, and the air force bombed the media centers outside of the two main cities. Two days later, the junta dissolved the Chilean National Congress."

There was a pause before John spoke. "What happened next?"

"Then," said Burdis, "the real nightmare began."

Chapter 12

Buenos Aires, Argentina

Patsy Bellocco stepped from the front entrance of his apartment building in the exclusive Recoleta neighborhood of Buenos Aires. He walked a few steps to a large black sedan idling by the curb of the wide boulevard. A bodyguard held the door as he climbed into the rear seat.

Bellocco was the 'ndrina boss, the santista, for a branch of a family business based in Plati, Italy. He had lived in Argentina for six years, and in general, Patsy liked the country. It had a warm, temperate climate, a European flair, and an Italian sensibility. He smiled to himself. Bellocco remembered his first introduction to Buenos Aires. A local explained that Argentina was a country filled with Italians, who spoke Spanish and thought they were English. Patsy reasoned that the local was mostly correct.

He tugged at his cell phone and dialed a number.

"Sí?"

"Twenty minutes," said Patsy before breaking the connection. The sedan turned right on Avenue Pueyrredon and quickly joined the midday traffic.

Bellocco's 'ndrina controlled a very profitable import-export company. The company specialized in all things illegal, as the family business was crime. The 'ndrina engaged in money laundering, usury, extortion, weapons smuggling, human trafficking, and skimming of public contracts—but its real cash cow was drugs.

Interpol estimated that 80 percent of Europe's cocaine supply entered the continent through either the Italian port of Gioia Tauro or the Iberian Peninsula. Patsy's organization acted as a major conduit for both locations.

Bellocco's sedan pulled to the curb on Tucuman near the Claridge Hotel. A second similar sedan was already parked in front of a large leather goods store. When Patsy arrived, two men stepped from the second car and fell in step behind him.

Bellocco entered the shop, walking straight to the back, passing racks of handmade leather coats, pants, and accessories as he made his way to a small office in the rear. Patsy barged through the door without knocking, and a middle-aged man looked up in surprise.

"Pasquale," said the seated man, a large binder of invoices spread across his desk, "what brings you here?"

Bellocco shrugged. No one ever addressed him by his nickname—Patsy— at least not to his face. "I was in the neighborhood." Bellocco moved forward and sat on the corner of the man's desk. "How's business?"

"Bueno," said the proprietor nervously. He leaned back as Bellocco hovered closer.

"That's important," replied Patsy as he reached forward and picked up a heavy crystal paperweight from the desk. Bellocco casually turned the paperweight in his hand, inspecting the ornament as he spoke. "Because when business is good, then one is able to keep their commitments. Comprende?"

"Sí," said the store owner, squirming uncomfortably in his seat.

Patsy looked at the Argentinean for a moment and then let his shoulders slump as he exhaled a long sigh. "Then please tell me," he said with a touch of melodrama, "where are my goods?"

"They are coming, Pasquale, I promise. I spoke with Bogata just this morning."

"My ship is waiting," said Patsy. "The delay makes my associates uncomfortable. It reflects poorly on my family. This is a problem. Do you understand?"

"Sí, Pasquale," said the store owner. "All is well—please, just a little more time."

Patsy took a final look at the paperweight and smiled. Then he offered the man the heavy ornament. As the proprietor reached up with his left hand, Bellocco slammed the paperweight down on the man's right wrist. The crack of bone snapping under the force of the aggression caused the man to shriek in pain. Patsy stood and placed the crystal ornament back on the desk. Then he pointed calmly at the Argentinean. "Remember, I'm waiting."

Bellocco turned and exited the office, followed by his two associates.

Chapter 13

Tucson, Arizona

CONSTANZA FINLEY PULLED her SUV into the driveway of her suburban home. She parked the vehicle and then took a moment to open the rear door. She plucked two brown shopping bags filled with groceries from the back seat.

A short distance away, two men sat in the front seat of a blue sedan under the shade of a guajillo tree. They watched Constanza. The driver quickly shuffled through a stack of full facial photographs as the passenger patiently held a camera equipped with a long telephoto lens.

"That's her," said the driver.

The passenger raised the camera to eye level and took several pictures as Constanza set one bag on the driveway and slid the rear door closed.

The camera continued to click as she retrieved the second bag and turned toward her home.

Chapter 14

Fayetteville, North Carolina

Calixto Lozen kept a small apartment in Fayetteville, North Carolina. It was close to Fort Bragg, the headquarters for Special Forces, and thus kept him close to the action.

Lozen was the rarest of soldiers, a Special Forces warrant officer and a full-time reservist. With the expansion of the army reserve system, various networks were created to retain highly qualified soldiers and officers. A reservist with flexibility—unencumbered by family or civilian careers—could fill vacancies in support of active-duty units.

Calixto dialed a toll-free telephone number in Saint Louis. It rang twice.

"Arpercen, Mobdes, Special Operations assignment desk, Captain Foster speaking," said a voice.

"Morning, sir, CW three Lozen calling," answered Cal.

There was a slight pause as the voice lost a touch of its formality.

"Morning, Chief. You've been out of the net for a while. Did you take a trip?"

"Roger that, sir. I was backpacking in the Andes—Peru."

"Well done," said the captain. "Did you take photos?"

"Only in my head, sir," said Calixto.

"Had to be sweet—high adventure. Are you ready to get back in the saddle?"

"Affirmative, sir. Been back a week; getting a little stir crazy."

"Okay," said the captain, punching a code into his desktop computer. "Let's see what we've got." He scanned the assignment postings and then spoke as he read. "We need an SF warrant in Kandahar to act as a liaison between special ops and the Tenth Mountain Division…It's a twelve-month rotation."

Cal hesitated. He recalled the emotional, almost panicked telephone call from his mother, Constanza, following his return from Peru. She was angry and scared. Constanza blamed Calixto for his sister Isabel's decision to take a trip to *Chile*. The fact that Izzy, an independent and responsible young lady, was now an adult was irrelevant. In any event, considering the crosscurrents, Cal felt it wise to keep things close to home. He answered the personnel officer, "Been there, sir. This time I'd prefer to keep it TDY if possible."

"Roger," said the captain as he scanned the computer screen for assignment postings that would keep Lozen on active duty for less than six months at a time. "Okay, I've got three or four openings that look interesting. All are TDY in rotation, and all match your qualifications. How about if I e-mail them to you?"

"That would be fine, sir."

"Same address?"

"Yes, sir."

"Okay, coming at you, Chief. Take a look. If any of these postings look good, let me know ASAP, and we'll hook you up."

"Thank you, sir," said Lozen.

"And, Chief," said the captain, "welcome home. Glad you're back in the net."

"Glad to be home, sir. Out here."

Calixto disconnected the telephone call.

Chapter 15

December 14, 2006
Gladwyne, Pennsylvania

PETER BURDIS SWIVELED the electric wheelchair toward his oversized desk. His eyes seemed to glow with a newfound energy as he continued to speak.

"In nineteen hundred seventy-one, Allende appointed Orlando Letelier ambassador to the United States. Then in the two years leading up to the coup, Letelier served in several senior ministerial positions. At the time of the overthrow, following Allende's death, Orlando was the first man arrested by the junta."

"It would appear that he was high profile," said Mike.

"Yes, both highly visible and very outspoken. Letelier spent the next twelve months in various political prisons and concentration camps. The secret police were brutal."

Burdis paused to catch his breath before continuing.

"Finally, in nineteen seventy-four, with political pressure from both Venezuela and the United States, Letelier was released and sent to Washington."

Their host took a shot of oxygen from his portable mask.

"And back in Santiago?" asked John.

"The streets were on fire," replied Burdis. "DINA, the Chilean Secret Police, arrested students, protestors, and subversives everywhere. Torture was rampant. Kidnap and disappearance were pervasive. Pinochet and his minions were going to stamp out dissent and eliminate Marxist ideology throughout Chile."

"Would it be correct to suggest that the Dirty War became *very* dirty," asked Mike.

"Indeed," agreed Burdis.

"But our side was in the right," said John as he edged his seat closer.

"Yes," answered Burdis with an extra measure of conviction. "We were in a war with the communists for the very soul of South America. Chile had become the linchpin."

"What happened next?" asked Mike, offering Burdis a sip of water.

He drank and then leaned back in his wheelchair, taking the opportunity to pause and gather his thoughts. "The most natural thing in the world, which gives us some insights as to how we got ourselves embroiled in the accident."

"The accident of six months ago?" said John.

"Yes," replied Burdis, "*that* accident."

Mike and John sat quietly, waiting for the mansion's owner to continue his explanation.

"Things *evolved*," said Burdis.

"How so?" said Mike in a whisper.

"Like-minded men, with like-minded goals, got together," answered Burdis. "They decided to cooperate and pool resources. The Dirty War suddenly extended beyond Chile's borders. The Southern Cone of South America became the new battlefield for the world's two great ideologies to compete— and each was supported by a world power."

Chapter 16

Vina del Mar, Chile

THE DARK SEDAN parked outside of the gated entrance to a lush villa. Well hidden, surrounded by a high wall and thick palm trees, the private residence boasted both seclusion and a wonderful view of the Pacific Ocean.

A man stepped from the sedan dressed in a blue suit and offered identification to the two private security guards. They waved, and he passed through the gate. Two minutes later he repeated the process at a side door to the main house.

"The colonel is expecting you," said a butler who greeted the new arrival in the foyer. "This way please."

They walked down the marble-floored hallway in silence and entered a small, private office in the rear of the first floor.

"Buenos dias, Captain," said the man seated behind the desk. He spoke his Spanish in the curious Chilean dialect, where the ends of words were dropped and *buenos dias* became *buena dia*. He stood to greet the visitor. "You have been busy."

"Sí," answered the captain. "Our friends in Washington have voiced some concerns."

The man in the blue suit was ushered into a chair, and the office occupant resettled behind his desk. In a strange quirkiness of protocol, both men continued to address each other by rank, even though neither man had served in the military in over a decade.

"So tell me, how was our new president's visit?" asked the colonel.

"Controlled, maybe even a little predictable. Her comments at the Letelier Memorial were emotional, but restrained."

The colonel shifted behind his desk, his thoughts wandering. Finally he asked, "Was the crowd large?"

"Forty or fifty people."

"Anyone of interest?"

"Maybe," replied the captain, "a person of interest from the past."

The colonel sat forward at his desk. "Who?"

"A former staff researcher at the Institute for Policy Studies. A woman."

The colonel frowned and considered the information. The admission seemed to draw an extra measure of pensiveness. "Letelier's old organization," said the colonel. "Not surprising, I suppose; they have been getting very vocal since Señora Bachelet was elected. Many want her to revoke the general's lifetime senatorial position and have him prosecuted."

The captain shrugged before responding. "It won't succeed: it's written into the constitution, and he still has many friends in high places."

"Sí," said the colonel, "but one never knows. Who is she?"

"Her name is Constanza Soto. She lives in Tucson, Arizona, with her husband and daughter."

"What is her interest after all these years?" asked the colonel.

The captain considered the question for a moment before answering. "We are not sure, but the election of Bachelet has opened a door and given new life to an old problem."

The colonel's expression turned serious. "Yes, it's probably inconsequential, but just the same, we should follow up. We have too much at stake to allow politics to interfere with our Empresa." He nodded his head toward the ceiling and alluded to the villa's owner occupant who resided upstairs. "After all, he's ninety, and he won't be around to protect us forever."

"I already took a few precautions," said the captain. "I have a contact back in the States checking things out."

"Bueno," replied the colonel. "Then we should know soon enough. Keep me apprised."

"Sí," said the captain as he stood and exited the first-floor office.

Chapter 17

ISABEL STEPPED ON to the tartan track of Drachman Stadium and started to stretch. Izzy had just completed her junior year at the University of Arizona, and though she failed twice as a walk-on candidate to the UA Women's Cross-Country Team, she still loved to run. It reminded her of Cal.

Isabel sat on the grass, and with a long, practiced motion, she began to massage her bare legs. The heat—always oppressive in Arizona—was especially difficult in summer, but it loosened the muscles.

Izzy's memories reverted to her older brother, and she wondered how Cal was doing. Growing up, despite the age difference, this had been their special ritual. Calixto would come home from high school, pick up Izzy, and they would run the track together.

Cal would run slowly at first, and then when Isabel tired, he would run several fast miles by himself. Finally they would stretch on the grass field, and Izzy would help her brother complete his workout. They played a game.

Calixto would extend his torso in a push-up position, arms spread at shoulder width, body flat, and Izzy would slowly turn over a playing card from a poker deck. One by one, she would flip a card and call out the number, and Cal would then pump out the matching number of push-ups. Face cards represented ten, and aces were eleven. Her brother continued nonstop until exhaustion.

If one were to multiply the total numbers on the playing cards, times the four suits, it equaled three hundred eighty repetitions per deck.

Isabel, the counter and coach, was more excited than her brother when, after seven months of daily exertion, Cal broke the deck without a rest.

Isabel finally stood and did a last series of stretches, kneading hard on her hamstring. She took a long drink of water and then turned on to the all-weather track and started to run.

Sitting in the stands at the track and field stadium, watching Izzy through a pair of high-powered binoculars, was the same man who photographed Constanza several days earlier. He consulted his wristwatch and then pushed several buttons on his cell phone.

"Yes," answered a voice.

"She just started her run," said the man with the binoculars. "She's typically good for five to six miles at a fast clip. She'll stretch at the end as well. If she doesn't shower here and we count travel time, you have at least one hour."

"Understood," said the voice.

"What's the status of the roommate?" asked the man watching Izzy.

"She just left for work in a waitress uniform."

"That's at least a three-hour window on her."

"Understood," replied the voice.

"Okay," said the photographer. "Work fast and be thorough."

He took a last look through his binoculars as Isabel rounded the tartan track, and then he disconnected his cell phone.

Chapter 18

December 14, 2006
Gladwyne, Pennsylvania

JOHN REMOVED HIS suit coat and folded it neatly across the back of his chair. He nodded at Peter Burdis. "As you were saying, things evolved. Please explain."

Their host leaned forward in his wheelchair, and a slight smile crossed his face before he spoke.

"The national bird of Chile is the condor. In November of nineteen seventy-five, a secret meeting was held in Santiago. Present were the leaders of the military intelligence services of Chile, Argentina, Paraguay, Uruguay, and Bolivia. Their common interests were discussed. They were powerful men. They established a plan to coordinate and share both information and assistance across national borders. Operation Condor was born."

Burdis leaned back in his wheelchair and took a breath of oxygen from his portable mask.

"The meeting evolved into an action plan," said Mike.

"Precisely," replied Burdis. "With the tacit approval of the United States, Operation Condor had real teeth. The intelligence services of the Southern Cone joined together to eliminate Marxist subversion."

"Leftists, socialists, political opponents," said Mike by way of clarification.

"Every trade unionist and relative of a dissident," answered Burdis. "For people in the business of secrets, the unchecked power held few restraints. Nothing was out of bounds."

"Was it just the five countries?" asked John.

"In the beginning," said their host. "But after the initial meeting in Santiago, the intelligence services of Brazil, Ecuador, and Peru joined Operation Condor."

A moment of silence enveloped the large study as the three men considered the implications. Finally Burdis spoke. "By nineteen seventy-six, the secret police of Chile and Argentina were taking the lead. Over the next few years, Operation Condor and the Dirty War would claim sixty thousand victims."

Chapter 19

Buenos Aires, Argentina

Patsy Bellocco walked down the long, lavish entranceway to the Faena Hotel. The five-star establishment suited Patsy's taste, complete with polished, hard woodfloors, exposed brick, and sheer silk draperies over long windows and graceful arches. A local fashion designer spent a fortune refurbishing the former wheat mill. Now it exuded chic elegance.

Bellocco turned right at the end of the long entranceway and angled toward a corner table in the hotel's *El Mercado* restaurant. His two bodyguards slid off to the side.

The restaurant served French cuisine, which was of no interest to Patsy. Rather, what drew Bellocco to the restaurant five times in the past two weeks was a dancer. The *El Mercado* doubled as a cabaret, and nightly, a troupe of tango performers graced the small stage with the most sensual, romantic show in Buenos Aires. One dancer in particular held Patsy's attention. He ordered a sambuca and leaned back in the comfortable chair to wait, allowing his mind to drift back to his childhood.

Bellocco was twelve and walking along a cobblestone street beside his father. They were in Plati, a small mountainous village in the south of Calabria, the proverbial toe on the boot of the Italian mainland. Plati spread along the slope of the Aspromonte Mountains three hundred meters above sea level, an inconspicuous hill town of less than four thousand residents.

Two areas in particular brought fame and notoriety to Plati: its delicious bread, and kidnapping. Plati was a central cog in the powerful organized crime syndicate known as the 'Ndrangheta.

The young Patsy walked in silence. His papa, a man of respect in Plati, was a strong advocate of formal schooling. He pushed his children—especially his sons—to be accomplished in both mathematics and languages. "Business," as Papa would say, "was about understanding the numbers and communicating." Which is why Patsy found it odd that his father insisted he take the day off from school for this excursion. Finally, the father spoke.

"Pasquale, I know you are not in school, but today is still part of your education. Capice?"

The youth nodded but looked confused. He gazed up at his father.

"You must pay attention," said Papa. "You watch, listen, and remember—but no talking. Do you understand?"

"Sí, Papa," answered Patsy, although his expression was doubtful.

The father touched young Bellocco's shoulder reassuringly and then added, "And you must be brave."

They turned down a small alley parallel to the town's sewer system and knocked on a heavy wooden door at the rear of a row house. The door opened from the inside. Papa led his son past a fat man holding a shotgun, down a flight of stairs, and into a long basement passage. At the far end, they entered a small room. Seated in the center of the room, tied to a chair, was a very nervous prisoner. He sweated profusely.

Hovering to either side of the chair were two men holding bladeless, wooden axe handles.

Papa motioned for Patsy to stay put, and paced across the room. He spoke to the prisoner in a quiet tone. Suddenly the man protested his innocence in a loud voice. Patsy's father replied by spitting in the prisoner's face. Then he walked back to the far side of the room and rested his hand reassuringly on Patsy's shoulder. He motioned.

One of the two guards positioned a cloth gag over the prisoner's mouth as the man started to squirm in his chair. He pulled at the ropes and begged for mercy. Then the captor took a two-handed grip of the axe handle, raised the wooden tool, and with a wide swing brought the heavy handle down on the man's right shin. The crack of bone echoed in the room. Then the second captor repeated the motion with his own axe handle on the left leg.

The prisoner screamed in agony with each blow as the two captors alternated, his cries muffled by the gag, his eyes bulging in pain with each repetition as his shinbones splintered.

At first Patsy turned his head and pushed his face into his father's thigh to hide from the carnage. Calmly Papa turned the young boy's face back toward the seated prisoner. He said nothing, but indicated that Patsy should watch.

It continued for ten swings. The prisoner's lower legs were shattered, with multiple fractures below the knees. Then the first captor pulled out a knife and cut loose the ropes securing the man to the chair. He tumbled forward and sprawled on the floor, semiconscious.

"Make sure you send for the doctor," said Patsy's father.

He led his son out of the room and down the long underground passage.

They walked in silence for a few minutes, climbing the stairs, leaving the row house, turning from the alley, and retraced their steps back on to the cobblestone streets of Plati. Patsy sniffled, shaken by what he had seen, and rubbed his nose with the long sleeve of his jersey.

"Are you okay, Pasquale?" asked his father.

"Sí, Papa."

"Did it scare you?"

"Sí," said the twelve-year-old.

"What are your questions?"

Young Patsy looked up at his father, an expression of bewilderment in his face. "Why, Papa? What did the man do?"

"He did not respect me, Pasquale."

"And this made you angry?"

The father paused in thought before answering. "No," he said calmly, "but it put my reputation at risk. It jeopardized my business."

They walked another few minutes in silence as Patsy digested the explanation. Finally the father asked, "And what did you learn today?"

Patsy considered the question. "If a man does not respect my business, I should cause him pain."

"Sí," said the father, "but remember, take no pleasure from causing pain. *Fear* is a tool—nothing more."

Young Patsy went back to school the following day. On occasion as he matured, his father would pull him away from his studies for a day, an afternoon, a long weekend, gradually interspersing a full curriculum of street education to supplement his formal subjects.

The combination of the two parallel bodies of knowledge fueled Patsy Bellocco's rise to the position of 'ndrina boss, the santista, of the Argentine faction of the 'Ndrangheta.

Patsy took a sip from his drink and watched as the troupe of performers entered the *El Mercado*. He took a long, appraising look at the third dancer, while unconsciously smoothing his slick hair.

Chapter 20

ISABEL FINLEY ARRIVED at her off-campus apartment and immediately knew something was wrong. Her computer had been touched, and no matter how many times Izzy asked her roommate, Sandy, to use her own laptop, the roommate often ignored the request. Girls were different. They shared clothes, food, and even sometimes secrets, but Isabel had a "thing" about her computer.

Part of Izzy's reluctance to come down hard was guilt. She attended UA tuition free, courtesy of her dad's employment. Arthur and Constanza Finley had promised Izzy that if she lived at home for her first two years and made honor roll, they would then allow her to live off campus. They supplemented both her rent and the cost of incidentals.

Sandy, on the other hand, needed every dollar of her part-time waitress job just to stay in school. There was little money left over to purchase a new, faster computer.

Isabel first noticed that her keyboard had shifted. She had a habit of sitting at her desk at an angle, one leg curled under her buttocks as she typed. Also, her notebook, containing the outline to her senior thesis had been moved. Finally, several of the flash drives that she used to back up her computer were missing.

Isabel stepped back from her desk and surveyed everything again. Then she turned in place and let her eyes roam her bedroom. The closet door was closed, but one of her bureau drawers was slightly ajar.

She didn't really care if Sandy borrowed a blouse or skirt, as they were close in size. She did, however, emphasize a concern about using her computer. Especially now.

The senior thesis was an Honors College requirement. It would certainly please her father, the academic. A well-researched and written course of independent study would also help position Izzy for graduate school selection.

Most importantly, however, was the subject matter of Isabel's senior thesis. It would aggravate her mother's sensitivity. She had chosen to research and write about the *Dirty War.*

Chapter 21

Columbus, Georgia

CALIXTO LOZEN SAT in the last row of the large auditorium at building number four at Fort Benning. Cal was twelve days into an eight-week temporary-duty assignment (TDY) at the Infantry School, and he was bored.

Lozen's job was to lead a four-man Special Forces cadre as they instructed fifty Latin American officers in small unit tactics at the SOA, the School of the Americas.

He yawned and checked his e-mails.

The SOA had existed for sixty years. Founded at the end of World War II in Panama, the exchange program moved to Fort Benning following the repatriation of the Panama Canal. It was steeped in controversy.

"Chief," said one of Cal's SF cadre in a loud whisper. Lozen looked to his left and saw one of his three senior NCOs standing in the aisle. The man jerked his head sideways. Cal stood and followed him through the auditorium doors into the hallway.

Each year, over fifty military officers from a dozen Central and South American countries came to Fort Benning for two months of instruction. The subjects were varied, and the Infantry School used translators to cover the formal lectures provided by their teachers. However, to add an extra level of intensity and elitism to the exchange program, the US Army provided several Special Forces soldiers to actually take the students out to the field.

"C. L.," said the SF trooper to Cal when they were in the hallway, "this is Major Ansen. He will act as the students' *advocate* when we put them through their paces."

The officer looked first at the SF NCO and then at Cal. "C. L.?" asked the major.

"Cal Lozen, sir—my name."

The major gave Cal a disdainful look. "As in *Chief* Lozen, correct?"

Cal sighed and nodded before answering, "Yes, sir, Chief Warrant Officer, Grade Three, Calixto Lozen."

He recited his formal rank without an expression. After nine years in Special Forces, Cal was inured to the informality that engulfed the regiment. Unlike their conventional military counterparts, rigid adherence to rank and protocol was often overlooked. In SF, one's reputation carried the day.

The major relaxed, a wrong corrected. "You are taking these students to the field at the end of the week. Which range?"

"Undecided, sir. We want to get deep into the swamps to teach raids and ambushes. We need to stress them a little to test their character."

"I see," said Major Ansen. "Well, let's remember, this is not a qualifications course. These Central American officers are our allies."

For a moment Cal remembered why he had taken this assignment. He wanted a short posting, and he wanted to stay stateside. This duty offered both.

"Well, sir," answered Lozen, "I'm not sure what an *advocate* actually does, but if these Latin American officers are to be leaders, then we need to push the envelope a bit. Don't you agree?"

The Infantry School officer stood rigid before responding, "I won't slow you down, Chief. I graduated ninth in my class at the Point."

Cal paused and stole a sideways glance at his SF NCO. Then he shrugged.

"Well, there you go, sir. I hope you like water moccasins."

Chapter 22

Vina del Mar, Chile

THE COLONEL LEANED back in his chair and studied the photograph. After thirty seconds, he turned it around so that the captain sitting across the desk could see the picture.

"This is Señora Constanza Finley?" asked the colonel, seeking confirmation.

"Yes, sir," answered the captain, adding a slight clarification. "It is Señora Constanza *Soto Finley*."

The colonel nodded and turned the photo around again so that he could continue studying the face. "Tell me about her," he said.

"Born in Curacavi, and moved to Santiago to attend the university. She got involved with protests. It went downhill from there. Soon after, she applied for political asylum in the United States. She went to work for Letelier at the institute in Washington as a staff researcher."

The colonel digested the information, and then with a roll of his free hand, motioned for the captain to continue.

"Following the Letelier incident," said the captain, "she left the institute and Washington and went in to hiding."

"Not an unusual decision for many of their staffers," replied the colonel.

"No," said the captain. "Six months later she quietly surfaced in Arizona. She secured employment at the University of Arizona in Tucson."

The colonel shrugged before speaking. "She is bilingual, educated, and foreign born. Did she teach?"

"No, Colonel, she worked in an administrative capacity."

"Young and idealistic, determined to change Chile—and then she came to grips with the real world."

"She was alone, no doubt shaken by the events. She met someone, a local."

"An American?" asked the colonel.

"Sí, a *Native* American. They began a torrid romance, and they had a son out of wedlock."

"Oh?" The colonel leaned forward at his desk, an extra level of interest in his voice. "So ethnically, her son is mixed blood?"

"Sí, Colonel, he is half Chilean and half Native American, the tribe known as Apache, to be precise."

The colonel laughed before speaking. "An American version of a mestizo?"

"Sí," replied the captain.

The colonel leaned back in his chair and asked, "And what became of this son?"

"He grew up in the Tucson area, being raised by his single mother, Constanza Soto, but he spent considerable time with his biological father. After finishing secondary school, he attended two years at a local junior college, and then quit and enlisted in the army."

"He volunteered?"

"Sí, there is no conscription in the United States," said the captain.

"And?"

"As close as we can tell, he has spent nine years in the army."

"Is he still active?" asked the colonel.

"We are not sure. It seems that he tried out for their Special Forces. Once that happens, the army segregates their records. If they fail to qualify, then their file resurfaces somewhere else in the army when they are assigned to another unit."

The captain handed the colonel a photograph of a young inductee with a shaved head.

"This is an early photograph, when he first enlisted."

The colonel looked at the picture of a twenty-year-old Calixto Lozen and frowned before speaking. "Continue."

"Constanza Soto then met and married an academic who worked at the same university."

The colonel raised an eyebrow as the captain offered him a third photograph.

"This," said the captain, "is Doctor Arthur Finley, a tenured Professor of Humanities at the University of Arizona." He paused for a moment. "Soon after they married, they had a daughter."

The captain handed the colonel a full frontal head-and-shoulders photograph of Izzy. "Isabel Soto Finley. She just completed her third year at the same university where her father teaches."

The colonel took an extra moment to appreciate Izzy's photo. He studied her long raven-colored hair, her violet eyes, and her striking features. "She is beautiful," said the colonel without hesitation. "She is also of mixed heritage?"

"Sí," replied the captain. "Her father, the professor, is a third-generation American of Scottish English descent."

"Is she another young idealistic university student?"

"Sí, Colonel," answered the captain, "and like her mother, she seems to have an unusual interest in Letelier."

The colonel waved his hand in a dismissive fashion. "The minister has been dead for thirty years. It is of no consequence."

The captain raised his hand politely. "But the daughter also seems to have an interest in *living* generals."

"How so?" asked the colonel.

The captain reached into his pocket and pulled out several flash drives and laid them on the desk in front of the colonel before answering.

"It seems that young Isabel has inherited her mother's penchant for research."

Chapter 23

December 14, 2006
Gladwyne, Pennsylvania

BURDIS SHIFTED IN his wheelchair and let his eyes wander. For a moment, he seemed to grow unusually pensive. Then with a wistful look, his thoughts and his attention returned to the two guests.

"Forgive me," he said. "It's been a long morning. Can I offer you something to eat—an early lunch perhaps?"

Mike and John exchanged a glance and shook their heads. The cripple nodded and continued his narrative.

"As I started to say, the initial coordination between the secret police forces that began with information sharing evolved into action steps. Operation Condor virtually denied asylum or safety to dissidents who fled their native countries. The purpose morphed into outright assassination across three continents."

"Yes," said Mike, "and there were some notable victims."

"Precisely," agreed Burdis. "The members became emboldened by their success. In addition to the thousands of killings and kidnappings of ordinary dissidents, Operation Condor targeted several high-profile citizens. First, in nineteen seventy-four, they murdered Carlos Prats and his wife, who were in Buenos Aires living in exile. Then in nineteen seventy-five, Operation Condor planned the elimination of Bernardo Leighton and his wife. A year later, the couple was gunned down in Rome." Burdis raised his portable oxygen mask and took a shot of air. "Finally," said the host, "in September nineteen seventy-six, Orlando Letelier, the most vocal and visible of the Chilean dissidents, was assassinated here in the United States, on the streets of our nation's capital." Burdis paused before whispering the final word: "Unbelievable."

"Did we render assistance?" asked John.

"No," answered Burdis quickly. "There may have been an element of paternalistic neglect in some corners, but we would never authorize such an act in our own backyard. South America is one thing, and even Rome is a bit dicey, but Washington, DC?" Burdis shook his head with absolute conviction.

Chapter 24

Buenos Aires, Argentina

PATSY BELLOCCO FANCIED himself a ladies' man, a charming rogue who attracted beautiful women. He liked to be visible around town, in the clubs and at restaurants, accompanied by desirable women. It made him feel good, and to be fair, there always seemed to be a list of comely partners who enjoyed his attention.

For Sofia, the tango dancer, this was new ground. It was not that Patsy was good looking. Actually, it was more that his appearance exuded a certain threatening quality. The santista moved with a predatory power that demanded respect—his walk, the slick black hair, the rigid set to his swarthy features. Patsy looked both important and in control. Some women liked the demeanor, the confidence, and this intrigued the dancer.

"My name is Pasquale," said the santista as he looked across the cocktail table and smiled.

"Yes," answered Sofia, "I have noticed you. It's difficult not to. You've been at three or four performances, and you always sit at the same corner table."

Bellocco unconsciously smoothed his slick hair and leaned forward.

"Actually, it's been five shows, but who is counting?" Patsy reached for his glass of sambuca. "Can I buy you a drink?"

"No, thank you," said Sofia. "I have another show in an hour."

Bellocco shrugged and changed the subject. "You dance very well. I would like to take you to dinner."

"Thank you," said Sofia with a polite smile, "but I am in a relationship."

"It's just dinner," replied Patsy.

Sofia's expression was a bit dubious. She was very pretty, fair of complexion, with light brunette hair and an engaging smile. Most importantly, Sofia had the lithe, toned figure and shapely legs that the 'ndrina boss coveted.

"I don't think it is wise," said Sofia.

"It's *just* dinner," said Patsy a second time. He spoke in a quiet but serious voice.

Sofia sensed his forcefulness, and it made her pause. Earlier that evening, she had been approached by the cabaret manager, her boss, who confided to Sofia that a special customer would like to meet her between shows. Repeat patronage was important to both the restaurant and the hotel, and thus, polite socializing between staff and clients was encouraged.

"Two shows per night, six nights per week, and I eat and drink very little before a show."

"I understand," said Patsy, "but I know that Raoul would approve, and I would be very appreciative."

The mention of the manager's name, the veiled threat, hung in the air.

"It will have to wait until next week for my next day off," answered Sofia.

"Of course," said Patsy. "What day?"

"I think Thursday, but *just* dinner," replied Sofia in a polite but firm tone.

"Sí," said Patsy as he offered a smile. "I will send a car and driver for you at nine in the evening next Thursday."

Sofia reached for a paper napkin and signaled to the waitress for a pen. "I live in Monserrat. I will give you my address."

"I have it," said Patsy in a confident tone.

Chapter 25

Tucson, Arizona

Izzy paused for a moment and scanned the open suitcase propped on her bed. She surveyed the stacks of neatly folded clothes, packed in several rows, placed efficiently inside the luggage. Then she turned back toward the desk and looked at her computer just as her roommate, Sandy, entered her bedroom.

"Take it with you," said Sandy, motioning toward the laptop. "You'll feel better."

It had become a small point of contention between them. Ever since Izzy had arrived back at their apartment following her daily run a couple weeks earlier, a small frost had hung in the air. Her computer had been moved, her senior thesis notebook opened, and her backup flash drives taken.

Izzy and Sandy were compatible as friends and roommates, but they were different. Where Isabel was shy and a little serious, Sandy was fun loving and carefree. They both were hardworking and attractive, although Izzy was by far the more committed student. Sandy's engaging smile and approachable demeanor attracted young suitors. Isabel's beauty, however, had the opposite effect—it often intimidated men.

"Do you think it will be too heavy?" asked Izzy.

"No," answered Sandy reassuringly. "It's only a laptop. People travel with them all the time. Stow it in your backpack." A moment of silence ensued before Sandy finally spoke again. "And I swear, I will not *touch* it." She held up her BlackBerry. "This is all I need."

Izzy relented, walked to her desk, and started folding the small laptop computer together.

"Besides," said Sandy as an afterthought, "then you can Skype your mom and fill her in on our travels, face-to-face."

Isabel saw the logic in Sandy's suggestion and knew it would offer her parents an extra measure of comfort. For so many personal reasons, this trip was more than a vacation.

Sandy smiled approvingly, and then as she walked past Izzy to leave the bedroom, paused and touched her on the shoulder. She whispered, "Iz, I know it's a sore subject, but I really *didn't* take your flash drives."

Isabel started to speak but Sandy held up her hand. "Please, I just want you to know." Izzy remained quiet as Sandy continued, "And I want to thank you for helping with my airfare. As soon as we get back, I am going to work extra shifts at the restaurant to pay you back."

Izzy smiled and waved her hand dismissively as Sandy raised her voice and spoke in an excited tone.

"Next stop for the ladies from Tucson: Santiago, Chile."

Chapter 26

Vina del Mar, Chile

THE FORMER CAPTAIN sat patiently in the small first-floor office of the villa overlooking the Pacific Ocean. He waited for his boss, a man he had served faithfully for over twenty years—ten as a junior military officer, and another decade in their lucrative private Empresa.

His eyes roamed the cluttered room, focusing on the military artifacts and mementos that spanned the colonel's thirty-year career. His mentor was a visionary, a leader who saw the potential for Operation Condor, its future, using the leverage inherent in a secret organization of powerful men, with like goals, similar beliefs, and stress-tested relationships. Military men were disciplined, obedient, and logistically capable. Most important, a military career quickly conditioned individuals to the trappings of authority. Rank had its privileges.

The door to the office opened, and the retired colonel entered. He was still dapper, despite his sixty-odd years, tall and lean, with trim hair and a pencil-thin mustache that showed flecks of gray. His bearing was formal and ramrod straight.

"Buenos días, Captain," said the colonel, circling his desk as the subordinate stood out of respect. "I kept you waiting." His eyes wandered up toward the ceiling, indicating the home's owner, who lived on the second floor. "My apologies; it was unavoidable."

"I understand, Colonel. How is he doing?"

The colonel leaned back in his chair and sighed. He took a moment before answering and chose his words carefully. "The general is doing well, especially so when one considers his age. Today he told me a story going back to the 'old days.' We discussed the success of his economic programs." The colonel leaned forward. "But this is your time, Captain. You suggested it was important."

"Sí, Colonel," replied the subordinate, smoothing the lapel of his blue suit. He had followed the colonel into an early retirement, cutting short a promising military career because of his confidence in the man sitting across the desk. He had been justly rewarded. "Did you have a chance to review the information on the flash drives?" asked the captain.

"Yes," said the colonel, his tone turning serious. "I do not like the focus of the daughter's research. What is the young lady up to?"

"We do not know, Colonel, but like her mother, she has an unusual interest in the man upstairs." The captain raised his eyes toward the ceiling.

"Yes," said the colonel, "it makes me uncomfortable, especially after all these years."

As the colonel's attention drifted into a different realm, the captain opened a plain manila envelope, pulled out a large stack of black-and-white photographs, and placed them on the desk. "We have located the son of Señora Soto Finley."

"Oh?"

The colonel picked up the stack and started looking at Calixto's pictures. He studied a very recent photograph of Cal, noting the square jaw, the high cheekbones, and the hard eyes of a man in his late twenties.

"He is still involved in the army," said the captain. "He is in their Special Forces reserve."

"Explain," said the colonel with a frown.

"Calixto Lozen is a warrant officer in an Active Reserve component. He only rotates into Special Forces assignments."

"That explains," said the colonel, "why it was difficult to confirm his current status."

"Sí, Colonel, but it gets more complicated." The captain paused for effect, waiting for his superior to wave a free hand. "The son is currently assigned to the School of the Americas in Georgia."

The colonel leaned forward and hunched his shoulders, taking a closer look at the stack of photographs. "The SOA," said the colonel in a quiet mumble. "Unusual, I attended the School of the Americas when it was in Panama."

The captain nodded. "As did I, Colonel, but by then it had relocated to Fort Benning, its current location."

"Many of our relationships are graduates of the SOA."

"Sí, Colonel," answered the captain. He gave his boss a moment to digest the information. "It seems an odd posting for a Special Forces officer, *especially* considering the controversy over the years."

The colonel leaned back and for an instant looked off into space before he spoke.

"This coincidence has my attention; it leaves me very unsettled."

"I agree," said the captain, motioning toward the stack of photographs. "And we must remember, he is Chilean."

"Half, on his mother's side."

"Same as the daughter," said the captain. "They share the same mother, and she is a known dissident."

"From thirty years ago," said the colonel with a frown. "So much has changed."

"Still..." answered the captain. He allowed his voice to trail off in a non-committal fashion. The tone prodded the colonel out of his reverie as a serious expression parted his lips.

Chapter 27

Tucson, Arizona

CONSTANZA FINLEY KNELT over the toilet bowl and dry-heaved for the third time that morning. She hadn't slept in days, and her face, haggard and drawn, depicted a woman under incredible stress.

"Connie?"

The voice from the hall was that of her husband.

"In here, Arthur," said Constanza in a mumble.

She stood and leaned over the sink to wash her face in cold water. Since Constanza hadn't eaten, the dry heaves produced no vomit, but her stomach still retched in involuntary spasms.

The professor entered the powder room and instinctively rubbed Constanza's back. "You okay?"

"Yes," replied Constanza. She straightened and managed a weak smile.

Today was the day. The proud parents would drive their only daughter to the airport with her roommate, and the two college students would travel to South America for three weeks.

It had been a tumultuous interlude filled with yelling, tears, accusations, and pleadings. In the end, her husband, Arthur, had convinced Constanza that Izzy had earned the right to cut the apron strings. The more Connie objected, the more her daughter rebelled. Isabel was a wonderful daughter—healthy, responsible, sincere, an honors student about to enter her senior year of college. She was an adult by any standard, having just celebrated her twenty-first birthday. To object to Izzy's choice of Chile as a destination, when everything in Isabel's past—her heritage, her upbringing, her cultural history—had programmed the young lady for just such a journey, defied common sense. Arthur Finley had counseled that this decision was precisely the link that signaled Isabel's passage into adulthood.

Constanza accepted the logic, and on a practical basis, she noted the strain that her misgivings were creating in her relationship with Izzy. Following the last explosive argument a few days earlier, Connie deemed it wise to remain silent. Nonetheless, her abdomen twisted in a deep, fathomless, implausible series of spasms, because Constanza knew instinctively that her daughter was at risk.

Arthur Finley hugged his wife and spoke in a reassuring tone. "Our little girl is a woman now. She is mature, and Sandy is a responsible young lady as well. Everything will be fine."

Connie fought back the tears. She knew her husband was right, and yet...

Arthur was a good husband and father—gentle, thoughtful, and calm. He provided both Connie and Isabel a secure threshold and a stable base from which to grow and develop. But what Constanza knew, and her husband never acknowledged, was that Izzy was as much her brother's sister as she was her father's daughter. Isabel had as many of Calixto's traits as she did Arthur's. There was an independent streak in Izzy, an unconventional nonconformist deep in her core, which reared itself occasionally in unusual ways.

Connie dried her tears with a face towel and said, "I'll be fine, Arthur. Let's get the girls to the airport."

Chapter 28

December 14, 2006
Gladwyne, Pennsylvania

PETER BURDIS LOOKED across his large study and gazed at the massive floor-to-ceiling bookcases for a full minute. Then he refocused on his two visitors and spoke.

"Joseph Stalin once said, 'Death solves all problems. No man, no problem.' It seems that Augusto Pinochet and the other generals of the Southern Cone took this philosophical approach to heart."

"So, the members of Operation Condor used the network to assassinate their political rivals, even on foreign soil," said Mike.

"Precisely," answered Burdis. "The very network they created significantly increased their reach."

"And now, with the assassination of Letelier, Condor made its most significant statement," said John, leaning in toward their host.

"Yes," answered Burdis as a light flashed in his eyes. "No one was safe. Not even a former ambassador living in the capital of the most powerful country in the world."

There was a pause as the three men let the weight of the statement settle. Finally Mike asked, "Were we involved?"

Burdis chose his words carefully.

"We were not responsible, *but* in some ways we were duplicitous. Think of the leverage in their action. The members of Operation Condor were drunk with power. They were self-righteous in their mind-set."

"Were they above the fray?" asked John.

"No," answered Burdis, "but they overestimated their position."

"Did it cause problems?"

"Yes," said the man with an extra measure of energy as he reached for his oxygen mask.

Mike helped Burdis with the equipment as John took the opportunity to unbutton the cuffs and roll up the sleeves of his own dress shirt. The clarity of the memories renewed their host's energy.

"The CIA had lost control of their stepchild. Letelier's assassination opened the shadow world of Operation Condor to the light of day. It brought the severity of the military dictatorships in South America *home* to our shores in a very real way."

"And did the CIA dive for cover?" asked Mike.

"They had to; the FBI was in full-fledged investigatory overdrive. The State Department was screaming. The media was having a field day. The Agency immediately shared intelligence that Ed Koch had also been targeted for assassination."

"The mayor?" asked John, a little incredulous.

"He was a congressman then," said Burdis by way of explanation. "Koch had sponsored legislation to cut off military assistance to Uruguay due to human rights violations. Needless to say, that didn't go over well in Montevideo."

"So the generals passed it to Operation Condor," said Mike.

"Yes," answered Burdis, "it was tasked to Condor for a solution."

"Is this the evolution, that you mentioned," said John.

"Precisely. Following each successive step, each turn of events, over a few short years, enthralled with the very audacity of their actions, Condor morphed; it grew—and it changed."

"They adapted," said Mike.

"Yes," said Burdis. "Within two years the FBI provided the grand jury with volumes of incriminating evidence on the Letelier assassination."

"Where did that go?" asked John.

"Indictments followed," replied Burdis, "and the courts exposed a clandestine organization sponsored by the military dictatorships of South America. Operation Condor was about to be forced to center stage for the whole world to see."

Chapter 29

PATSY BELLOCCO TREATED Sofia to a whirlwind of fancy dinners, private cruises, and expensive gifts. He was an energetic, somewhat irrepressible suitor of romantic intent, and it was all a bit overwhelming to the dancer.

Sofia smiled. She was used to attracting attention. Her lithe frame and shapely legs often drew a lustful interest from both men and women alike. But years earlier, Sofia had resigned herself to a career of modest income. She loved to dance. Tango was Sofia's passion, but the tradeoff to being a professional dancer was a lack of money. Patsy changed all that.

The black sedan pulled to the curb in front of two enormous polished brass doors. Patsy's bodyguard in the front seat quickly jumped to the sidewalk and waved off the valet. Then he tugged open the rear door and guided Sofia from the car.

Inside was the Casa Cruz, one of the most expensive restaurants in Buenos Aires. The trendy establishment, conspicuous by the absence of a sign over its polished brass doors, beckoned a privileged clientele. It was always crowded with the beautiful people.

The brass doors opened from within, and the maître d' greeted Patsy by name.

"Señor Bellocco, a privilege," said the man deferentially with a slight bow. Then he repeated the motion to Sofia. He quickly noted her graceful posture and the style with which she exposed a leg through the thigh-high slit in her long gown.

"Señorita, a pleasure. I am Rinaldo. You are with Señor Bellocco, so please, anything you need." He used a wave of his hand to finish the sentence.

Patsy and Sofia followed the maître d' into the modern interior, looping around the huge round bar filled with floral arrangements and into the spacious dining room. All eyes were on the attractive woman with swanlike balance and her swarthy, bull-chested escort. They were the center of attention. The maître d' guided them to the middle of the wood and red upholstery decorated dining room. Immediately, several waiters appeared and started fawning over the couple, lighting candles, spreading napkins in their laps, and moving silverware around their table. Each of them greeted Patsy by his last name. Then the sommelier approached with an ice bucket and a bottle of champagne.

"Señor Bellocco, good evening." He offered a view of the label, *Dom Perignon*. "As always, only the best for you."

Smoothly, the sommelier popped open the champagne and poured the bubbly into two elegant flute glasses. He wrapped the neck of the bottle in a napkin, placed it in the bucket, and gave a slight bow with his head as he drifted away.

Sofia considered the moment as Patsy leaned forward, his eyes riveted on her face.

"You look beautiful tonight," said Bellocco.

The dancer smiled. This was heady stuff. Patsy was a bit overpowering, and at once she was both flattered by the attention, yet also leery of the control. Everywhere they went, people jumped. Bellocco was rich and demanding in a quiet sort of way, but underneath there was an animal magnetism that was somehow attractive in its quality.

Patsy's two bodyguards faded into the background and sat at a small table in the shadows, from where they could watch the entire room.

"Gracias," answered Sofia as she reached for her flute glass. They toasted, and she sipped the expensive champagne. He held her gaze.

One of Bellocco's charming qualities was his ability to focus. When he was with Sofia, he seemed to have eyes only for her. As subordinates responded and sycophants groveled, Patsy assured that nothing impeded his attention. He placed Sofia at the center of his universe. As seductive as it was, it created a conflict from the beginning. Sofia stressed her involvement in an existing relationship. Patsy clearly ignored the information. Sofia held Bellocco at a distance, but like a runaway train gathering speed going downhill, he would not be slowed. He wanted what he wanted, and the dancer sensed that few denied Patsy his desires. This, of course, was part of the aura. Bellocco was handsome in a brooding, rugged type of way, but more than anything, his demeanor held Sofia's attention. He exuded power.

Sofia decided that tonight she would finally invite Patsy to her bed. For the past two weeks, she had deftly turned back his advances, forcing him to earn her affections, but each polite side step increased his ardor. Patsy was clearly not a man conditioned to disappointment, yet the denials actually deepened his interest.

It also gave Sofia a chance to sort out the conflict of her existing lover. It was not exclusive, but it was important. The dancer found that dual emotional bonds clouded her judgment, and therefore, she used the time to consider her feelings. In any case, Sofia concluded that now she would reward Patsy's patience.

Sofia reached across the table and touched the back of Patsy's hand.

"This is a special evening, Pasquale, and I want to remember everything tomorrow morning when we have coffee together on your balcony."

A slight glint of understanding crept into Patsy's eyes, and then he seemed to relax and actually smile. He raised his champagne flute a second time.

"To memories," he said, and without looking, lifted his free hand toward the waiter.

Chapter 30

Columbus, Georgia

CALIXTO LOZEN WADED into the swamp. He raised his arms as each step sank him deeper into the chest-high water. The murky ooze filled his boots, and within seconds the warm wash soaked his fatigues. The complaints started.

Fort Benning was never a pleasant place, but in the summer it was particularly hostile. It was hot, sticky, and filled with poisonous reptiles. The nights were worse than the days.

Cal led a twenty-man student platoon of SOA junior officers on a training maneuver, and it wasn't going well. These future leaders didn't like the field. They were educated, but too often the pampered children of powerful families. A little adversity, and they broke down. The swamps of Georgia exposed one's character.

Suddenly, halfway across the swamp, Cal froze. Clearly frustrated, he turned and spoke in a low but very clear voice. "Silencio. Acallar."

A hushed silence fell over the students. They represented a dozen Central and South American military organizations, but in Lozen's estimation, these junior officers lacked commitment.

One of the Special Forces cadre pushed his way along the single-file line that stretched across the swamp, and caught up with Cal.

"Everything okay, C. L.?" asked the sergeant in a whisper.

"No," said Lozen, "what's the problem back there? Do any of these guys understand noise discipline?"

The SF NCO smiled in the moonlight before answering.

"I think they're afraid of the dark. They talk to hide their fear. It's a Latin thing."

"It's constant," said Lozen.

The NCO grinned before adding, "And they forgot we speak Spanish."

Cal gave the NCO a curious look.

"They think you are hard on them," said the NCO. "You're getting a reputation."

Lozen smirked before responding, "They haven't seen anything yet. How's our advocate doing?"

"Okay," said the NCO with a shrug, "but be careful of him, C. L.; he's on their side. The major is more interested in keeping the students happy. It's a diplomacy thing."

Lozen frowned knowingly. "No surprise there. Tell our young officers to keep a lid on the jabbering. If I hear any more noise, then we're going to stand right here in the swamp until daybreak."

The Special Forces sergeant stifled a laugh before whispering "Well, C. L., that would befit their new nickname for you."

Lozen studied his NCO before asking, "Nickname?"

"They are calling you Jefe el Loco."

Chapter 31

Tucson, Arizona

THE RETURN RIDE from the airport was difficult. Constanza was distraught, and no amount of reasoned discourse could calm her nerves. Connie's only daughter, her little girl, Izzy, was outbound on a plane to South America, to Chile.

Constanza shifted uneasily in the passenger seat as her husband negotiated the traffic. Another quiet minute passed before Arthur Finley reached across the front seat and gently patted his wife's knee.

"She's a young lady now," said Arthur.

"I know."

"She's mature and reliable."

"I know," said Constanza.

"Sandy is fun loving, but has good common sense. They'll be fine."

Connie looked at her husband bleary-eyed and let out a long sigh before responding, "If you say so."

The professor saw no point in trying to talk his wife through an emotional chasm. Logic could not bridge the thirty years since Constanza had fled her home and the wrath of the generals. In Connie's mind, three decades hadn't really transpired. It was yesterday, and the threat of arrest, torture, and assassination was real and still existed. Whenever Arthur offered a contrary opinion on the matter, Connie pointed to the fact that Augusto Pinochet, the leader of Chile's Dirty War and the primary force behind much of South America's evil era, was still alive and active in Chilean politics. He was a senator for life. He could not be prosecuted, and he was protected by a circle of powerful people, politicians, and military men with like interests. *Nothing* had changed.

"He's ninety years old," said her husband.

"He's still in power."

"Michele Bachelet is the president of Chile, and she was a dissident."

"And *she* cannot arrest Pinochet," said Constanza in a sharp rebuke. "Please, Arthur, you don't know these people the way that I do."

They drove the final ten minutes in silence, and as Arthur turned down their quiet street, he passed an empty blue sedan parked under the shade of a guajillo tree. He pulled the SUV into their driveway and turned off their car.

Once inside their split-level ranch, Constanza walked down the hall past her husband's small home office on the way to her kitchen. Suddenly she stopped. Something had caught her eye. Connie turned and backpedaled softly to the open door of his study.

Constanza stood motionless in the entrance, her gaze shifting curiously in a semicircle, her mind trying to absorb what seemed odd and out of place.

Arthur's computer was on. Connie watched as every few seconds the screen lit up with the University of Arizona logo and then reverted again to a black façade. It was a screen saver, but it only worked if the computer was left on, and her husband *never* left his computer on.

Constanza exhaled. Her husband had two computers, a laptop at his university faculty office and this desktop model at home. As a tenured professor, Arthur had access to secure university websites through his personal password. He also kept confidential files for exams, test results, and academic papers. He could only access this information from one remote location at a time. Therefore, to assure he never inadvertently boxed himself out or to prohibit hacking by a curious student, Finley always logged off and shut down his computer—at either location—when he was finished.

Arthur was finicky about his computer, a personality trait mimicked by his daughter, Isabel.

"Arthur?"

"Back here, Connie," answered her husband from the rear of the house. He turned into the hallway, his face twisted in a baffled expression, and approached the study. "Rather odd."

"What is?" asked Connie.

"I was the last one out of the house when we took the girls to the airport. I was sure I locked up."

A deep expression of concern crossed Constanza's face. She turned in the door of his study. "Were you working in here before we left?"

"Yes, I was grading papers."

"Did you leave your computer on?"

"Of course not," said Arthur. "Never. Why?"

Constanza motioned with an open hand toward his desktop computer. It sat sideways on the corner of the desk, partially facing the door. The black screen lighted with the UA logo for a few seconds and then went black, on and off, repeating the sequence.

Arthur shook his head as Connie ran to the front of the house. She stood motionless behind the full-length drapes in her living room, and peered up and down the quiet suburban neighborhood street.

Off to her right, she saw a blue sedan parked along the curb under a guajillo tree start to pull away. Two men sat in the front seat.

Chapter 32

En Route to Santiago, Chile

Isabel and Sandy huddled in their coach seats on the American Airlines flight from Dallas.

This was the final lap on their trip from Tucson to Santiago. Sandy was immersed in a Frommer's guidebook as Izzy took the opportunity to kick off her shoes and stretch her legs. The weather was reversed in South America—summer was winter—but the bristling Arizona heat compelled them to wear shorts until they arrived.

Isabel massaged her bare thighs and calves, moving her knees and ankles in tandem. Like most avid runners, Izzy stretched regularly.

Sandy was thin and full breasted, but not as athletic as her roommate, and for a moment she paused and dog-eared a page in her tourist guide. "You okay?"

"Yes," said Izzy with a smile. "Just cramping up a bit because of all the sitting."

Sandy watched Isabel stroke her legs before speaking again. "You have such great legs, Izzy. They are so toned. I wish I had your legs."

Isabel looked at her friend with an embarrassed expression. Self-consciously she stopped kneading her sore legs.

Sandy laughed. "Well, don't get uptight. You know I'm not gay. It was just an observation."

Isabel blushed and placed an index finger across her lips. Her eyes shifted to her right. "Sandy," whispered Izzy, "someone will hear you."

Sandy shrugged and changed the subject. "I think that Buenos Aires is going to be more fun than Santiago or Lima." She held up her guidebook. "Lots more of a party atmosphere in BA. It's the whole Evita thing."

"We'll check it out," said Isabel, "but remember, I have a list of places to see in Chile when we get to Santiago."

"Of course," answered Sandy.

"And we need some flexibility in our schedule in case I get an audience."

Sandy looked over at Izzy with a slightly puzzled expression. "Come again?"

"An audience," said Isabel.

"An audience with whom?"

"The president."

"What president?"

"Michelle Bachelet, the president of Chile."

Sandy sat up in her airline seat and looked squarely at her roommate. Her eyes were wide in amazement. "What makes you think you can get an audience with the president of Chile? Why?"

"For my senior thesis," said Izzy. "I sent her a letter a couple of weeks ago. I told her of my background, my mom's history, and that I saw her speak in Washington at the Letelier monument on the thirtieth anniversary of the assassination."

Sandy was clearly chagrined. "So you sent a letter to the president of Chile and asked for an audience when we arrive?"

Isabel looked at her friend curiously. "Yes."

"An American college student from Arizona?"

"A person of Chilean descent. A woman whose mom was, like her, a dissident and fled the generals. A young student who wants to understand and do a thorough research paper on the Dirty War and its aftermath."

"Wow," said Sandy, leaning back in her seat. "You've got brass."

Izzy looked blankly at her roommate, confused by the statement.

"You are just like your brother," said Sandy.

"Why do you say that?"

"Because all of this academic stuff is to please your dad, but you *think* just like Cal. That's a Cal move—no fears."

Isabel studied her friend for a moment. She was a little perturbed at Sandy's misgivings. "I don't see what the big deal is."

"It's the incongruity, Iz—the audacity of the request. Think about it. We're not diplomats or CEOs or world leaders. We're just two college seniors from Tucson. President Bachelet is running a whole country. Do you actually think she has time to meet with us?"

Isabel considered the question for a minute before answering. Then she looked calmly at Sandy and lifted her two open hands in the air. "What's the worst thing that can happen?" said Izzy. "She says no?"

Chapter 33

December 14, 2006
Gladwyne, Pennsylvania

Peter Burdis shifted in his wheelchair and folded his hands in his lap before speaking.

"So, under the full glare of the world stage, the generals did the common-sense thing: they dragged Operation Condor underground."

"Buried their activities," said Mike.

"Hid them from view," said Burdis. "It didn't stop the pattern, mind you. The kidnappings and torture continued. People still disappeared. But now, instead of the secret police openly abducting someone in broad daylight in full view of a hundred citizens, Condor's henchmen became masters of the midnight raid."

"Did they become *less* brazen?" asked John.

"They became *more* secretive," replied their host, "more sensitive to the unwanted glare of the spotlight."

"But no less committed to their goals," said Mike.

"No," answered Burdis as a smile crept to his lips, preceding the shared pun. "They evolved."

The two visitors laughed before Mike finally asked, "And the assassinations—did they stop?"

"No," said Burdis, raising his hand in the air. "There's a perfect example of how they adapted." The mansion's owner coughed several times before continuing. "The Chilean secret police hired a biochemist to experiment with poisons. So instead of noisy car bombs or blazing gun battles, Condor began to quietly poison their enemies."

John took a sip of water and leaned toward Burdis. "What obstacles developed as a result of their new, lower profile?"

"Money, the cash flow, dried up. Condor needed funds to operate, and we, the United States, the largest benefactor to these staunch anti-Communists, shut down the money tree."

"The generals had slashed their own wrists," said Mike.

"Precisely," answered their host. "There was no appetite for overt support. The Letelier incident had everyone diving for cover."

"So what did they do?" asked John.

"The members of Operation Condor began an exploratory campaign. They needed to identify alternate sources of financing."

Chapter 34

Buenos Aires, Argentina

SOFIA STOOD IN front of the gold-plated mirror and reached for a bottle of lotion. Like so much in Patsy's world, the bathroom was ornate, complete with imported marble, gilt-crafted fixtures from Europe, and hand-stitched fabrics from China. She wrapped her torso in a towel from breasts to hips and extended a shapely leg on the countertop.

The last few weeks had been a carousel for Sofia. Patsy practiced the good life as only a few wealthy Argentineans could enjoy. He spoiled her with attention and enveloped her body with passion. The rugged Patsy was a sexually charged lover, more energetic than gifted, who couldn't keep his hands off the lithe tango dancer. Truthfully, Sofia loved Patsy's lust for her. She started rubbing the expensive body lotion onto her exposed thigh.

A minute later Patsy entered the bathroom. She looked up and saw him in the mirror's reflection, sensitive that he had caught her in a compromising position. Bellocco stepped forward and pressed his clothed body against her partially covered back. He nudged her neck and ears with his lips from behind. "You are so beautiful," said Patsy in a whisper. Then he ran his right hand over the skin of Sofia's extended leg and stroked her from ankle to thigh, rubbing the body lotion deeper into her limb, savoring the feel of her toned muscles and sensual flesh.

She reached back and kissed him as he nibbled on her neck, feeling his hand as he groped under the towel to grip her buttocks.

"You have the most incredible legs," said Patsy.

"I think it is your favorite part of me," replied Sofia softly.

Patsy reached up with both hands and cupped her breasts through the towel. "I love it all," he said, "but yes, my first attraction is *always* the legs."

She had started to kiss him, when surprisingly, Bellocco pulled away.

"I'm sorry; I am late. I have to go," said Patsy.

Sofia looked perplexed. "Where?"

"Away—business. You can stay here. My people will take care of you."

"How long?" asked Sofia.

"A few days. Maybe a week."

Sofia was puzzled. This would be the first time in several weeks that she wouldn't see Patsy on a daily basis. It was clear he wasn't asking her to accompany him. "Will you call?"

"Maybe—if I can," said Patsy.

The sudden announcement seemed to catch her off guard.

"You've been taking plenty of time away from the restaurant," said Patsy. "Raoul will be happy to have you back for more performances. He has been very accommodating."

"I will miss you, Pasquale."

"And I will miss you," said Bellocco. He smiled and walked from the bathroom.

In the master bedroom, Patsy grabbed for a leather jacket in his closet just as he heard Sofia's cell phone ring. Instinctively, he looked at the bathroom door, and then quickly crossed the bedroom and opened her purse. He tugged the cell phone free and examined the glass face. The ringing phone identified the caller simply as *Dan* and printed the number. Bellocco grimaced in frustration. He marched into the bathroom and held up Sofia's cell phone as she looked in the mirror.

"You have a call," said Patsy as the phone continued to ring. "The caller is Dan. Who is *Dan?*"

Sofia turned and looked directly at Patsy, and for the first time experienced his edge. He was angry, but still under control.

"I told you, Pasquale, when we first started to date, that I was already in a relationship."

"So?"

"I was very honest with you."

"That was then," said Patsy. "Things have changed. You are with me now. You are mine. I don't share."

Bellocco's stance was both rigid and confident.

"The relationship with Dan existed first. It predated ours. Dan helped me, and therefore, it's complicated."

"No," said Patsy with an air of finality, "it's quite simple. Have I treated you well?"

"Yes," said Sofia, "very."

"Then tell Dan it's over. I am going away for a few days. When I get back, you are moving in. I will take care of you. Understood?"

Patsy tossed the cell phone, which had stopped ringing, on the marble countertop next to the sink. Then he turned and exited the bathroom.

Chapter 35

Vina del Mar, Chile

THE COLONEL LEANED forward at his desk, rested both elbows on the black blotter, and gently touched the tops of his fingers together. Across the desk sat his subordinate, the captain, who was finishing the report in his typically terse, frill-free manner.

"Then, Soto Finley and her friend took a bus to the Pajaritos Metro Station and transferred to Baquedano. They checked in to the Mito Casa Hotel on Providencia."

The colonel stroked his thin mustache and motioned for the captain to continue.

"They settled in for a few hours, probably napping from jet lag, and then ventured out for a late afternoon stroll around the neighborhood. They had dinner in Bellavista at a local café, stopped for a drink at a couple of pubs on the way back to their hotel, and retired early," said the captain.

The dapper colonel spread his arms wide and looked at his subordinate. "It all sounds so routine, Captain—two young adults on a holiday."

"Sí, Colonel." The captain paused for effect before continuing. "Except the young Soto Finley woman called La Moneda."

"The Palace?"

"Sí, Colonel, the Palacio de Gobierno."

"Why?" The colonel's expression turned quizzical.

"She referenced a letter. She seeks an audience with Señora President."

"With Bachelet?" replied the colonel, taken aback. "She is a student."

The captain shrugged and looked blankly at his superior.

"What's in the letter," asked the colonel in a perturbed tone.

"We don't know."

"Then we need to find out," said the colonel. He frowned, his features becoming quite pensive. "These inconsistencies are becoming the norm, and they make me very uncomfortable."

"Sí, Colonel."

"Why *now*, Captain?" asked the colonel rhetorically. "After all these years, just when we are transitioning our Empresa?"

The captain shrugged a second time as the colonel stood. The senior officer quietly looked out of his small office window to the rear of the villa. Finally he turned back to the desk and motioned. He seemed to be resolute.

"I want a very tight net around these two young ladies. And get me the names of the junior officers we have assigned to the School of the Americas' exchange program in the United States."

Chapter 36

Tucson, Arizona

ARTHUR FINLEY STEPPED from his home office just as his wife walked down the hall.

"When did you get in?" asked the professor.

"I just got back," replied Constanza. She continued toward the kitchen.

"You missed her."

"Who?"

"Izzy."

Constanza suddenly stopped and turned toward her husband. "She's here?"

"No; she called."

"From Santiago?" asked Constanza.

"Yes, on the computer. She Skyped me from her hotel room."

"Is she okay?"

"She's fine; she looked a little tired."

"Well, get her back on," said Constanza, pacing quickly back down the hall toward her husband.

"She signed off," said Arthur. "She was going for a run."

"In Santiago?"

Arthur Finley looked curiously at his wife. "Well, yes, Connie, she runs every day. Why wouldn't she?"

"She'll get lost. She's in a strange city. She doesn't know Santiago. Something will happen."

"It's morning there. The streets are filled with people. She said there are sidewalks and a small park near their hotel."

"Arthur, *please*," said Connie.

The professor looked at his wife in frustration. The edge in her voice heightened the frost that had enveloped them for the past two days. Constanza was convinced that someone had surreptitiously broken into their home and searched Arthur's office. She wanted him to contact the Tucson police and report the crime. She wanted the blue sedan checked out.

Arthur, on the other hand, was not convinced. He felt a modicum of ambivalence about the situation and therefore was reluctant to sound an alarm. His nature was toward reasoned judgment, where Constanza was given to emotional reactions.

In retrospect, the professor conceded that it was unlikely that he would both leave his computer on and not lock their back door. However, he could find no sign of unusual computer tampering or forced entry. Arthur was no expert, but in logically thinking through the situation and the questions the police were likely to ask, he favored restraint. "Professor Finley, is it possible that in your rush to get the girls to the airport, you forgot to turn off your computer? In all the commotion, could you have forgotten to lock your back door? Mrs. Finley, could you tell us the make and model of the suspicious blue sedan? Did you happen to get a license plate number?"

Most importantly, under questioning, Arthur feared that his wife's irrational fears of a thirty-year-old conspiracy come back to life would not play well.

Finally, Arthur started to wonder whether with all the emotional turmoil of the past few weeks on the advent of their daughter's first international trip, he could have forgotten to turn off his computer and secure their home. Maybe he and Connie were experiencing a delayed empty-nest syndrome. Most parents felt this a few years earlier, but insofar that Izzy lived at home for her first two years of college and since she stopped by regularly even while living away at an off-campus apartment, maybe this was their reaction to Isabel's absence.

"Connie," said the professor, "the girls are fine. I saw them on Skype. Sandy said hello. Izzy's going for a short run, they are having breakfast, and then they will be tourists for the rest of the day."

"Arthur," said Constanza in a strident tone. Her eyes were bleary.

"Please," replied her husband, cutting her off, "let Isabel be an adult. Let her *enjoy* this experience."

Connie grimaced, whirled on her heels, and paced from the hallway.

Chapter 37

Columbus, Georgia

AT DUSK THE Special Forces cadre separated the exchange students into groups of six and gathered them around small campfires with an instructor. They huddled together in the dense tree line to discuss strategy.

This was nontactical time. Give-and-take in a relaxed atmosphere was part of the SF tradition. It allowed the junior officers in the SOA to let down their hair and absorb the day's lessons without rigid protocol and the fear of reprisals. They chatted for an hour.

"So, what other questions do you have?" asked one of the NCOs.

A slight hesitation ensued, and finally a student from Paraguay raised his hand. "Sergeant, may we ask about your leader, the warrant officer?"

"Chief Lozen," said the NCO.

"Sí."

"Sure; what about him?"

"Is he American?"

"Of course," said the SF NCO with a nod.

"Where is he from?"

"Originally, Arizona. But he lives somewhere near Fort Bragg. Why?"

The SOA student grinned sheepishly. "He does not look like a typical American."

The NCO laughed. "What does a typical American look like?"

"Different than him," said a junior officer from Bolivia. "He looks mestizo."

The NCO smirked. "Well, I guess he is. Welcome to America." The instructor lowered his voice and said in an amused tone, "But trust me; he's about as red-blooded an American as it gets."

The small group of students looked confused. A junior officer from Argentina spoke. "You call him C. L. Is that for Chief Lozen?"

"No," said the NCO, spitting a wad of chewing tobacco onto the campfire. "We call him C. L. because of his name, Calixto Lozen."

The SOA officers absorbed the informality before a student from Brazil spoke.

"Calixto is a Spanish name."

"Yup," replied the SF NCO. "His mother was Spanish, somewhere down your neck of the woods." Then the NCO leaned forward and, in a quiet, conspiratorial tone, lowered his voice to a whisper. "And we know about your nickname for him: Jefe el Loco."

The students all sat forward, nervous, their secret exposed, their concerns for reprisals apparent.

"Don't worry," said the SF NCO, enjoying the drama. "That is, as long as you don't piss him off."

"Would he hurt us?" asked the student from Paraguay.

"Only if you crossed him," said the NCO. He lowered his voice another full notch. All six of the junior officers leaned forward and strained to hear his explanation. "You see," said the SF instructor, "C. L. has two meanings. To us, it's Calixto Lozen, his birth name. But to his father, it's Canus Lupus, or Gray Wolf, his warrior name."

The SOA students sat enthralled.

"His mother is Spanish," said the NCO, "but his father is a Chiricahua Apache. C. L. grew up learning how to track. If you offend him, he will find you."

"Even here?" asked a student from Honduras, his open hand indicating the dense foliage of the Fort Benning swampland.

"Anywhere," said the NCO. "A forest, a mountain, in the sand of a desert. C. L. has instincts. He could find anyone."

The junior officers sat in silence and tried to form a visual picture. Finally the SF NCO smiled and leaned back against his rucksack.

"It will be dark soon. In thirty minutes we go tactical, so heat up some grub now if you're hungry. Then put out the campfire and post security. Three-man teams on two-hour shifts. You'll get your new Ops order at twenty-two hundred hours."

The NCO shifted his patrol cap to cover his eyes and quickly fell asleep.

Chapter 38

Santiago, Chile

To Isabel's surprise, she was emotional about seeing Santiago. For two days they had walked the streets of the city, exploring the sights and sounds, absorbing the rhythm, behaving as tourists.

For Sandy, the kaleidoscope of Chileans in and around the *Plaza de Armas* was the show; artists, musicians, chess players, and shoeshine vendors interacted in a variety of manners with the tourists and gawkers. She watched the people. The soul of a culture was in the citizens. It told her the history.

Izzy's sensitivities were more basal. They were spawned by her mother's stories, which mirrored Isabel's current travels, with a thirty-year lag. Constanza Soto Finley had been a young university student in her early twenties, protesting in these very streets. The overlay of the moment added a poignancy to Izzy's trip. It offered a context to both the Dirty War and the continued existence of the very same buildings and institutions that surrounded her.

"Okay, Iz," said Sandy, tired of posing. "*Vogue* is not calling, and I need a beer."

"Just one more," replied Izzy as she turned from the twin spires of the Metropolitan Cathedral and lowered the camera. She made a handoff to her roommate and walked in the opposite direction.

"Take me from this side," said Isabel. "It will give us a different perspective for the other view of the square."

Sandy focused the camera on Izzy standing in front of a large equestrian statue.

"So who's the guy?" asked Sandy.

Izzy looked over her shoulder at the statue of a man sitting on a horse. Then she smoothed her blouse. "Pedro Valdivia, the founder of Santiago."

"Figures you would know that," said Sandy. "Some Spanish guy?"

"Yes, a conquistador. The first governor of Chile."

"Smile," said Sandy.

Izzy forced a weak grin. As beautiful as she was, Isabel found it hard to pose for a picture. She was too self-conscious to appear natural.

"Lousy," said Sandy, looking at the photo. "It doesn't do you justice." Then she laughed. "But the guy on the horse looks great."

Sandy zipped up her sweater against the late afternoon temperature change. August was winter in Santiago, and although the South American city had a Mediterranean-style climate, her winters sometimes got a bit cool. Most days the sun was plentiful, and thankfully for the girls from Tucson, it snowed only in the mountains.

The roommates navigated the streets to the intersection of Paseos Ahumada and Hue'rfanos and sat at a quiet sidewalk café. They ordered two local Chilean beers. Sandy took a long sip and settled back in her chair before speaking.

"Best part of the day."

"We covered a lot of ground," said Izzy, as two well-groomed business-men dressed in expensive suits slid in to the table next to them. The men ordered wine.

For the next ten minutes, Izzy and Sandy chatted about the day's experiences, and then Izzy turned her attention to a street map.

"Excuse me," said one of the men finally in English, leaning toward their table. "Are you Australian?"

Sandy looked first at Izzy and then at the man. She shook her head and spoke.

"Right language, wrong accent."

"Sorry," said the man politely. "I couldn't resist. I don't get much of an opportunity to practice my English." He paused. "Great Britain?"

"Wrong again," replied Sandy, smiling, enjoying the guessing game. She was a natural flirt with men, more friendly than sexual in her banter. Yet her pretty features and nonthreatening demeanor made men comfortable.

He shifted in his seat, turning his torso toward their table. "Well, then, it's either the US or Canada."

"Pick one," answered Sandy.

"Canada."

"Wrong," said Sandy, making the sound of a fake buzzer. "You lose. You buy the next round."

The two men smiled obligingly and motioned for the waiter. The first man pointed at the two Cristal Pale Lagers.

"Do you like our Chilean beer?"

Izzy, who had been attentive but quiet during the conversation, quickly held her hand over the top of her glass and shook her head sideways.

"It's okay," replied Sandy diplomatically. She motioned toward their wine. "We like the wine better, especially the Carmenere."

The second man leaned forward and quietly spoke to Izzy in broken English.

"You must try a special drink then. It is very popular in Chile. I think you will like it."

"What is the drink?" asked Izzy effortlessly in Spanish.

The man's eyes opened wide in surprise. "Your accent sounds Chilean."

"On my mother's side," said Izzy.

He nodded approvingly. "But you are American?"

"Sí."

"From where?"

"Tucson," answered Izzy.

The location confused the man, and rather than admit he wasn't familiar with the city, he answered the drink question. "It is a pisco sour," he said in Spanish, clearly more comfortable in his native language, "and I admit, it is from Peru."

Chapter 39

December 14, 2006
Gladwyne, Pennsylvania

PETER BURDIS TURNED his wheelchair in place so that he could see the early afternoon sun from across the study.

"What happened next?" asked Mike.

"We made it clear that Operation Condor was a very hot topic on the Beltway and there would be no funds coming from Washington, so they asked for our advice," replied the cripple.

"And did we advise them?" asked John.

Burdis hesitated before answering, "Sort of."

"Please explain," said Mike, leaning forward in his cushioned chair.

"The military dictatorships of the Southern Cone were isolated, cut off from the rest of the world," answered Burdis.

"They needed funding, and they didn't know where to turn," said Mike.

"They needed alternative sources of financing for their operations," said Burdis.

"They needed a direction," said John. "Did we put them in touch with certain organizations?"

"With certain people," answered Burdis, "people who had affiliations."

"Did we make the connections?" asked Mike.

"We made suggestions," said their host. "We helped with introductions, and nature took its course."

"Why?" asked John.

"*Why?*" said Burdis with a touch of indignation. "Because, despite the flaws inherent in their system, the generals had made great strides in protecting the continent from communism. We had saved South America, and we were not going to give it back."

"So we introduced them to some businessmen," said Mike.

"Not just businessmen," said Burdis, somewhat incredulous at their naïveté. "To the architect, a financier of incredible vision."

Chapter 40

Plati, Italy

PATSY BELLOCCO WALKED down the cobbled streets of Plati. Several young men, soldiers in a rival locale or family, stopped and respectfully acknowledged the 'ndrina boss of Buenos Aires, knowing he was only in town for the annual meeting to be held in San Luca.

Each year, all of the 'Ndrangheta clan bosses from all over the world descended on the small village of San Luca, in Calabria, for a gathering at the Sanctuary of Our Lady of Polsi during the September feast.

This year, in an attempt to thwart the constant surveillance of the Italian military police, the Carabinieri, the meeting dates were moved forward into the summer.

The annual meeting in San Luca provided a forum for the 'Ndrangheta families to iron out differences, impose a structure, and force decisions on the disparate, competitive clans.

Followed by two bodyguards, Patsy turned right at a small intersection and entered a door guarded by several men in collared shirts, casually displaying their lupara shotguns. He descended a flight of stairs into a private wine cellar.

As soon as he entered the cellar, a hush fell over the crowd. Then suddenly, the dozen men milling around a rectangular table started to clap. Their applause grew, and Patsy accepted their congratulatory handshakes and slaps on the back.

He took a full two minutes to respectfully work the room, sure to angle toward the far corner, where an old man waited patiently at the head of the table. As Patsy approached, the old man smiled, stretched his arms wide, and opened his hands toward the ceiling.

Finally, Bellocco stood before the old man, who gripped Patsy by both shoulders and mumbled his name in Italian. "Pasquale."

"Zio Ciccio," replied Patsy respectfully as he folded into the old man's arms. They exchanged kisses on both cheeks. The old man motioned toward the seat on his left, and then as Patsy sat, he addressed the room full of guests.

"Amici," said the old man in a clear voice, "tomorrow I have the honor of representing all of you, the Bellocco-Pelle Famiglia, at the annual meeting of the Capobastones in San Luca. Each of you, as a 'ndrina boss, understands the importance of this gathering at the sanctuary." He took a moment to assure he had everyone's attention. "For years," said the old man in a thoughtful manner, "our famiglia, based here in Plati, has earned a reputation through all of the 'Ndrangheta as the 'cradle of kidnapping.' Human traffic has made the Bellocco-Pelle clan rich and powerful."

The old man was interrupted by a chorus of 'ndrina bosses as they slapped their open hands on the wooden table in agreement. He waited until they quieted down.

"I am proud to add," said the old man, "that my brother's son, Pasquale, has created a new chapter in the reputation of our famiglia. It is known throughout the 'Ndrangheta. Our South America 'ndrina, based in Buenos Aires, has for the past three years produced incredible profits. For this reason, tomorrow when I go to the sanctuary, I will be accompanied by our newest *quintino*, my nephew, Pasquale."

The wine cellar again erupted in cheers and table-pounding as the other men, many of them older than Patsy, stood to acknowledge the huge promotion.

Finally, the old man held up his wineglass in a toast as he patted the still-seated Patsy on the shoulder. "I only wish," said the proud uncle, "that Pasquale's papa, my brother, could see this day. God rest his soul. Salute."

The old man tipped his glass and drank as the other 'ndrina bosses for the family followed suit and toasted Patsy in unison.

Chapter 41

Santiago, Chile

THE MAN'S NAME was Alvaro, and he clearly showed an interest in Sandy. He was polite and easygoing, a man comfortable in himself and around pretty women. He smiled a lot, which immediately put him on the same wavelength as Izzy's roommate.

They had chatted for an hour, sharing another bottle of wine, and then the men invited the two young ladies to an early dinner at a casual restaurant.

Alvaro spoke good English, which was helpful, as Sandy's Spanish was only passable. The pairings seemed natural, as the second man, Juan, enjoyed the fluency of Izzy's Spanish. It helped to offset his broken English.

At first, Izzy was reluctant to go to dinner. She had no interest in Juan. He was nice enough and it was easy for them to converse in Spanish, but she didn't quite accept that they were *only* in their midtwenties.

In fairness to her friend, however, Sandy and Alvaro were hitting it off. For Isabel, the trip to Chile was a personal quest, but to her roommate, the lure of South America was for the experience. Sandy was fun loving and people oriented, and therefore it was important to be sensitive to her needs as well.

They went to dinner and spent another couple of hours relaxing and conversing. The men suggested continuing on to a nightclub for dancing, at which point Izzy begged off. Sandy caught the cue and followed suit.

"And tomorrow," asked Alvaro curiously, "what are your plans?" He smiled at Sandy as he asked the question. She looked at Izzy, who had planned their itinerary.

"Tomorrow," said Isabel, "we have some nontraditional places to visit."

"Then let me take you," said Alvaro. "I know Santiago; I have lived here my whole life."

"Don't you have to work?" asked Sandy with a laugh.

The two men exchanged a glance, and then Juan answered in his broken English. "I have to work," he said. "The bank is very strict about vacation time." He pointed to Alvaro before continuing. "But he is an independent consultant. He makes his own hours."

"Then it is settled," said Alvaro warmly. "Tomorrow I will be your tour guide."

Sandy looked at Izzy with an open expression and cocked her head.

"We wouldn't want to impose," said Isabel politely.

"Not at all," replied Alvaro. "It would be my privilege."

Izzy turned to look at Sandy as she considered the offer. The three-way conversation had just become a two-way conversation. After a minute of silence, Isabel spoke directly to Sandy. "I'll run early. Then we can have breakfast. We can meet him there."

"I can pick you up," said Alvaro, interjecting his thoughts, not realizing he had been momentarily excluded from the dialogue. "It is no problem."

Sandy ignored him. She understood that Izzy was less adventurous and less trusting and therefore wanted a cautious approach. Finally, she turned back toward Alvaro and repeated Izzy's response as if he hadn't heard it. "It's okay," said Sandy. "We can meet you there."

Alvaro began to protest and then quickly relented. "Fine. Where shall we meet?" he asked.

"Estadio Nacional," answered Izzy, speaking for both of them in Spanish.

There was a flicker in Alvaro's eye, and he couldn't help but sneak a look across the table at Juan. "The national stadium in Nunoa?" asked Alvaro.

"Sí," said Izzy, "antes de las diez de la mañana."

He nodded in agreement before speaking. "Before ten tomorrow morning." He stood. "I look forward to our day, Señoritas."

Everyone followed Alvaro's lead and stood, and they shook hands all around. In parting, Alvaro snuck a quick peck onto the back of Sandy's hand and winked.

The girls watched as the two Chileans waved goodbye.

"Spanish guys are so charming," said Sandy in a wistful tone. "They are perfect gentlemen."

"Yes," answered Izzy. "They can be."

"And tomorrow will be fun. You don't mind, do you, Iz?"

"No," said Isabel. "I know you like him. I just prefer to take things slower. Clearly he has eyes for you. We'll see what tomorrow brings."

Chapter 42

ARTHUR FINLEY STOOD at the door of his study and called down the hallway to his wife. "Connie, Izzy is on the line; she's on Skype."

He turned back toward his desk and sat facing the computer screen. "How are you, Iz?" asked the professor. He looked at a full-screen picture of his daughter. "You getting enough sleep?"

"I'm good, Dad," said Isabel. "We have busy days, but I've been taking a lot of notes, pictures of course, and even dictating some tapes. It's been really interesting, and we've met some nice people." Izzy intentionally downplayed their time touring with Alvaro. It was uneventful and although the Chilean was curious as to their choice of destination he seemed to have eyes only for Sandy.

"What people?" asked Constanza, suddenly entering the small home office from the hall. "Who are they?" She peered over her husband's shoulder so that she could see Izzy on the computer screen.

"Hi, Mom," said Isabel. "Just some guys that we met a couple of days ago. One of them has a crush on Sandy."

They heard a laugh in the background of the hotel room, and then Sandy was smiling for the camera. "Hi, Mr. and Mrs. F. Don't listen to her; he's been a real gentleman, and his English is better than my Spanish."

"Have you contacted your mom?" asked Constanza.

"Yes, I sent her an e-mail last night," said Sandy.

"Where are you off to today?" asked the professor in a conversational tone.

"Izzy's the itinerary planner," said Sandy. "Yesterday we checked out the national stadium,"—she lowered her voice to a conspiratorial whisper—"and it's *smaller* than UA's Wildcat Stadium." She yawned. "And today we are going to some villa. Got to go."

In a blur, Sandy's face disappeared from the computer screen.

"You went to the national stadium, Izzy?" asked Constanza, curious. "Do you know what happened there?"

"Of course, Mom. It's open to the public."

"And what villa—are these guys you met rich?"

Isabel sighed. She didn't want to alarm her mother, but she didn't want to lie either. "No, Mom, they're not rich. We're going to the Villa Grimaldi."

Constanza gasped. "Izzy, *why?*"

"It's a park now," said Isabel. "The government made it a national monument to honor the victims during the dictatorship. I need to understand. That's why I'm here."

"But, Izzy, you *know* what they did there. The torture, the murder."

"Which is why I need to go." Isabel paused before continuing. "Did you know that Michelle Bachelet was held as a prisoner at Villa Grimaldi?"

"She can't control these people."

"She's the president," said Izzy.

"The general is *still* in charge," said Constanza in a sharp tone.

"Dad," said Isabel, appealing to her father's ability to temper the conversation with her mother.

Arthur Finley sensed, more than knew, that his daughter was researching the Dirty War for her senior thesis. Isabel had not said so directly, but she did hint around the edges when discussing possible topics. To the professor, Izzy's destination and focus seemed to support this view. "I'll handle it, Izzy. What are you up to now?"

"Just going to get in a quick run, and meet Sandy for breakfast before we hit the road."

"Izzy," said Constanza in a heightened state of anxiety, "can you please…"

"Mom," replied Isabel, cutting the conversation short, "everything is fine. I've got to go. Love you."

The computer screen went blank.

Chapter 43

Vina del Mar, Chile

THE COLONEL SAT at his desk absorbing the report, and more importantly, its implications. He was uncomfortable with the timbre of the captain's information and interrupted to make a point. "But nonetheless, Captain, even with the unusual itinerary and this predisposition to the old days, we have no reason to believe they have connected us to the Empresa."

"Nothing specific, Colonel," replied the captain, "but their intention is to come here tomorrow."

"Here, to Vina del Mar? Why?"

The captain swiveled as he adjusted his glasses. "We do not know, Colonel. We can only surmise." He let his eyes drift up toward the ceiling.

The colonel followed his eyes and then spoke. "You think they know the general resides here?"

"It is not such a big secret. We must presume that young Soto's mother has contacts here in this country. She is a native Chilean."

The colonel considered the fact for a moment and then seemed to dismiss the concern. "They are young college students; they are coming to the coast because it is beautiful. You even said that romance was in the air," said the colonel.

"It is an unusual coincidence when one considers all of the other facts, none of which by themselves is all that important. But when taken as a whole, there is a disturbing connection." The captain paused to frame his thoughts before continuing. It was important that his superior understood. "With respect, the general is old and sick. Soon he will die. As we speak, the Supreme Court in Santiago is attempting to strip him of his immunity from prosecution. For the past two years, we have been strengthening deep relationships with our associates throughout the Empresa."

"It has been very productive," said the colonel.

"Sí, but above all, our associates are businessmen. If they doubt for a moment our resolve, our ability to guarantee certain protections to their operations, they will look elsewhere for partners."

The colonel bit his lip in thought. "Do we have reason to believe that these tourists have made any connection between us and the associates?"

The captain swallowed before answering the question with a question. "Colonel, why are they coming here to Vina del Mar tomorrow, and then flying to Buenos Aires the very next day?"

The colonel sat forward, surprised, and stroked his thin mustache. "They are going to Argentina?"

"Sí, in two days," said the captain.

"Why?"

The captain shrugged in response, preferring to remain silent for the moment. The hush in the small office was so pronounced that one could hear the sweep second hand of the wall clock as it rotated. Finally the colonel spoke.

"Captain, please." He raised an open hand.

The subordinate fiddled with his glasses, taking a moment to clean the lenses with his handkerchief before answering.

"Colonel, maybe this research is nothing more than a thirty-year-old history lesson for the daughter. But the mother is native Chilean, and I don't understand why she would concern herself with the Argentinean side of the Dirty War. Has someone, some organization, made a connection between the man upstairs and the relationships we developed through Operation Condor?"

The captain clearly had the colonel's attention. They were trained to be suspicious of anomalies. These were too many loose ends, too many seemingly unrelated threads to be ignored.

"Why are they going to Buenos Aires, Colonel?" asked the captain, continuing the discussion. "Why not Lima or La Paz?"

"Why not Rio de Janiero?" said the colonel, interjecting his own question. "Isn't that the carnival capital for college students?"

"Precisely," answered the captain before continuing. "And why is Soto's half brother, a Special Forces officer, suddenly involved with the SOA?"

"Sí," said the colonel in agreement. "The School of the Americas has proven an excellent recruiting point for our future relationships. Many of them are now involved in the Empresa."

"And *why*," said the captain with an extra measure of discomfort, "does young Soto keep calling La Moneda for an audience with Señora President?"

The colonel leaned forward.

"How many times?"

"Four."

"In a week?"

"Sí," said the captain. "She is quite persistent."

"Do we know what she said in the letter?"

"No, Colonel, we have not been able to obtain a copy."

They lapsed into silence again. The colonel considered the various points and the captain's analysis. In truth, the colonel did not like the incongruity either. Were these young students on holiday, probing history for the purpose of scholarly research, or were they part of a much larger effort to connect the past of Operation Condor to the present Empresa? Was the organization at risk? Were their friends up north changing the landscape? In years past, he had acted much more decisively on considerably less information. Intelligence analysis was far from an exact process.

He pulled open the thick folder on his desk and fished through the dossier until he found a large black-and-white photograph of Izzy. The colonel studied the picture for a few seconds. "She *is* quite attractive."

"Sí, Colonel," answered the captain.

"Her traveling companion, is she presentable?"

"I am told that she is a lovely señorita in her own right," replied the captain, "and more vivacious than the young Soto."

The colonel placed Izzy's photo back on top of the dossier with a very deliberate snap. He had been spurred to action. "Take them, quickly, quietly, *before* they leave for Buenos Aires." The colonel looked hard at the captain and then off to the distance before continuing. "I must think of how I want to handle this. Use good people. Cover our tracks. We *must* assure that the members are safe and that the Empresa remains hidden."

The captain stood. "I shall see to it immediately, Colonel." He clicked his heels deferentially and exited the small office.

Chapter 44

Buenos Aires, Argentina

PATSY BELLOCCO STEPPED from the plane at Ezeiza International Airport, followed by two young Calabrians. They were his nephews, each in their early twenties, and they were sent to Argentina to learn the ropes. They would help Patsy expand the family business.

Word had traveled fast from Plati. The 'ndrina boss of South America, Pasquale Bellocco, had been promoted from *santista* to *quintino.* He was now one of the five privileged members of the Bellocco-Pelle Famiglia who reported directly to the clan boss, his uncle, the capobastone.

It was a rare and deserved honor, and it reverberated throughout the 'Ndrangheta world the way a lofty corporate promotion would echo through the halls of competitive industries. Patsy's success enhanced the standing of the entire Buenos Aires 'ndrina.

"Pasquale," said his brother-in-law as he passed through customs. The older man greeted Patsy with a hug and a whisper. "Mi quintino." He kissed his cheek.

They smiled. Ettore was a good husband to Patsy's older sister, and an even better lieutenant in the 'ndrina.

"And who are these picciotti d'onore?" said the brother-in-law, pointing at Patsy's nephews while using the Calabrian term for soldiers.

"Our newest additions to the locale," answered Bellocco. "They are my brother's two sons. We are expanding."

Ettore pointed at Patsy's bags, which were secured by an associate, and they walked from the international terminal.

The addition of the two nephews brought to four the number of blood relatives working for Patsy in Buenos Aires: the brother-in-law, a cousin, and now his older brother's two sons. In addition, Bellocco's 'ndrina boasted a dozen local associates in Buenos Aires and another twenty pledged subordinates spread throughout Central and South America. Patsy and Ettore climbed into the rear seat of a Lincoln Continental Town Car.

"How is your mother doing?" asked the brother-in-law.

"Bueno," said the new quintino. He changed the subject. Patsy was not by nature a patient man, and his promotion to quintino seemed to amplify this personality trait to a new level of intensity. "All is quiet?" asked Patsy.

"Sí."

"And our new friends in Tamaulipas, you have set up the meeting?"

"Sí."

"On neutral ground?" asked Patsy.

The three-car motorcade sped north along the Riccheri highway. "Sí, in Guate." Ettore used the slang term for Guatemala City, the capital of Guatemala. The Central American country sat midway between Tamaulipas, Mexico, and Buenos Aires, Argentina.

In many ways, Patsy's promotion to quintino was due in large part to his 'ndrina's performance. In the world of the 'Ndrangheta, promotions followed profits. Over the past six years, Bellocco had streamlined and amplified the Colombian cocaine pipeline. It flowed from Bogota to Buenos Aires to the Calabrian port of Gioia Tauro.

Luck was in the air. The European appetite for the drug had doubled in the past decade. There were now five million customers demanding the product. So Patsy made the logical business decision. He would expand the traffic routes and partnerships of his cocaine supply from the Colombians to other, additional sources. He chose a particularly aggressive Mexican cartel known as Los Zetas.

"Bueno," said Patsy, "and cancel any appointments for this afternoon. Did we set up a 'ndrina dinner for tonight?"

"Sí, Quintino, all the underbosses and associates will want to congratulate you."

"And meet our newest members," said Patsy, referring to his two nephews, who rode in the car behind them.

Five minutes later, Patsy walked into his penthouse apartment in Recoleta. Sofia turned and smiled as she saw him drop his suitcase and cross the foyer. She was dressed in a short negligee that seductively exposed her shapely legs. Sofia waited as he crossed the room.

"You look beautiful," said Patsy, scanning her figure in appreciation. Sofia moved forward, turning to greet him, her eyes focused on his face.

"Your trip was good?"

"Yes," said Bellocco, his expression smug and satisfied. He never talked business.

"I've missed you," said Sofia.

She reached up and gently placed a hand behind his neck. Sofia looked deeply into Patsy's eyes.

"Did you handle the cell phone issue?" asked Patsy in a sarcastic tone.

For a moment, Sofia looked confused.

"Your caller," said Patsy.

"You mean *Dan?*"

He nodded.

"Yes, we spoke," answered Sofia. "It was difficult and it did not go well, but it is finished."

Patsy's eyes flashed in a moment of anger. "Will he be a problem?"

"Shh," said Sofia gently, touching her index finger to Patsy's lips. "I told you it is finished. I am *only* with you." Bellocco seemed to relax as Sofia reached up and whispered in his ear, "I've missed you so much, Pasquale."

She started to nibble on his earlobe, her breath warm to the touch. She probed his inner ear with her tongue. Sofia knew what Patsy wanted from a woman, what he *needed* to hear. Her hands became active as she stroked his back.

"Take me, Pasquale, please, take me now. I need you *inside* of me."

Bellocco responded by grabbing for Sofia's buttocks. He pulled her close, placed one hand under each cheek, and started to lift.

Quickly the lithe dancer straddled Patsy with her legs, wrapping them around his hips as he tore at her thong, gripping his shoulders as she kissed him passionately with an open mouth.

"Please," said Sofia again, an urgency in her tone. Bellocco yearned to have his lovers beg for him sexually. To hear them plead for him was a huge turn-on, and Sofia understood. For Patsy, there was nothing quite like a beautiful woman who craved his manhood. It was the ultimate aphrodisiac to the quintino—the ultimate power.

Bellocco continued to tug at the negligee as he carried Sofia backward into the bedroom.

Chapter 45

Santiago, Chile

THE VILLA GRIMALDI Park for Peace was located in the Penalolen outskirts of the city. Hidden from the road by high concrete walls and thick foliage, the property originally belonged to a wealthy Chilean family whose daughter ran afoul of the army. A trade was soon made. In weeks, the property transitioned and became the center of internal repression for the new military junta.

"As we circle past the small isolation chambers, the Casas de Chile," said the guide, a woman in her early thirties, "we approach the wall of names. This commemorates those who were executed."

Isabel listened intently, absorbed in the narrative. The guide spoke first in Spanish and then in English. She was the daughter of a survivor. Her father, a former prisoner at the villa, had endured gruesome conditions and lived to tell his story.

"Five thousand prisoners were detained and tortured here," said the guide, "but over two hundred prisoners just *disappeared*."

Izzy took notes and spoke into her pocket-size tape recorder. For her, this was a particularly poignant tour, as she realized that many of the villa's prisoners were just college students—young idealists who disagreed with the government of Augusto Pinochet.

"Please note the site markers," said the guide. "They are on the ground, which forces you to look down, as the prisoners did because they were blindfolded."

Sandy looked at Izzy with a serious expression. A somber mood had over-taken the naturally happy roommate. "This is tough stuff, Iz,'" said Sandy. "No wonder your mom wanted to get out of this country. Did she know anyone that was here?"

Izzy snapped a photograph of a colorful mosaic before answering.

"She never said, but I think she did know some people that were detained here. She certainly knew all the stories."

Sandy looked at the stone wall in the distance, the grass-covered brick walkways, the leafy ombu trees. She shuddered. "This was a bad place," said Sandy. "It's sinister."

"They were bad people," replied Izzy.

The guide stopped in front of a tall, oblong, wooden building that loomed high above the compound.

"This is the tower," said the guide. "In addition to holding cells and tor-ture cells, many important prisoners were executed here."

She motioned, and the small group followed her in to the tower.

"Torture," said the guide as they all gathered together in a small room, "was the primary method used to elicit information."

She lowered her voice and made sure that everyone squeezed into the room. They formed a semicircle around the metal frame of a bed, its springs coiled and connecting, void of any mattress or bedcover. The guide spoke again.

"The torture was both physical and psychological. The food was poor and insufficient, hygiene sparse. Beatings, near drowning, cigarette burns, dry asphyxiation, and puncture wounds were prevalent. The prisoners were always blindfolded. The fear of the unknown was deliberate and constant."

The guide continued to switch her narrative from Spanish to English. All of the dozen tourists in the room were fixated on the metal rack bed frame to their front.

"But," said the guide in a quiet voice, "the secret police were sadists. Their specialty was *la parrilla*." She pointed down at the metal rack. "It's a Spanish word for a cooking grill," said the guide. She took a moment to look at every woman in the room. There were five. Sandy self-consciously reached for Izzy's hand.

"The secret police were especially brutal to female prisoners," said the guide. "They believed it was easier to break a woman, and thereby gather more information."

The guide paused for a few seconds before continuing. "First, they would bring the female prisoner here, blindfolded, and strip her totally naked. They would rape her, repeatedly, taking turns, to degrade her, to destroy her dignity." The guide indicated the metal bed frame to her front. "Then she was laid here on the rack, still naked. Straps were used to secure her arms and legs, forcing her to spread wide, defenseless and vulnerable."

The guide moved toward the wall and pointed to a control box. "The current flowed from here through two wires with electrodes on their tips. This box allowed the torturers to control the voltage, and thus the severity of the electric shocks, the amount of pain."

The guide moved back to the *parrilla*, the metal rack in the center of the room. "Sometimes the secret police would fix an electrode on one sensitive body part, such as the earlobes, the nipples, the feet, and repeat the electric shocks to the same location for the entire session." She took a few seconds to catch her breath. The narrative was clearly affecting the group. "And sometimes the torturers would attach a wetted, steel wool pan scrub to the electrode, and push the rod into the woman's vagina."

The group cringed, as even the men winced at the verbal portrait painted by the guide. She had touched them with the horrors of life at the Villa Grimaldi.

Sandy tapped Isabel on the arm and walked from the tower.

Izzy stayed with the group, listening to the final few minutes of the guide's explanations, taking a photograph, and absorbing the significance of such a place. She was a first-generation American of Chilean descent, yet she lived in a serene, blissful, stable environment, void of fear and instability.

Outside, she approached Sandy, who was standing alone by the center of the park looking at a decorative fountain.

"You okay?" asked Isabel.

Sandy looked up. "Yeah, Iz, sorry, I needed some fresh air. You okay?"

Izzy nodded and touched her roommate's arm. "Yeah, it's a lot to process. Had enough for one day?"

"Yes," said Sandy with a laugh. "I need a drink."

"Beer is on me," answered Izzy, turning her friend toward the gated entrance.

"Forget the beer," said Sandy, starting to cut across the grass-covered stone walkway. "I need a shot of tequila."

Chapter 46

December 14, 2006
Gladwyne, Pennsylvania

PETER BURDIS SPUN his wheelchair in a circle. The movement surprised his two guests; Mike and John looked at their host, curious.

"Sorry," said their host. "I felt a surge of adrenaline." He leaned forward and managed a smile. "That's the extent of my aerobic activity."

Burdis continued the story.

"As I was saying, we introduced them to the architect." He took a moment to look toward his bookcases across the study. "You must understand that if history is written by the victors, then *laws* are written by those in power." Burdis shifted his gaze back toward his guests.

"The generals were in power," he said, "in every sense of the word, and they were *not* going to let go."

Mike leaned forward and whispered a question. "So they changed the laws?"

"However it suited them," answered Burdis. "They preserved the framework, the pretense of legitimacy. Constitutions were torn up and rewritten, legal procedures were abdicated under the premise of martial law, and statutory protections were either shredded or ignored."

"And how did this play out?" asked John.

"Slowly," said Burdis as he stifled a cough. He took a moment before continuing. "Mind you, the leadership of Operation Condor had long since crossed over morality bridge, but this was different. This was new ground for the generals. The 'Ndrangheta was a truly criminal organization. These disciplined law-and-order military men needed to adjust their thinking."

"And they needed money," said Mike.

"Yes," answered the cripple, "so the architect set up the Empresa, and then he contacted the Calabrians."

Chapter 47

Santiago, Chile

THEY SAT ON the patio of the Santo Remedio Bar off Providentia, each nursing a beer, ate a light lunch that was more liquid than solid, and enjoyed the last warm rays of August.

"You want another shot?" asked Sandy.

"No, I'm good," said Izzy.

It was quiet time, and the two roommates were comfortable enough together to be silent as they reflected on the day's events.

"I feel so naïve," said Sandy, sipping at her beer. "Sheltered."

"You're not," replied Izzy. "We were never exposed to this type of world." She looked around the bar. It had an artistic flair to the décor. "Cal always said that the more one travels outside the US, the more one appreciates living in the US."

"He should know," said Sandy, cracking a smile for the first time in hours. "He's been, like, everywhere. Have you spoken with him?"

"Tonight. I knew I would want to talk after today," answered Izzy.

"What does he think about all of this?"

"All of what?"

"Chile, South America, our trip."

Isabel made a noncommittal expression and shrugged. "Cal is an experienced traveler. He believes I should try new things as long as I think it through and use good sense."

"Do you ever talk to him about your mom?"

"Sometimes," answered Izzy. "She's his mom too."

"And what's his take?" asked Sandy. "Does he know the stories?"

"I think so, but Cal is philosophical about people and events."

"And women," said Sandy.

Izzy laughed and took a sip of beer. "He's my brother. We don't talk about those things."

"Why?"

"It's different," replied Izzy.

She gave her roommate a playful punch on the arm as Sandy lowered her voice and whispered with a mischievous smirk, "Well, I bet he's really *hot* in bed. He's got that great bod and all that Apache blood."

"Sandy," said Isabel, feigning annoyance. She couldn't hide her grin.

The roommate took another long swig of beer.

"Speaking of tonight," said Sandy, "Alvaro sent me an e-mail wondering if we could meet him and Juan for dinner."

Izzy thought before responding. "Sure, if you want…but tell me, Sandy, how old do you think they are?"

"Alvaro and Juan?"

"Yes,"

"Older than they said," replied Sandy. "There is no way they are only a couple of years older than us."

"That's what I thought. Why do you think they lied?"

Sandy considered the question and then answered, "Well, I figured they wanted to hook up, but when they learned our ages, they were afraid we would be scared off."

Izzy thought about the answer.

"Alvaro and I are getting along pretty well," said Sandy.

"I noticed."

"He knows that you and I are leaving for Argentina soon."

"And you like him."

"Well, *yeah*," said Sandy sarcastically, "but you're not digging on Juan."

"He's nice, but no, I don't have any interest," replied Izzy.

"Well, I was wondering," said Sandy, "Alvaro's been hinting pretty hard about me staying over one night."

Izzy smiled her natural smile. It was beautiful. "So go ahead," she said.

"Do you mind?"

"Of course not," said Izzy. "You're a big girl. Why would you ask me?"

"Well, you'll be all alone at the hotel."

"So?"

"You'll be okay?" asked Sandy.

"Of course." Izzy reached across the table and gave her roommate a hug. She was by nature a little reserved, but Isabel was a sincere person and genuine in her warmth to family and friends. "Thanks for thinking of me, Sandy. Will *you* be okay?"

"I'll be fine. I'll set it up that after dinner we'll drop you off at the hotel, and then I'll go back to Alvaro's apartment."

"Good. Just make sure I get the address. Send me an e-mail."

"And tomorrow, we'll meet for breakfast?" asked Sandy.

"Yes, and then we'll drive to Valparaiso and the coast for the day."

"You're sure you'll be all right, Iz?"

"I'll be fine," said Izzy, stifling a laugh, "but does Alvaro know what's in store for him?"

Chapter 48

Columbus, Georgia

CALIXTO LOZEN SAT in the rear seat of the SUV as his cell phone rang. He recognized the number and answered. It was Izzy. "Hey, where are you?" he asked.

"Santiago. Can you hear me okay?"

"Crystal clear," said Lozen.

"Can you talk?"

"Sure."

Just as the SUV turned on to Marne Road, the passenger in the front seat turned and spoke over his shoulder.

"C. L., what are you in the mood for?"

Lozen lowered his phone and covered the speaker as he replied.

"I'm up for anything. You guys choose. This is my kid sister. She's in South America."

He raised the cell phone back to his ear.

"Is it a bad time?" asked Izzy.

"No, I'm with a couple of friends. We just got in from the field, and we're going to get something to eat."

"Where are you?"

"Fort Benning. That's in Georgia. They sent a few SF guys here to do some work with an international school."

"Is it interesting?" asked Isabel.

"Not in the way you'd think. But how are you doing?"

"Good, it's really something, Cal. Eye opening. Even with Mom's stories, it's hard to imagine how it really was."

"Touring a lot?"

"Yes, we visited lots of historic sites and some of the bad places too. It's pretty scary what happened here."

"You doing okay?"

"Yes, I'm at the hotel. We went out to dinner with some guys we met a couple of days ago. They're nice; they've been showing us around a little."

"Use your head," said Calixto.

"I am. I'm sitting here on my bed typing stuff into my laptop. I took lots of notes and a bunch of pictures—I know you don't take photos. Anyway, I just sent them to my dad."

"How long will you be there?" asked Lozen.

"Another couple of days here in Chile, then off to Buenos Aires."

"You glad you took the trip?"

"Oh yeah," said Izzy. "As interesting as it is, travel is tiring, but I've got a much better understanding as to how things work."

There was a slight lull in the conversation before Izzy asked, "Have you been able to run?"

"Yes," answered Cal with a laugh, "when we're not in a swamp. How about you?"

"Every morning before breakfast," said Izzy.

Cal sensed the pride in her voice. It was just chitchat, an excuse to talk. Both were avid runners, and this was a piece of their childhood connection. "Iz, is everything *okay*?"

There was a slight hesitation on the line before Izzy answered, "Yeah, just thinking about a lot of stuff. Can we talk when I get back to Tucson?"

"Of course," said Lozen. He let the moment pass and changed the subject. "How's Sandy?"

"She's good," said Isabel, suddenly looking at her cell. There was an incoming text message from her roommate as they spoke. "She just stepped out for a few minutes." Izzy wasn't going to discuss Sandy's romantic dalliance. "I've got to go—that's her calling," said Isabel. "Love you."

"Stay in touch," said Cal as she disconnected.

Chapter 49

Santiago, Chile

SANDY LAUGHED AS Alvaro easily maneuvered the midsize Chevrolet through the streets of Santiago. It was late, but it had been a pleasant evening, complete with dinner, drinks, and relaxed conversation.

The four had dined at a popular local restaurant in the upscale El Golf neighborhood, and then Juan departed before Alvaro dropped Izzy off at their hotel.

"It's good to hear you laugh," said Alvaro, reaching across the front seat to touch Sandy on the knee.

"It's been quite a day," said Sandy.

She seemed relaxed, having worked through the history of the Villa Grimaldi, and now focused on their pending assignation. "Where is your place?" asked Sandy.

"The Queen," answered Alvaro.

"That sounds like an interesting location," said Sandy. Her face brightened into a smile.

Alvaro continued to be quite charming, pulling out all the stops in an effort to seduce the visiting American. Truthfully, Sandy was every bit as interested in bedding the handsome Chilean. She was no prude, but the excitement of an international romance while traveling was offset by Izzy's natural wariness of strangers. Sandy made friends easily, where Isabel was shy and held back.

"Is Juan upset?" asked Sandy.

"About Isabel? No," answered Alvaro. "He sensed that they would never progress. She is beautiful, that one."

"Gorgeous, and a true friend," replied Sandy with a nod.

"Is she committed?"

"No, she's between relationships, but I don't think the timing is good. She has a lot on her mind this trip."

"I understand," said Alvaro.

"Plus, she has a lot of her brother in her." The statement was made in a matter-of-fact way.

"Her brother?"

"He's quite a bit older, same mom, different dad, but they are very close."

"Is he back in the US?"

"Most of the time," answered Sandy.

Alvaro turned on to Avenida Larrain and crossed Tobalaba.

"I know he's been to Iraq at least twice, and I think Afghanistan as well," she said.

Alvaro seemed surprised before asking, "Is he military?"

"Oh yeah," said Sandy with a smirk. "Some big hush-hush job. He's the real deal."

They lapsed into silence for a couple of minutes as Alvaro reached over and affectionately stroked Sandy's thigh.

"Is it much farther?" she asked with a smile, all the while keeping mental notes on the street names and turns.

"Soon," answered Alvaro. "We are almost there."

"To the Queen."

"Sí, Señorita," said Alvaro. "In Spanish, La Reina. It is a quiet neighborhood on the residential side of the city. It has a beautiful view of the mountains."

Sandy looked seductively at Alvaro.

"I don't think we'll be spending too much time looking at the mountains."

Alvaro smiled in anticipation. "Just a few more minutes," he said.

They made another turn on to Avenida Jorge Alessandri. After a short ride, they turned onto a small side street. There were buildings and homes, lush trees and vegetation. Alvaro turned left into a driveway that led to a walled courtyard hiding the residence from the street. He pulled the Chevy forward and parked next to an old Range Rover beside the house.

"This is your place?" asked Sandy as she stepped from the passenger seat.

Alvaro placed his index finger across his lips and motioned. He took Sandy by the hand and led her to a stone walkway that circled toward the rear of the house. Once inside, he led her to a set of large floor-to-ceiling picture windows that offered them a spectacular view of the snow-covered Andes Mountains.

"Wow," said Sandy, absorbing the impressive prominence of Cerro El Plomo in the distance. "It's wonderful, like a postcard."

"Fitting for such a pretty señorita," said Alvaro.

Sandy kicked off her shoes and reached for her purse. She pulled out her BlackBerry and began texting. "What street was this again?"

"What are you doing?" asked Alvaro, clearly surprised by her action.

"Sending Izzy a message. Telling her about the view—why?"

"Why do you need the address?" He looked perturbed.

"Just for a point of reference," answered Sandy, taking a moment to snap a photograph of the mountain scene with her BlackBerry.

Sandy could see that Alvaro was annoyed. She was afraid of ruining the romantic moment. "I'm sorry," she said. "I was just bragging a little. It's kind of a girl thing."

He seemed to relax. Sandy reached up and passionately kissed him on the lips. "The mountains are quite impressive," said Sandy. "How is the view from the bedroom?"

"Not as good," answered Alvaro.

"I'll be the judge of that," said Sandy, "but first, I need to use the ladies room."

She touched his neck, and he smiled before leading her down the hall.

"This way, Señorita."

Chapter 50

December 14, 2006
Gladwyne, Pennsylvania

THEY WAITED FOR a few minutes as John stepped into the hall just outside the study and used the washroom. It had been a long morning, and Peter Burdis displayed unusual stamina. He was old and sick, but he seemed energized by the process.

"Sorry," said John, once he had returned from the interruption. "You were saying?"

"The 'Ndrangheta is different," said their host.

"How so?" asked Mike.

Burdis considered the question before speaking.

"Let me digress for a moment before answering." A minute of silence ensued. "The word *mafia*," said their host, "has become a euphemism for the Italian-based crime syndicates. In many ways, the term has become synonymous with organized crime in general."

He watched as Mike and John sat attentive, digesting the story.

"To be pedantic, the word is Sicilian, and accurately refers to *La Cosa Nostra*," said Burdis. "The Mafia controls Sicily, the *Camorra* Naples, and the *'Ndrangheta*, the region of Calabria. They are similar and there is contact between them, but they are not interchangeable. They operate under independent structures."

"And the vision thing," said Mike, turning the conversation back to a previous statement.

"Well," replied Burdis, "to oversimplify, the Sicilians are known for being tough and aggressive, but they have a short attention span, and they rarely think beyond tomorrow."

"And the Camorra?" asked John.

"Crude, insular, a blunt instrument, not interested in venturing far from their stronghold in Naples. If a member were to go overseas, he would lose influence back at home," replied Burdis.

"Which bring us back to the Calabrians," said Mike.

"Yes. Clearly, the 'Ndrengheta are every bit as virulent as their counterparts, but they are also capable of being subtle."

"Subtle," said John.

"Yes," answered Burdis. "They are men who perceive the *fear* of violence to be every bit as valuable as the violence itself. To them, it is a tool, and when coupled with their global appetite for business, they proved a fortuitous selection."

"The timing was good," said Mike, clarifying the statement.

"Exactly. Just as the generals were in need of financing, the 'Ndrengheta was expanding beyond Calabria."

"Glove to hand," said John.

"And then some," answered Burdis. "As important, the 'Ndrengheta understood the long-term potential of gaining a foothold in foreign countries on distant continents."

"And they understood how to be patient," said Mike.

"Yes," replied Burdis. "They moved slowly, they cultivated the relationships, and they seduced the generals with money."

"And Operation Condor transformed itself again," said John.

"Yes," said their host. "The Calabrians gave them a chance to digest their new actions. Remember, the generals still wanted to sleep at night secure in the *legality* of their decisions."

Chapter 51

Santiago, Chile

THEY LAY IN bed together, snuggling, Sandy's leg wrapped over Alvaro's hip as he gently stroked her long hair.

"Wow, that was worth waiting for. You really know your stuff," she said.

Alvaro blushed. It was a common compliment. He was an experienced lover and aware of his reputation.

"How old are you?" asked Sandy as she kissed Alvaro on the chest.

He looked at her, puzzled. "I told you—twenty-four."

Sandy grinned and rolled her tongue along his skin.

"No, how old are you *really*?"

Alvaro hesitated before answering. "Twenty-seven."

Sandy reached up and looked deep into his eyes, their faces barely inches apart.

"Really?" she said. "You seem so much older."

He laughed, making a joke out of the inconsistency.

"Do I seem decrepit to you?"

"No," said Sandy. "Worldly."

Alvaro continued to stroke her hair, kissing her gently on the cheek.

"Is this place really yours?" asked Sandy.

He looked at her with a curious expression and then shook his head. "No, actually it belongs to a friend of mine. He is away on business, and I am keeping an eye on things for him. Why?"

"Just wondering," said Sandy. "I didn't see anything personal. It seems sort of sterile."

Alvaro leaned toward her and whispered, "I wanted to impress you with the view of the mountains, and my apartment is not nearly so big."

Sandy nibbled on his neck. "They are beautiful. It's a wonderful view, but I would rather have seen your apartment, because it would be *you*."

"Next time," said Alvaro as he tapped her on the arm. "Excuse me, but I need to use the bathroom."

Sandy lay back on the pillow, the sheet half covering her naked torso. She gently touched her own breast. "Hurry back," she said as Alvaro paced from the bedroom.

After a couple of minutes, Sandy heard a small commotion and then what she thought was a quiet voice.

"Alvaro," said Sandy, calling out the open door toward the hallway. "Is everything all right?"

A few seconds later, Alvaro reentered the bedroom, with a towel wrapped around his waist and a strange expression on his face. He looked at Sandy.

Then, two men dressed in black, their faces covered, darted into the room from the hall and rushed to either side of the bed. Before Sandy could scream, one man covered her mouth with a gloved hand, and the second man pressed a handheld stun gun to her upper shoulder. He pulled the trigger.

Fifty thousand volts of low-amperage electricity crackled between the electrodes and into Sandy's body. The three-second blast disrupted her system, and her muscles started to twitch and spasm. Quickly, while she was still helpless, they duct-taped her mouth and ankles and handcuffed her wrists behind her back.

Sandy was alert, but not able to respond as her muscles failed. She looked up at Alvaro with a confused expression, but he wouldn't meet her eyes.

The first man lifted Sandy and threw her over his shoulder, as the second man grabbed at her clothes, her pocketbook, and the few pieces of jewelry she had removed and placed on the nightstand. They pulled a cowl over her head.

Then they spoke to Alvaro, who nodded and led them to the back door.

It was four in the morning, and the neighborhood was long asleep. The two men carried Sandy across the drive to the old Range Rover parked near the house. The walled courtyard provided excellent privacy.

The men opened the rear hatch and placed Sandy on a tarpaulin in the back. Then they covered her naked body, her clothes, and her possessions with a blanket. Finally, the two men removed their ski masks, climbed into the vehicle, and under cover of darkness drove away.

Chapter 52

Santiago, Chile

IZZY AWOKE THE next morning, freshened up, and dressed in her regular jogging clothes. Even though it was winter in Santiago, it wasn't particularly cold. As in Tucson, the early mornings and evenings could get a little crisp, but otherwise, her typical attire of shorts, T-shirt, and running shoes was fine. She supplemented the ensemble with a light, nylon windbreaker.

It had been a tough night for Izzy as she tossed and turned in bed, restless, her thoughts reflecting on the day's events. Sleep had been elusive.

Isabel now understood the fear that propelled her mother to the United States. To see friends arrested and detained at a place like the Villa Grimaldi, and then to hear their stories of torture, would prompt anyone to flee.

Her mom settled in at the institute in Washington, DC, with Orlando Letelier. They were doing good work, exposing the abuses of the Dirty War, when the generals had him assassinated.

Constanza escaped again, fleeing across the country, feeling afraid, alone, cornered, envisioning a secret police agent around every corner. She settled in Tucson, far from the political epicenters of Santiago or Washington.

Izzy imagined her mom, like her, a college student in her early twenties, having her life turned inside out. What confluence of emotions could cause a young adult to abandon everyone and everything she knew in search of calm and a sense of safety?

It was a terrible ordeal for Isabel's mother, but one that directly contributed to Izzy's existence. Constanza's experience and her decisions resulted in her parents meeting and marrying.

As Izzy electronically flipped the last series of photographs taken by her and Sandy to her dad in Tucson, the hotel room telephone rang.

Surprised, thinking it was the hotel staff, she plucked the phone from the cradle and answered in Spanish. "Hola?"

"Isabel," said a voice back in Spanish, "it's Juan."

"Sí," replied Izzy.

"Did I wake you?"

"No," said Isabel, "I've been up. I was about to go for a run. Is everything okay?"

"I am afraid not," said Juan. "I just got a call from Alvaro. He is at the hospital. He was driving Sandy back to your hotel when there was a car accident. He is hurt, but I think Sandy is in a bad way. She is asking for you."

"My God," said Izzy, pausing to catch her breath. "Do you know which hospital?"

"Yes," answered Juan, "the Integramedica in Las Condes. I was en route. I could pick you up."

"Where are you now?"

"Only a few blocks away from your hotel, but the traffic is very busy on Providencia. It would be easier if we could meet a few blocks farther south."

"Okay," said Izzy. "Where?"

Juan paused.

"Let me think...okay, we could meet at the corner of Avenidas Seminario and Francisco Bilboa. They are only a few blocks from your location. Can you make that?"

"Yes," said Izzy, "corner of Seminario and Bilboa. I'm leaving now."

"Do you remember my car?"

"Yes."

"Hurry, Isabel; it did not sound good."

The line clicked dead, and Izzy turned. For a moment, she debated changing her clothes, but in the rush of the moment, she realized time was crucial. She stayed in her running outfit, zipped up her nylon windbreaker, and grabbed for her pocketbook and cell phone. Izzy hustled from the hotel room.

In the lobby she double-checked directions with the front desk clerk and quickly exited the hotel.

It took Izzy five minutes at a fast pace to speed walk the distance. She saw Juan, standing beside his idling Volvo, his emergency lights flashing. He waved.

They piled into the front seat, and he quickly merged back into the traffic.

"Thank you," said Izzy.

"No problem," answered Juan, tugging at his suit coat. "I was on the way to work when I got the call."

"What do you know?" asked Izzy in a worried voice.

"Only that it happened about an hour ago, and Alvaro is in pain. But it sounds like Sandy is serious."

Izzy's emotions muddled together. "Is the hospital far?" she asked.

"No, but the traffic is heavy. I know some shortcuts."

Juan threaded the car through the less-traveled streets of Santiago, continuing to work them east and south of the Mito Casa Hotel and the main thoroughfare of Providencia.

Ten minutes later they turned into a quiet side alley, and Juan entered a fenced lot. He pulled straight into a large open bay garage and slammed on the brakes. The garage door began to electronically close behind them.

"Where are we?" said Izzy, a touch of alarm in her voice. Something was wrong.

"One minute," said Juan as he jumped from the car.

From the shadows, two men, dressed in black and wearing ski masks, paced toward the Volvo. The first bounded through Juan's open door into the front seat next to Izzy, as the second man stood outside her passenger door, blocking escape.

"No," said Izzy in a loud voice. She lashed out at the man beside her in the car.

The man blocked her blow, grabbed her forearm, and yanked upward. Then he shoved a handheld stun gun against her exposed rib cage and pressed the trigger.

The electricity crackled for four seconds. Izzy's muscles twitched, then contracted, and she slumped back in the front seat, helpless. The first man reached across Izzy and unlocked the passenger side door.

The second man opened the door and went to work. He wrapped Izzy's mouth and ankles in duct tape. Then he handcuffed her wrists behind her back and lifted her out of the car. He blindfolded Izzy, and finally she was carried to the rear of a Ford minivan parked in the garage next to Juan's Volvo. They covered her limp body and her pocketbook with a painter's canvas and climbed into the van as Juan got back into his car.

Three minutes later, the two vehicles exited the garage, crossed the fenced lot, and drove off in opposite directions.

Chapter 53

Tucson, Arizona

CONSTANZA FINLEY MET her husband at the side door near their driveway. It was early in the afternoon on a hot August day. She instinctively looked over his shoulder, searching for strange cars or unknown people along their quiet suburban street.

"Hi, Connie," said the professor, a little surprised. He shifted the briefcase to his other hand and kissed Constanza on her cheek.

"Have you heard from Izzy?" she asked.

"No," answered Arthur. "Why?"

"You went to the office for a few hours today. I just hoped she had skyped you."

"No," said her husband, squeezing past Constanza into the mudroom, "but I didn't necessarily expect her to."

Connie shut the door and followed him down the hall. "Well, check again. See if she called."

Arthur Finley stifled the urge to reply. Instead, he entered his home office, put down his briefcase, and turned on the desktop computer. He punched in his password and then an access code. Finally, he checked for messages.

"Nothing. No e-mails, no voice mails. Just another set of photos sent early this morning."

Constanza shifted uncomfortably before responding, "That's not like her."

"It's not?"

"No, we haven't talked since yesterday," said Connie.

Finley leaned back in his chair with a baffled expression on his face. "Connie, we've talked to Izzy more over the last eight days while she was in Chile than we did the last month when she was home here in Tucson. She's having fun."

"Fun?" said Constanza. She gave her husband a stern look. "Arthur, she went to the Villa Grimaldi yesterday. That's *not* fun."

The professor didn't want to argue. He held up his hand in surrender. "Wrong choice of words. Izzy is probably *busy*."

"Yes," replied Constanza in a snappy tone, "but when she was four miles away, it wasn't an issue."

"Point taken," said her husband.

"Please find me when she calls," said Connie. She whirled on her heels and exited the office.

Chapter 54

Santiago, Chile

IT WAS LATE at night when two men approached the empty hotel room on the third floor. The first carefully worked the lock of the refurbished room, while the second kept watch in the small hallway.

They were what was known in the business as "cleaners," people who typically followed assassins into a crime scene and sterilized the environment for any DNA or incriminating evidence. In this case, no crime had been committed in the room, but their trained eyes and techniques were used to assure that it appeared Izzy and Sandy had checked out. The lock popped, and the two men quickly entered and rebolted the hotel room from the inside.

Down the hall, a surveillance specialist had checked into the Mito Casa Hotel a day after the girls. He specifically requested the same floor under the pretense of an old anniversary from years past. He placed a *Do Not Disturb* sign from his room on the girls' doorknob as he casually walked by and positioned himself at the end of the hallway.

Inside the room, the two cleaners each put on a pair of surgical gloves and surveyed the layout. Then they started. The men moved fast, opening the girls' suitcases, gathering clothes, possessions, Izzy's laptop, stuffing everything together, cleaning out drawers and toiletries as they searched furniture cushions and under chairs. They tossed the bedcovers and double-checked the closet.

The Mito Casa Hotel was a small hotel that maintained a twenty-four-hour front desk service, but no express checkout. This required some extra planning. The first man placed a short note, written in Spanish on hotel stationery, on the desk top, with a modest tip in Chilean pesos for the maid. The note was in a woman's cursive and simply stated that their travel plans had changed and they needed to catch an early flight. The invoice should be settled to their credit cards already on file.

The final piece was the room keys, and the cleaners had to wait until those were separately retrieved from the two different snatch teams. They were placed with the note.

The men stopped and stepped back to opposite corners of the hotel room. They scanned everything. Then each man grabbed a full suitcase, and the first man cracked open the door. He signaled the surveillance specialist, who quickly paced the hallway and opened his own door three rooms down.

The two cleaners exited Izzy and Sandy's room carrying the girls' possessions and entered the surveillance specialist's room. Over the next hour, all contents, including the girls' suitcases, would be concealed inside different suitcase covers and walked out of the hotel when the surveillance specialist went through a normal checkout later that morning from his own room.

Chapter 55

Tucson, Arizona

CONSTANZA FINLEY STORMED into the kitchen as her husband poured himself a glass of orange juice. "Something's wrong," she said.

Arthur set down the glass on the counter and replaced the pitcher of orange juice into the refrigerator. He faced her with a patient expression. "Why do you say that?"

"Have you heard from her?"

"No," said Arthur, "but she's traveling."

"She should have arrived in Buenos Aires hours ago. I have her schedule."

"Maybe there's a delay on the airline?"

"I checked," said Constanza. "I compared the airline schedule against the flight. It left on time from Santiago. The flight to Buenos Aires is two hours long. It *arrived* ten minutes late in Argentina. That was four hours ago. Have you received a text message?"

"No," said the professor, understanding the reason for his wife's discomfort. "Maybe there was a delay at customs? They're probably checking in and getting settled."

"Arthur," said Constanza; there was fear in his wife's eyes. "Something is wrong. I can feel it."

The husband put a hand in the air. "I will call their hotel in Santiago. Then I will call their hotel in Buenos Aires. If we know the plane traveled on time, we can track the movements."

"If they even got on the plane," said Constanza.

"Well, why wouldn't they?"

"I'm calling Cal," answered Constanza.

"What? Why?" asked Arthur.

Arthur Finley was not especially close to Calixto. He didn't understand what drove the young man, his interests, or his motivations. It's not that Arthur and Cal weren't cordial; they were. They were just different. It was due to Naiche, Cal's dad. He and Arthur were as opposite as two men could be. Naiche was physical, intimidating, a hot-blooded individual filled with street smarts and aggressive tendencies. Finley, on the other hand, was academic, highly educated, cultured, and calm—a thoughtful man given to logic and reason.

As Calixto aged, Arthur's influence waned. The biological father, Naiche, dominated Cal's adolescence.

Additionally, part of Arthur's sensitivity to the situation was that he felt Constanza still kept an emotional tie to Naiche. They shared a son, and that son, Calixto, despite the eight-year age difference, held an unusual sway over his younger sister, Arthur's daughter.

"Because Cal needs to know," said Constanza. "Please, Arthur, call the hotels."

Chapter 56

Vina del Mar, Chile

THEY SAT IN the colonel's office at the rear of the villa. He seemed unusually pensive, his mind analyzing the various implications of their action. The colonel had made a decision, one that the captain not only agreed with, but in some ways, prodded him into. They appeared to have a problem at a critical juncture, and they needed to protect their Empresa. The die was cast.

"They have been secured?" asked the colonel.

"Sí," answered the captain. "They are in the basement of a farmhouse outside the city."

"The location is discreet?"

"Sí, and it is guarded around the clock by our people."

"Did they put up a struggle?"

"Young Soto tried," said the captain, "but she was overwhelmed. The other woman was abducted without incident."

"Rendered," said the colonel, "she was *rendered* without incident."

"Sí," answered the captain, accepting his superior's choice of words. When possible, they always preferred the use of political or military terms to couch their language. This abduction, or kidnapping, was an *irregular rendition* in their world.

"They are unharmed?"

"Sí, Colonel," replied the subordinate.

"Keep them that way. I am formulating several options depending on what we learn next. Have we secured the computer, the cell phones, and their handheld devices?"

"Sí, Colonel. It will take a few more days to follow up on the information, but we should soon know who they are in contact with."

"It is important that all persons of interest *here* are immediately put under surveillance."

The captain nodded as the colonel, in an uncharacteristic motion, placed a highly polished shoe on the desk and leaned back in his chair. The colonel paused before offering, "The meeting between our associates in Buenos Aires and the new organization in Tamaulipas has been set for neutral ground in Guatemala."

"There is much at stake," said the captain in a deferential tone.

"This new venture," replied the colonel, "could expand the scope of our Empresa to an immense level."

Chapter 57

Santiago, Chile

IZZY STIRRED, SUDDENLY alert from her slumber. She realized she was bound, spread-eagled, and secured to a piece of furniture that squeaked each time she moved. Izzy tried to sit up but was unable. She was blindfolded and gagged, and her thoughts were foggy as she realized they had drugged her.

Izzy recalled the abduction in the garage, Juan, the two masked men in black, and the stun gun as memories came flooding back. She tried to take inventory. Other than a throbbing headache, she felt no pain, but she felt cold. There was a chill in the room, and she sensed metal against her skin, quickly realizing she was still dressed in her running attire.

Izzy strained to listen. There seemed to be another person in the room, muffled sounds, movement, squeaking to her left. Isabel thought she smelled a faint whiff of Sandy's perfume, but she couldn't be sure. The whole predicament felt surreal—like a nightmare that she would soon awake from. She shook her head sideways, trying to physically clear the cobwebs.

The incongruity of her situation receded to fear. It made no sense, but the improbability of her abduction, so many years after the height of the Dirty War, rattled her equilibrium. She worked at controlling her emotions and tried to think through her problem.

Izzy tested her wrists and ankles again and shifted her buttocks. She heard the squeak and felt the cold steel on the back of her exposed thighs. It was a metal bed frame. She was clothed, but her limbs were spread to the four corners. Izzy felt vulnerable. Even worse, the similarity of her captivity to the stories she heard at the Villa Grimaldi was disturbingly vivid.

Chapter 58

Tucson, Arizona

ARTHUR FINLEY SAT in his small home office and reviewed his notes. His cell phone was on the desk, next to their home telephone and his desktop computer.

He had made countless telephone calls and sent many e-mails using all three devices, and he wanted to assure that he documented all the contact names, dates, and times.

Truthfully, although the professor's demeanor was given to thoughtful interaction, he was becoming concerned. This was unlike Izzy. It's not so much that she would feel the need to connect, as much as her sensitive nature would prompt her to do it for their sake. Isabel would make contact to allay her mother's fears.

Constanza entered his office and sat across the desk from Arthur. She looked haggard. The lack of sleep and incessant stress etched deep lines in her face. In thirty-six hours, Constanza had aged a decade. "Any news?" she asked.

Arthur shook his head before speaking. "I've called our congressman, and her office has people looking into the matter through congressional channels. I also have a call into Senator McCain."

Constanza frowned. Their congresswoman was a fine lady and would push buttons, and McCain was a very senior US senator, a war hero, and a potential presidential candidate. But they needed pressure.

"I've also contacted the State Department and the US embassy in Santiago," said Arthur. "Izzy's hotel, the Mito Casa, confirms that the girls checked out early on the morning of their flight. They left a note that their travel plans had changed."

There was a doubtful look in Constanza's eye. "A note? Did anyone *see* them check out?" she asked.

"I don't know," said Finley, accepting the inference. "Have you spoken with Sandy's mother?"

"Yes," answered Connie. "She has not heard from Sandy since the day before checkout. She received a short e-mail with some photographs. She lives in Flagstaff, so her congressman is from the first district. She's reached out."

Arthur Finley considered the information before speaking. "LAN Chile, the airline, confirms that the flight left on time, and the girls never boarded. The hotel in Buenos Aires confirms that the girls had a reservation, but they never checked in. What about the hospitals?"

"Nothing," said Constanza. "There are numerous hospitals and clinics in the city, but only two are prepared to deal with international patients in Santiago. I checked them, as well as called every other medical facility I could find; there is no news of any girls fitting their description or under their names."

"And the police?"

"The *police*?" said Constanza in a suspicious tone. "Are you serious?"

The professor looked at his wife with a blank expression. "Connie, don't you think that's appropriate?"

"No, Arthur, they're the ones responsible. Do you think they would tell us the truth?" She broke into tears, the anxiety of the past two days amplified to an extraordinary level as memories of past indignities filled her head.

"They're going to hurt our Izzy," said Constanza, lowering her voice. "My God, what they'll do to her." She trembled as the tears flowed unchecked.

Arthur reached across the desk to his wife, but she pulled back, recoiling away, tucking her knees up under her chin, and wrapped her arms around her legs in a ball.

"Connie," said Finley, trying to remain calm and logical, "it doesn't make sense."

She glared at her husband. "Don't you think that it's unusual, Arthur, that the day after they visit the Villa Grimaldi, they disappear?"

"A coincidence. She's been touring the country. It's a park now, a memorial."

"It's a message."

"Why?" he asked. "You heard some stories. Everyone did. But you were lucky: you escaped out of the country." The professor leaned back in his chair.

"No," said Connie in a quiet voice. Her breathing turned shallow.

"No, what?"

"I didn't escape," replied Constanza in a whisper.

Arthur looked across the desk at his wife for a moment before responding. "I don't understand."

"I never escaped. The secret police arrested me. I spent four weeks at the Villa Grimaldi."

Arthur Finley's face lit in surprise. Clearly, he was caught off guard. "I'm confused. I thought your parents smuggled you out of the country when the trouble began."

"No," replied Constanza, "I lied. Calls were made after my arrest. My father was a businessman. He knew someone high up in the military. A pay-off was made with the understanding that I would immediately leave Chile. Otherwise, I would disappear for good."

The professor looked perplexed. "You never told me that."

"I know."

"Why?" asked Finley with a touch of exasperation in his voice.

"Because I was afraid you wouldn't want me," said Constanza.

"That doesn't make sense."

"Of course it does," said Connie with a quiver of emotion. "You were kind and patient with me. You had a good job. People respected you."

Arthur leaned back in his chair and tried to absorb the new information. "They held you for four weeks?"

"Yes."

"Did they question you?"

"Yes."

Finley hesitated before asking the next question. "Did they torture you?"

"Of course," answered Constanza.

He swallowed hard as he looked at his wife. "Like some of the stories we heard?"

Constanza looked at her husband with an expression of disbelief. Was he in denial? Shock? Was his academic life so insulated from the real world that he could not assimilate the reality of her ordeal? Finally she spoke in a halting voice. "Arthur, they ruined me. Do you understand? As a woman I can't feel anything. It's a miracle Izzy was born."

"What about Calixto?"

"The same thing. I didn't think it was possible for me to have children, so I took no precautions."

"And Naiche?"

"He doesn't know. I felt safe with Naiche. He was rugged. He would protect me, but men have needs. Then Cal happened."

"And me?" asked Finley.

"You were a different kind of safe. You were gentle. But you're a decent man, and I knew you wanted a family."

"So you tricked me?"

"No," said Constanza sharply. "Never. My love grew over time. I hoped that after Calixto's birth, I could get pregnant again. And I did, with Izzy. But I was afraid that if you ever learned the whole truth, you would see me as damaged goods."

Arthur Finley shook his head in dismay. After twenty-two years of marriage, he felt that a huge unexplainable void in their relationship had suddenly surfaced. He sat in silence and looked at his computer screen. Finley was numb. Finally he spoke.

"Was it as bad as everyone says?"

"Worse," said Constanza. "It was beyond anything I ever said or you ever read. These people are monsters. They enjoy it." Connie stood before her husband could respond. She looked at him with sorrow in her eyes and mumbled, "I got hold of Cal. He's coming."

She turned and walked from Arthur's office.

Chapter 59

Santiago, Chile

SANDY WAS AFRAID. She tossed sideways on the bed, her bare legs and back pinched by any movement to the metal springs and coils. Her arms and legs were stretched in four directions, and each was secured with very little slack for movement. A dusty blanket was draped across her naked torso for warmth.

It was cold in the room, and it smelled musty. Sandy was both blindfolded and gagged, which caused her to focus on her other senses for information. Occasionally, she heard a squeaking noise to her right, the sound of someone shifting their body on a metal bed frame, much like her own. Due to the blindfold and gag, Sandy couldn't see or speak to the other person, but she surmised it was another prisoner.

In an odd and selfish moment, Sandy realized that just the knowledge that she wasn't alone, the fact that someone else was suffering a similar plight, helped her through the ordeal. Sandy was scared and disoriented. She could make no sense of the multiple factors that engulfed the current situation. To her it was all a movie with a bad ending. At the center of the events was Alvaro. He was complicit in the abduction, and this, as much as any other fact, jarred Sandy's emotions.

How could she have so misjudged Alvaro? He was sweet and charming and worldly. He seemed the perfect gentleman. Sandy liked him, and he knew she did. They spent countless hours together—talking, laughing, drinking, and making love. It confused her. This turn of events left her dazed and angry. *Why?*

Her thoughts shifted to Izzy. Sandy was sure her roommate was focused on finding her. Isabel, the cautious one, had insisted on Sandy forwarding Alvaro's address. Despite Sandy's mildly promiscuous ways, she and Izzy always practiced dating sense—whether at a UA campus bar in Tucson or in the company of new friends in a foreign land. Sandy hoped and counted on Izzy's resolve. Her good friend was more relationship driven than Sandy, but she was sincere and never judgmental.

A door opened to Sandy's left, and multiple footsteps approached her bed. She felt someone standing to either side, and then a hand grabbed at the dusty blanket that covered her torso and ripped it away.

Sandy gasped as a brisk wave of cold air chilled her body. Her naked skin began to bubble in goose bumps. She felt incredibly vulnerable. A tingle of anxiety surfaced, and she began to tremble. Sandy tried to talk through the gag.

Two sets of hands reached down and unfastened the straps securing Sandy's wrists and ankles to the bed. Then they stood her up and faced her toward the door.

She stood naked on a cement floor, still gagged and blindfolded, as unseen captors stared. She felt their eyes study her. Her pulse quickened. A hand from the front touched her breast. It was cold and callused. It startled her, and Sandy jumped. She bit her lip as the rough fingers slowly circled her nipple, and then just as quickly, it stopped.

One of the two men drew closer. She could smell his sweat, the presence of his torso. Sandy tensed. The man leaned forward and whispered in her ear, "Tell me about the Empresa."

Empresa? The word meant nothing to her. Sandy swallowed through the gag, unable to answer. She fought off a wave of panic and managed a shrug.

There was a pause of ten seconds, and then she felt clothing pressed into her hands, and the person to the rear helped her put on her blouse, her wool slacks, and her shoes. They were the clothes Sandy had worn the night of her abduction. When was that—yesterday, the day before?

The hands guided her back to the bed, the *metal*-framed bed, and they refastened her limbs to the four corners. Then she heard the footsteps recede across the room, and the heavy door opened and closed. They were gone.

Chapter 60

Guatemala City, Guatemala

THE THREE STRETCH Lincoln Continentals sped through the streets of Guate, the locals' name for the capital city of the small Central American country. They were already in zone ten, the financial district, a scant twelve minutes from the airport. A moment later, the cars turned into the circular drive of the posh, fifteen-story Real Intercontinental Hotel.

Patsy Bellocco yawned as the heavy precipitation pelted their car. It was the rainy season in Guatemala, and the clouds burst daily, drenching the country in copious amounts of water. The cars pulled to a halt.

"Have we double-checked procedures?" asked Patsy before stepping into the rain.

"Sí, Pasquale," said Ettore. "The security is guaranteed by the Guatemalans."

"And our associates in the Empresa have also given us assurances?"

"Sí, Santiago has been quite explicit."

Patsy considered the information as one of his bodyguards brushed aside the hotel doorman and opened an umbrella beside the car.

"We've checked the hotel and meeting room?"

"Sí," answered his brother-in-law. "We have had people on-site for several days. You are staying in the presidential suite."

This was the planning stage of a new business venture for the 'Ndrangheta. Patsy had mushroomed the Colombian cocaine connection into a major pipeline between South America and the Italian mainland. Yet Europe still clamored for more product. The appetite for illegal drugs was huge. Recently, with the help of their associates in Santiago, Patsy's 'ndrina started exploring additional avenues of distribution. The 'Ndrangheta controlled the Calabrian port city of Gioia Tauro and the trafficking of cocaine throughout Europe. Up to now, this had been exclusively with the Colombians.

Capacity was not an issue, provided of course that Patsy could secure another pipeline. Their associates introduced some folks in Mexico that were looking to expand. The Mexican cartels already controlled storage and transit points to the United States. Most of the marijuana, methamphetamines, and cocaine heading north passed through the Mexican shipping lanes, even when initiated by the Colombians.

If Patsy could establish a second pipeline of cocaine flowing from North America, in addition to his current pipeline from South America, then supply could match demand in Europe and profits would soar.

Bellocco stepped from the rear seat of his Lincoln and motioned. Everyone followed as the bodyguard kept pace, looking ahead and holding the umbrella.

Sitting in a third-floor room, peering through a picture window at the hotel's front entrance, were two DEA agents. The first snapped his fingers several times.

"Chris, I think this is our guy."

The second drug enforcement agent focused hard on Patsy's entourage through a pair of high-powered binoculars. "Bingo," he said, moving to take several photographs through a tripod-mounted camera. He focused the zoom lens. "The big man himself."

The first agent speed-dialed a number on his cell phone and spoke. "Look alive," he said. "November One is coming your way."

A man reading a newspaper in the hotel lobby replaced his cell phone and looked at his female companion as he stood. "We're on."

The couple strolled to the entranceway of the spacious reception area and stood in front of the doors as Patsy entered the hotel.

The female agent had one hand in the crook of her partner's arm, the other draped over a shoulder bag that concealed a hidden camera lens mounted in a brass clasp. She pressed a button that activated the camera shutter several times.

After a short pause, allowing Patsy's entire group to first enter the lobby, the two DEA agents walked from the hotel like a couple on a holiday.

Chapter 61

Tucson, Arizona

THE FRONT DOOR opened, and Calixto Lozen looked at a middle-aged man with a square jaw and straight, shoulder-length, black hair.

"Hi, Pop," said Cal.

Naiche motioned with a jerk of his head and then moved back. Lozen stepped in front of his father and crossed the threshold. He was three inches taller and considerably leaner than Naiche, but his father was thick and knotty, and with his weather-beaten skin, he looked like a grizzled rock cut from granite.

"How is your mother?"

Calixto dropped his civilian duffel bag on the floor and shrugged before answering.

"She's pretty uptight," said Cal.

"How long were you there?"

"Four hours."

Naiche led Cal into his living room and sat on a leather couch. Then he picked up the huge Randall Bowie knife that he had been sharpening, and inspected the blade. "Was the teacher any help?"

Calixto sat before responding. "Actually, he was." Lozen pulled out a notebook from his satchel. It was bulging with notes, photographs, itineraries, and copies of e-mails from both Izzy and Sandy.

"He helped me put the information into perspective. That was useful."

Naiche dripped a little kerosene on his coarse-grit whetstone, used to apply a keen edge to a knife.

"You don't like him," said Calixto.

Naiche grunted. "Not my kind of guy, but your mother's happy." He looked up at his son. "Life is a journey, Gray Wolf; the path has many twists and turns."

"How about something to drink?" asked Cal.

"There's mesquite iced tea in the fridge," said Naiche. "I'll have some too."

It had been an abrupt exit from Fort Benning and Cal's assignment teaching at the School of the Americas. Time was crucial. Fortunately for Calixto, he had an excellent military record and top OERs to grease the skids. His performance over the years earned some leverage, and thus a quick call to his personnel officer in Saint Louis generated an emergency change of orders to paper trail his sudden absence.

Lozen returned with two tall glasses of iced tea.

"Speak your mind, Gray Wolf," said his father, smoothly stroking the eleven-inch blade over the whetstone. "The silence is deafening."

Cal sat again. "Did you know that Mom had been tortured in Chile?"

Naiche looked up and fixed his son with a steady gaze. "She said she escaped as soon as her friends were arrested."

Cal frowned and spoke. "She *said*. Now she says different."

Naiche gently placed his knife on the coffee table before answering. "I always suspected. I could tell, as a man can sometimes tell, but she offered a story, and I accepted the story. It was not my place to do otherwise."

Calixto considered the information as Naiche looked at his son. "You think it somehow relates?"

"Mom does," said Lozen.

His father rolled his head from side to side in a noncommittal fashion. "She is a mother; Isabel is her daughter. What do *you* think happened?"

"I don't know," answered Cal. "I was hoping to go over my notes with you, see if you had any thoughts."

"Sure. What time is your flight tomorrow?"

"Early, around zero eight."

Naiche stood and started for the kitchen. "After dinner. Chicken okay?"

"Yeah, Pop, that's fine," said Lozen.

Calixto's father fixed him with a very serious expression. "I know you are very close to your little sister, Gray Wolf. You know her better than anyone. People are people. Remember, that is your advantage."

Naiche walked from the room.

Chapter 62

December 14, 2006
Gladwyne, Pennsylvania

Peter Burdis coughed several times before John offered a glass of water to help clear his throat.

"At first," said the wealthy mansion owner, "it was just passive assistance. It was 'ignore that package' or 'look the other way' or 'pretend that didn't happen.' There was no pressure placed on the membership of Operation Condor to do anything. No overt acts."

Burdis leaned forward in his wheelchair and spoke in an admiring tone. "That's where the Calabrians are subtle. Their pattern is insidious."

"And it paid off," said Mike, hovering toward the cripple.

"Yes, human nature is curiously predictable," answered Burdis. "The 'Ndrengheta, unlike their counterparts, saw the advantage of corrupting people in authority, and they were willing to take the time to draw them in."

"Do you mean that they gave a lot and asked for very little?" questioned John.

Burdis's eyes glinted, he raised an index finger, and he whispered, "For a while."

"So now the cash is flowing," said Mike, "the generals are still in power, the relationship is developing. Then what?"

"Then the passive assistance turned into active participation. It became 'could you help us with this' or 'could you take delivery of that' or 'we need you to sign these papers.' All the while, the Calabrians kept ratcheting up the money."

"It evolved," said John.

"Yes, and *yes*," said Burdis with a grin. "In the next few years, Augusto Pinochet ordered the army to build a secret laboratory in Chile to mix and process 'black cocaine.'"

"Coca Negra," replied Mike, "camouflaged product, easy to smuggle."

"Precisely, and the chemist in charge of this endeavor was none other than the same scientist who was producing poisons to assassinate the enemies of Operation Condor."

"They'd made the transition," said John.

"All the way. They were past the pretense of legal propriety or philosophical necessity. Operation Condor became a full-blown criminal *enterprise*. They had the structure, the power, and the money."

"And the 'Ndrengheta had their fix," said Mike.

"Deep," said their host. "For the Calabrians, nothing was out of bounds if it made money; drugs, weapons sales, human traffic—it didn't matter. They were very egalitarian when it came to generating revenue—illegal revenue."

Chapter 63

Santiago, Chile

IZZY FELT UNSETTLED. They had neglected her for hours. She slumbered, pulled on her restraints, and stirred semiconscious as her muscles cramped and her thirst increased. It was the fear of the unknown, and in a cognitive sense, Isabel understood its intent. Nonetheless it still disturbed her. She was angry, uncomfortable, and afraid—all at the same time.

Izzy tugged on her shackles. She felt numbness in her arms and legs from being stretched and immobile in the same spread-eagle position for so long. She swallowed. Blindfolded and gagged, Izzy shifted her torso so the metal coils squeaked. She raised her head to the left. The other prisoner moved, and the bed squeaked in return. It was an attempt to communicate, and Isabel took solace in knowing she was not alone.

Hours earlier, there had been some movement, and she was sure someone had entered the musty room from the far left and moved the person around in the bed next to her. In the intervening time, Izzy heard breathing, and more metal bed squeaking. It sounded like there were only two of them in the room, and she wondered in her moments of clear thinking if it could be Sandy.

It made sense. Juan had used the pretense of her roommate being in a car accident to abduct Isabel. Why? What was the reason for any of this? Did they kidnap Sandy as well?

The heavy door across the room opened, and two pairs of shoes crossed the cement floor. Izzy tensed. She felt a presence standing on either side of the bed, hovering, looking down at her. Suddenly hands were at work, unfastening ankle and wrist restraints, pulling at her arms, lifting her stiff body from the metal rack. They stood her to the side of the bed, and Izzy felt a rush of blood flow back into her limbs. She felt dizzy, but the person to her rear held Isabel steady, gripping her at the elbows.

The person to the front slowly unzipped Izzy's windbreaker, and she braced, fearing what was to happen. Hands moved, and her running shorts were yanked downward to her ankles, exposing her panties. Izzy stiffened, still not in control of her numb muscles. The hands to the rear increased their grip, easily controlling Izzy's movements, as the hands to the front reached under Izzy's T-shirt and started rubbing her skin. She tried to object through the gag, but the muffled plea only brought increased pressure from the person to her rear.

The hands stroking her flesh were cold and callused. They started at her shoulders, pressing, kneading her muscles, massaging her body downward over her back and waist and hips. There was a pause, and then Izzy felt the rough touch squeezing her breasts through her sports bra. She inhaled, her body tensing again as the hands fumbled crudely over her chest. The palms cupped her breasts in a full grope and then quickly descended to her legs, massaging Izzy's thighs and calves. It became more clinical now, a task to accomplish. Her running shoes and socks were tugged off, and for the first time, she felt the cold concrete floor under her now-bare feet.

Izzy steadied herself as each foot was lifted, rubbed, and rotated in place. Then the running shoes, without the socks, were placed loosely back on her feet. Finally, Izzy's running shorts were pulled back up to her waist and her windbreaker rezipped.

For a moment, Isabel relaxed. Her worst fears hadn't transpired, and the raw rubbing forced new blood into her stiff muscles. She felt the cramping recede, and the tingle of numb limbs started to fade.

A person on either side gripped one of Izzy's arms and stretched them loosely as she was led blindfolded in a wide semicircle around the basement. They rotated her arms in step with the movements. After two minutes, Izzy was guided into a seat in the corner. She smelled food.

The gag was removed, and a hand was cupped over her mouth, a clear signal not to talk. Then as her arms were held on her lap, a straw was placed between her parched lips. She sipped. It was water. Izzy drank in earnest, feeling the cold, tasteless liquid wash over her dry throat.

When she finished the cup of water, a wooden spoon was held to her mouth with some type of lamb stew. She tasted, then ate, realizing that besides her hunger, she needed sustenance. Izzy had to keep up her strength.

She ate slowly, taking her time, allowing them to spoon-feed her the way a parent might nourish a child. Her mind was racing, and her emotions teetered between an expected sexual assault and now a benevolent series of acts. She was confused as to her captor's intent.

In ten minutes they were finished, and before standing Izzy up, her captors gave her another cup of water through the straw. Then they repositioned the gag.

They walked her around the basement again for a couple of laps before leading Izzy into a small room. The change in pattern alerted her senses. She felt the rough hands grab at her running shorts and jerk them downward to her ankles. Then the hands pulled down her panties.

Izzy gasped and clenched her fists, prepared to resist, afraid of what would follow. She stood naked from the waist down, unable to see her captors, vulnerable.

"Tell us about the Empresa," said a voice in a quiet whisper.

She froze, confused, not understanding the question. The Empresa?

Seconds passed, and then Izzy was pushed backward and forced to sit. She realized it was a toilet. A moment later, Izzy relieved herself. Her embarrassment at being naked and without privacy in the presence of unseen, probably male, strangers was offset by her hope that they wouldn't hurt her. That it was just a necessary body function.

Izzy was redressed and walked back to her bed. They laid her down, stretching her limbs in four different directions as before, but this time allowing much greater slack in the restraining straps that bound her ankles and wrists. The metal-framed bed squeaked under her weight, and she felt the coils and springs push against the back of her legs.

Once she was resecured, just as Izzy sighed a sense of relief to the whole experience, she felt the cold callused fingers again. They stroked the flesh of her inner thigh, rubbing her naked skin, tracing a path upward under her running shorts to her crotch. The hand fondled Izzy's vagina through her panties. She swallowed, biting her lip. Then the hand was gone, and the two captors seemed to move away from her bed toward the prisoner on Izzy's left.

Chapter 64

Mexico City, Mexico

EIGHTEEN DRUG ENFORCEMENT Administration supervisors sat in a large, sealed conference room on the sixth floor of an office tower in downtown Mexico City. They represented the nine country offices of South America, the four resident offices of Mexico, the Houston Division Office, and Headquarters in Washington, DC.

The ASAC, or Assistant Special Agent in Charge, of the Mexico City Country Office stepped to the podium. "Thank you for joining us on such short notice," said the ASAC. He nodded at the various supervisors. Many were familiar faces from years of working together at the DEA. He clicked the remote control, and a bold disclaimer page stamped "Top Secret" flashed onto the video screen. The ASAC paused to heighten the moment. "This is huge," he said. "It could totally reconfigure the power and the pecking order in the distribution of cocaine."

He clicked the remote control again, and a clear picture of Patsy Bellocco flashed on the screen. The 'ndrina boss, dressed in a $3,000 suit, with his bull-like chest and slicked-back hair, glared at a subordinate.

"This is 'November One,'" said the ASAC, "the 'Ndrengheta's top man in South America. He was recently promoted to quintino. For years, his family back in Calabria specialized in human trafficking and kidnap for hire." The ASAC took a sip of water and surveyed the conference room. He had their attention. "Six years ago, he arrived in Buenos Aires, bringing the full array of illegal activities with him. He built on his predecessor's relationships and expanded. His work with the Colombians proved formidable."

"And now?" asked a senior supervisor in the rear of the conference room.

"And now," said the ASAC, "we have contact between the 'Ndrengheta and Los Zetas."

Several supervisors gasped, and the general look of surprise of the room's occupants was palpable.

"Roy," said a supervisor to the left, "maybe some background first."

"Sure," said the ASAC. "Our first piece of information was developed through a deep undercover confidential informant through our Monterrey, Mexico, office." The ASAC nodded to the Monterrey supervisor in the audience. "Then, the lead was corroborated through the Joint IA Task Force in Key West. Finally, we analyzed the data at the El Paso Intelligence Center. Two days ago, a team from our Guatemala Office confirmed our worst fears."

He flicked the remote control, and a photograph of a short, unshaven Mexican in an ill-fitting leather suit flashed on the screen.

"This is Zulu One," said the ASAC. "He, like November One, was confirmed by our own people. They met at the Real Intercontinental Hotel in Guatemala City last Wednesday."

The senior field supervisor from Washington walked to the front of the conference room.

"Thank you, Roy," said the headquarters representative. He turned to face the room. "This is without question the most significant new development to occur in the international supply of cocaine in a decade."

The Washington supervisor took the remote control from the ASAC and continued the briefing.

Chapter 65

CALIXTO CHECKED INTO the Mito Casa Hotel on Providencia. Time was crucial, and he needed to immediately put himself in Izzy's footsteps.

During the flight, Cal used the duration to double-check known facts from suppositions. In tracking, the hunter needed to quickly assess and separate what happened from what appeared to happen.

Naiche had been very helpful in rummaging through Cal's notes and Izzy's itinerary. His father was a font of experience and good practical sense. He knew people and their tendencies, and he understood the dark side of the human condition.

Arthur Finley, in turn, had proven a valued asset as well. The professor, equally concerned in Izzy's plight, had brought his keen intellect and organizational skills to the process. It gave them a head start as Cal departed Arizona with a satchel full of collated information. Even more important, Finley would keep the heat turned up. His standing at both the university and in the Tucson community would intensify the awareness. Calls to congressmen and senators, media interviews, State Department contacts, diplomatic channel overtures, and blogging would all contribute to the visibility of the disappearance of Izzy and Sandy.

Finally, Cal's mom, Constanza, would prove a vocal irritant. Her own experiences would prove to be highly newsworthy, regardless of whether Izzy was the victim of a Chilean government cabal or it was merely coincidental. The power structure in Santiago would get involved either to disprove her allegations or to bury them. Either way, the intense scrutiny would force actions.

Lozen dropped his duffel bag on the bed and consulted his asset list. Before leaving the United States, Cal had rustled up every personal or professional contact he had ever made in government or the military for names of people working south of the border. SF was a tight-knit community. Friends of friends often paved the road in helpful and unseen ways.

He noted a couple of individuals and their current postings. Cal picked up his international cell phone and made a call.

Chapter 66

Santiago, Chile

SANDY LISTENED TO the activity on her right. She heard the other prisoner being moved around, released from the confines of the metal rack, and being forced to stand. There were muffled sounds of discomfort, and Sandy wondered, feared, that the captors might be sexually molesting her fellow prisoner. She heard clothing being pulled, squirming, heavy breathing, and then they seemed to all walk away. Time passed.

The noises faded to the other side of the room. Furniture was moved, smells of food seemed to drift her way, and then a toilet flushed.

Sandy felt disoriented. She couldn't seem to gauge time. She was thirsty and hungry. She needed to go to the bathroom. Her arms and legs were stiff and numb, and she mostly wanted an explanation. Why?

A short time later, they were back, and the other prisoner was repositioned on the squeaky bed. She heard the shackles being secured and then a gagged sound of distress, a woman's plea, more anxiety than pain, as she held her breath and strove to listen. Then it ended.

They hovered above her. In seconds two pairs of hands were pulling at her wrists, then her ankles. They tugged at her body, and Sandy was hoisted upward and supported as she stood on the floor. She was shaky. The sudden rush of blood flowed into unused limbs.

In seconds her wool slacks were unfastened and yanked downward to her ankles. Simultaneously her blouse was unbuttoned and pulled back. Sandy was virtually naked. Hours earlier she had been redressed without her underwear. Now her mind raced, fearful of the purpose.

Hands started stroking her skin from both front and back, rubbing flesh, kneading muscles, pinching at her breasts and her buttocks. At first, she thought it a crude method of foreplay, but then realized it was a hasty massage. Arms were flexed, knees and elbows bent, feet and ankles rotated. They held her arms out to the side and then paused. She started to relax.

The hands from behind circled Sandy's breasts and squeezed, just as the callused hand in the front rubbed her crotch. She started to squirm.

She felt the hot breath of the captor to the rear on her neck. He pulled and gripped at her nipples just as the captor to her front started to probe Sandy's vagina. She wanted to scream. Then suddenly it stopped. She was redressed and walked in circles several times around the basement.

Minutes later, Sandy was sitting at a wooden table; her hands were held at her side. She smelled food. Then her gag was removed, and a meaty palm clamped her mouth. She understood. A straw was placed between her lips; Sandy tasted the water and drank. As she finished the cup, she nodded and politely uttered a *"thank you."*

A rough hand lashed across Sandy's face. The sudden sting caused her to shriek in pain, and then as she started to apologize for the unintentional break in etiquette, a second hand lashed her cheek from the other side.

The hands to her front clamped Sandy's mouth closed, as the hands to her rear gripped her arms to the side. The pressure was applied for ten seconds until she froze. Sandy was crying, surprised, frightened by the ferocity of the response.

She took a breath and nodded, and the two sets of hands seemed to ease, withdrawing from their intensity. Sandy nodded again. She understood: no talking.

The straw returned to her lips, and then a wooden spoon. It was a stew, meaty and hearty. They spoon-fed her for ten minutes before finally standing her up and walking Sandy around the musty basement for several more laps. They took her to the toilet and then finally back to the metal rack.

Sandy was resecured to the bed, but this time, they seemed to allow a much greater slack in her shackles, which permitted more leg and arm flexibility and range of motion. She moved her ankles and wrists. Sandy's stomach was in a knot. Physically she felt better, due to the movement, the food, and the toilet facilities, but emotionally she was rattled. What did they want?

She felt a presence kneel at her side and whisper in her ear, "Tell us what you know about the Empresa."

That word again: *Empresa*. What did it mean?

Sandy felt their eyes staring down at her. Then a hand started to grope at her body, touching Sandy through her clothing as she lay helpless on the metal coils. She squirmed. In a few seconds it stopped, and she heard them leave the room.

Chapter 67

Santiago, Chile

CALIXTO STOOD IN the lobby of the Mito Casa Hotel holding two photographs up to the front desk clerk. "Do you recognize them?" he asked in a friendly tone, speaking in fluent Spanish.

"Sí," answered the woman with a smile, "the two American university students. Nice young ladies; they were very friendly. Do you know them?"

"Yes," said Cal. He pointed at the picture of Izzy. "She is my sister."

The front desk clerk gave Cal a somewhat hesitant look. "Your sister?"

Lozen realized he and Izzy did not look related. "Same mother, different fathers," said Cal. "You know I'm American; you saw my passport at check-in."

The woman waved with a gracious motion.

"I need your help," said Lozen.

The clerk folded her hands and set them on the countertop.

"The girls checked out?" said Cal, seeking confirmation.

"Sí, several days ago."

"Were you on duty?"

"Sí."

"Did you help them check out?" asked Cal.

"No, they left a note in their room. It was a little unusual, because we always have someone on the desk."

"So no one *saw* them check out?"

"Not that I am aware of. I was on duty, and I did not see them," said the woman.

"Do you have the note?"

"I don't know," replied the clerk. "Is there a problem with the bill?"

Cal lowered his voice and pointed at the two photographs.

"They have disappeared."

"Disappeared?" The clerk looked alarmed.

"They never boarded their plane after checking out, and they never arrived in Buenos Aires," said Cal. "Can I see the note?"

The clerk thought for a minute, and then turned and reached for a drawer behind the counter. She tugged at the appropriate file and offered Cal both the hotel invoice and the handwritten note. Cal studied the documents.

The invoice was settled to Izzy's Visa card and stamped in red ink: *Pagado.* (Paid.)

The note, drafted in a woman's penmanship on hotel stationery, was written in fluent Spanish. "May I?" asked Calixto.

He took the two documents and laid them flat on the countertop, side by side. Then he held up his cell phone and took two photographs. "We are very worried," said Cal.

"I assure you," said the woman, "the Mito Casa is a small hotel, but we have a fine reputation."

"I understand; it has nothing to do with the hotel, except that this is the last place they were seen."

She seemed to be sympathetic.

"Is there anything you can remember?" asked Cal.

"This one," said the clerk, pointing at Sandy's photograph, "she was always smiling and laughing. She had a lively personality. She didn't seem concerned with anything."

"Sí," answered Cal, "that's Sandy."

"This one," said the woman, pointing at Izzy's picture, "your sister, she was quieter, but very polite. Her Spanish is excellent."

Cal nodded and then added, "Our mother is Chilean."

The clerk digested this piece of information as Cal sought to build a rapport, hoping for more information.

"She did seem a little preoccupied the day they checked out," said the clerk.

"How so?"

The woman shrugged. "She ran every morning. On her first day, when they checked in, she asked me to suggest a couple of safe running routes near the hotel. I gave her this." The woman pulled a complimentary strip map from a drawer that depicted several choices for five-, seven-, and ten-kilometer runs that started and finished near the hotel. "She always ran near the park, then came back and changed before breakfast."

"And on this morning?"

"She was in her running shorts and shoes, but she didn't go for a run. She was carrying her pocketbook, and she wanted directions to an intersection several blocks south of here. She seemed distracted and concerned."

"Where is this intersection?"

The woman paused. "I would have to think, but it was not where she would go to run—and she was not wearing her iPod. Your sister always ran with her music."

Chapter 68

San Antonio de Areco, Argentina

THE THREE LARGE sedans negotiated the winding drive that connected Patsy's ranch to the main road. This was Bellocco's country home, a late-colonial-style mansion surrounded by acres of grazing cattle and rolling pastures in the heart of the Argentine pampas. The drive had taken them a little over an hour to wrestle the traffic from his apartment in Buenos Aires to the fertile grasslands. Patsy felt the stress slowly melt away.

He looked over at Sofia and managed a smile. The tango dancer had never been to his estancia. She knew this was a new chapter in their relationship. Bellocco reached across the back seat and stroked Sofia's neck. "You look beautiful," he said.

She kissed his hand.

This ranch was a part of Patsy's private life. He was secretive by nature, given to long taciturn moments where Sofia found him protected by a high, impenetrable wall. But she knew he was also introspective, and as much as he thrived on the energy of Buenos Aires, he needed to leave the city for short periods of time to control his natural impatience—to think. She sensed something big was brewing.

"We're almost there," said Patsy, indicating the pastoral scene as they turned another corner. "This is much quieter than Recoleta."

"Pasquale, I am with you," answered Sofia. She always seemed to calm his concerns and say the right thing.

Six years earlier, when Patsy arrived in Argentina, he was surprised to find a country endowed with such a magnificent coastline that consumed so little fish. For Bellocco, a Calabrian from Italy, his diet growing up was fresh vegetables, pasta dishes, and seafood. Occasionally a little lamb or rabbit was mixed in when available.

In Argentina, beef ruled. They were a country of steak eaters, and they owed their pride and their obsession for red meat to the free-range, grass-fed cattle that roamed this vast lowland countryside.

The three sedans pulled up to the front door of the main house, and Patsy stepped from the rear seat and held out his hand for Sofia.

She climbed from the Lincoln and stood on the gravel drive. Her eyes roamed the cluster of eucalyptus, palms, centennial oaks, and araucaria trees that surrounded the entrance. "Pasquale, it is amazing."

Bellocco shrugged as he pointed to a cabin in the distance. It stood on the far side of a small lagoon, several hundred meters across the spacious grounds. "That building is *off limits*, Sofia. I keep it for our gauchos. They take care of the ranch. I let them have their privacy. Everything else is available."

She nodded, and Patsy motioned to his bodyguards to grab their luggage from the trunk as he guided Sofia by the hand. "Everyone lives with us in the main house. Tonight we will have a leisurely dinner, and tomorrow morning we can go for a ride before breakfast. You do ride?"

"Horses?"

"Of course," said Patsy.

"A little."

"We'll keep it light. It's a wonderful way to see the property."

They stepped first into the foyer, which had richly tiled floors, and then into a spacious living room filled with late nineteenth-century period furniture. It had a huge fireplace ablaze with logs and a crackling stone hearth.

He walked her through the room and down a series of cascading steps into a covered gallery. In the center of the gallery was a large, ornate hand-carved billiards table, surrounded by distressed leather furniture. Sofia was quiet but clearly intrigued. Patsy motioned toward the staircase and whispered, "You realize, you are the first woman I have ever brought here."

Patsy's statement was meant to emphasize a point to Sofia. She understood and hugged his arm. The tango dancer was a little overwhelmed, but also sensitive to his need to impress her. She whispered back, "Pasquale, I will be sure to remember that."

Chapter 69

Santiago, Chile

MICHELLE BACHELET SAT in a conference room on the second floor of the national palace known as La Moneda. It had been five months since Michelle assumed the presidency of Chile, and she had a full agenda.

The first hundred days in office had been consumed with her thirty-six measures, campaign promises, and some unfavorable turnover in her new cabinet. The last two months found her reacting to a variety of domestic issues.

Bachelet leaned back in her chair and touched her trademark pearl necklace. She looked out the bay window to the south, her eyes scanning the newly opened Citizenry Square. "Then we should provide information on our positions, and bring it to a vote in the assembly," said Michelle. "Do you agree?"

"Sí, Señora President," answered the Minister of Health.

It was difficult to disagree with Bachelet on many issues, certainly health, as she was eminently qualified in the discipline as both a medical doctor and a former health minister.

Michelle took a final fleeting look at the pigeons sitting on top of the statue of Arturo Alessandri in the square. Then she refocused on the faces circled around the table. "Are there any other issues that require our attention?" asked the president.

The room turned quiet as several of the cabinet ministers exchanged glances. Finally, the Minister of Foreign Affairs spoke. "Señora President, we had an inquiry from the US embassy regarding the disappearance of two American college students."

Michelle twisted in her chair to face the minister. "Disappearance?"

"Sí, we received a request for assistance through their consular officer here in Santiago."

"What happened?"

"Evidently they checked out of their hotel but never boarded their plane."

"They were going back to the US?"

"No, Señora, to Buenos Aires."

"Have you contacted the Carabinieri?" asked Bachelet.

"Sí, Señora, the investigative police are involved."

Michelle leaned forward on the conference table and peered through her wire-rimmed glasses. Something was not being said. She opened her hands in an inquisitive manner. "What else?" said Michelle.

The Minister of Foreign Affairs glanced across the conference table at the president's appointment secretary. The secretary picked up the conversation. "One of the young ladies wrote you a letter seeking an audience, Señora President."

"A letter? Have I seen it?"

"No, Señora. She also called several times. I explained how busy you were."

"Where is the letter?" asked the president.

The appointment secretary opened a file in his folder and pulled out Izzy's original letter. He stood and walked it over to Bachelet. She gave him a perturbed look and reached for the correspondence.

For the next two minutes, Michelle read Izzy's one-page typed letter. She paused, looked up, and then read the letter a second time. It was well constructed, poignant, polite, and used grammatically perfect Spanish. She set the letter down on the conference table. "I think this is a young lady I would like to meet."

The secretary bristled. "With respect, Señora President, she is a student, and your schedule is replete."

"Sí, that it is. So first, we need to find her."

Chapter 70

Santiago, Chile

CALIXTO SAT AT a corner table in Duke's bar at the Grand Hyatt Hotel. There was an English décor to the small lounge, but more important than its ambience was its proximity to the US embassy in the Las Condes commune of Santiago.

This was a courtesy contact. David Shields was a civilian who worked for the Defense Intelligence Agency. He had spent ten years in Special Forces and was recommended by a mutual friend who knew that Lozen needed help.

Shields entered Duke's and glanced around the bar. There were only a few customers in midafternoon. He spotted Cal and approached the table. "Lozen?"

"Yes. David, right?"

Shields nodded and signaled to the bartender as they shook hands. "Clap mostly had the description correct, although I was expecting some type of a ponytail."

Cal smirked. "I just got off active duty, so the hair needs to grow out."

"Anywhere interesting?"

"No, we had a few SF guys who spoke Spanish assigned to the SOA at Fort Benning."

"How did those young students acquit themselves?"

"Not very well," said Calixto with a laugh. "How long have you known John?"

"Clapper?" said Shields, looking off into the distance as he thought about their mutual friend. "Shit, probably about fifteen years. I met Clap back in Seventh Group. He's a *good* man."

"He said the same about you," replied Cal. "I met him when we were on an MTT to Costa Rica. They sent a couple of teams down to train their Special Intervention Unit."

Shields nodded. "Their UEI. You're working through MOBDES now?"

"Yeah, I'm in an IMA slot. It allows me to choose my SF assignments with more flexibility. There's plenty going on."

The bartender brought their drinks, and Shields loosened his tie. "Cheers," he said, raising his glass.

Cal lowered his voice. "You're over at DIA?"

"Yes," replied Shields. "I'm on a deployable HUMINT team out of DX Center in Washington. We rotate through embassies and do most of our work with the folks from Langley."

"You like it?"

"Yes," replied Shields in a somewhat ambivalent tone, "most of the time."

"Do you miss SF?"

"Yes. I mostly miss the clarity of the mission."

There was a moment of silence between them before Shields spoke again. "Clap said you needed help."

"Yeah, but to be fair to you, David, this is personal. I'm traveling on a blue passport."

Lozen's allusion to private citizen status struck a chord. US diplomats and those with immunity carried black-colored passports. Those on official US government business used red, and regular citizens traveled with blue.

Shields opened his hand in a wave. "I understand. Good to know. What's the deal?"

"My sister and her roommate, two college seniors, disappeared four days ago."

"From here?"

"Yes, here in Santiago, somewhere between their hotel and the airport."

Cal pulled out two photographs of Izzy and Sandy and laid them on the table facing Shields. Lozen pointed at each of the girls and repeated their names.

Shields picked up Izzy's picture and studied it. "Your sister got all the looks in the family," he said sarcastically.

"That she did," answered Cal with a smile. "Same mother, different fathers. I've got a few years on her."

"Any suspicions as to what happened?"

"Only conjecture, but our mother is native Chilean. She fled the country during the Dirty War."

"The plot thickens," said Shields. He leaned back in his chair and lowered his voice. "Clap said that you deserved the best I could offer."

"John and I went through some stuff together."

"So I gathered. He thinks highly of you. He said you can find anyone, that you've got some innate sixth sense."

"He's probably stretching things, but I have done a lot of tracking."

Shields took another sip of his beer. "Okay. No promises, but show me what you've got, and I'll see what I can do."

Chapter 71

Santiago, Chile

THE VOICE IZZY heard was Sandy's. As Isabel listened, her roommate mumbled two words: *Thank you.* That courtesy was followed by a swift, sharp crack of a hand. Sandy shrieked and began to apologize to her captors. That mistake brought a second hard slap to the opposite cheek.

Isabel rustled on the metal bed frame. She knew Sandy was afraid, but her friend needed to stop talking or they would hurt her. Izzy heard a muffled sob, and she could tell they were squeezing Sandy, gripping her into quiet submission. The noise subsided.

Izzy's mind raced as she considered the new information. It was her and Sandy. They were apparently alone as captives. What did that mean? What was the purpose of the abduction?

They each lay strapped to metal bed frames, to a parrilla, just like at the Villa Grimaldi. There was no way for Izzy to see if there was a wall-mounted electric power source beside the bed. The blindfolds and gags certainly did the trick. The lack of sensory information and human contact heightened her anxiety.

Additionally, the threat of sexual abuse was constant in the touching: callused hands, probing fingers on their skin, rubbing their genitals, reminding them of their captivity, their powerless position as prisoners.

Finally, the most recent events, where Izzy was massaged, fed, exercised, and allowed use of the toilet, seemed to indicate that the captors intended to keep them alive. At least until they gave up information on the Empresa. What was that?

The sounds from across the room sounded consistent with Sandy being fed. There was walking around, and then the flushing of a toilet. They returned.

Sandy was laid back on the squeaky metal coils and secured to the bed.

Izzy heard fabric being shifted, some stroking, and then Sandy's muffled discomfort. Isabel suspected her roommate was being molested, hands groping at her body, an act of intimidation and control.

It turned quiet, and then they were alone. Izzy counted to ten and listened. She bounced a little on her metal coils and made them squeak. Sandy copied the motion as an answer. Izzy needed to signal Sandy. They couldn't talk or see each other, but Izzy had to somehow let her roommate know they were together.

Isabel started to hum through her gag. She hoped that the sound Sandy heard resembled the song Izzy was trying to sing. Her roommate would remember. It was the song that Sandy had repeated in their apartment as the friends prepared for their trip.

Chapter 72

San Antonio de Areco, Argentina

SOFIA CLIMBED FROM the large double slipper cast iron tub and wrapped herself in a long towel from chest to thigh. The bath felt luxurious.

She and Patsy had taken long rides on the property two mornings in a row. In the afternoons she would stretch and rehearse dance steps as he met with his associates in private. The evenings had been quiet dinners at home and relaxing games of five pins, a popular Argentine cue sport played on Patsy's billiards table. Sofia failed miserably at the game.

Tonight he was taking Sofia into town for a romantic dinner at a restaurant overlooking the Areco River.

Sofia took some skin cream from her luggage and walked toward a large multipaned colonial window. She extended her leg, raised a bare foot, and propped it on the windowsill, letting the afternoon sun warm her skin as she started to apply the lotion.

In the distance, Sofia noticed Patsy returning from an afternoon ride, accompanied by two of his gauchos. But instead of the three men riding around the small lagoon toward the horse stable next to the main house, the cowboys led Patsy toward the distant cabin.

She momentarily stopped using the skin cream and watched as her paramour got off his horse and handed the reins to one of the gauchos. Sofia was intrigued, primarily because Patsy had emphasized the off-limits status of the cabin. That in itself increased her curiosity.

Sofia was not confrontational by nature, but she did have a streak of independence that occasionally pushed back at Patsy's controlling personality. In some ways she liked being a kept woman, and in other ways she just needed to be herself.

Patsy walked up to the cabin door and knocked in a pattern: three sharp thumps, a pause, and then two more. He waited for the door to open. Then, one of his bodyguards appeared from the inside and took a look over Patsy's shoulder. He nodded and stepped back so that the 'ndrina boss could enter the cabin. The two gauchos took up positions on the front porch and lit cigarettes.

Sofia found the whole scene rather odd. Pasquale said the cabin was home to the cowboys, yet they never entered. In addition, Patsy knocked and waited to be admitted to the cabin, which was not his usual demeanor. He could be courteous, but he was also brusque. This was his property, and it was unusual to see him wait patiently for anything under his domain.

Sofia continued standing in the window and watching the cabin for another ten minutes. There was no more movement at the gauchos' home. Finally, when Sofia finished applying the body lotion, she turned and started to get dressed.

Chapter 73

Santiago, Chile

CAL SAT IN the front seat of the rental car and studied the home. He was doing a hard reconnaissance during daylight hours. For the thirty minutes he sat watching, there was no movement. The residence appeared quiet and uninhabited.

Spread across the dashboard was a street map of La Reina, the Queen commune of Santiago. If questioned, Cal was a lost tourist.

This location came as an overlap. In piecing together Arthur Finley's timeline, it appeared that on the evening of their last known contacts, the girls had separated. They were apart, but apparently it was by choice. The dates and times of all e-mails, cell phone use, and computer photo files were electronically recorded.

In fact, Lozen himself had spoken to Izzy the evening before her disappearance. She sounded reflective, but unafraid. The following morning, the day of her abduction, she had forwarded a photo file to her father in Tucson *and* been seen by the front desk clerk in the lobby.

The good fortune here was that Sandy had taken a picture of the Cerro El Plomo Mountain, a towering peak in the Andes that was visible from parts of the city. Attached to the photograph that she sent Izzy was a short text message describing "A's" home, its walled courtyard, and several of the streets in La Reina leading to the location. Who was "A"—Sandy's friend?

Somehow in her haste, Izzy had merged the photo—with text—to her picture file and flipped the entire download to her dad.

Lozen compared the photograph of Cerro El Plomo to the home. Rising up behind the walled structure was the same view. It was the same angle.

He flipped through a series of photographs taken by the girls and sent to Arthur of their travels in Chile. He paused and focused on a picture of Izzy, Sandy, and two young men. Then he came across another photo of Sandy and one of the two men. She was smiling and leaning on his shoulder. Cal wondered if this was the "A" of Sandy's text message, the home's owner.

Cal turned on the ignition and put the car in gear. He didn't want to attract undue attention. Lozen would drive the neighborhood one more time and commit to memory during daylight all pivot points. Cal was sensitive to the distortions of darkness.

Calixto believed his sister and her roommate were the victims of foul play. Clearly his mother thought so. To Constanza, it was the general and the secret police still pressing their Dirty War.

To Naiche, Cal's dad, however, Lozen needed to be grounded in hard fundamentals. Thirty-year-old conspiracies sounded diabolic, but time was their enemy. To have any reasonable chance at success, Calixto needed to take shortcuts. He needed to track instinctively, as he had neither the resources nor the manpower to proceed by the numbers.

Cal shifted in his seat as he recalled the dinner with Naiche the evening they spent together in Tucson. His father took a long look at Izzy's and Sandy's photographs before turning away.

"Pop, what is it?" asked Cal at the time.

Naiche had turned and stared at his son, his weathered skin pulled taut as he spoke. "Beauty can be a blessing, Gray Wolf, but it can also be a curse. To find your sister, you cannot think like her brother." He hesitated before continuing. "But you must think like a man."

Calixto looked at Izzy's and Sandy's photographs one last time. They were two very attractive young ladies, Izzy especially so. Naiche hinted at the dark heart of men.

Lozen pulled from the curb and started down the quiet street, retracing onto Avenida Jorge Alessandri, to Tobalaba, to Larrain, and headed back to the Mito Casa Hotel.

Chapter 74

December 14, 2006
Gladwyne, Pennsylvania

PETER BURDIS YAWNED as he looked out across his lawn. The midafternoon sun cast a gentle shadow over his manicured gardens.

"Tired?" asked Mike in a solicitous tone, offering a drink of water.

"I'm fine, thank you," said their host, swiveling in his wheelchair. "Where were we?"

"The partnership," replied John.

"Ah yes," smiled the man. "The members of Condor and the Calabrians were firing on all cylinders: graft, embezzlement, gunrunning, the sex trade, and of course, drugs. They used over twenty international bank accounts to launder the money."

"A well-oiled machine," said Mike.

"Yes," replied Burdis, "but like any organization, they wanted to grow."

"They already had the power *and* the money," said John.

"Yes, but they needed new energy. They needed to build on their foundation. They needed new blood."

"A succession plan?" asked Mike.

Burdis smiled, a twinkle in his eye. "They were capitalists. They studied business models."

"Example," said John.

"The years flew by. In Argentina, the junta pushed the Falklands issue too far, and they had to step down. In Peru, the chief of the intelligence service was caught bribing an elected official, and the president resigned. Finally in Chile, Pinochet stepped aside as dictator, but stayed on as commander in chief of the army."

"So," said John, "the members of Operation Condor needed new blood to continue their partnership with the 'Ndrengheta."

"Yes," said Burdis, "they had to prepare for the future. They needed to grow, to evolve."

The joke hung in the air as now, only a tired pun could. Mike smiled before asking, "So what did they do?"

"They were military men," said Burdis. "They fell back on the common denominator of their training. The generals established a pool of qualified candidates to be brought into their Empresa from the graduating students of the SOA, the School of the Americas."

Chapter 75

San Antonio de Areco, Argentina

PATSY ENTERED THE gaucho cabin with his bodyguard. The outer room was larger than it appeared, a living room-kitchen combination filled with amenities: on one side a sturdy wooden table with seats beside a refrigerator, stove, microwave, and large sink; and on the other side, several comfortable couches and thick chairs circled around a large flat-screen television.

He followed the bodyguard down the hall past a toilet, complete with a shower, and entered the second door. Inside, sitting on yoga mats but shackled to long chains over their heads, were two young women. They were pleasant to look at, reasonably attractive in an ethnic sort of way, and clearly bathed, shampooed, and perfumed for inspection. Both had received makeup and lipstick as well.

Patsy glanced around the familiar room. It had no furniture, but could hold as many as eight captives spread along the walls in the chain-shackle setup.

Bellocco stepped forward and bent over the first girl, almost kneeling, and raised her chin up so their eyes could meet. The prisoners were not blindfolded, but they were gagged. The young girl, maybe eighteen years of age, mumbled imploringly at Patsy as he loosened her gag. Her eyes darted nervously from side to side. She whispered in Spanish and started to cry. Bellocco raised two fingers and placed them on the girl's lips, studying her dark olive skin and her thin peasant frame.

"Where did you say they were from?" asked Patsy.

"The Dominican Republic," replied his bodyguard.

Bellocco grunted and slid over to the second girl. She was similar in ethnic coloring and a little stronger in build. She met his eyes and never wavered as Patsy gently tugged at her gag. He touched her cheek as she kept her head straight to meet his gaze. Then she opened her mouth and curled her tongue around Bellocco's index finger. The second girl started licking, pulling his digit into her mouth, sucking his finger with her lips in a long, slow rhythm. Her message was both suggestive and intense.

Patsy's eyes lit in surprise. He looked over his shoulder at his bodyguard. "I think this one wants me."

"Sí, Quintino, she craves your verga," replied the bodyguard with a laugh.

Bellocco stood and motioned toward the first girl. "Give her to the gauchos. She is still fragile. She needs to be broken."

Patsy turned and looked down at the second girl, who had sucked on his finger. "This one may be ready to go. You take her and tell me what you think."

The bodyguard started to politely object. "Quintino, it is *you* she wants."

"Yes," said Patsy, looking at the girl. "But she's not quite up to my standards."

Bellocco turned, walked from the bedroom, and then exited the cabin.

Chapter 76

Santiago, Chile

CALIXTO PARKED THE rental car two blocks away, next to a curb, squeezed among several other nondescript vehicles on a small side street.

He had formulated an action plan in his head, complete with contingencies, and in the process considered the equipment he would need. Earlier that afternoon he stopped at a local Easy Hogar home improvement store and purchased several types of common construction tools for cash. Lock-picking sets with various torsion wrenches and picks were always carried in the movies, but in the real world, burglarious tools resembled items found at the neighborhood hardware store.

Lozen stepped from the car carrying a small bag. He was dressed in dark colors, wearing gloves, black running shoes, and a navy stocking cap. It was three in the morning, and the neighborhood was asleep. He slung the bag over his shoulder, positioning the bulk of the bag at the small of his back, and darted between the homes.

Cal reasoned that Izzy disappeared on the streets of Santiago somewhere south of the hotel in broad daylight. Either the hotel staff was involved in her abduction, which he doubted, or she knew—at least peripherally—her captors. Isabel was not a rambunctious individual who would flit away with strangers.

Conversely, Sandy was a bit more adventurous with people. In this case, the private residence with the walled courtyard in La Reina appeared to be the last-known location of the roommate before she disappeared. Yet again, the implication was that Sandy knew her captors and was here by choice.

He approached the seven-foot wall from the south side of the courtyard through a neighbor's backyard. Earlier that afternoon Cal noted several trees near the wall. These were strong, multibranched, easy-to-climb deciduous trees. He shimmied up the thick tree trunk until he reached a strong branch that could support his weight and also clear the wall. Lozen sat and surveyed the home.

All was quiet. The residence itself appeared vacant. Cal considered the known facts, careful to let his natural instincts guide his thoughts without jumping to conclusions. Just as in land navigation, it was important to let the map fit the terrain, not vice versa. The ground did not change: mountains were mountains, and valleys were valleys. This residence fit all the criteria for a low-profile safe house. A private home, in a quiet neighborhood, close to the downtown area, with a walled courtyard. A secure location for an abduction. As important, Sandy's e-mail provided a description, a photograph, and street names in a close proximity to the residence.

Fortuitous? Lozen considered those facts. He guessed that it was a romantic liaison and Sandy was using common sense at Izzy's insistence. He let his breathing slow and studied the grounds from above.

There were no cars parked in the courtyard, no motion detectors, lights, or ground strobes. No dogs outside or movement inside that he could see. The home looked empty and quiet.

Calixto stretched out on the tree branch, over the wall, and hung toward the ground. Then with feet and knees together and a gentle bend to his torso, he dropped the remaining four feet to the ground and rolled in a practiced form. The controlled tumble, known to parachutists as a PLF, diffused the energy through leg and hip muscles as he landed.

In seconds, Lozen was alert and in a crouch. He listened, waiting in silence a full minute before moving toward the house.

Cal's senses were on peak alert. Earlier that afternoon, with the benefit of daylight, he studied the home's and neighborhood's layout. Then he planned several contingencies and escape routes for each part of his excursion. Now, as Lozen moved toward the rear door, he examined the ground to his front, sensitive to trip wires or alarm systems. He didn't expect any, as such measures would alert the neighbors to strange ownership. Such was the antithesis of a low-profile safe house. The wall appeared to be a structure that had existed for years and most likely preceded the current ownership. No one in the neighborhood would think twice about a walled courtyard that seemed to be there forever, but unusual and extensive security measures? That would suggest to the neighbors either criminal or government ownership. It would draw the wrong kind of attention.

Calixto withdrew a thin, black, pen-size Mini Maglite from his shoulder bag, closed one eye, and started to trace the seams of the doorjamb and the window frames. He searched both the outside and as much of the inside of each portal as he could see. Then, with a thin putty knife, he felt inside the seams, tracing the narrow cracks up and down, gently feeling for a magnetic strip or contact point.

His plan was to use an unlocked window if possible. Barring that, he would force the door. If the windows were alarmed, then so was the doorway. He checked both as a matter of confirmation.

He paused, stepped back, and reconfirmed his escape route should he trip an alarm. Then he pulled a steel woodworking chisel and rubber mallet from his bag, and placed the penlight between his teeth. Cal positioned the blade of the chisel squarely in the center of the doorjamb, beside the lock, and swung the mallet at the head of the chisel. It took two strikes before the door gave way, splintering the lock mechanism and frame inward. Lozen froze and held his breath.

This was an inflection point. The sound of the mallet, though muffled, or an alarm would alert occupants to an intruder. He waited twenty seconds with the door cracked open, and listened.

Then Calixto stepped across the threshold and quickly scanned the side foyer, his eyes searching for blinking lights or silent alarms. There were none. He was in.

Chapter 77

Santiago, Chile

SANDY HEARD THE melody and tried to sit up. The shackles prevented a full change in posture, despite the extra slack, so she leaned to her right, straining her head toward the other prisoner. It was very familiar, despite being hummed through a gag...*all my bags are packed, I'm ready to go, I'm standing here outside your door, I hate to wake you up to say goodbye...*

Sandy bounced on the metal springs to signal. Then she started humming back the melody. It was *her* song, the one she had excitedly adopted in the two weeks preceding their departure. It was the popular travel tune recorded years earlier by Peter, Paul, and Mary...*leaving on a jet plane, don't know when I'll be back again...*

She drove Izzy crazy, breaking into the melody on a whim and adding her own cheerful lyrics to the original sad score. It was Izzy. It had to be. Only her roommate would know that song.

This was their private joke. Sandy heard the song one day and channeled the melody into her own special adventure of international travel. She felt a rush of adrenaline, of hope, and hummed through her gag, knowing now that her friend was near.

Sandy's initial excitement triggered a sense of comfort. She knew that she was not alone, but now she also knew that it was Izzy who shared her dilemma. In a sharp reversal of mind-set, Sandy's elation turned sullen. If Izzy was here, then who was looking for the two college roommates? Who was available to guide the rescue effort? Who would expose Alvaro and his accomplices? Who would free them?

Sandy hummed louder while simultaneously rocking her metal bed frame. She received back the same enthusiastic reply from Izzy. They had connected.

The control of their captors, however, seemed more ominous. For several days, the two young women had been held prisoners, only four feet apart. Yet due to the gags, the blindfolds, and the shackles, neither was aware of the other's proximity. They had a problem, and still, both friends were unable to offer strength or support to the other.

Chapter 78

Vina del Mar, Chile

THE COLONEL STOOD and ushered his subordinate into the small office. They exchanged pleasantries, and then the captain sat across the desk from his superior and opened his briefcase. He pulled out a notebook and turned to a specific page, which included a list of line items, before setting the briefcase on the chair to his right. It was a familiar ritual, and the colonel waited to receive the organized, methodical report.

Finally, the captain began. "The two rendered females in our suburban farmhouse are holding up. They are physically in good health."

The colonel rolled his hand, and the captain proceeded to the next line item on his list.

"An inspection of their electronic equipment, including laptop computers, cell phones, and handheld devices, indicates only routine contact with family members, each other, and our two romanticos," said the captain. The last word referred to Alvaro and Juan, who had been used to befriend and, if possible, seduce the girls.

"Any contact with locals, with dissidents here in Santiago?"

"None, Colonel."

"Any chance meetings or passed communication with the police or the judiciary?"

"Nothing we could detect."

"What of the letter to Señora President?" asked the colonel.

"We never obtained a copy of the letter, but evidently the request for an audience was ignored. There was never a return contact from the palace to young Soto." The captain looked up from his list. There were still several line items to be checked off, and he tried to anticipate the colonel's questions.

"What of the travel itinerary? Why was a visit planned here to the coast, and why the trip to Buenos Aires?"

"The coast seems coincidental," replied the captain. "The time scheduled to tour Valparaiso was minimal, and there is no indication that they knew of this residence or that the general lives here. Buenos Aires also appears to be conjecture. An examination of their scheduled reservations indicates a week spent in Argentina as well as a week in Peru. At face value the choices appear to be random."

The captain sat patiently as his superior considered the information. They may have overreacted to a series of coincidental, if unusual, events.

"And the Empresa?" asked the colonel.

"There is no evidence yet to indicate that they even know that it exists." The captain made another check mark on his list.

"What are we *not* reviewing?" asked the colonel.

"The brother," said the captain without hesitation.

"Ah," replied the colonel, "yes, the Special Forces officer at the School of the Americas."

"Sí."

"His status?"

"He is here, Colonel."

"Here, in Chile?" asked the colonel in surprise.

"Sí, in Santiago. He checked in to the same hotel. He is asking a lot of questions."

The colonel's demeanor grew very pensive. He raised both index fingers to his lips as he pondered the information. A few seconds passed before the captain continued.

"In addition, the PDI is involved, and the US embassy has become quite vocal in their requests for assistance. Evidently, the family of young Soto has engaged both their media as well as influential elected officials back in Washington. Some of the mother's past experiences are being mentioned."

"The PDI," said the colonel as he ruminated on the involvement of the Chilean Investigations Police. They reported to the Ministry of Public Security, and as such, acted more like a detective bureau than a national police force. Their structure was much more independent and far less military in their bearing.

"We have yet to directly question the two rendered subjects under duress," said the captain. "Do you wish us to proceed?"

The colonel considered all the information, and in his head, he overlaid the burgeoning stickiness of the abduction versus the success of the recent meeting in Guatemala.

"No, Captain, this issue is becoming too hot. There is too much risk to our Empresa." He sat forward at his desk and folded his hands together. "We reacted correctly, given the facts at the time, but now we know differently, and therefore we must revise the plan."

"How so?"

"By extricating ourselves from the problem, and in so doing, turn a liability into an asset."

The captain looked dutifully at his superior, unsure of how this would occur. Clearly the colonel had a strategy.

"We present our two very attractive young ladies to our associates in Buenos Aires, as a gift."

"A gift?" replied the captain, a little confused.

"Sí. A gift to applaud our associate's recent promotion to quintino. To recognize our many years of successful collaboration together. To acknowledge the next important development in the Empresa."

The subordinate sat, absorbing the colonel's thought process.

"Do you understand, Captain? We had an issue, and we reacted to safeguard our organization. Now we have a different type of issue."

"Our associate traces the success of his family business to its origins in human trafficking," replied the captain.

"Precisely. What could be more respectful than an acknowledgment of their history? He is very proud."

"So we present him with a gift that salutes the family tradition," said the captain.

"Two beautiful young ladies. A thoughtful gift to a man who has everything—a man who personally stays involved in all aspects of the family business."

"It is brilliant, Colonel. It removes a problem from our ledger, and if blood is spilled, it occurs in another's backyard. It also protects the relationship with our friends up north." The captain exhaled. He had a newfound appreciation for his superior, who always seemed to be thinking a step ahead. The subordinate made several notes at the bottom of his list.

"Shall we use the Paso Los Libertadores border crossing?" asked the captain.

"Sí. It is the most direct and gets the heaviest use—even in winter. Make preparations."

"Sí."

"And draft the letter yourself. It is important that our associate receives notice of our gift prior to their arrival in Mendoza."

"Sí."

"And one final thought, Captain."

The subordinate looked up from his notes and gave the colonel his utmost attention.

"Assure that when our associate receives the gift, it is presented in the most favorable light."

Chapter 79

Santiago, Chile

CALIXTO FIRST TOOK a walk through the home to assure he was alone. The one-floor structure was a medium-size ranch, with high ceilings, hidden behind the wall that circled the courtyard, the driveway, and most of the home.

Lozen did a quick but thorough room-to-room search, stopping to check every closet and cubbyhole, assuring he would not be surprised by a hidden occupant.

Then Cal slowed his movements, absorbing the layout, pausing to double-check the huge floor-to-ceiling picture windows that looked at the Cerro El Plomo and the Andes. He compared the angle of Sandy's mountain photograph to his live view. It matched.

Next Calixto walked around and surveyed the rooms again, at a slower pace, sweeping his Mini Maglite over the walls and furniture as he continued to keep one eye closed to preserve his night vision. This review was for feel.

He noticed the very same sparse décor that Sandy noticed. The home lacked a personal touch. It presented as a transitory location, like a hotel room, void of personality, as opposed to a personal residence replete with mementos and keepsakes.

Lozen started pulling open drawers and checking bureaus. He was not concerned with the effects of a perceived burglary. The splintered frame on the rear door already spoke to the forced entry issue. He was looking for paperwork or hidden information. If this was a safe house, used by people or an organization for a secret purpose, then the type of data would support his belief.

The medicine cabinet was bare, the toiletries basic and small in size, as would be furnished for multiple users. The kitchen utensils were few, and the refrigerator was only stocked with easily preserved, long-duration food items. The bedcovers were clean and recently made up. The curtains were drawn.

Cal found a locked cabinet in the rear of the utility closet and used his chisel to snap the drawer fasteners open. He rummaged through the cabinet drawers until he found a thick, sealed, brown manila envelope. He picked up the envelope just as he heard a noise toward the front of the house. A car had pulled into the courtyard. Lozen extinguished his Maglite and quickly moved toward the side foyer.

Cal considered the situation. At three in the morning, it was either the owner returning from a night of partying, it was a caretaker performing a routine check, or there was some type of hidden, silent alarm that he'd failed to detect that had alerted the wrong people.

Lozen watched closely from a side window as a single man climbed from the car and circled along the stone walkway toward the rear of the house. He would soon be at the broken door. Cal reached into his shoulder bag and pulled out the rubber mallet as he eased back into the shadows.

The man was heavyset, short, and older than Cal. As he raised a set of keys toward the lock, he noticed that the frame was splintered and the door was slightly ajar.

His first mistake was not stepping back from the entrance and calling for help. His second mistake was reaching inside the foyer to flip the light switch on the wall.

In a blur, Calixto grabbed the exposed forearm with one gloved hand and swung the mallet overhead, landing it on the top of the man's shoulder. He let out a shriek as the heavy blow fractured his scapula. The man crumpled in place, partially paralyzed, trying to turn toward Cal as Lozen punched him hard in the kidney. The expulsion of air rendered the man silent.

Lozen duct-taped the man's mouth, ankles, eyes, and wrists. Then Cal searched through his pockets and clothing and took anything of value, including money, jewelry, wristwatch, cell phone, and most importantly, his identification.

Calixto stuffed the items into his shoulder bag along with the unopened manila envelope from the utility cabinet. He dragged the man into the center of the foyer floor, stepped over the battered body, and exited the home.

Chapter 80

Santiago, Chile

DAVID SHIELDS SAT in the DIA office, clustered with the other members of his team, down the hall from their CIA counterparts. The intelligence wing was behind a heavy steel door, protected by marine guards, in one corner of the five-story tower that wrapped around a central atrium of the US embassy.

The buildings, built of granite, stood alone on top of a small plateau, surrounded by a wall, a patch of grass, a circular fountain that resembled a moat, and a trapezoid tower that connected their private section to the public departments. It looked like a fortress. The whole feel of the facility was that of an impregnable castle, standing alone as a sentinel in an occupied country.

Shields's telephone rang, and he could see by the internal number that it originated at the LEGAT offices. The LEGATs were the FBI's legal attaché officers, special agents scattered through sixty foreign countries, who acted as liaisons between the host country law enforcement and US governmental agencies back in Washington.

"Yes," answered Shields as he plucked at the receiver.

"How about a cup of coffee?"

"Sure; where?"

"I'll meet you downstairs."

"Ten minutes," said David as he hung up.

The FBI agent was standing in the formal two-story rotunda holding two Styrofoam cups when Shields got off the elevator.

Embassies were cesspools of infighting and politics. Not surprisingly, everyone had an agenda. In theory, the US ambassador, a State Department employee, was the senior US officer in any foreign country. Ambassadors reported to the secretary of state, who reported to the president. In practice, little of substance occurred in a foreign nation without the knowledge or tacit approval of the CIA station chief.

The FBI agent jerked his head toward the lobby, and David followed him out of the embassy onto the south lawn.

"Sorry about the drama," said the FBI man as he handed Shields one of the coffees, "but I know your team is here on rotation, and I didn't know if our friends from Langley would share."

David popped the plastic lid on the Styrofoam cup and blew on the coffee. "Thanks; go ahead," said Shields.

"I'm sure you know the history of the general and his long reign of power."

"Yes."

"And I know you've been read into the current state of affairs."

"Yes, as I understand, things are slowly coming to an end."

The FBI agent frowned. "I think *slowly* is the operative word. The current government of Chile is trying to indict him, but it's tough sledding. He's in his nineties, and the odds are he'll die before he ever spends a day in prison."

"And your take?" asked Shields.

"Hard to say. Clearly he pushed too far. Back in the day, when he assassinated Letelier in DC, it became the classic in-house fight between my people and Langley. The lines are blurred now—which is a good thing. We are all on the same team."

"And yet," said Shields, "here we are, meeting at a picnic table in a grass courtyard outside the building, rather than in my office."

The FBI agent laughed. "Yes, such is the sensitivity of old wounds. I won't dismiss the politics of the times—neither of us was around back then—but I know you have been poking around asking about those two college kids that disappeared."

"Yes."

"What's the interest, if I may ask?"

Shields hesitated before answering. "It's personal. A friend of a friend, but it's important."

"Why? Is he military?"

"Yes," said Shields without hesitation.

The FBI agent considered the information for a moment. He seemed to be deliberating how much to share. Finally, he spoke. "Well, I get that."

"Were you military?" asked Shields.

"Yes, marines before I went to law school."

David leaned forward and opened both hands, palms up.

"Our friends at the DEA," said the agent, "are on to something big. *Very* big. It could change the landscape, and the power structure, of the international narcotics pipeline."

Shields sipped at his coffee, quietly absorbing the information.

"Somehow," said the agent, continuing his explanation, "there's a connection to the general's people here in Santiago. They have military contacts throughout Latin America, and it is believed they made introductions that joined together various drug-smuggling syndicates."

"And our friends at Langley won't share this?"

"I don't know. I thought it best to meet away from the wing." He alluded to the old rivalry between cops and spooks. The FBI, like the DEA, was a law enforcement organization. The CIA and DIA were spy types, who sought information but rarely concerned themselves with arrests or prosecutions.

"They may have shared," said Shields, referring to the CIA.

"Maybe," replied the FBI agent. "It's a different world, but many people at Langley, and many Chileans, still hold the general in high regard. They believe that he and his minions protected the continent from communism."

"He probably did," replied Shields, exhibiting a neutral expression. "I guess we'll let historians debate the political cost."

"Fair enough."

The FBI agent pulled a sealed envelope from his suit coat breast pocket and handed it to the intelligence officer. "I know there's been a lot of noise back home, as well as pressure here at the embassy, over these kids disappearing."

"They're just students," said Shields.

"Exactly."

"Why would someone grab them?"

The FBI agent bit his lip before answering. "Senior supervisors at the FBI would tell us stories about the old days. Hoover ruled by fear. Everyone was afraid of embarrassing the Bureau. No one wanted to get fired before they clocked in their twenty."

Shields leaned forward and sipped his coffee. "I'm not sure I follow."

"Well," said the FBI agent, "when people have something to protect, they tend toward paranoia. They see a ghost around every corner."

"It causes people to overreact," said Shields.

The FBI agent grimaced. "It could be that these Pinochet people dove in to the pond, thinking it was deep." He stood and started back toward the Rotunda. "I hope that helps," said the FBI agent, pointing at the envelope. "Good luck to your friend."

Chapter 81

Izzy awoke with a start. For a moment, she lay on the metal rack, taking a few seconds to get her focus. She tested her shackles and found to no surprise that she was still a prisoner.

Isabel controlled her movements, listening first for any general noises in the basement, and then she leaned to her left. She could hear Sandy breathing.

Izzy opened her eyes under the blindfold and thought she detected ambient light in the room. After a few seconds, she admitted to herself that it was probably wishful thinking. The blindfold was much too thick to be permeable to light.

She considered their plight, wishing to talk with Sandy, hoping to share impressions, seeking to compare experiences. It came back to Alvaro and Juan. They were an integral part of this whole situation. If somehow the roommates could talk, then maybe they could figure out who their captors really were and, more importantly, what they wanted.

As much as Izzy worried about her own fate, she also worried for her mother. Constanza possessed an innate fear for her daughter's safety. What Constanza dreaded would happen, happened. Now, in light of the bizarre events, Izzy wished that she had not doubted her mom's concerns. She also wished that they had not argued daily prior to her departure.

To her left, Isabel heard the bed squeak. Sandy hummed a few bars from the melody "Leaving on a Jet Plane." Izzy hummed back through the gag. Sandy bounced on her metal springs, and Izzy squeaked back. They were together.

The door to the left opened, and Izzy heard the two sets of heavy footfalls enter. She sensed them hovering over her bed. Then, on either side, hands started to pull at her limbs, loosening the shackles, standing her up.

Isabel felt dizzy. The captors took a few seconds to steady her body, allowing the blood to flow into her torso. One person on either side gripped her wrist, and still blindfolded and gagged, they walked her across the cement floor to the far side of the basement.

Izzy speculated that it was dinnertime again, but they led her into the bathroom. They rotated her in place before she realized where she stood. It was the confined space of the now-familiar toilet room.

Callused fingers grabbed at her running shorts and panties. The clothes were yanked downward, exposing the bottom half of her body. Then, Izzy's windbreaker, T-shirt, and sports bra were pulled off. Finally, her running shoes, loosely laced, were tugged from her feet.

For a brief moment, Isabel had hoped that this was a toilet call, but she realized that something was dramatically different. She was totally naked, and the routine had changed.

Izzy held her breath. There was something especially vulnerable about being exposed to unseen captors. What was their intent? Would they abuse her, take her, subject her to rape and defilement as at the Villa Grimaldi? Would they hurt her, torture her, as Izzy now suspected had happened to her mother?

A set of hands removed Isabel's gag, and fingers cupped over her mouth as a signal. She understood. Izzy exhaled and exercised her facial muscles in silence to remove the numbness in her lips.

Then the other set of hands loosened and removed her blindfold. For the first time in days, Izzy could see. She stared at two burly men. They were dressed in overalls, their faces hidden by stocking masks as they crowded into the bathroom, blocking the doorway. Her anxiety swelled.

Up until this point, the unseen eyes of Izzy's captors had created a strong trepidation. Now, however, she felt a different foreboding. Looking at her captors for the first time, with their labored hands and rough-fabric clothes, Isabel sensed a more personal danger. There was something in the cold eyes and hidden facial features that harbored dark urges. They studied Izzy, scrutinizing her from head to foot, sullen in their silence.

One of the men pointed at the shower stall to her left, and then offered Izzy two plastic bottles, one of liquid soap and one of shampoo.

Isabel nodded. She had not bathed in days. She took the two bottles and turned on the shower faucet. In seconds, the hot water fought through the pipes to the nozzle.

Izzy stepped into the stall and slid the shower curtain closed. She felt the warm water trickle down her neck as the steam soothed her shoulders and the stiffness of inactivity seeped from her body. It felt wonderful, and Izzy marveled at how an act as simple as a hot shower could alter one's mind-set.

Isabel took a copious squirt of shower gel into her palm and then spread the liquid soap over her skin. She worked the cleanser into a lather, savoring the feel of hygiene. Suddenly, a callused hand reached into the stall and violently swept back the shower curtain. The abrupt movement startled Izzy. Her eyes popped open, and she gasped. She pushed back into the stall and cowered with hands raised in the corner.

The masked captor pointed first at the plastic curtain and then at the shower nozzle. The unspoken message was clear. There was no privacy. She would bathe, and they would watch.

More unnerved than embarrassed, Izzy started to resoap as her two captors stood in the bathroom door and eyed her movements in silence.

Chapter 82

CALIXTO WALKED INTO the Mito Casa Hotel carrying a newspaper. The front desk clerk waved him toward a quiet corner of the small lobby. They exchanged pleasantries, and then the woman lowered her voice as she spoke.

"Señor Lozen, I missed you earlier, but I wanted to advise that some men were here asking questions."

It had begun. Cal's break-in of the safe house in La Reina had stirred an interest. Suspicious people, people with something to hide, had been galvanized to action.

"Men—what kind of men?" asked Cal.

"Men in suits, official looking," said the clerk.

Calixto's face feigned ignorance. "Police, the PDI?"

"No," replied the clerk, "not the Investigations Police—more secretive."

She said the last word with a touch of discretion, as if mentioning it at all was disclosing a solemn confidence. He had hit a nerve. Only one day had transpired since his assault on the man at the La Reina residence and his theft of the man's valuables.

At the crime scene, Cal had exfiltrated through the backyards and driven away. Within ten minutes, he had pulled the rental car into a half-filled parking lot and changed his attire in the dark. Then he stuffed the stolen valuables, the identification, and the sealed manila envelope in the bottom of a gym bag and covered everything with maps and a tourist camera.

Lozen had continued east toward the mountains, taking photographs of the sunrise over the Andes from different locations. It was a loose cover to explain his presence in the early morning dawn hours. It also gave him an opportunity to study the information and identification. He memorized names, dates, and addresses. Then he gathered all of the stolen articles and, with the exception of loose cash and the man's ID, deposited everything in a roadside trash bin. He wasn't interested in the man's wristwatch or valuables, but to have not taken everything would be to confirm that the break-in was not a burglar caught in the act.

"What did they want?" asked Calixto with a baffled expression.

"I don't know," said the clerk conversationally. She was trying to be helpful. From the beginning, she had empathized with Lozen's efforts to locate Izzy and Sandy. "But they did not ask about your sister. They were interested in *you.*"

"Me?" Cal frowned in a casual way. "Really?" he said.

The clerk lowered her voice another notch as she answered, "I didn't like their questions. They seemed very sure of themselves. Arrogante."

The Spanish pronunciation of the word struck a chord. She was turned off by their demeanor. She felt a kinship to Cal, a protective instinct to the hotel's guest. It was valuable information to Calixto. At the very least, it confirmed his suspicions.

"Thank you," said Cal with sincerity. "I can't imagine what they want, but please let me know if anyone else comes asking questions."

"Of course."

Lozen lowered his voice and held the woman's gaze. "And please let me know if you find out anything about my sister, Isabel."

Chapter 83

Buenos Aires, Argentina

PATSY WAS PREOCCUPIED, and Sofia was intuitive enough to understand that she was neither the reason nor could she help. She let him fester in silence.

They sat at the Dominga Restaurant in the Palermo Hollywood barrio of Buenos Aires. The Dominga exuded a quiet charm, contrasting shiny black tables against white wood floors and softly illuminated walls. It nestled among the trendy bars and clubs of the popular neighborhood known for cool chic and television stations.

Sofia reached forward with chopsticks and selected a piece of sushi from the platter between them on the table. She met Bellocco's eyes. "Pasquale, is everything okay?"

For a moment, he descended from the internal ice mountain and focused on the tango dancer. "Sí, just some things going on at work. It isn't you."

"How can I help?"

With a wave of his hand, Patsy cut her off. He had made it clear on more than one occasion that his business was private and therefore never open to discussion. Sofia did not like the condition, but she understood. Part of Bellocco's world operated behind a huge impenetrable wall of secrecy, and he would not open the gates.

Sharing was important to Sofia. In relationships, she was both sensuous and sensitive. For her to be intimate, Sofia needed to feel physical closeness and emotional closeness at the same time. Anything less left the tango dancer feeling unfulfilled.

Sofia was not naïve. She grew up in the arts, surrounded by music and dance, but understood that clubs and bars were often controlled by people who worked on the fringe of legitimacy. The cash operations attracted a different type of business owner. It was clear to Sofia that Patsy was rich and powerful. He insulated himself with a cadre of tough-looking associates. They did his bidding and watched his back, but he never went to an office. He did, however, spend an inordinate amount of time in bars, clubs, and restaurants— and everyone seemed to know him.

One of Patsy's bodyguards approached the table, bent over, and whispered quietly into Bellocco's ear. Patsy stood. "Con permiso," said Bellocco, excusing himself. He followed the bodyguard across the dining room toward a long hallway.

Sofia watched Patsy walk away. She sighed and leaned back in her chair, taking a sip of champagne. In the early days of their courtship, the dancer found Patsy's furtive nature mysterious. As time passed, however, she felt the frosty barrier prevented them from getting closer. Sofia was at heart a romantic. She loved the attention Patsy demonstrated, except when he became preoccupied with business. Lately, this seemed to take a much greater amount of their time.

As Patsy turned down the hallway at the far end of the dining room, Sofia's cell phone chimed, advising her of a new text message.

Bellocco entered a small office at the end of the hallway and waited as the restaurant manager motioned Patsy toward a desk. Then the manager exited the office, leaving Patsy alone with his brother-in-law. The bodyguard posted himself in the hallway and closed the door.

Patsy hugged Ettore and sat behind the restaurant manager's desk. "You said it was important."

"Sí, Pasquale, important enough to interrupt your dinner."

Bellocco looked around the office. "We are alone." He folded his hands casually on the desk.

"We received a letter today," said the brother-in-law, "from our associates in Santiago."

"A letter?"

"Sí, Quintino, and like you, I am surprised at the form of communication." He opened a letter, typed in Spanish on plain stationery, with no signature. "Good friends," said Ettore, as he began reading the letter aloud, "We wish to acknowledge your recent promotion with a special gift, thoughtfully packaged in respect to your long family tradition. It will arrive through the regular channel. We hope it conveys an appreciation of our long association and all the new developments soon to come."

"A gift?" said Patsy with a curious expression on his face.

"Sí, Quintino."

"This letter was received today?"

"Hand delivered and unsigned. The original postmark is Santiago."

Patsy bit his lip in thought. He was a little confused, but also wary. "Read it again."

His brother-in-law read the letter a second time. Then he refolded the typed letter and handed it to Bellocco. "A gift, Quintino, for your promotion. A gesture of respect."

"Sí," replied Patsy as he placed the letter into his inside breast pocket. Then he smoothed his suit coat and stood. "I guess we will have to wait and see." Bellocco patted Ettore on the shoulder and kissed his cheek. Then he opened the door and exited.

The bodyguard walked Patsy across the dining room from the hallway as Sofia looked up. She paused for a moment and then erased the following text message.

Sofia,
I miss you. I want to see you. Please call.
Dan.

Chapter 84

Santiago, Chile

CALIXTO SAT IN an overstuffed chair in the corner of the Cordillera lounge at the Marriott Hotel. He idly sipped a beer as he considered the known facts of the girls' abductions:

In the hours preceding their disappearance, the roommates were separated by choice.

In both cases, Izzy and Sandy seemed to know their abductors. They appeared to be in the company of familiar people, men they felt comfortable around.

Sandy went to the residence in La Reina voluntarily. Izzy got into a car at the intersection of Seminario and Bilboa during morning rush hour voluntarily.

They never personally checked out of the hotel. Their flight had not changed. Izzy was the Spanish linguist, and she did not write the note, as both Arthur and Constanza confirmed that the penmanship was not Isabel's.

There was something very methodical and well organized about the twin abductions. It demonstrated a precision.

Cal looked up and saw David Shields enter the bar. It was midafternoon, between lunch and dinner, and the intelligence officer took his time circling the garden-like setting of the lounge. Several guests sat scattered on sofas amid tall plants reading newspapers and using laptops. Finally, Shields took a seat across from Cal. "Lozen."

"David, do you approve?"

"I better," smiled the DIA officer. "I selected it."

He motioned toward the cocktail waitress and ordered two more beers.

"Low key, middle of the day, big international hotel, close to the embassy," said Cal. "Hide in plain sight."

"Still works," replied Shields. "Habits are habits."

The waitress brought two bottles of imported beer and fresh pilsner glasses.

"So," said David, "your timing was excellent. I have something for you, but you called for the meet, so you go first."

Calixto sipped his beer and started. "I'm on to something. I've made some inroads, and I'm drawing attention."

"Well, I would hope so. There's been a lot of noise over at the embassy. Back home, there's a buzz in Washington, and the media won't let it go. It's a hot topic."

"I had some visitors. They made a trip to my hotel, asking questions."

"Isn't that the same hotel where the girls were last seen?"

"Yes."

"Makes sense."

"These were in addition to official channels. These were not the Investigations Police, who had already been to the hotel."

"I see," said Shields. "So, you want out of the hotel?"

Cal nodded. "I need to go to ground. Somewhere that doesn't require me to check in using a passport."

Shields thought to himself before answering, "Langley's got a couple of safe houses on file, but since I'm on rotation, I'd have to sign for them."

"That would bring questions."

"For sure. They'd want to be read into the operation," replied Shields.

"And of course," said Cal, "there is *no* operation."

"Well," said Shields with a shrug, "nothing that's been sanctioned."

"The Agency always gets their way."

"Well, not always, but often. Langley has the big budget. It's their world." They lapsed into silence until David finally spoke again. "What else?"

"I need you to check someone out."

"Who?"

Cal slid a folded piece of paper across the table. Shields unfolded the paper to behold a xeroxed copy of a Chilean National Identification card, known as a *Cedula de Identidad*.

The card was required to be carried at all times by every citizen over eighteen years of age. It was the only official form of identification in Chile. It provided the owner's full name, gender, date of birth, national identity number, right thumbprint, a small photograph, and a signature. It was widely used in bank transactions, legal contracts, voting, and travel within Chile. The card was presentable on demand to law enforcement personnel.

Shields refolded and pocketed the piece of paper. "I won't even ask," he said.

"Thanks."

"Don't get caught with the original."

"I won't," replied Cal. He didn't mention to Shields that the original was already destroyed.

"What else have you got?" asked Shields.

Calixto slid another piece of folded paper across the table. "Could you check out these two companies for me?"

Shields studied the names of two Chilean corporations printed in plain block letters on the page. "I'll see what I can find out. What are you expecting?"

"I'm not sure," said Cal, "but I seriously doubt they're legit. I know they own real estate."

"Straw companies? Front organizations?"

"Probably."

David leaned forward and took a long drink of his beer. "Anything else?"

Cal hesitated before answering. "I feel a little naked, and I could use some armament."

"I anticipated that. It will have to be local hardware, but I'll make sure it's reliable."

"Thanks," said Calixto.

"My turn," said David. Shields opened his briefcase and pulled out a file. "Read this. Ignore the typos; I was working fast. Then burn it. Understand?"

"Yes."

"It can get a little technical, so I'll give you the two-minute version."

"Go ahead," said Cal.

"The generals never gave up their power," said Shields. "They converted their intelligence organization into a criminal enterprise, an *Empresa*. They partnered with a tough faction of the Italian mob. Their infrastructure is staffed by a cadre of former military officers and NCOs from all over Latin America."

"Interesting."

"It gets better," said Shields. "They recruit their newest members from the best and brightest of each country's armed forces—most of whom are graduates of the School of the Americas."

"You're kidding." Cal sat forward, leaning toward the DIA officer. He was clearly surprised by the revelation. "How do you figure that piece?" asked Lozen.

"Not sure. Most young officers who are selected to attend the SOA are rising stars. It's a shared experience. Friendships are formed at a young age, and there are over twenty Spanish-speaking countries that send students."

"So how does this involve my sister's disappearance?"

"A major expansion is in the works. The Empresa is brokering a huge deal between the Italian mob and a Mexican drug cartel. Everyone's on edge—including our own DEA. If this flies, look out…somehow your sister got caught up in the process."

"Izzy? No, it doesn't make sense."

"I agree. But read the file, then burn it." Shields stood. "Thanks for the beer. I'll be in touch on the other stuff."

He winked at Cal and walked from the lounge.

Chapter 85

Santiago, Chile

SANDY WAS ALONE again. Thirty minutes earlier, they had taken Izzy into the toilet, run the shower, and then removed her from the basement. Now, standing huddled in the shower herself, naked, Sandy felt unsettled by the new pattern.

The hot water soaked the tension from her shoulders as she studied her captors for the first time. They had removed her blindfold. Sandy could see, and for a moment, she wanted to look at everything that up until now, she had only felt. The sensory deprivation was acute. But she could only stare at her captors blocking the bathroom door as they watched her bathe, their faces hidden by stocking masks.

They were brutes, with bulky bodies, weathered hands, and rough movements. Sandy lathered the shampoo deep into her scalp, washing her long hair, forcing her eyes to stay open. This was voyeurism at its most intimidating, and she found it more disturbing than standing naked and being touched on previous occasions. Now she could see their withering gaze. The anonymity of her blindfold was gone.

Sandy rinsed the soap from her hair and washed the lather from her skin. She was a little afraid to stroke her body to wash properly, for fear that any action might be perceived as enticing to her captors. She feared a sexual reaction.

As Sandy turned off the faucet, still dripping in shower water, one of the men tossed her a bath towel. It was damp, and Sandy realized as she patted her face that it had been used by Izzy. It was comforting to know that they had another shared experience.

She finished wiping herself dry, feeling a little refreshed, and started to wrap the towel around her torso, instinctively covering her breasts and hips. A callused hand reached forward and ripped the bath towel away. Startled, Sandy recoiled into the corner as the second captor offered her a makeup kit and pointed at the wall-mounted mirror.

Her angst grew. It was her own kit, taken from their hotel room at the Mito Casa. Sandy was being bathed and beautified. Earlier Izzy had been taken from the basement. Now, Sandy presumed it was under the same preparations, the same change in pattern.

Her stomach knotted further as the first man handed Sandy clean, lace underwear and her favorite red dress, complete with a short hem and a plunging neckline. Then he pointed a stubby finger at her and spoke in broken English. "Before we are finished, you will tell us everything you know about the Empresa."

Chapter 86

December 14, 2006
Gladwyne, Pennsylvania

PETER BURDIS TWISTED in his wheelchair to face Mike before speaking. "So the School of the Americas, officially the Western Hemisphere Institute for Security Cooperation, became their recruitment pool."

"Their inventory to develop associates," said John.

"Yes," said Burdis. "The key to the Empresa's success, like any organization, was its people. The SOA was a known source. It offered a standard, and a connection from which to recruit."

"Maybe some background?" said Mike.

Their host took a shot of oxygen before continuing. "It started at the end of World War II, in Panama, the Canal Zone. The goal was to foster strong bilateral relations between our military and their Latin American counterparts."

"Conceptually it made sense," said John.

"It still does," said Burdis. "The Cold War had begun. What better way to influence our neighbors than to share our curriculum? The SOA literally took US military doctrine and translated our lesson plans into Spanish."

"Then the goals were noble," said Mike.

"They still are," replied their host. "Where the SOA takes a bad rap is in the application of the lessons."

"Due to misuse of skill sets,?" asked John.

"Of course. If the school teaches counterinsurgency, drug interdiction, and small-unit tactics, who is to stop the students from practicing the same methods for different purposes?"

"So over the years, the Empresa identified future associates at the SOA," said Mike.

"It was a natural. If you were a young Latin American officer, your selection to attend the school was a mark of distinction in your country."

"And an inordinate number of SOA graduates populate the elite military units of these respective countries," replied Mike.

Burdis took a sip of water and wiped his chin with a handkerchief. "Yes. One thing the 'Ndrengheta had taught the members of Operation Condor was the power of money."

"So it was only a matter of time," said John.

"Exactly," answered Burdis. "The Empresa picked off a few recruits in strategic countries before things really heated up."

"Example?" asked Mike.

"The Gulf Cartel lured a top lieutenant in *GAFE*, the elite unit in the Mexican Army. They offered him ten times his government pay. He deserted the army with thirty *GAFE* soldiers. Most were SOA graduates. They became a private mercenary army for the cartel."

"So the game was on," said John.

"Yes," answered Burdis, "in a big way. Soon this group of ex-soldiers, who went by the nickname Zetas, hungered for more."

"They tired of wages?" asked Mike.

"Yes. They knew their value. They wanted *profits*. They split off from their employers and started their own cartel."

"Named Los Zetas," said John.

Burdis cleared his throat to continue. "The leadership of Condor, now running the Empresa, reached into their SOA Rolodex to set up an introduction between the 'Ndrengheta and Los Zetas. The meeting took place on neutral turf, in Guatemala. The Empresa guaranteed everyone's safety."

"Using SOA contacts?" asked Mike.

"Of course. There was a cadre of rogue Kaibiles to provide security," replied Burdis. "The Kaibiles were the elite soldiers of the Guatemalan army."

"So money is flowing in all directions," said John.

"Big money," said their host. "The architect had layered together a montage of front companies with interlocking directorates to launder the cash flow. Once the Calabrians took their cut, the largesse was spread throughout the Empresa."

Chapter 87

Santiago, Chile

CAL RETURNED TO the Mito Casa and stepped in to the lobby. He had been busy. Rising early, Lozen had done an hour of freehand exercises in his hotel room: thirty minutes of push-ups, sit-ups, and flutter kicks, followed by another thirty minutes of aerobic running in place and stretching.

After showering and eating a quick breakfast, he had walked several blocks south to stand at the intersection of Seminario and Bilboa during morning rush hour. There was no way that Izzy was snatched against her will at this time in this location. She entered the abductor's car willingly.

Then he returned to the hotel and had a nice conversation with the housekeeping maid who had retrieved the room keys, the handwritten letter, and a modest tip—all purportedly from the girls who had checked out to catch an early flight. The Mito Casa was a small, family-owned hotel, and news circulated quickly. Everyone remembered the two American college students, and everyone knew of their disappearance. The older woman liked Izzy, calling her the *hermosa señorita*, the beautiful young lady. This was consistent for Cal, as Isabel treated everyone well. His sister always took time to engage in polite conversation, and he surmised that her speaking fluent Spanish with a Chilean accent brought added attention. Sadly, no new information surfaced from this conversation, but the maid reaffirmed Cal's impression: Izzy departed the hotel the morning of her abduction alone, but in an agitated or worried state. The maid sensed that Izzy had received some bad news and was in a rush to meet someone.

Finally, a breakthrough occurred. Cal reasoned that the girls had been set up by their abductors, and fortunately, Izzy took numerous photographs of their trip. She periodically sent them in bunches to her father. Arthur constructed a succinct timeline from the date-time stamp on all Isabel's text messages, photographs, and Skype calls. Several sources confirmed a farewell dinner with male friends the night preceding the roommates' disappearance. Cal even recalled his brief conversation with his sister that evening.

Lozen located and visited the restaurant in the upscale El Golf section of Santiago. He spoke to the manager and then the staff. Cal showed photographs. He hit a nerve. One of the waitresses not only remembered the American girls, but also recalled *Alvaro*. She confirmed that Alvaro and Sandy appeared to be infatuated. Was Alvaro the "A" of Sandy's e-mail the night of her disappearance from the home with the walled courtyard in La Reina? It seemed likely. The puzzle was fitting together, and any qualms Cal may have felt in taking hard action to get to the truth were quickly dissipating.

--->==◉ ◉==<---

"Señor Lozen," said the front desk clerk, motioning Calixto to the side of the counter.

She was Cal's new friend—a responsible woman who liked Lozen and empathized with his plight. He was fairly confident that no one at the hotel was involved. They worried about their guests' safety and about the Mito Casa's reputation.

"Sí, Señora," said Cal.

"A package arrived one hour ago. A special delivery that I signed for."

Cal was surprised and watched as the clerk bent over and retrieved a rectangular package the size and shape of a shoe box. It was wrapped in coarse brown paper and bound by tight string. Calixto's name and the hotel's address were printed in plain block letters. There was no return address.

"Thank you." He smiled and took the package.

"How does it go?" she asked.

"It is starting to fit together," said Lozen. "You've been very helpful."

The woman tapped the countertop reassuringly as Cal walked to the elevator.

In his room, Lozen inspected the package first in the sunlight and then under a desk lamp. He snipped the string with a small pair of scissors and then tore a corner of the brown paper. Using his Mini Maglite, Cal looked into the hole between the paper and the shoe box. There appeared to be no wires or powder. He gingerly sniffed at the hole. Nothing. Calixto cut off the brown paper. He traced the outside of the shoe box and then took a deep breath before popping the lid.

It was a care package from David Shields. Inside, taped neatly to the floor of the shoe box to avoid jostling, was a weapon and a notebook filled with information. Cal pulled the handgun from the shoe box. It was a CZ-75, a reliable nine-millimeter semiautomatic pistol from the Czech Republic. It was also the standard sidearm of the Chilean Army. Lozen inspected the weapon and the two loaded, staggered-column box magazines of ammunition. Then he did a quick function check. Satisfied, he stood and placed the pistol at the small of his back, under his belt. He looked sideways in the mirror. Then Calixto reached back, withdrew the handgun, and aimed. He repeated the process several times before increasing the speed. After ten practice repetitions, Lozen loaded the weapon and chambered a round. He engaged the safety and replaced the pistol in the small of his back.

Calixto turned his attention to the notebook. The identity of the man he assaulted at the home in La Reina was first. He was a retired master sergeant of the Chilean Army, now employed as a security consultant for Industrias Comercial SA. The company was also one of the two names listed on the paperwork that Cal had recovered in the sealed manila envelope from the cabinet in the same La Reina residence.

Even more interesting, Industrias Comercial SA was a holding company. It owned title to four addresses—including the La Reina home—and several unrelated businesses. It felt all wrong. Cal made a note of the other real estate locations.

Finally, Shields included the name and address of a private home in Santiago that discreetly took in temporary tenants, for cash, and didn't require identification or ask questions. Lozen smiled. David had backstopped him in a big way. Friends of friends.

Chapter 88

Santiago, Chile

THE PATTERN HAD changed. At first Izzy wondered if it was merely psychological, a tool to mess with her head. Then she realized that the inactivity and sensory deprivation of her captivity in the basement prison just evolved into a new phase. Isabel had been beautified, and she felt oddly like an Aztec princess being prepared for sacrifice.

Izzy considered the crosscurrents. The captors had permitted her to see them—albeit masked—as she showered and applied makeup from her own cosmetics kit. If the goal was to intimidate her, it worked. Just like the open fondling of her genitals, the threat was unsettling. Thus far, the touching had been surface molestation. Thankfully it halted prior to penetration. Yet Isabel found the constant gaze of their masked faces equally unnerving. The voyeuristic aspect of them watching her shower and apply her makeup standing naked before them subdued her confidence. As physically attractive as Izzy was, she was still modest around strangers.

Now she analyzed the second message. The hot shower and shampoo refreshed her spirits, but providing cosmetics from her own luggage said that they had visited her hotel room at the Mito Casa and taken control of her personal possessions. The clothes clinched the concern.

The captors took away Izzy's running shoes, gym shorts, T-shirt, and windbreaker. They replaced them with clean underwear, high-heeled shoes, and the one expensive cocktail dress she had taken on the trip. It was a form-fitting silk piece that clung discreetly to Isabel's figure.

She had been bullied and intimidated for days in a dark basement prison, but left essentially unharmed. Now Izzy feared the change in pattern; cleaning them up and primping their appearance felt ominous.

The captors placed Izzy in the special compartment of an SUV, laying her sideways inside a metal seat covered with blankets. She was gagged, blindfolded, and handcuffed to a bracket at hip level. She had a range of motion, but could not escape. To her side, staggered head to foot like sardines, was Sandy. The closed compartment gave them warmth and the ability to touch at knee level. Izzy smelled her roommate's favorite perfume and knew that Sandy had been beautified as well. They continued together in the same predicament.

A lid covered the compartment as the empty seat frame slid into place and the vehicle started to move. Sandy hummed through her gag, and Isabel returned a few verses from their song to confirm.

Sandy let out a sigh of relief and touched Izzy knee-to-knee. Somehow, despite their inability to converse, the gentle human contact was comforting. Izzy nudged her roommate back.

Isabel needed to think. The venue was changing, the pattern altered. The stun-gun shock and drugs had long since worn off. Either the abductors' original plan had changed, or *this* phase always was the plan. She was scared, and down deep she knew she would have to escape. Izzy would find an opportunity, because she also knew that somewhere out there, her brother Cal would be searching.

Chapter 89

Santiago, Chile

CALIXTO WAS A loner. He always had been. It was not just that he looked different, which he did, but in addition to his multiethnic features, there was a cultural thing. He acted different.

His Spanish ancestry from Constanza was Chilean, which was a different type of Hispanic posture than typically resided in Tucson. When added to Naiche's Apache bloodline, steeped in both the physical and spiritual lessons of the warrior breed, Cal evolved into a curious mix of an outsider. But it suited him.

Special Forces was a natural for Lozen. His fellow teammates—officers and NCOs alike—valued Calixto on his ability and reputation, not on his rank or his pedigree. He was rawhide tough, but leather flexible. If SF taught its men anything, it was the need to bend to the culture while rising to the occasion. There was a time and place to push the envelope.

Naiche echoed this mind-set. His dad always taught Cal to never broadcast his toughness. It would surface when needed, like a sudden storm that swept aside the unsuspecting. Things were getting to that point.

Isabel was the flash point. She was Cal's weakness, his Achilles' heel. Lozen felt a special, protective instinct toward his little sister, and her safe return was paramount. Izzy's absence and perceived danger brought back a flood of memories from their collective youth. His tall, gawky, prepubescent sibling had developed into a beautiful woman—a smart and strong young lady who could be warm and sensitive, yet instinctively was wary of strangers. Izzy's disappearance was difficult to fathom. She was street smart.

Calixto studied the information from David Shields. Earlier that afternoon, Cal had checked out of the Mito Casa Hotel and traveled across town to the Barrio Concha y Toro. It was a quiet neighborhood of cobbled, narrow streets and three-story homes of neoclassic design. Hidden among the fading mansions was a small side alley between Escala and Brasil, with an unmarked wooden door to the rear of a large, gothic residence. The front of the home was faded, its stone edifice in disrepair, its windows grimy and dark, but the rear was surprisingly unaffected—sterile, sublime, vacant. It was here that Calixto rented a modest one-room studio apartment by the week, complete with bedroom and private toilet. The contact was a landlord known to David Shields who had sealed off the maid's quarters from the main house and rented the room for cash, with no questions asked.

Lozen parked his rental car down the small alley and lived out of his duffel bag. Each time he left the apartment, he initiated several silent alarms that would warn him should he have an intruder: unseen trip wires that could give him a moment's notice: a piece of paper stuck in the doorjamb, a thread stretched across a drawer, a square knot on his bag zipper strings.

Cal plotted the addresses of the four real estate properties in the name of the front company *Industrias Comercial*. He fixed their locations on a map. Then he planned his drive-by review of each address using the rental car. It would be a sweep of the exteriors, neighborhood by neighborhood. His gut told him that just as the walled courtyard residence in La Reina had been the scene of Sandy's abduction, these other locations would hold clues to the girls' disappearance as well. They were connected—the security man with the now-fractured shoulder, and Alvaro, the handsome Chilean dinner companion from the photos.

There were two things that Cal was certain of: one, given an opportunity, Izzy would try to escape, and two, his sister would know that Cal was coming.

Chapter 90

Tucson, Arizona

ARTHUR FINLEY LOOKED every bit the college professor. When he spoke, he projected an aura of intelligence, a seasoned, articulate lecturer that could logically present the case for his daughter's criminal abduction. His interviews, whether in newsprint or on television, were cool dissertations on Izzy's timeline and a dispassionate recitation of the facts.

But the star of the show was Connie. Isabel's mom had aged a decade in a few short days. Stress lines and premature gray hair invaded the once-attractive features of the Chilean-born Constanza, her beauty quickly fading through sleepless nights and a sparse appetite. It caught the camera lens.

As Izzy's mom spoke, her raw emotion and deep concern transcended to the viewer. She told a story, exhibiting an unwavering certainty as to Izzy's fate. There was gravitas in her voice. Constanza believed that Isabel's disappearance was intentional, a planned abduction by persons connected to officials in the Chilean government. Somehow, it mirrored her own ordeal as a young college student in Santiago thirty years previous.

Arthur had prevailed in his desire to suppress the odd occurrences at their home. The suspected surveillance or break-in by unknown, unreported perpetrators sounded too Orwellian. It would undermine their credibility.

In retrospect, the professor wished he had followed Connie's instincts on the matter. However, to broach the issues now might cause his wife to be portrayed as unstable—especially given the lack of a paper trail.

Constanza discussed the Villa Grimaldi. She told the viewers of torture and depravity, while offering nothing of personal specifics. Even so, the story provided enough texture and factual accuracy to rivet the public's attention. Their imaginations filled in the blanks. Viewers could picture the young Constanza undergoing a horrendous ordeal, and when she held up a full frontal photograph of her daughter Izzy, the story was particularly poignant. This was the here and now. It went viral.

Television, national news, weekly periodicals, investigative reporters, the Internet, and lawyers all surfaced to carry the sound bites and flesh out the story. It had legs.

Connie exited the broadcasting studio in downtown Tucson, paused to turn on the sidewalk, and thought for a moment where she had parked her car. It was her seventh taped interview in as many days for television or human aid groups. An innocuous-looking man in sunglasses, a porkpie hat, and flowered shirt bumped into Connie and quickly apologized. He handed Constanza a sealed, unmarked envelope as if she had dropped it, politely tipped the brim of his hat, and crossed the street before she could see his face. A yellow cab pulled to the curb, pointed in the opposite direction. The man jumped into the rear seat, and the cab sped away before he could close the door.

Connie stood motionless on the city sidewalk, frozen by the swift interlude, not knowing what to make of the event. She stared down at the envelope, turning it over in her hand. The outside was blank—no name, no title, no address.

An uncomfortable twitch started in Constanza's stomach as she rotated the envelope. Then she tore it open, withdrew a single folded piece of paper, and read the one-word message stamped in large, bold, oversize block letters:

STOP

Chapter 91

Santiago, Chile

CALIXTO WOKE WITH a start. He lay in bed, eyes suddenly open, as his right hand quickly grabbed the CZ-75. He gently released the safety on the pistol and pointed it across the bedroom toward the door.

Lozen was bone-tired, having just returned to the studio apartment an hour earlier. He had spent the better part of the afternoon and evening surveilling the real estate properties owned by Industrias Comercial. This reconnaissance took Cal deep into the night, offering a different perspective on each location and its potential use as a safe house for the front organization.

Cal took a deep breath as he focused in the dark. Something had stirred him—some unseen, gut-tightening twist deep in his abdomen. It warned Lozen of pending danger. Naiche called it wolf sense, an unusual animal instinct that surfaced at odd times in odd ways to warn Calixto of trouble. Early in Cal's childhood, his father noticed the attribute. Naiche was a true Apache, steeped in the mysticism of his ancestral heritage, and therefore never missed an opportunity to develop a bond with nature. He believed Cal had a gift.

Lozen heard a scuff outside, a shoe scratching on the cobblestone surface of the alley. He rolled smoothly off the bed, crawled to the far corner of the apartment, and positioned himself in a crouch behind the one cushioned chair. Cal waited, his senses alert, dressed in skivvies and a T-shirt, his arms resting on the furniture as he drew a breath and aimed at the entrance. The advantage of a one-room apartment was the single point of entry, the door. It took four seconds.

The portal splintered with a deep thud, and three men dressed in dark clothes and masked faces stormed into the studio. They instantly fanned out, spreading sideways as they entered.

Cal shot the first man twice in the rib cage as he stepped in front of the empty bed. The assailant keeled forward, dropping his stun gun.

The second man whirled in place, quickly aware that he was outgunned. He tossed aside a wooden truncheon and handcuffs and reached for his side-arm. Lozen continued firing in rapid succession from his crouch. He triple tapped the assailant, hitting him twice in the chest as he turned and once in the forehead.

The third interloper was the largest of the three. He reacted by tossing the heavy battering ram, used to shatter the door, across the room. The thirty-five-pound steel cylinder smashed into the chair and Cal's forearm as he shifted his aim. The pistol flew sideways, and Cal stumbled under the weight of the ram and the chair. It set off a scramble.

The third man dove forward, surprisingly agile for his bulk, and grabbed at Cal's foot. He yanked hard at the leg, twisting, snapping, and keeping Lozen off-balance as he tried to dislocate his ankle. Calixto kicked with his free foot, trying to squirm, keeping the man at bay while he reached for the weapon. A bare heel to the chin momentarily stunned the assailant, but then the grip on Cal's foot tightened and the man started to stand, pulling Lozen by his leg, forcing him upside down.

He raised Cal on to his shoulders, controlling Lozen's balance by the angle of the lift, using his superior strength and leverage to drag Calixto across the floor. Cal thrashed wildly with his free leg while pulling on his raised foot. The man absorbed the kicks and kept lifting until Lozen was nearly off the ground. Desperate, Calixto rolled hard to the right in a series of body spins until the assailant lost his grip. Cal crawled hard for the weapon as the man charged. He gripped the handle and swung the pistol sideways. The metal barrel smashed across the assailant's forehead, stunning him, offering Cal just enough room to turn the weapon and fire two rounds at point-blank range. The man's face exploded.

Cal shifted his aim toward the broken door. He waited. Ten seconds elapsed before he stood and peeked into the alley, searching for more accomplices. No one. Then he turned his attention back into the room and frisked each man. After assuring that each was dead, he calculated the situation: three men, moving as a team, using stun guns, a police-style battering ram, plastic handcuffs, a wooden truncheon, and no identification. They also knew the layout of the one-room studio. It didn't look good. These people were there to capture and question him. They were there to take him alive. In turn, Cal had fired seven rounds in fairly rapid succession in a small apartment. His ears rang in protest.

Calixto dressed, replaced a fresh magazine in the nine-millimeter pistol, and stuffed the few loose possessions into his duffel bag.

Out on the street, Lozen checked the alley. He had been in the new location less than thirty-six hours when the snatch team came calling. It didn't make sense. Cal needed to think and sort things out.

Walking quickly, Calixto negotiated the cobblestone street while shifting his gaze in all directions. The rental car would have to go, but for now, it was the quickest method to put distance between himself and the bloody scene back at the apartment. Cal checked his watch. From the moment of forced entry until his time on the street, four minutes and thirty-seven seconds had elapsed.

Cal threw his duffel bag in the back seat, climbed behind the wheel, and drove away.

Chapter 92

Vina del Mar, Chile

THE CAPTAIN ENTERED the small office in the rear of the villa. He stood and waited as his boss swiveled in his chair. Finally, the colonel motioned, and the captain sat.

"Colonel, we have a problem," said the captain, leaning forward. His body language was stiff and halting.

"Please explain."

"Our gift was packaged for delivery and transported yesterday. Unfortunately, there was a late seasonal snowstorm, and the pass was closed. They were forced to turn around and return to the safe house."

"I see. Everything was in order?"

"Sí, Colonel. I am confident that our associate in Buenos Aires will be most appreciative once he receives our gift."

The colonel leaned back with a satisfied expression on his face. He took the news in stride. "There are always unexpected variables, Captain. We cannot control the weather. Los Libertadores is difficult even in the summer months."

The central border crossing of Paso Los Libertadores was the most direct route between Santiago, Chile, and Buenos Aires, Argentina. It was the only high-quality road in the entire section of the frontier. Despite the highway and a tunnel beneath the point of the route where the mountains were particularly high, winter snowstorms were a constant threat to close the pass.

"Sí, Colonel, but there is more."

"Explain."

The captain pulled out his notebook and referred to several bullet points.

"As you know, we have been keeping our eye on the brother. He has been quite active. Then, following the incident in La Reina, we decided to tighten the net. We believe he was involved."

"Why?" asked the colonel, leaning forward again.

"He checked out of his hotel and went off the grid."

"He went to ground?"

"Sí, but we located him in Barrio Concha y Toro," replied the captain.

"So quickly. How?"

"We were fortunate. The unregistered rental is owned by a family with long-standing ties to one of our associates in the Carabinieri. We were alerted. When the gift was turned back before the vehicle could cross the border, we needed to adjust. We were afraid the brother would become an impediment. We sent in a team to interdict his progress, to slow him down."

The colonel looked at his subordinate with a blank expression. He knew the captain's speaking style well enough to know that the worst was still to come. "Continue."

"The team is dead, and the brother has disappeared."

"Dead? How many?"

"Three men."

The colonel fidgeted in his chair and grimaced. He was surprised by the new development. "Who did you use?"

"Our own people. They were well trained. We needed to assess how much the brother knew. We needed to assure he didn't interrupt the delivery."

"No sign of him?"

"None."

"Three men," said the colonel, almost to himself. "Impressive. Was he warned?"

"How? Such would indicate that he had breached the Empresa. That is highly doubtful."

"But possible."

"Sí," replied the captain, conceding the point.

The colonel lowered his voice to a whisper. "Then we must find him, Captain. Two incidents in only a few days. The trial shipment is en route. The Mexicans are impatient with disruptions. If we cannot control a minor issue in our own backyard, our associates in Buenos Aires will lose confidence."

"I will make it go away, Colonel."

"By any means necessary, Captain. Understood?"

"Sí, Colonel." The captain stood, buttoned his suit coat, and with a polite nod, exited the office.

Chapter 93

Santiago, Chile

CALIXTO SLEPT IN the car. He was tired, but conditioned to operating on little sleep and less food. So much of Cal's training stressed the need to think clearly under less than optimal conditions. First in Ranger School, and then in the Special Forces' "Q" course, Lozen had learned to perform under pressure while averaging three hours of sleep per night.

The training served him well. In both Iraq and Afghanistan, Cal led a split team of operators tracking high-value Al-Qaeda targets. They slept by day and worked at night, putting "eyes" on suspected terrorists hiding among the peaceful villagers. When identities were confirmed, he either called for a CIA drone strike or guided a heavily fortified black team in to take prisoners. In both scenarios, Cal and his men stayed in the field for weeks at a time, functioning around the clock.

Cal lay across the front seat and slept with his weapon at the ready. He pushed the vivid memories of the recent firefight out of his head and willed himself into a couple hours of REMs. The body needed rest to recuperate, and the key to deep sleep was a state of rapid eye movement.

He rose from his slumber before dawn, waking during nautical twilight, and slipped from the car. Then he rechecked the camouflage, adjusting some of the shrubs and bushes he used to hide the vehicle off a dirt road leading to the farmhouse.

Cal chose this location for further reconnaissance because it was the only remote address outside of the city limits and he needed to get away from

Santiago. All of the other real estate tied to the front company Industrias Comercial was closer to the action in the Barrio Concha y Toro neighborhood. Lozen dug his hands into the soft loam of the woodline and smeared the rear windows and the license plates.

Earlier, he had spotted an opportunity to swap his plates with a car parked at a late-night roadside restaurant. It was a temporary precaution. Eventually he would abandon the car, call the rental company, and report his vehicle stolen. In the interim, the different plates could buy him time.

He carried his pistol, the tool belt, and his shoulder satchel as he worked his way through the tree line to a clear view of the farm. It looked different than a day earlier. The main house wasn't quite as large in the early light of dawn, and the barn appeared more dilapidated. A few cows sat on the hill in the distance, and a tractor looked broken and rusted beside a mud pen housing two old pigs. Not exactly a working farm.

Cal reached into his satchel and withdrew a small pair of civilian-style binoculars, the kind that drew little attention from a customs officer, especially when carried next to a camera. It suggested a tourist.

He scanned the farmhouse from the cover of the trees. It mixed a stone and wood façade with a poured concrete foundation. The structure sat on the pitch of a hill, which created a split-level effect, and it seemed to have a thick door offering access to a functioning walkout basement.

As Cal circled the farm, he studied the windows and door placements and memorized the exterior of the property. Suddenly, a light popped on and illuminated the front porch. Then a burly man in his midfifties stepped from the house dressed in bib overalls and a soiled shirt. He spat, and then leaned impatiently on the handrail as he sipped a mug of coffee.

Cal heard a vehicle in the distance. Someone was driving up the dirt road, approaching the farmhouse. Then a black Volvo jutted into the clearing and spun in a short semicircle on the muddy gravel that fanned across the lawn in front of the porch. The driver stepped out and motioned to the man in the overalls.

For a moment, Calixto thought the driver looked familiar. He tried to place the face, studying the visitor from a distance through his binoculars. Who was he? Where had he seen the driver before?

In a spark of memory, Cal took out his BlackBerry and started flipping through the e-mail messages and photographs assembled in a timeline by Arthur Finley. It was the dinner attended by the girls on their final evening in Santiago, the night that Sandy disappeared. Izzy, Sandy, and two male friends ate at a restaurant in El Golf. One of the waitresses remembered Alvaro, Sandy's handsome suitor. Cal looked hard at the other man, Izzy's date.

Lozen shifted his gaze back to the binoculars. He focused the lens. Then he looked back at the picture on his BlackBerry.

The visitor and the farmhand spoke for a few minutes, but the distance was too great for Cal to hear the conversation. The discussion seemed to heat up, as if the man in the bib overalls didn't like what he heard. Then he dumped out his mug of coffee on the ground and turned back toward the house.

The driver climbed back into his Volvo, and with an acceleration, spun up bits of gravel and mud as he backed away from the farmhouse. He turned and guided the car back to the dirt road.

Cal made a quick decision. He grabbed his gear and started to race back through the woodline, picking his spots as he kept an ear to the Volvo, winding its way along the dirt road in the distance. He made it to the rental car and crouched behind the shrubs just as the visitor turned onto the main thoroughfare and headed back to Santiago. Calixto jumped into his sedan and followed.

Chapter 94

SANDY WANTED TO scream. She felt the urge to reach out and grab the face of her closest captor and tear the mask off his head.

Minutes earlier, they had lifted her from the hidden, coffin-like compartment in the SUV and stood her on solid ground. The midmorning sun warmed her cheeks, and she heard the gravel underfoot scratch at her high heels. They held her upright, allowing the blood to flow into unused limbs, shaking her arms and smoothing the ruffles from her clingy party dress. She felt human, almost normal again.

The ride had been an ordeal. It seemed like hours elapsed as she and Izzy huddled together, fastened under the seat. The temperature started warm, then turned cold, and finally warm again. It corresponded with the pitch of the SUV, as the vehicle left their basement prison, climbed into the mountains, and then descended again.

A couple times there were brief, unintelligible conversations spoken quickly in Spanish. Sandy dozed through the process. Now, finally, amid all the drama, they had arrived at their new destination.

Sandy was, by nature, a fun-loving, life-embracing coed more interested in completing college and flirting with cute men than solving the serious issues of the day. She was not inclined toward politics, the economy, or world peace. If she could pay her bills and get her degree, then everything else would fall into place. For this reason, she could not fathom why any of this was happening. She had a good heart, was a good friend, and bothered no one. Her mom had no money, so ransom made no sense.

For days on end, they had been held prisoners in a moldy basement, strapped spread-eagled to a metal bed, and subjected to constant indignities. Her captors had stripped her naked, fondled her, and slapped her silly for minor infractions. Then they permitted Sandy to shower, shampoo, apply makeup and perfume, and dressed her in a pretty dress with high-heeled shoes. From sexual innuendo and humiliation to beautification. It was all one big mind game to intimidate. Why? What could she have that they wanted? No one spoke, except to ask her a question about the Empresa. What? Sandy craved five minutes of conversation with Izzy. She was sure her friend could make sense of the whole situation if they could talk.

They led Sandy through a heavy door onto a cement floor that felt oddly familiar. The smell of the dank basement permeated her nostrils, but the real confirmation to Sandy that they had returned to the original holding place was when they lay her back, party dress and high heels untouched, onto the metal-framed bed. She heard the springs squeak and felt the cold steel coils pinch at the exposed skin of her legs. They spread Sandy's limbs and secured her to the four corners. What were they doing? What was the point of the entire beautification process and the endless ride in a stuffy secret compartment? They brought them right back to their cold, dungeon-like prison. Why?

Sandy's emotions got the better of her. She started to shake. Her strident voice tried to yell through the gag as she wiggled her limbs. Her body bounced up and down on the metal coils. She was stressed. Sandy wanted no part of this game. The whole ordeal was starting to take a toll.

Within seconds one rough hand clamped down on her mouth, while a second reached up under her dress and grabbed her crotch. Both hands squeezed. Sandy winced in pain and relented. After a few seconds, the hands relaxed.

Lying still, feeling hurt and confused, in a moment of understandable self-pity, Sandy started to cry. They were small sniffles of helplessness, tears of hopelessness, from a large well of frustration.

Chapter 95

Santiago, Chile

CALIXTO FOLLOWED THE black Volvo back into the city. He was sure to keep at a safe distance until Santiago metro traffic clogged up the early morning streets and provided sufficient cover to his rental car. He felt conspicuous in the sedan, despite the stolen license plates. An extra level of vigilance kicked in. They had tried to grab him at the studio apartment in Barrio Concha y Toro and failed. It was prudent to assume that someone had raised an alarm and they were searching for him. But he couldn't pass on the opportunity to tail the Volvo, driven by Izzy's dinner companion, to wherever it led.

Thirty minutes of rush hour weaving and bobbing brought the Volvo to a neighborhood several blocks south of Izzy's last-known destination, the intersection of Bilboa and Seminario streets. The driver took a circuitous route, turning east, but didn't seem concerned with being tailed. Cal reasoned that the firefight of the previous evening was not common knowledge.

Finally, the Volvo turned onto a quiet street that Cal recognized. It approached the known address from the opposite direction, but the location was fixed in Lozen's head. It was one of the addresses that he had surveyed on a drive-by recon the previous day.

The driver pulled in front of a gated chain-link fence that secured a vacant lot in front of a metal building with closed garage doors. The car idled for a moment, and then the gate started to electronically open. The Volvo pulled forward into the lot. Simultaneously, the garage doors to the building opened, while the gate to the chain-link fence slid closed. The Volvo drove forward and entered the metal building.

Cal slowed his sedan as he cruised by the facility, taking the opportunity to study the layout without drawing attention. The garage doors closed, assuring the Volvo was not visible from the sidewalk.

At the far end of the quiet street, Lozen turned right and circled the block. There were security procedures in place at the address, and a connection among people, properties owned by Industrias Comercial, and his sister's disappearance. Cal had learned long ago to be suspicious of coincidences.

Lozen approached the street from the opposite end and slowly eased his sedan into a position where he could view the front gate from a distance. Cal slumped down in the seat and adjusted the mirrors to his new height. Then he pulled out his cell phone and dialed a memorized number.

"Two, six, one, three, four, two, four," answered David Shields.

"Can you talk?" asked Cal.

They spoke cryptically, never using names or specifics.

"Hey, stay with me…"

Lozen heard the DIA officer shuffle some papers and then slide his chair back. Cal knew that Shields was walking from his office in the intelligence wing to enter a different part of the embassy. Finally, the familiar voice returned. "How's it going?"

"Still kicking," said Cal.

"You all right?" asked Shields.

"It was close."

There was a pause from Shields as he lowered his voice. "What happened?"

"I was at the new place. I received a visit."

"From who?"

"Professionals," said Cal. "They knew what they were doing. They came prepared."

"What did they want?"

"Me," answered Cal.

Cal could hear Shields's mind working in overdrive. "A takeout?"

"No, a snatch operation."

Shields mumbled a profanity before asking, "Are you impaired?"

"No. Did you share my location with anyone?"

"Never."

"Then I would suggest you keep an eye on the contact that rented me the place. He's working both sides of the fence."

"Shit," said Shields in frustration.

"And that company is definitely dirty. It's all coming together."

"I'm not surprised. Are you making headway?"

"Yes."

"How can I help?" asked Shields.

"Run some interference. Don't let them paint me into a corner."

"I will. What's the status of your visitors?"

"They're gone," said Calixto.

He could hear Shields exhale before responding, "That's news. It hasn't hit the intel wire. Maybe these people have the ability to keep it under wraps."

"That would suggest a high level of influence in official circles."

"Yes," answered Shields.

"They set the bar. I need to do what I've got to do. I don't want you hurt by this."

"I understand. You let me worry about my side. You take care."

"Will do," said Cal as he hung up his cell phone.

His eyes first checked his mirrors and then shifted to the tall chain-link fence at the far end of the street.

Chapter 96

December 14, 2006
Gladwyne, Pennsylvania

"THE YEARS FLEW by," said Burdis, the memories causing his eyes to flicker, "and we hit some rough patches."

"It was tough sledding," said John.

"Yes, too many politicos with an agenda."

"Like when Jimmy Carter sat in the White House," said Mike.

"And Carter appointed his classmate from Annapolis to be the director of the CIA," said Burdis.

"Stansfield Turner?" asked John.

"The admiral himself. A self-righteous prig who gutted the Agency of experienced operators and dug in to the black-ops budget."

"And the result?" asked Mike.

Burdis took a shot of air before answering. "The Agency warned the members of the Empresa that it was only a matter of time before each of their countries was confronted with a similar plight—hostile politicians that would withhold necessary funds and undermine the gains they had made in controlling communism."

"So the architect offered a plan," said John.

"He convinced the members of the Empresa that they needed a contingency fund."

Chapter 97

Buenos Aires, Argentina

SOFIA SAT IN front of her vanity mirror, half dressed in her underwear, applying moisturizer to her face. This was quiet time, when the dancer could take a few minutes to relax and think.

She smiled. Men had it easy. A quick shower and shave, a little cologne, and they were ready to go. Women, however, were expected to progress through a retinue of beauty steps to dazzle their partners with the finished product. Sofia was no feminist, but there did seem to be a bit of inequality in those expectations.

Sofia finished her foundation and eye shadow before using a pencil to apply eyeliner. She thought about Patsy and their relationship. Things had changed in several ways. Bellocco was still attentive and passionate toward the dancer, but he seemed to have so much on his mind. Something very important was adrift with his business. In addition, Patsy acted different around his nephews, Beppe and Lino. She didn't like the nephews—two young, testosterone-fueled family members from the old country. She didn't like the way they leered at her, or their aggressive demeanor. Patsy himself had an edge, yet her lover added a touch of refinement to his personality. He seemed to control his impulses. The nephews, however, postured like two arrogant attack dogs.

Sofia curled her long eyelashes and brushed on mascara. She understood Patsy was a private person, but his secrecy ate away at their connection. For Sofia to feel a special bond, there needed to be trust. Odd things, like the mysterious use of the gaucho cabin at Patsy's estancia, bothered her. She wondered where their relationship was going. Recently, Dan, her former lover, contacted Sofia. Dan wanted a rendezvous, but she refrained. Relationships and feelings were always so complicated. Sofia kept the dialogue to cell phones and text messages.

The dancer added blush, lip liner, and a dab of perfume. Then she stood and took a final look in the mirror. Sofia had to admit she was a very desirable woman. Finally, she turned and walked into the large bedroom that she shared with Patsy—and suddenly stopped.

To her right, Beppe sat in a cushioned chair, while Lino circled her unmade, king-size bed. He plucked a cotton leg warmer from the sheets and raised it to his nostrils.

"What are you doing here?" said Sofia.

"Pasquale sent us," said Beppe from the chair.

"Why?"

"To fetch you," replied Lino, making a point to inhale, smelling her leg warmer. "He was detained."

"How *dare* you," said Sofia, angered by their invasion of her privacy. "Get out. You have no right to be here. This is my bedroom."

"Oh, we know," said Beppe. He stood and took a long, exaggerated look at Sofia in her bra and panties. "But the boss told us to find you and bring you to dinner."

"Get out," said Sofia again.

Lino dangled the long leg warmer over the sheets and casually dropped the dancer's clothing on her bed. "We couldn't find you," said Lino, "and the door was open."

The two nephews sauntered past Sofia as Beppe spoke. "We'll be waiting in the living room."

Lino deliberately winked at the irate dancer as they exited. It caused Sofia to slam her bedroom door behind them.

Chapter 98

Santiago, Chile

CALIXTO LOOKED AT his wristwatch as he approached the three-hour mark. Surveillance work, whether military reconnaissance or police stakeouts, combined long moments of boredom with short bursts of extreme activity.

In the time that Lozen watched the fenced lot, only two pedestrians passed his rental car. Neither seemed to notice Cal slumped in the front seat. Just as important, neither person stopped anywhere near the gated, chain-link fence.

The garage door to the metal building opened, and the Volvo backed into the open parking lot. The driver executed a three-point turn and waited. Then the garage door closed as the gated fence slid open.

Cal sat forward in his seat and readjusted his mirrors. He started the car and shifted the sedan into neutral. Then as the Volvo turned on to the side street, Cal followed.

They headed south, into the neighborhood of San Joaquin, a Santiago commune of ten square kilometers inhabited by a hundred thousand residents of average income. Over the last few years, the area had started to attract younger urban professionals due to its proximity to the financial district and the Catholic University extension campus.

The Volvo made several turns, threading easily through the midday traffic, until finally the car turned into a residential area of apartment blocks and small, multiunit homes off Rivera Street. Unlike the wealthy communes of Vitacura and Las Condes, most of the young residents of San Joaquin either worked, went to school, or did both. There were few stay-at-home moms or domestic workers tending to the properties.

Calixto waited as the driver turned into a short driveway and parked. He studied him from afar—thirty years old, well groomed, gray suit and tie. The same man that sat next to Izzy in the farewell dinner photograph from the restaurant in El Golf. He disappeared around the corner, presumably toward a side door.

Lozen waited twenty minutes. It was decision time. Alvaro's friend was either at home, visiting a friend, or had entered an unmarked safe house owned by Industrias Comercial. Time was becoming crucial, and Cal was very sensitive to the realities of abduction. He had neither the inclination nor the luxury to wait until nightfall. Every hour that elapsed closed the net tighter on Cal and put Izzy in greater danger. He would stay on the offensive.

Calixto donned a baseball hat that he purchased at a local street vendor. It displayed the name and logo of a popular Santiago soccer team. Then he adjusted the pistol in the small of his back and put on the shoulder satchel before wrapping the tool belt around his waist.

Cal climbed from the rental car looking very much like a local tradesman. He walked down the street and approached the side door used by the Volvo's driver. With a quick glance around the small yard, he knocked on the door and consulted a small pocket notebook. It actually contained relevant information, some written in English, some in Spanish. In this case, Cal was using it as a stage prop.

He knocked a second time, and to his relief, the Volvo driver paced toward the door dressed in a bathrobe. He was either sleeping or in the middle of an assignation. Cal studied Juan up close, marveling at how much he resembled the man in Izzy's photograph.

The driver looked at Cal in his work clothes, carrying tools and wearing the Club Universidad de Chile baseball hat. Lozen mumbled in street Spanish and held up the notebook. The man ignored the question and waved Cal off. He started to turn as Lozen rapped on the door again, referencing his notebook and then motioning over his shoulder at the street.

Juan raised his voice and shook his head through the glass portion of the door.

Lozen turned several pages in his notebook, pointing over his shoulder, insistent, and still speaking in a rough dialect.

Juan argued for a minute until in exasperation, he flung open the door to end Cal's interruption. That was his mistake.

Chapter 99

Santiago, Chile

CAL SNAPPED FROM the hip, punching the Volvo driver flush in the mouth with a short, sharp jab. Juan stumbled backward, his bathrobe popping open, and Lozen jammed the CZ-75 automatic pistol under his chin. Juan raised his hands toward the ceiling in alarm.

Cal walked him back from the threshold and quietly closed and bolted the door. Then Lozen whispered in fluent Spanish, "Are you alone?"

The voice of a woman from the other room answered his question. "Juan?"

The driver shook his head as a worried expression crossed his face. Cal grabbed a fistful of Juan's hair, turned him around, and pushed him toward the back of the apartment.

It was a small efficiency, a one-bedroom with a kitchen-living room area and a full bathroom. Lozen scanned the different corners and absorbed the layout with a trained eye. All the while, Cal kept the muzzle of the weapon against the base of Juan's skull, pushing him forward, using the Volvo driver as a human shield. He walked him toward the bedroom.

"Juan, is everything okay?" asked the woman in a nervous voice.

"Sí, Marita," said Juan. "A workman; he was lost and needed directions. I sent him away."

Five seconds later, Cal shoved Juan into the room and pointed the pistol at a naked woman patiently lying in her bed. She gasped as Cal held up his free hand.

"No noise. If you scream, I will kill you. Comprende?"

The woman swallowed hard and nodded, working to control her surprise. She was afraid.

"Is there anyone else in the apartment?" asked Cal.

"No," answered both Juan and Marita in unison. Cal studied the woman and took the answer for true based on her expression and the rapidity of their simultaneous response.

He motioned for her to relocate from the bed to a large chair in the corner. She stood and self-consciously covered her breasts with folded arms. Cal's interrogation of Juan just became more complicated, but he decided to use her presence to his advantage. First he needed to dispel the notion that she was at risk. Marita needed to understand that if she cooperated, things would work out.

Cal shoved Juan onto the floor, where he could keep an eye on him. Then he pulled duct tape from his satchel and started to secure the woman to the large chair. She started to panic, and Lozen raised an index finger to his lips and whispered. She nodded.

Next Cal walked across the bedroom and plucked a wooden chair from beside the desk and carried it to the center. He placed it ten feet from the woman. Then he tugged off Juan's robe and sat him naked in the chair. Finally he used Juan's bathrobe to cover Marita's bound torso.

Cal was much less solicitous of the man. He controlled Juan by pulling his hair and yanking hard on his limbs. He duct-taped Juan to the chair and also covered his eyes, ears, and mouth. The woman watched him manhandle Juan and noted the contrast in his voice when he spoke to her. Cal knelt beside Marita and took a moment to reposition the robe to more adequately cover her exposed body. He drew the pistol from the small of his back and set it on a side table within easy reach.

"Take anything you want," she said, "but please don't hurt me." Her eyes filled with tears, but she was able to keep under control.

"I don't want money," said Calixto, fixing her with a steady gaze. "I want information." He reached over and fingered the pistol. "And I will do anything to get it."

Marita's eyes riveted on Lozen as he casually handled the weapon. She started to cry.

"If you lie, I will know, and then I will hurt you. Do you understand?"

"Sí," replied the woman, nodding her head. She was young, maybe midtwenties, attractive, and spoke in an educated accent. The woman seemed to have every reason to want to live. He hoped that was the case.

Cal paused and then asked her a series of rapid-fire questions that offered Marita little chance to think—or lie. "What is your name?"

"Marita Flores."

"Do you live here?"

"Sí."

"Alone?"

"Sí."

"What do you do?"

"I am a graduate student at the university."

"What are you studying?"

"Social sciences."

"Are you married?"

"No."

"How do you know *him*?" Cal pointed across the room at the duct-taped Juan, who could not speak, see, or hear their conversation.

"We met at a coffee shop six months ago."

"What is his name?"

"Juan Guzman."

"What does he do?"

"He works at a bank."

"Which bank?"

The woman paused, suddenly in a minor panic. "I forget."

Cal squinted at Marita with a serious expression. He started to reach for his pistol.

"Please," she said, a pitch of anxiety in her voice, "I don't remember; one of the big banks in Santiago."

Lozen waited before asking the next question. "Do you love him?"
The woman hesitated and then sort of shrugged. Cal read her eyes.
"I'll take that as a no."

Chapter 100

Santiago, Chile

CALIXTO REACHED INTO his satchel and pulled out the duct tape again. He covered Marita's eyes, ears, and mouth. The new changes caused her to stir. The woman's anxiety level increased. So Cal touched her reassuringly on the forearm before he stood.

Lozen paced back across the bedroom toward Juan. He tore the tape off Guzman's eyes, ears, and mouth. "I am going to ask you questions," said Cal. "If you lie, you will regret it."

Juan watched Lozen pace quietly to his front. The crude dialect was gone, replaced by a fluent Castellano Spanish. It was the formal speech of an educated man, a Castilian dialect.

"I understand," said Juan.

"What is your name?" asked Cal, using the same fast-paced interrogation style.

"Juan Guzman."

"Where do you live?"

"Here in San Joaquin, about three blocks past Avenue Rivera."

"What do you do?"

"I work at a bank."

"Which bank?"

"Banco de Credito."

"What is the girl's name?"

"Marita Flores."

"How do you know her?"

"We met months ago, at a restaurant."

"A restaurant?" asked Cal, repeating the answer in a suspicious tone.

"Sí," said Juan. He squirmed, naked in the desk chair, straining his wrists and ankles, which were duct-taped to the wooden frame. "A coffee house over on Homera." Juan's eyes shifted at the discrepancy as Cal watched.

"Do you work for Industrias Comercial?" asked Lozen.

A flicker of comprehension lighted Juan's expression for only the briefest of moments, but it was enough. Cal walked over to the television set and increased the volume.

"Do *you* work for Industrias Comercial?" said Lozen a second time.

In the corner, although she could not hear or see, Marita sensed that something in the room had changed. She squirmed in her seat.

"I work for Banco de Credito," said Juan. There was a hitch in his voice.

"Sí," said Cal, "but you *also* do work for Industrias Comercial, correct?"

Juan swallowed as Cal studied his reaction. "I do not know that company."

"Really?" said Cal with a touch of theater.

Juan started breathing heavily. "Sí," said Guzman.

Cal reached toward his tool belt and tugged out the rubber mallet. "Are you sure?" asked Calixto. Then he repositioned the gag of duct tape.

Juan's breathing broke into a pant. He watched Cal tap the hammer lightly against his fingertips. There was something ominous in the action. "Are you *sure?*" repeated Cal.

Juan swallowed before nodding.

Lozen spun and swung the mallet in a wide arc, landing the head of the hammer squarely on the front of Juan's bent knee.

Guzman screeched, bouncing in the chair; the muffled agony of his pain caused his eyes to bulge and his cheeks to flush. He crashed to the floor, and tears streamed down his face, a desperate wounded animal unable to touch his shattered patella. Juan howled through the gag.

Calixto reached forward and picked up Juan, righting the fallen chair as he continued to convulse. "You need to understand how serious this is," said Lozen.

Cal reached into his satchel and extracted the picture of the girls and their dates on the evening of the farewell dinner in El Golf. Then he removed his baseball hat and knelt close to Juan. He showed him the photograph.

Guzman clearly recognized the people in the picture. Sweat mixed with tears as he panted in pain, his blood pressure pulsed, and he gasped, trying to focus on Calixto's comments. Cal pointed at the four people from left to right.

"This is your friend Alvaro," said Cal in a quiet voice, "this is Sandy, and this is you." Lozen paused to study Juan's reaction before continuing. "And *this*," he said, pointing at the last person in the photograph, "is Isabel, my *sister*." That piece of information surprised Juan. Lozen stood, raising himself to the full height of his six-foot frame. He towered over the seated, restrained Guzman. "Now do you understand? We are going to talk, and you are going to tell me things."

Juan began to sob. He started to nod, pleading as he choked on his own saliva.

Chapter 101

Santiago, Chile

ROUGH HANDS GRABBED at Izzy, pulling at her wrists, tugging at her ankles. They stood her next to the bed, forcing the blood to flow into unused limbs. She felt the familiar wave of dizziness.

Isabel was groggy. She had been in a restless sleep for hours, never fully relaxing, her sense of clarity muddled with inactivity and lack of stimulation.

They held Izzy at arm's length, extending her limbs, inducing her to walk in her high heels around the uneven floor. Then the captors sat her down and fed Izzy a small meal with plenty of water. Finally, they took her to the toilet. This was a practiced ritual, but it felt rushed. There was a pronounced impatience to the captors' steps, and it seemed to Isabel as her head cleared that they were on a schedule.

They walked her from the basement prison into a cool brisk air. The rush of early morning dew caused Izzy to shiver, and she felt the scrape of gravel under her shoes. Izzy tried to remember and process everything, despite the time imbalance.

She and Sandy had returned to the room after a long, claustrophobic ride. Why? Something had changed, and now it had changed again. Their captivity progressed from days strapped to a metal rack in a moldy basement, to being stuffed into a metal box with blankets, hidden under the seat in a large SUV. Izzy was confused and frustrated, but Sandy seemed worse. Her roommate had a bit of a panic attack.

At first, Isabel thought that Sandy was being sexually molested or tortured, but then she realized that her friend was having a meltdown. Sandy's muffled outburst while secured to the metal rack felt more like a scream of despair than an actual assault. The incongruity of their situation was forcing a reaction.

The captors positioned Isabel in the coffin-like compartment, careful to protect her cocktail dress from stains or tears. She would be traveling again.

Isabel understood and accepted that she would need to be the catalyst to their escape. Fortunately, her brother had taught Izzy many things. Physical discipline conditioned one to mental discipline. Cal showed her how to temper emotional balance.

It started with her running. Izzy learned to push herself a little farther each time she ran. One mile, then two, then five K. As she got comfortable with a reasonable distance, she stepped up the speed. Then she ran ten K and finally a half marathon. The increasing distances gave Isabel confidence. Next, she would ease back the length—knowing she could run far—and pick up the speed.

Izzy never stopped. Running became a daily ritual as important and habitual as brushing her teeth. Days without a run left her feeling lazy and tense, although Cal also taught his sister that the body needed rest. The key lesson of her activity was the self-awareness that she could endure. Izzy could press through obstacles and finish. Pain could be ignored. Frustration could be overcome.

The captors fastened Isabel at hip level into a pair of handcuffs. Then they secured her ankles. She was on her side again, but had leg and arm mobility.

She lay by herself for a few minutes, feeling the cool predawn air on her cheeks. Izzy surmised it was still dark outside. She shifted, enjoying the crisp weather despite her restraints. She knew it was only a matter of time before the secret compartment was resealed and the stuffy but breathable air closed back around her.

More noise, and then she felt them piling Sandy back into the same compartment next to her. Izzy felt slightly relieved, despite their predicament: the roommates were still together. Isabel knew that she was the stronger of the two. She would need to buffer her friend.

A few minutes later the metal lid closed above, and the SUV started. It shifted into gear and slowly crept across the gravel drive until it turned onto a dirt road and drove away.

Chapter 102

Santiago, Chile

CAL DROVE ALONG the rural route north of the city, heading back to the farmhouse. Traffic was sparse, and the farther he traveled outside the city, the fewer cars he passed.

It was dark outside, a couple hours before dawn. Lozen first wove the sedan in a circuitous path through the downtown, careful to place the call to the rental company that the vehicle had been stolen while still in the city limits. He was more concerned with the cell phone relay station fixing his whereabouts than he was with any vehicle locater devices.

The interrogation of Juan Guzman had proved fruitful. The banker admitted many things, all under duress. Cal was now acting on that information. Ironically, he was driving right back to the same location where the sighting of Juan began.

Calixto slowed as he passed a now-familiar bend in the road. He estimated that the dirt entrance turnoff was just a short distance ahead. A large SUV passed Cal's rental heading in the opposite direction. A single driver sat behind the wheel focusing on the road. He handled the turn with ease. Lozen glanced over as their two vehicles passed each other in the night. Neither the driver nor the SUV looked familiar.

Two minutes later, Cal slowed his sedan and searched with the aid of his headlights for the small sign that alerted deliverymen to the partially hidden dirt road that led to the farmhouse.

The interrogation session with Guzman had lasted nearly two hours. Cal had inflicted more fear than pain, but the torture was still in contravention of his training as a soldier, the Geneva Conventions, and the Rules of Land Warfare. He didn't care. This wasn't a military operation; it was criminal. And it was about Izzy.

The facts were that in the absence of drugs, unlimited time, and skilled psychological interrogators, torture worked. The knack came in deciphering at which point it became counterproductive. Torture failed to be effective when the incessant nature of pain caused the prisoner to say anything, admit to anything, in order to make it stop.

Unfortunately, most interrogators who used torture were sadists. They enjoyed the act of causing pain. Calixto was quite the opposite. He needed quick answers, accurate facts. Cal needed to find his sister, and he didn't have many options. He had no qualms about the violence. They picked the fight, and Lozen felt morally justified to perform any act that would rescue Izzy.

Part of the drama with Juan Guzman was his comprehension that Lozen was both committed and desperate to find his sister. The pain was not about punishment; it was about information. The banker needed to place fear of Calixto before fear of his employers. He also needed to believe that Cal could smell a lie. Guzman admitted, but downplayed, his involvement in Izzy's abduction. He feared retribution, but in his hope of currying favor and mercy, he offered detailed information on the organization behind the front company of Industrias Comercial. Guzman called it the Empresa.

Lozen turned at the familiar small sign and burrowed his rental car into a thicket of shrubs in the gully next to the dirt road. He hopped from the rental, taking all of his personal equipment, belongings, and the vehicle identification papers. Then he recamouflaged the car with loose bushes and tree branches. Cal retraced his steps into the woodline from less than a day earlier and circled to the east behind the farmhouse.

He did not kill Guzman. This was a debate that played out in Lozen's head. He considered the tactics of such an action. At this point it was still a rescue mission, not a revenge mission. If Izzy was alive, and according to the banker, she was, then to eliminate Guzman might provoke her murder. The three dead men in the midnight raid in the studio apartment of Barrio Concha y Toro was self-defense, and therefore a different matter. The banker stressed the military background of the organization's personnel. In Cal's mind, they would draw a distinction.

Cal took up a position in his previous perch. He pulled out his minibinoculars and scanned the farmhouse. There was a light on in the basement of the stone foundation that spilled into the lower level of the gravel drive.

Chapter 103

Santiago, Chile

CALIXTO USED THE darkness as he hugged the tree line. He circled to the far side of the farmhouse, hoping that the occupants were not watching from a darkened window. If his luck held out, he could cross the one hundred meters of open ground between the woods and the building in a short time.

Lozen left his duffel bag and tool belt hidden in the woods. He opted for speed. Light and motion attracted the eye, but he wanted to reduce the chance of detection by embracing the night. Cal sprang from the trees and double-timed across the pasture. Fifteen seconds later he hugged the stone foundation under a darkened double window and took a moment to catch his breath.

Juan Guzman confirmed that the farm functioned as a safe house. Two retired military NCOs were employed as live-in custodians. Juan also emphasized that the girls were alive and had been held in the basement since their abductions. Recently they were scheduled for relocation, but the plans were interrupted. Guzman swore he didn't know the destination.

A light spilled from under the heavy door and a small basement window. Cal slid along the foundation, his pistol held to the front, careful of his balance as he crept along the mixture of gravel and mud. He studied the door. It was thick, solid oak, and the barrier swung inward. He heard faint noises from the room.

Calixto had questioned the banker about the layout of the farmhouse. Guzman readily offered this information, but was much more reticent about the follow-on plan for the girls. That worked for Cal. If he could save Izzy, there would be time later on to consider motives.

To breach the door, Lozen needed to draw the occupants out. The caretakers needed to open the basement door from the inside. Cal leaned back against the wall, looking around the property, thinking.

He noticed a rusty tractor parked on the side of the yard a short distance from the farmhouse. On the ground, beside the piece of abandoned equipment, were two metal fuel cans. An idea developed.

Cal replaced his pistol in the small of his back and hustled the short distance to the tractor. He picked up the cans and jiggled for fuel. Both were partially filled. Then he grabbed several stained rags beside an old toolbox and carried the items back to the stone foundation. A light snapped on, spilling illumination through a bedroom window high up on the second floor. Lozen froze.

Calixto counted to twenty before turning his attention back to the plan. He needed to create a diversion. Cal would start a fire. He didn't want a blazing, highly flammable, destructive bonfire, as that would put the girls at risk. Calixto wanted a smoky, slow-moving, containable fire. He just wanted the two custodians to react.

Fortunately, farm equipment used diesel. The tractor fuel had much lower vapor and volatile content than gasoline. The combustibility was controllable. It burned very slowly, creating thick black clouds of choking smoke rather than explosive flames.

Calixto rummaged within arm's distance of the stone foundation. He started to collect burnable materials stored or abandoned along the base. He found a broken window shutter, several paint cans covered by a soiled tarpaulin, and a stack of wooden fence slats. Cal started soaking the items in diesel fuel and carefully placed everything in a loose pile several feet from the wall. The materials were between the basement door and the small side window.

While still in a crouch, Cal pulled out his BIC pocket lighter and held the flame to the soaked rags. Then he placed the accelerator inside the loose pile of stacked materials. It took several minutes before the fire jelled. The smoldering, diesel-soaked items set off a billowing black smoke. Cal stood and pounded on the heavy door. He yelled twice in a clear, loud voice, "Fuego, fuego," the Spanish word for fire.

From the corner of the stone foundation, Cal saw a shadow pass by the small window. Someone had peered out. Then he heard the bolt on the basement door slide sideways, and the portal popped open.

Human nature proved predictable. One of the two custodians rushed out carrying a fire extinguisher. He was reacting to the destructive force of fire, rather than the incongruity of the situation. He turned left and focused his attention on the smoldering pile of debris; then Cal swung. The barrel of the CZ-75 caught him flush in the face, fracturing his nose and knocking him unconscious. The caretaker went down, and Calixto dashed into the basement, aiming his pistol.

Lozen scanned the lighted room, sweeping his weapon in a controlled arc, searching the hidden corners. He noted the layout, the cement floor, the sparse furnishings, the toilet in the rear, but mostly the two metal-framed prison beds mounted with shackles. They were empty.

"Mateo," said a voice from upstairs. The second caretaker was calling to his friend. There was a noise on the stairwell, and then Cal heard the distinctive cocking sound of a pump-action shotgun. Heavy footfalls sounded on the stairs.

Lozen looked toward the open basement door to see the first man still lying outside next to the fire extinguisher. The black smoke curled into the room as the breeze shifted. Cal sank into the far corner away from the stairs. He took a shooter's crouch and aimed.

"Mateo," repeated the man on the stairs. His voice was quieter, more suspicious. There were several more creaks on the stairs, and then the barrel of the shotgun protruded a few inches past the wall. This telegraphed his position.

As the caretaker abruptly spun in to the room, swinging his shotgun, his eyes focused on the open basement door and the scene of his friend lying prone next to the fire. The slight edge was all Cal needed. He shot twice, just as the man twisted and fired the shotgun. The twenty-gauge let loose as the nine-millimeter bullets tore into the caretaker's sternum and knocked him sideways.

Cal felt a sting in his left thigh. He had also been hit. As the custodian went down, Lozen moved forward and fired a third shot at the man's forehead. He took a breath, listening for more caretakers, lest Juan had lied. Everything seemed quiet.

Calixto extinguished the fire, dragged the semiconscious caretaker back into the basement, and shackled him to one of the metal rack beds. Then he set about searching and securing the rest of the farmhouse.

Chapter 104

Tucson, Arizona

ARTHUR FINLEY OPENED the front door of his home and looked at the two men dressed in conservative business suits standing on his doorstep.

"Dr. Finley?" asked the first man, politely removing his sunglasses. He held up his laminated credentials with a practiced motion. "FBI, Special Agents Phillips and Trent. May we come in?"

The professor examined the two men. Each held up his identification for inspection. Arthur stepped aside and allowed the two men to cross the threshold.

"I suspect you'll want to speak with my wife as well," said Finley.

"Actually, sir, that would be best," replied Agent Phillips.

Arthur nodded and called out to his wife. Then he led the two federal agents into his living room. "Make yourselves comfortable. Some coffee?"

"Coffee would be fine," said Trent.

The FBI agents sat as Arthur moved toward the kitchen. Phillips pulled out a small pocket-size notebook. A minute later Constanza entered the living room and introduced herself. She looked drawn and haggard. Izzy's mom seemed surprised at their presence, but she waited until Arthur returned.

"Is there any news?" asked Arthur as he set down a tray of cups and saucers on the table between them. He poured all around.

"Nothing definite," said Phillips, "but we have been in touch with our liaisons at the embassy, and they in turn have been in close contact with their counterparts in the Chilean National Police. Everyone is engaged in the search."

"A waste of time," said Constanza in a soft voice.

"Why do you say that, ma'am?" replied Trent.

"Because everyone knows," said Constanza, sitting forward on her couch, "that in Chile, the military and the national police work together. They are part of the same regime."

"What regime is that?" asked Phillips.

"The Pinochet regime," said Connie.

There was a frosty edge to her reply. Arthur reached over and touched his wife's knee. "Special Agent Phillips, my wife's ordeal of several decades ago is well documented at this point. So is the assassination of her former boss, Orlando Letelier. We were hoping you had some information relating to the disappearance of our daughter."

"Unfortunately no," said Trent. "But we were hoping you could tell us about this." The second agent opened a copy of the anonymous warning letter handed to Constanza on the downtown Tucson sidewalk.

Arthur looked at the piece of paper lying on the coffee table with one word printed in bold block letters: **STOP**. "What is that?" said Finley.

"We understand it is a message, a warning," said Agent Phillips. He looked directly at Constanza. "Is that your understanding as well?"

"Where did you get that?" asked Constanza, with a surprised expression.

"Unfortunately, ma'am, we can't discuss that."

"What is going on?" said Finley, raising his voice. He looked at his wife with an air of frustration. The agents exchanged a glance. "Connie?" asked Arthur.

Constanza looked at her husband and shook him off. The conversation would hold for a private moment. She returned her attention to the two FBI agents.

"Have you heard from your son?" asked Trent.

"Actually no," replied Constanza, "I rarely do. He is in the military. I'm sure you know that."

"Yes, ma'am," said Phillips. "He's in the army. In Special Forces actually. I understand he is decorated for valor. A very capable individual."

"What's your point?" said Finley, still irate at being in the dark about the warning letter.

"Our point," said Trent, turning his attention back to the professor, "is that your son went to Chile to search for your daughter, and his involvement may be complicating our diplomatic efforts."

"First of all," replied Arthur with an edge to his voice, "he is *not* my son. Secondly, how could anything Calixto does serve to derail your efforts?"

"Mrs. Finley's son," said Agent Trent, correcting his miscue.

"Clearly you have nothing new to report," said the professor. "I fear that if not for the publicity our efforts have generated, we would be no further along in finding my little girl."

"I'm sorry you feel that way, Doctor," replied Phillips, "but please rest assured, we are working to locate your daughter and her friend in the hope to bring them home safe."

A moment of silence enveloped the four adults, and then Agent Trent pointed at the copy of Connie's warning letter. "Mrs. Finley, if you can think of anything or anyone that this relates to, please call." He placed a business card on the coffee table next to the warning letter.

"Thank you for the coffee," said Phillips. The two men stood. "We can find our way out."

Chapter 105

Santiago, Chile

CALIXTO POSITIONED SEVERAL carving knives on the side table next to the metal-framed bed. Slowly, with a practiced hand, he sharpened the edges on an old kitchen oil stone. The captured caretaker watched with interest.

Lozen had taken nearly thirty minutes to check the farmhouse and tend to his wound. First he had searched every closet, corner, and odd angle for hidden doors. There appeared to be no secret rooms or hidden persons. Then he found a first-aid kit and, using tweezers, pulled several lead pellets from his thigh. Cal was lucky that the shooter used a small-bore twenty-gauge with a birdshot load. He cleaned and disinfected the wound before wrapping it in a clean dressing.

Finally, Cal heated a burner on the seldom-used basement stove as he sharpened the carving knives. "Do you know who I am?" asked Calixto in Spanish.

The caretaker nodded. His fractured nose made it difficult to breathe while he spoke. His eyes had noticeably blackened, and he was still dazed from the assault.

"Speak," said Cal.

"Sí."

"That's better. Do you know why I am here?"

"I never touched your sister," said the caretaker. A look of fear twitched in his face.

"Oh?" Lozen studied the man. He was shackled to the very bed that had been Izzy's prison. Cal slid a filleting knife along the stone. "Which one is my sister?"

"The pretty one."

"They're both pretty."

"The beautiful one."

Cal leaned forward and lowered his voice. "You mean you never touched her sexually?"

"No, no sex, no torture. I swear."

Cal slid the knife back across the oil stone. There was an ominous touch to his motion. "Who told you about me?" asked Lozen.

"My people."

"At Industrias Comercial?"

"The Empresa."

Calixto hesitated. That word again—the Empresa. That was the organization behind the front company. "What did they say?"

There was a pause in the prisoner's explanation as he tried to clear the blood and spittle from his throat. Finally, he spoke in a halting voice. "They said that you were dangerous, a highly trained soldier."

"What else?"

"They said you looked like a mestizo, but acted like a Mapuche."

The mestizo were Chileans of mixed blood that shared ethnic similarities with both European colonists and local Indians. The Mapuche were a fierce tribe of indigenous people who never surrendered to the Spanish conquistadors.

"My father is Chiricahua," said Cal in a quiet voice as he checked the edge of his knife. "He taught me many things—for instance, how to *skin* an animal."

The caretaker's eyes popped wide. The gravity of the situation coalesced. He watched enthralled as Lozen continued honing the knife's edge.

"You and I have a problem," said Cal. "My sister is not here, and I need to find her. Do you understand?"

"Sí, but I did not touch her. Our instructions were to scare them, to see what they knew about the Empresa." The man started to shake. "We only held them a couple of days—just long enough to check through their computers and cell phones."

"We don't have much time," answered Cal as he slid the knife across the stone.

Chapter 106

Mendoza, Argentina

IZZY FELT THE vehicle slow. It had been in a descent for some time, and the interminable ride had again gone on for hours. She yearned for a breath of fresh air.

The pattern of confinement and transport in a stuffy boxlike structure stretched Isabel's patience. Yet she sensed her roommate was having an even tougher time. On several occasions, Izzy heard Sandy crying. They were soft, muffled sniffles, cries of anguish, of despair, rather than those of pain. Isabel quickly reached out to touch Sandy's knee. Then she tried to tap her leg to calm her.

It could always be worse. That was Cal's motto. Whenever things looked bleak, when the body broke down, when the mind wanted to quit, he would look up, laugh, and mumble that it could always be worse. It was an old SF joke. The tenet of the training was to select individuals who had strong minds. Being physically fit was a given. The Qualification course broke down candidates' bodies. Special Forces wanted soldiers who would not mentally quit. Ever.

Isabel thought of her brother. She could have been raped. She could have been tortured. She could be dead. Things *could* be worse. Izzy needed to support her friend. An opportunity would come, and Izzy would get them to safety.

Ten minutes later, the SUV came to a stop. The engine turned off, and a garbled conversation took place. The doors slid open, and then their coffin-like compartment popped its lid. A wave of fresh, cool air billowed Izzy's torso, flushing her cheeks and crinkling her skin. Strong hands lifted her from the boxlike structure and stood her on solid ground.

Izzy wobbled. Her ankles buckled as her high heels fought for stability on a cement floor. Then she was passed to a different set of hands, a smaller, softer touch to the grip.

They led Isabel down a corridor into another room. She was positioned upright, sitting in a metal chair, secured by a series of buckles and straps.

The small hands touched her forehead, and then two fingers reached for a pulse at her neck. Izzy felt the same two fingers touch her skin at the wrist, the back of her knee, and then at her ankles.

A cold circular medallion touched her skin, moving around her breasts inside her bra, and then shifted to the skin on her back. Izzy felt a palm thump on her shoulders, her forearms, and her thighs. The person with the small hands had some medical training. Isabel caught a faint hint of perfume. Was it a woman?

High heels were tugged off, and the hands touched and massaged Izzy's feet, feeling her toes, checking for frostbite. Then the shoes were replaced, and the process was repeated on her fingers and her earlobes. For a period of time, the journey had turned cold in the SUV. The vehicle had heat and extra blankets, but the temperature seemed to change in conjunction with the pitch of the vehicle. Now Izzy understood. They had taken her and Sandy to a new location in the mountains.

Minutes later, Isabel heard someone bring Sandy into the room and strap her into a chair to Izzy's right. The small hands moved away and repeated the inspection on her roommate. The pattern had changed again.

Chapter 107

Santiago, Chile

IN THE END, the caretaker broke down before Cal inflicted any pain. It was the anticipation that got him. When Calixto sliced open the pant leg of the man's overalls in preparation for skinning, the prisoner caved. He wanted no part of it.

The caretaker was in his sixties, tired, and already feeling considerable discomfort due to the fractured nose. Cal noted the weariness in the man's eyes, the resolution of personality that sets in when older folks accept they are on the downside of the mountain of life and the hunger of youth has long since subsided.

In Lozen's favor were his enemies. Someone at the Empresa, the secret organization behind the straw company called Industrias Comercial, was fomenting fear. To get everyone's attention, they had embellished the threat. They were making Calixto into a larger-than-life adversary.

The caretaker mumbled in fear. He knew of Jefe el Loco, the renegade brother of the beautiful girl. He had never touched her. He was only following orders, and now they had taken the sister and her friend away to a new location.

Cal tried a different tack. He spread a large map of Chile across the wooden table and positioned it next to the metal bed. Then he sat the caretaker up on the steel coils so that he could see the map. Finally, with his index finger, Calixto traced the four corners of the country. "Where are they taking my sister?" He slid his finger down the west coast of Chile, along the Pacific Ocean, pausing to point out various cities along the way. He watched the caretaker as his finger moved: La Serena, Los Vilos, La Ligua, Valparaiso, Cartagena...

Gradually Cal started to ascend north, touching the few cities in the middle of the long, thin country, arching back to the right, along the eastern border buffered by the Andes mountain range. "Where is the new location?" asked Cal in a rhetorical tone, as if he was alone and speaking to himself. All the while he watched the caretaker.

Lozen hesitated around Santiago, circling the city for a few seconds, before on a whim, he moved his index finger right and started touching a few border towns in Argentina. At the city of Mendoza, the caretaker looked away.

Cal stopped and squinted at his prisoner before speaking. "Mendoza?"

The man didn't speak, but his expression confirmed the answer. It was an involuntary verification.

Cal turned the large map around and studied the route from their current location to downtown Santiago. Then he checked the routes between Santiago and the border crossing. Mendoza was the closest and most direct city between the Chilean capital and the country of Argentina. It made sense. This farm on the outskirts of Santiago made for a perfect safe house location. But why? Why Argentina?

Chapter 108

December 14, 2006
Gladwyne, Pennsylvania

"Tell us about the contingency fund," said Mike.

Burdis shifted in his wheelchair. "It was a back door, a sweep mechanism set up by the architect to funnel all the loose cash in the Empresa to a central location—a single depository."

"And who controlled this contingency fund?" asked John.

"The Agency," answered Burdis with a shrug.

The three men shared a moment of silence before Mike finally asked, "How did this new development sit with the Empresa?"

"It appeared seamless, so the members agreed. The cash from the Calabrians grew in both size and frequency; the money flowed without interruption, and extra cash was always available to fund their sensitive operations."

"It felt the same," said John.

"Even better," replied Burdis.

Mike stood. "So the Agency figured out a way to get a little payback for all their advice."

"They needed nonsource funding to continue some of their black operations."

"A nest egg that was untraceable," said John.

"But necessary," replied Burdis. "Congress was unpredictable. Budgets were political."

Chapter 109

Santiago, Chile

DAVID SHIELDS WAS studying the report from DX Center in Washington when his cell phone rang. He looked at the calling number and stood. Then he paced toward the door, dropping the classified file on the desk of another DIA officer as he exited the large office. "Pat, babysit this for me. I have to take a call."

The coworker grabbed the file with a red "Secret" stamp on its cover and placed it in the middle of his desk. He waved.

Shields turned in the corridor and answered his cell phone as he continued walking from the intelligence wing. "Stay with me," said Shields. He took the elevator down to the ground floor at the embassy. "What's your status?" asked Shields finally as he walked outside.

"Ambulatory," replied Cal, wincing at the ache in his left thigh from the shotgun pellets.

"Are you in a secure location?"

"For now."

"Did you make progress?"

"Yes," said Lozen, thinking of the discussion he had with the compliant farmhouse custodian. Once the retired soldier revealed Izzy's next destination, the information flowed pretty freely. The fact was, the older man with the fractured nose had done his time. He saw little valor in protecting powerful men who needed no protection. They allowed him to be threatened by a renegade American soldier engaged in a personal vendetta. Each time Cal touched the blade of the sharpened knives, the custodian offered more data. "I just missed the girls," said Lozen.

"Really?" replied Shields, surprised by the information. "How close?"

"Ninety minutes, give or take."

"Can you make up the time?"

"I don't think so. There's a complication."

"Which is?" asked Shields.

"Mendoza is the pivot point."

"Shit," said Shields, hesitating. "That changes the equation."

"Totally. Whatever game is in play, it just became a bigger canvas."

"It's the organization," said David. "Don't think political; think criminal."

"I have an address, but I need to go east."

"I understand. Do you have clean transportation?"

"Yes," answered Cal. He fingered the keys to the farm's Range Rover. "I reported the disappearance of my first vehicle last night, and I have secured new wheels. But I'll need help with paperwork to cross, and I'll have to leave my equipment behind."

"I need some time. Can you hold up for a few hours?"

"Yes," answered Lozen.

Then Shields asked as an afterthought, "Is the body count increasing?"

Cal thought of the dead caretaker lying in the middle of the basement floor next to his imprisoned partner. "Plus one from the previous total."

"I'll be back to you," said Shields.

The cell phone clicked off.

Chapter 110

Mendoza, Argentina

SANDY WAS BY nature a friendly person. She engaged in conversation easily and without pretense. She enjoyed the interaction. Therefore, the silence forced by the gag was especially difficult. Her inability to talk to Izzy, or anyone else for that matter, made this whole strange ordeal extradifficult. Not being able to see or touch or understand only compounded the problem. It clearly started to unnerve the roommate.

Earlier, she had been fed a small meal, a heavy drink of water, and then taken to the toilet. Now the new captor was back. A person with small hands and a clinical touch. Things felt different in the new location. The ever-present threat of sexual molestation seemed to dissipate. The rough callused hands had disappeared, and they had been replaced with a gentler approach, almost a medical orientation.

Her blindfold was removed, and Sandy looked at a hood with two large eyeholes. The new captor was a woman. The small hands rubbed softly at Sandy's cheeks with a cotton ball and wiped away the streaks of mascara caused by her crying. The woman grunted beneath the hood. Then she reapplied some pressed powder and blush. Sandy tried to talk through her gag. The hooded face never wavered. Sandy was ignored.

In minutes, the blindfold was replaced, and dabs of perfume were touched to her neck, between her breasts, to her wrists and ankles. Finally, a second set of hands, stronger, reached from behind and unfastened the security straps. Sandy was raised to her feet and guided across the cement floor.

They walked her into the cold. She sensed it was nighttime. Car doors slid open, and Sandy was positioned sitting upright in a cushioned seat. They fastened her in shackles at the ankles and wrists and walked away.

Several minutes elapsed before the captors returned, and a second person was strapped into the seat on her left. Was it Izzy? As the two doors slid closed, she took a chance and hummed a few notes from their song. Quickly her roommate hummed back.

"Silencio," said a brusque voice from the front seat.

The girls froze, but they were still together. The van started to move.

Chapter III

Mendoza, Argentina

CALIXTO SLOWED THE Range Rover as he zigzagged through the mountains along the Paso Los Libertadores. The stolen vehicle was rugged and reliable, well suited for travel through the snowbound Andes.

Earlier, Cal had gone back into the woodline and retrieved his duffel bag and possessions. Then he returned to the farmhouse and rechecked his prisoner. He left the caretaker alive, next to the decomposing corpse of his partner, again using the rationale of rescue versus retribution.

David Shields delivered. It took four hours, valuable time, but the DIA officer arranged for a roadside rendezvous. A courier met Lozen, and they exchanged packages. Cal received new identification and travel documents, including a fake Chilean passport, National Identity Card, and working papers. He was listed as a construction contractor, which allowed him to keep his tools and duffel bag. In return, he gave up all his US identification and the CZ-75 pistol.

Calixto reflected on the description of the large SUV he was tracking to Mendoza. The caretaker stressed that the vehicle was used routinely to transfer contraband from Santiago to Argentina. Occasionally, as in the case of Lozen's sister, that included people. The SUV always ended its journey at the same address in Mendoza and returned to the Santiago area. What happened to the goods from there, the farm custodian did not know.

Cal recalled the large SUV he passed on the rural road north of the city the previous night. Could Izzy and Sandy have been hidden inside? Did Lozen miss a golden opportunity to rescue the girls? Such speculation could fluster. It was what it was.

Calixto looked over his shoulder at Aconcagua, the highest mountain in all of the Americas. The scenery was beautiful and snow was everywhere, but the road was clear. The east side of the border crossing seemed a little less arduous than the hair-raising turns of the west.

Traffic was heavy. Customs officers on both sides worked feverishly to reduce the backlog created by the closing due to the recent snowstorm. It worked in Cal's favor. He crossed the border without incident, and for a brief moment, he regretted waiting for the new identity and abandoning his weapon. Cal excused the decision. That was a mind trap—would have, could have, should have. He knew that he acted tactically correctly. Calixto had lost valuable time, but if someone in Chile alerted officials and he was caught traveling under his true identity, with an illegal weapon, all would be lost. Lozen would never be free to rescue Izzy.

Calixto negotiated the mountain pass, traversing the foothills of west central Argentina on the east side of the border. The address he sought was on a dirt road, off of Ruta Nacional Seven, twenty kilometers south of Mendoza.

Chapter 112

Buenos Aires, Argentina

Patsy's two-car caravan traveled south along Paseo Colon into San Telmo. The Barrio was the oldest neighborhood in Buenos Aires, and therefore the narrow cobblestone streets and decaying colonial buildings showed the ravages of time. However of late, San Telmo began to effuse a bohemian chic, boasting starving artists, offbeat curio shops, and eclectic antiques. Every third door was a café. It was quaint but edgy.

The large Lincolns turned left on Avenue San Juan and threaded through the midday traffic. Patsy was tense. He was expecting news on their recent run of cocaine to Europe. The network shipped from Mexico to Spain, and then continued to the northern Italian cities of Milan and Turin. His new partners, Los Zetas, controlled the trafficking lanes.

Bellocco glanced out the window as they turned toward Humberto Primo. Several locals spontaneously stood and danced in Plaza Dorrego as an accordion played in the background. He watched in amusement as the older folks of San Telmo bore their hardscrabble life with a marked stoicism, craggy faces stretched firm, serious demeanors stepping to the tango. The poor in Argentina took respite in simple pleasures.

The cars slowed just past the intersection at Chacabuco, and Patsy stepped from the rear seat of the first Lincoln. His bodyguard joined him on the sidewalk as his two nephews climbed from the second car.

Bellocco walked past an old stone façade with blue awnings, and several balconies trimmed in wrought iron fencing. A colorful sign next to the glazed oval windows advertised *Antiques*. Patsy and his entourage paced around the corner to a narrow pedestrian alley, and the bodyguard knocked on a heavy, unmarked oak door. It opened from inside. A burly Argentinean stepped back, mumbling as Patsy strode down the narrow hallway at the rear of the antique shop and entered a small office.

"Pasquale," said his brother-in-law, standing to greet the quintino. He kissed the younger Bellocco on the cheek.

Patsy waved his two nephews into the crowded room and motioned to the bodyguard, who closed the door and remained outside. Patsy sat in the chair behind the desk.

"Some good news, Pasquale," said Ettore. "Some *very* good news."

Bellocco settled in the chair as his brother-in-law took a hard-shell briefcase from the corner, positioned it atop the desk, and snapped open the locks. Then he turned the attaché toward his boss and, with an open hand, motioned for Patsy to take the honors. The quintino opened the briefcase and let out a large, satisfied exhalation.

Ettore beamed in pride as the two nephews looked on in amazement. They had never seen so much cash in one briefcase.

Packed end to end in neat, crisp stacks of one hundred euro currency paper notes was the equivalent of $2.4 million US.

"Our take in gambling operations for Buenos Aires, Montevideo, and Asunción for the past six weeks," said the brother-in-law.

Patsy looked at his nephews and explained further. "Of course, the take is higher, but we must pay a vigorish to clean the money. When we ship, it is only in dollars or euros."

"And also," said Ettore, "we must pay the Famiglia in Plati and the Principale in San Luca."

Patsy closed the top of the hard-shell briefcase and slid the attaché to the corner of the desk. "What else?" he asked.

"The trial run of our new product lines proved quite reliable. The entire shipment passed through the Iberian Peninsula to our twin destinations in Italia. Everything went as planned," answered Ettore.

For the first time in a long while, a large smile broke across Patsy's face, and he stood to hug and congratulate his brother-in-law. "Bueno," said Bellocco. "Who could foresee that our 'ndrina would be in business with the *Mexicans*?" He said the final word with an extra measure of emphasis.

The two nephews shared in the success of Patsy and Ettore. Everyone was in a good mood.

"There's more, Quintino," said Ettore with a sheepish grin.

"More?"

Patsy sat back down behind the desk, running both hands through his thick, black hair. He could hardly contain his enthusiasm.

"Sí, Quintino," said Ettore. "I spoke with Mendoza this morning. They received and inspected your package."

"The gift?" asked Bellocco.

"Sí. It is en route, and should arrive at the Estancia late tonight."

"Interesting." Patsy mused in silence, still a bit intrigued by the letter and the extension of a special "gift." He looked at Ettore with an odd expression. "Did Mendoza offer any insights?"

"Only that they felt you would be very pleased. They said that our friends in Santiago had outdone themselves."

Chapter 113

CALIXTO WORKED HIS way south along Ruta Nacional Seven. The thoroughfare connected the border crossing to Mendoza and Mendoza to the east.

During the downtime preceding the exchange with David Shields's courier, Cal studied several maps. It was apparent that the girls would not remain in the Mendoza location for very long. It acted as a pivot point to redirect contraband to various locations in Argentina and beyond.

The small city served as a provincial capital, popular with adventure tourists for climbing, hiking, skiing, and rafting. It also enjoyed a deserved reputation as a wine region, boasting several varietals produced on ancient vines in century-old bodegas that dotted the river and rolling foothills.

However unknown to the general public, another piece of notoriety existed. Mendoza functioned as a major way station on the smuggler's map. Ruta Nacional Seven ran through Mendoza, connecting the two capital cities of Santiago and Buenos Aires.

Lozen found the address in Agrelo, twenty kilometers south of the city. He turned on to a dirt road that threaded through a working vineyard, passing rows of spaced vines and trellises en route to the wine lodge. With a final turn, the road opened to a large Spanish colonial-style home with rounded walls that wrapped around common spaces and a half dozen individual casitas scattered about the property in a semicircle around the main house. So far, it matched the farm custodian's description.

Cal walked through a set of double glass french doors into a reception area filled with baroque European furniture. He approached the front desk. They had a small suite available in one of the casitas, so he checked in, paying cash in advance for two nights. Truth be told, Lozen expected to be gone long before that time expired.

As a porter guided Calixto to his distant casita, he reflected on how well the wine lodge satisfied several necessities for a pivot point: it was a remote setting, but with easy access to the main highway; it received regular visitors, but it managed to keep them separated and private through the use of individual casitas; it maintained several legitimate businesses as cover for illegal activities. All in all, the farmer's recollections proved accurate.

Cal would take the afternoon to explore the grounds and survey the vineyards. He had a specific description from the caretaker of a petite, elderly woman who was the family matriarch and controlled the large smuggling operation. He had yet to see her.

Lozen listened to the porter as the man explained the various amenities in the suite. With a polite thank-you and a small tip, Cal escorted the man from the room and turned his attention to his duffel bag. He had a lot to do.

Chapter 114

December 14, 2006
Gladwyne, Pennsylvania

MIKE AND JOHN both leaned toward their host. Peter Burdis gazed off into the distance, as if he was focusing on some unseen but highly important event. He began to speak without making eye contact. "Back to the abduction of the two girls. The error of that initial decision morphed. It was their own insecurity combined with an inherent paranoia."

"When they realized they had overreacted, why didn't they just release the girls?" asked Mike.

"And be done with it?" said Burdis with a grimace. "Thirty years of ingrained military protocol. Admit a mistake? Release prisoners without compensation? It would have appeared incompetent, or worse, *weak*."

"They feared the reputational blowback," said Mike.

"Exactly," replied their host, "right at the time when the Empresa was organizing a major operation—a new relationship they had promoted between the Calabrians and the Mexicans."

"The 'Ndrengheta and Los Zetas," said John.

"Who could have imagined," replied Burdis. He started to drool, and Mike helped him with his handkerchief to prevent the embarrassment.

"So when they realized they had already fomented a storm," said Burdis, "the Empresa pushed the envelope. They hyped the brother to explain their difficulties."

"Something that could explain the problem," said Mike.

"Something their partners would accept," said John.

"Calixto Lozen," replied Burdis. "A Chiricahua Apache descended from Cochise and Geronimo. A Special Forces soldier with unique military training. A young man boasting of renowned tracking skills."

"And a touch of mysticism," said Mike.

"Latinos tend toward the superstitious," replied Burdis.

"It worked," said John.

"Yes." Burdis shifted in his wheelchair. "The fact was, the perception became the reality. The brother was totally committed to finding his sister. Who could have foreseen that siblings growing up separated by so many years would be so close?" The man paused before continuing. "Calixto Lozen, the Gray Wolf, proved relentless. He didn't care who got in the way."

Chapter 115

Santiago, Chile

DAVID SHIELDS'S TELEPHONE rang. He stared down at his desk, debating whether to answer. On the third ring, he plucked the handset from the cradle. "Shields."

"Cup of coffee?" asked the familiar voice.

"Sure. Usual place?"

"Five minutes."

The line clicked dead, and David stood. He exited the large DIA office and paced down the corridor. At the heavy steel door, he nodded at the marine guard and approached the elevators. Three minutes later he was sitting at a wooden picnic bench across from the FBI legal attaché. The agent popped the lid on two cups of coffee and passed one to the DIA officer.

"I'm a cheap date," said David.

"Nice for a change," replied the FBI agent with a laugh. "I used to have a CI in New York that expected me to cover his mortgage payment every month."

The reference to a paid confidential informant brought a smile to David's lips before he answered, "It hasn't changed. Langley has all the money. When I'm working a source, I can't tell them I'm a different department with a smaller budget."

They sat in silence for a moment as Shields looked off into the distance. The FBI agent took a few seconds to gather his thoughts.

"Speaking of Langley, I think you'll be getting a visit from some folks down the hall."

Shields shrugged, acting unconcerned. "The wing is as prone to politics as anywhere. Someone giving you grief?"

"Me?" said the FBI agent. "No, I don't know anything. But…I did get a call from Headquarters."

"Oh?"

"It seems that the Agency was approached by some contacts back in the States. They were asked for help in toning down the rhetoric."

"The mother is Chilean," said Shields. "She's been very vocal."

"I noticed that it's gaining some airtime here as well."

"Yes," replied Shields.

"The Internet has changed everything," said the FBI agent with a frown.

"What did the Agency say?"

"Release the girls, and it would go away."

Shields laughed before responding, "That's about as simple as it gets."

"Yes. Naturally the Chilean contacts backed off and played dumb. They claimed only to be asking on behalf of old friends."

"Of course," said David.

"But then they approached the mother in Tucson."

"Directly?"

"Handed her an anonymous warning letter."

The DIA officer studied the FBI agent before speaking. "That takes balls."

"Yes it does, but remember, these are the people who whacked Letelier in Washington."

Shields took a sip of coffee and leaned back on the picnic bench. "And now?" asked David.

"Now they're trying to extricate themselves from a problem. They claim the authorities dispatched the National Investigations Police to no avail and that no one can locate the girls. To the best of their knowledge, the coeds are not even *in* Chile anymore."

"That would be convenient," said Shields.

"It would if the noise would stop. What they fear, of course, is that the spotlight will focus on their business venture."

"The Empresa," replied Shields.

"So they went to Langley again and implored their old friends to please call off the dogs."

"And Langley said?"

"What dogs?"

The two men broke into laughter. For David, it was a deep, hearty laugh. He leaned back and rubbed the tears of mirth from his eyes as the FBI agent sipped coffee. Finally the agent continued with his explanation. "Needless to say, someone is wreaking quiet havoc on the Empresa's personnel, and your neighbors down the hall don't have the foggiest idea what the fuck is going on?"

"Oh, I can hear them screaming now," said Shields. "This is rich."

"You're going to get cornered by some pissed-off amigos."

A quiet moment passed before David asked, "So where does it lead?"

"Hard to say. But DEA confirmed that this new partnership between the Calabrians and the Mexicans is real."

Shields whistled. "Look out below."

"No shit," said the FBI agent. He stood and dumped the remainder of his coffee on the grass. "Unofficially, a few of us are really pulling for your friend." He turned. "Just remember, the boys at the Agency know everything about Operation Condor, but when it comes to organized crime, that's our game."

David Shields absorbed the comment as the FBI agent spoke over his shoulder while walking away. "Don't be afraid to reach out."

Chapter 116

Mendoza, Argentina

CALIXTO WORKED BOTH quickly and methodically. First he stopped by the lodge to procure an overview of the property. The front desk provided him with a colored, preprinted strip map. It highlighted the amenities, buildings, hiking trails, and vineyards that stretched in various directions from the main house. The lodge itself maintained the restaurant, a café, an arcade room, some offices, and the front desk.

Cal spoke with the clerk, appearing curious, asking innocuous questions, engaging in polite small talk. She was a local and proudly offered tidbits of information about the bodega. It had been owned by the same family for over ninety years. The matriarch was in her seventies and the daughter of the founder. She lived on the property with her oldest son.

Lozen studied the map in the café, sipping espresso and getting a feel for the staff and the few other tourists. Then he explored the lodge, roaming the public rooms, committing their layout to memory, watching, listening, and showing polite interest in the art and furnishings. He appeared every bit a Chilean tourist taking a few days to relax in the countryside. Cal carried his camera slung over a shoulder.

Next, Calixto walked the grounds, comparing the strip map to the dirt roads, the marked vineyards, and the various buildings scattered about the property. He paid particular attention to the paths that crisscrossed the winery, connecting the rows of varietals and vine trellises that could be traveled by a vehicle smuggling goods away from the main house. For contraband to be offloaded and stored pending redistribution, they needed a private, semi-remote facility.

Cal hiked the bodega property in various directions for over two hours to no avail. He returned to the lodge.

"What a beautiful establishment," said Lozen to the front desk clerk in Spanish.

"You had a chance to explore?" asked the woman.

"Sí, it is quite impressive. I was wondering, is it permitted to go upstairs for an overhead view?" Cal held up his camera.

"No, I am sorry. Upstairs is the private residence of the owner."

"I see," said Lozen. "Well, is there any place to get a higher angle?"

The clerk thought for a moment before her face brightened. She motioned for his map. "Here." The clerk pointed at a building on the strip map. "This is where we store our equipment—the tractors, pruners, hedging attachments, and basket presses. It has a loft on the second floor, but it is high up, with a walk-around patio. If you'd like, I could call over to Frederico, and he could take you to the loft for a few minutes?"

"That would be wonderful," said Cal.

"It is about a ten-minute walk from here."

Calixto thanked her and left.

Seven minutes later, Cal was led up a winding wooden staircase at the rear of a large barnlike storage facility, housing the specialty equipment for wine making. He walked onto a circular patio with views in all directions and stopped beside an old adobe fireplace to take a picture of the vineyards. Then he oriented his map and started comparing the building locations and casitas to the scene before him. In his head, Cal matched impressions from his foot reconnaissance earlier that afternoon to what he now saw. He took a few more photographs.

Then in the distance, a kilometer from the main house, Lozen noticed a small building nestled among several squares of different vines. It seemed out of place among the rows of matching varietals, each positioned to maximize the grapes to the soil and the angle of the sun. He looked at the map and then back at the building. The dirt road on the map seemed to end, but as he looked in the distance, it seemed to circle around the far side of the squares. Cal pointed. "Frederico, what is that?"

The employee looked over and then shrugged. He looked nervous.

"Is it a casita?" asked Cal.

"No—abandoned."

Cal tried to appear uninterested. He memorized the view and then continued to pace around the patio looking in various directions. Calixto made it a point to appear nonchalant. Then he took several more photographs, tipped the employee, and descended the wooden staircase.

Chapter 117

San Antonio de Areco, Argentina

I<small>ZZY SAT ON</small> a yoga mat shackled at the wrists to a heavy overhead chain. She could stand, stretch, or recline provided she didn't try to wander too far from her place on the wall. To her surprise, she was gagged but there was no blindfold.

Isabel looked to her left. Sandy was next to her, barely six feet away, but beyond reach. The setup in the furnitureless room allowed for eight prisoners, but they were alone.

Their eyes met. For the first time in ten days, the two roommates could see each other. It had been a difficult period, but one that Izzy had weathered better than her friend. The fun-loving personality that always brightened Sandy's features was now replaced with a look of fragile helplessness. Sandy was clearly battered by the ordeal.

The door opened, and Patsy entered the room, followed by his two nephews. As Isabel studied the bull-chested 'ndrina boss with the slick black hair, he snapped his fingers and spoke in Spanish. "Stand up."

Izzy looked at her roommate and motioned.

The girls stood, gaining balance in their dresses and high heels, attempting to preserve decorum as they struggled with the chains and shackles.

Lino stepped forward and removed their gags before stepping back behind his uncle.

Patsy turned and addressed Sandy. "Do you speak Spanish?"

"Not very well," answered the roommate in English.

"Where are you from?"

"The United States."

"Americanos?"

"Yes."

Patsy turned toward his nephews and spoke in a language that Izzy couldn't understand. It sounded a little like Italian. Beppe's and Lino's faces lit in surprise. Bellocco made a funny expression and then reached into the cleavage of Sandy's tight dress and grabbed her breast. Sandy quickly backpedaled, caught off guard by the sudden grope.

Instead of stopping, Patsy stepped forward and pushed Sandy against the wall, fondling both her breasts with two hands. He increased the pressure as Sandy squirmed, making a point. She winced and bit her lip as Bellocco pawed her nipples.

"Stop it," said Izzy as her roommate struggled on the verge of tears.

Patsy broke into a laugh before saying in broken English, "Scream if you want, Americano; no one can hear you."

Izzy watched the quintino as he shifted from broken English back into the strange dialect, and then Spanish. She couldn't place the accent, but it was not Chilean. Then she looked at the two nephews. They were enthralled with their uncle. Beppe and Lino had a glazed, predatory look in their eyes. The young men watched Patsy as he toyed with Sandy's emotions.

The quintino shifted his attention. He stepped sideways and took a long, lustful look at Izzy. He studied the tone of her shapely legs, the cling of her silk dress, and the balance of her lithe frame. Then he examined her beautiful face. He noted the raven hair, the violet eyes, the porcelain skin. All the while, Izzy said nothing. She stood motionless and returned his gaze.

"You speak Spanish?" asked Patsy.

"Sí."

"What is your name?"

"Isabel."

"You are Americano?"

"Sí."

Patsy took a final head-to-toe look at Izzy before speaking. "You are my gift."

"What?" Isabel's face tightened in confusion.

Bellocco chuckled without explaining. Instead, he asked another question. "Are you a dancer?"

"No."

"What do you do?"

"I go to college."

"You have beautiful legs. What do you do?"

Izzy looked at the 'ndrina boss with a strange expression before answering. "I don't understand."

Patsy reached forward and traced his index finger around Izzy's lips and whispered, "You want me, don't you?"

Isabel looked at Bellocco like he was from another planet.

"Don't you?" said Patsy a second time. He started to gently push his finger into her mouth. "Say it. You want me."

Izzy twisted her face away, separating her lips from his index finger. "Want you?"

"Say it," replied Bellocco again.

Izzy remained silent and looked at Patsy with disdain. A sudden twist of anger flashed across his face, but the quintino held his temper. He shrugged in an overly exaggerated fashion. "Have it your way."

The 'ndrina boss took a final glance at Izzy and then pointed at Sandy. "Take that one," he said.

The two nephews stepped forward and aggressively started to unfasten Sandy from her shackles. The roommate's Spanish was weak, and she had difficulty following their conversation, but Sandy suddenly realized something fundamental had changed as Beppe and Lino each grabbed an arm.

"What's going on?" asked Sandy. She started to panic and looked at her roommate. "Izzy, what's happening?"

Isabel struggled with her own shackles as she grasped the situation. Somehow her denial had imperiled her friend. She yelled at Bellocco in Spanish. "What are you doing? Leave her alone."

"Iz," said Sandy, dragging her feet as the nephews half pulled, half carried her from the room. "Help me, Izzy." She started to cry.

"Stop," said Isabel in a loud voice. "Please, stop."

Patsy took a slow turn around the room before settling his eyes on Isabel. Then without expression, he exited the room and closed the door.

Chapter 118

Mendoza, Argentina

CAL WAITED UNTIL dark. Fortunately, it came early due to the season. All good Argentineans ate dinner late, in the Spanish tradition, which allowed Lozen the opportunity to take a walk to examine the unmarked building he noticed from the rooftop patio of the equipment barn.

On Calixto's earlier return to his room, he made a point to circle each casita on the property. The half dozen adobe guesthouses appeared to be occupied and in use. In addition, they sat clustered in a wide semicircle with easy, direct access to the main lodge.

By contrast, the "abandoned" building sat hidden a kilometer to the north, far from the tourists or vineyard workers, and apparently situated at the end of a dirt road that led to nowhere. Cal's instincts told him that the lone unaccounted-for building offered the most privacy for a contraband storage facility.

Calixto surveyed his carpenter tools. He felt naked without a firearm. Thankfully, however, his Chilean cover identity listed him as a construction contractor; owning carpenter equipment fit the profile. Cal also knew that in the long evolution of history, most tools and weapons developed simultaneously with a dual purpose. If he couldn't risk transporting real weapons over a border crossing, carpenters' tools were the best alternative.

Cal selected the wood chisel, a Phillips-head screwdriver, a pair of small nail nippers, and a carpenter hatchet. He arranged the tools between his leather belt and his jeans. Then he donned a long-sleeved shirt and draped the tail outside his pants.

Lozen slung the hatchet in a case on his belt and covered the long handle with a sweater knotted at his waist and draped over his hips. Finally Calixto took his shoulder satchel filled with incidentals and started for the door.

He walked in the dark—a lone traveler taking an early evening stroll around the property before dinner. Cal was careful to follow the dirt roads that bisected the sprawling vineyard, with an eye toward the unmarked building. It took him ten minutes to locate the mismatched vine squares. Lozen was convinced that the unusual pattern of cultivation signaled a cover pattern more than a desire to experiment with different varietals. He circled the squares, hugging the trellises until the building came into view.

Cal crouched in the dark and surveyed the adobe walls. They were pockmarked and decaying. Oddly, however, all the windows appeared intact, and a heavy wooden door looked both usable and sturdy. A faint glimmer of light dipped from inside, as if someone was watching a television in a darkened room. In the distance, Cal heard the whine of an engine downshift gears, and the low rumble increased as the vehicle turned down a narrow dirt path and approached the building using only parking lights.

Calixto hunkered down into the base of the vines twenty meters in front of the building. A Chevy van cruised to a halt and killed the engine. Two men jumped from the front seat as the wooden door to the "abandoned" building opened. A beefy, middle-aged man dressed in a leather jacket and carrying a clipboard appeared and motioned toward the van.

Cal watched as the two men slid open the door to the van and started offloading and stacking several dozen unmarked boxes. His instincts were correct.

Twenty minutes into the process, the man with the clipboard walked over and examined the contraband with a flashlight. As the man inspected the product, randomly checking several boxes, a light spilled from the open door of the building. A short, wire-thin woman with cropped gray hair and a lined forehead appeared smoking a cigarette. She stood surveying the scene, shifting her gaze from the boxes to the men and back to her cigarette. Then she turned and walked into the building as the men started to carry the boxes through the door.

Cal watched from the vines. The woman matched the description provided by the farm custodian. She was the matriarch, the head of the Mendoza smuggling operation used by the Empresa to sneak contraband across the border.

It took another twenty minutes to carry all of the boxes into the building. Finally, the two men returned to the van, slipped the Chevy into gear, and crept back down the dirt path. The heavy wooden door slammed shut from the inside.

Cal counted to one hundred. Then he backtracked through the vines and took a few minutes to circle the building from the outside, checking for other points of access. It appeared to have only the one door, facing away from the main lodge. To the best of Lozen's knowledge, inside was one middle-aged man and an elderly lady. He began formulating a plan.

Chapter 119

San Antonio de Areco, Argentina

THE DOOR OPENED, and Izzy watched in horror as Beppe and Lino dragged Sandy's naked body into the room.

Her roommate was limp and bruised, showing a streak of dried blood along the inside of her thigh. Sandy's hair was disheveled, matted in clumps, and wide blotches of seminal fluid splattered her breasts and neck. She moaned.

The nephews laid Sandy on the yoga mat next to Izzy, spreading her legs, allowing the roommate to view Sandy's ravaged torso. They shackled her wrists to the chain above and stood.

Isabel looked at the two nephews with a mixture of fear and loathing. "What did you do to her?" said Izzy in Spanish.

Beppe licked his lips suggestively as Lino gave Isabel an exaggerated wink. Then the two Calabrians broke into laughter and sauntered from the room.

Izzy turned toward her roommate, who lay prone on her back. Sandy's chest heaved in anguish, and a tremor shook her right leg.

"Sandy, what happened?"

The roommate just cried.

"Sandy, please tell me. What did they do?"

Izzy scooted as far to her left as the chains and manacles would allow. She tried to turn her body sideways. It took a moment for Sandy to focus. Finally, her friend was able to formulate words. She started to whisper. "They hurt me, Iz. They did bad things."

Isabel was concerned that she was unable to touch her friend. Tears welled in Izzy's eyes as she beheld her roommate's plight. "What did they do?"

"They raped me," said Sandy, "again and again. The two men—they wouldn't stop." She choked in tears. "Why, Izzy? What did you say?"

Isabel looked surprised. "Say? I didn't say anything."

"He said it was because of you," replied Sandy.

"Me? Who said that?" asked Izzy in confusion.

"The older one. He sat and watched. He gave them things to use. He wouldn't let it stop. He said that it was your fault." Sandy broke into a deep sob, and her body convulsed in pain. "My insides hurt," cried Sandy.

Isabel looked mortified. What had happened? She had said nothing, no reply to Patsy, yet he took the rejection out on her roommate. They had sexually tortured her friend because Izzy had not stroked his ego. What sickness was this? "I said nothing," replied Izzy.

"He said only you could make them stop." She started to shake again. "Please, Izzy, you're my friend. Don't let them hurt me anymore."

Isabel started to cry, partly out of empathy toward Sandy, partly out of frustration. She bit her lip. "I understand," said Izzy. She stretched her face as close to her roommate as the chains would allow. "I understand."

Chapter 120

Mendoza, Argentina

CAL HID NEXT to the wooden door, alternating between a crouch and leaning against the wall. His wristwatch ticked off the minutes. This was a raid, pure and simple, and like the military operation, he would use speed, surprise, and violence of action.

Calixto knew that the smugglers would need to open the door from the inside to leave the abandoned building. The alternative was a tunnel escape that connected this far-flung location to another building. Lozen calculated this possibility as highly unlikely.

As always, there were risks. The first was that there were more than the two people he had seen inside the building. The second was that another load of contraband would arrive along the dusty dirt road.

He considered the odds and decided to wait. It took twenty-four minutes before Cal heard voices from inside, and then a latch was thrown and the portal opened. A man stepped through the door, and Cal immediately thrust sideways with the Phillips-head screwdriver. The tool penetrated the man's chest two inches deep into his sternum. He gasped. As the man fell, Calixto pushed him backward, using him as a human shield, and forced his way into the building.

A second man, the guy with the clipboard, yelled in astonishment. He reached under his leather jacket toward his waistband. Lozen swung the carpenter's hatchet in a short arc and sliced through the exposed hand. The man fell to the floor clutching at the wound.

The elderly woman stood third in line. She froze, her mouth agape; a lit cigarette fell to the ground. Cal punched her in the face, and she crumpled.

Lozen turned and bolted the door. Then he made a quick assessment of his captives and went to work. He found the prisoner room at the end of the hall, complete with heavy chairs and security belts. He strapped the woman and the clipboard man into two chairs. Then he duct-taped and gagged the first man on the floor.

If there had been any doubts in Cal's mind about the smugglers' involvement in the disappearance of Izzy, the room clarified the point. The winery was set up to transport human contraband as well as product.

Cal looked at the three captives and pulled a chair up next to the woman. The matriarch sat dazed, yet surprisingly conscious considering her age and the blow he had delivered. He leaned forward and removed her gag. She eyed Lozen warily.

"Do you know why I am here?" he asked in Spanish.

The woman gave Calixto a contemptuous look before speaking. "To rob us."

"Wrong."

A line furrowed along the woman's forehead. "Then what do you want?" she asked.

"Information," replied Cal in a serious tone.

"I have nothing to say."

"Then I'll be forced to hurt you."

The matriarch sneered in Cal's face. He sat back, surprised. The elderly woman had courage. He took a moment to wipe his brow. Then he motioned at the man on the floor, who was gagged, duct-taped, and had the screwdriver protruding from his chest. "Your friend is dying."

She shrugged, indifferent.

"You don't care?" asked Cal.

The woman motioned at the man in the leather jacket, who trembled in pain. He was strapped to the other chair, gagged and bleeding heavily from the hand wound. He was missing several fingers and half his palm. "He needs medical attention," she said.

Calixto looked at the second man. Her advice seemed pragmatic, but something suggested a deeper concern. He looked back at the woman. "Do you care?"

The matriarch coolly studied Cal before answering, "Take what you want and get out."

"I told you," said Cal, shifting his stance. "I am not here to rob you. I want information. Where did you send the girls?"

Cal saw a flicker in the woman's eye, but she played dumb. "What girls?"

Lozen reached into his satchel and withdrew a photograph of Izzy and Sandy. He held the picture four inches from the woman's face. "These girls."

The matriarch looked at the photograph and then started to laugh. "What are they to you? They are Americanos."

Cal didn't answer.

"You're a mestizo," said the woman, gazing at Lozen's mixed ethnic features. "Your accent is different. Where are you from?"

Calixto ignored the question before asking again, "Where did you send the girls?"

The woman smirked in an arrogant display of confidence. "To someone you can't touch. Don't you know who protects us?"

"No. Should I care?"

"He'll make sausage out of those two. Especially the beauty. She's the perfect gift. Just the way he likes them."

Calixto slapped the woman across the face. "Where?"

It took the matriarch a moment for the sting to subside, but her insolence never wavered. "You're a fool. You'll never find them. He has people everywhere."

Cal leaned back. This diminutive little grandmother was a tough old bird. She showed more gumption than any three men on the Empresa's payroll. He picked up the carpenter's hatchet and the nail nippers for effect. "You will tell me what I want to know," said Cal.

She swallowed, but preserved the appearance of indifference. "Go ahead. Nothing you do could compare to what he'll do."

"Who is *he*?"

"The quintino."

Lozen leaned back in silence. The threat of pain or violence didn't seem to faze her. He thought for a moment. Everyone had a button. Cal just needed to figure out what it was. Something earlier had caught his attention. At the time, it didn't quite register. He looked at the middle-aged man in the leather jacket. Then he looked back at the woman. Her eyes opened wide as she seemed to suddenly take an interest. Cal slid his chair over toward the other prisoner. The matriarch watched him closely. Then Lozen reached over and squeezed the man's injured hand. He yelped through the gag. More interestingly, the old woman jumped in her chair. She caught her breath before speaking, but her mouth formed a nasty snarl.

Calixto recalled that the front desk clerk mentioned earlier that the matriarch ran the winery with her son. She was in her seventies. The injured clipboard man was in his forties. It made sense. "He matters to you," said Cal to the woman.

"Leave him alone," she said in a serious tone.

Lozen had figured out the woman's weakness, and she realized her conundrum. He reached back with the carpenter's hatchet and deftly spun it in the air. Cal put on a little demonstration of his skill with the tool.

"You said that I was a mestizo," said Cal. "You were sort of correct, but there are things you don't know about me."

Lozen stood and moved behind the injured son. He touched the man's shoulder with his free hand, while dangling the hatchet in the other. The old woman studied Cal.

"My father taught me many things," said Calixto, "including how to use one of these." Cal twirled the forged steel tool ominously. "Except he called it a tomahawk."

Chapter 121

San Antonio de Areco, Argentina

It had been a sleepless night for Izzy. She spent most of the time trying to comfort her physically abused and emotionally distraught friend. So much fear and angst had been imposed on Sandy, and by extension, Isabel.

The two young nephews had battered her roommate, knowing the ordeal and the blame would settle into Izzy's psyche. Izzy felt horrible, and yet, her options were limited. She knew her friend would crack if they took her again. However, to willingly accept rape and defilement of herself to satisfy the bull-chested man's desires was equally abhorrent. She felt trapped.

Isabel knew that she was helpless to control their actions. They were animals. She also knew that she had done nothing wrong. Yet the blame and the feeling of guilt caused her to struggle with the dilemma.

Izzy's thoughts reverted to Cal. Her brother always counseled to be true to yourself. Calixto was never afraid of failure, but he always gave things his best effort. She would too.

Patsy Bellocco entered the room, followed by his two nephews. He walked up to Sandy, and she started to tremble. Her voice turned desperate.

"No," said Sandy. "Please."

Beppe and Lino smirked in anticipation of another session. They watched as Sandy looked to Isabel for help. Izzy grimaced as Patsy shifted his attention toward her.

"Do you want me?" he asked.

Isabel bit her lip, controlling her own fear.

"You do, don't you?" said the 'ndrina boss.

Izzy looked at Bellocco from her sitting position. He waited for an answer. When none came, he motioned toward Sandy. The two nephews stepped forward and started unshackling the roommate.

Sandy started to beg. She squeezed her legs together and cried out in a strident voice, "Help me, Iz. Please, don't let them take me."

Suddenly Isabel spoke in Spanish. "Wait."

The Calabrians paused and turned toward Izzy. She stood up and looked directly at Patsy. He moved closer. In her high heels, she matched Bellocco's height. Izzy fixed the quintino with a steady gaze, which he returned, curious. Patsy reached forward with an index finger and traced her lips.

"Do you want me?" he asked.

"Leave her alone."

"Do you want me?"

"Will you leave her alone?" she asked.

In a strange way, Patsy was excited by Izzy's challenge. He was not used to people acting defiant, much less a woman.

"Do you *want* me?" asked Bellocco a fourth time.

A few seconds elapsed before Izzy answered, "Yes, but *only* you." She nodded at Sandy. "Leave her alone, and send them away. It's not a show."

Patsy reached forward and grabbed Izzy's breast. She flinched, but then quickly recovered. Isabel touched her tongue to her lips and said, "I want you but only you."

Bellocco looked into her violet eyes and then he motioned toward Sandy. "Forget her." He pointed at Izzy. "Free this one."

Beppe and Lino hesitated, causing Patsy to snarl. The two nephews stood. They turned their attention away from Sandy and unshackled Isabel. As they marched Izzy from the room, Sandy realized she had been given a reprieve. She started to panic for a different reason.

"Izzy...where are you taking her?" Sandy continued to yell until the door closed and she was alone.

Down the hall, Patsy opened a different door and shoved Isabel inside. Then he turned toward his nephews. "Go back to the house."

Beppe started to protest, but Patsy held up his hand. "I'll be fine; now go."

The two nephews looked dejected, but they obeyed. He closed the door.

The room was nearly empty except for one chair, a large bed with a soiled sheet, and thick leather shackles positioned at the four corners. To the left was a large window with wooden shutters, and to the right, a small bathroom stall with a toilet and sink.

Isabel stood in the center of the room and started to tremble. "I need to use the toilet."

Patsy motioned with an open hand. Izzy entered the stall and closed the door.

She stood motionless and looked around the bathroom. It was bare. Izzy sat on the commode fully clothed and tried to slow her racing heart. She started to hyperventilate and began counting by twos. Then she thought of her parents, her brother, Cal, and Sandy. She squeezed her eyes and prayed.

Bellocco banged on the door. Izzy stood and flushed the unused toilet. Then she turned on the faucet and splashed her face with cold water.

Isabel opened the door and strutted back into the bedroom. Patsy sat in the corner, in the lone chair. Their eyes met, and Izzy walked over to the bed, sat sideways, and stretched her long, shapely legs to the front. The silk dress automatically hiked upward as her feet touched the floor. It exposed several more inches of Izzy's thighs.

Bellocco ogled before crossing the room. He crouched below Izzy and lifted an ankle with each hand, starting to remove her shoes.

"No," said Isabel, looking down at Bellocco. "I feel sexier with them on."

Patsy shrugged, and then with an exaggerated motion, he spread her legs apart.

The quintino worked slowly, savoring the feel of Izzy's smooth skin. He slid his palms upward, over her calf, to her knees, finally stroking her inner thighs. It caused Izzy's feet to rise off the floor.

"You are so beautiful," said Patsy in a quiet voice. "You want me, don't you?"

Isabel looked down at Bellocco from the bed as he fondled her legs. His groping became more intense, and she sensed Patsy was getting aroused. "Yes, I want you," she said in an aroused voice.

Patsy's fingers slid up under her dress, reaching for Izzy's panties. She leaned back and raised her legs even higher off the floor, bending her knees, exposing her fabric-covered crotch. Izzy started to moan. Bellocco leaned forward, felt for the waistband, and pulled at the lacy fabric. Suddenly Isabel snapped out with both legs, kicking hard, and drove her three-inch-high heels flush into Patsy's face. He fell back in a heap, clutching at his left eye.

In an instant, Izzy jumped off the bed and ran to the window. She pushed open the wooden shutters and looked outside. It was a cabin set in the middle of a rolling pasture.

Isabel shimmied up and crawled through the window, hitting the soft grass on the other side. Her adrenaline was pumping. She looked right and saw a large manor house in the distance. She looked left and saw a horse trail. Then she heard Patsy gasp from inside the bedroom. Izzy took off her high heels, held one in each hand, and did the only thing she could think to do. She ran.

Chapter 122

Mendoza, Argentina

IN THE END, it was about a mother's love. The petite matriarch, barely a hundred pounds soaking wet, didn't care a whit about her own well-being, but the moment she believed Calixto would carve her son into bite-size pieces, she babbled like a drunken adolescent. Two deft nicks with the carpenter's hatchet, and the old woman caved.

She told him everything. In effect, it was information overload, more than Cal needed to know. Yet extra intel always added value. The matriarch recounted the eighteen years of her smuggling operation, including the extra refinements that occurred six years previous, when Patsy Bellocco, the new 'ndrina boss arrived. It was a trove of useful information, and it forced Lozen to recalibrate his mind-set. David Shields had said it best: "Don't think political; think criminal." Cal adjusted.

The Argentine side of the Empresa was not aware of Lozen. They did not understand his relationship to Izzy, their mother, Constanza, or the family ties to the nation of Chile. They also didn't care. These were mobsters, pure and simple, who received a "gift" of two pretty young hostages, who happened to be Americans. Their goal was profits—human trafficking for the sex trade. Bellocco turned his prisoners into broken, drug-controlled prostitutes for his string of bordellos.

Calixto was incensed. It had always been personal to the brother, but now Cal felt an extra urgency. There was no military code or soldier's respect. The

Chileans were not sharing everything with their associates. Therefore, Lozen would not give up his advantage. He changed tactics.

Calixto did a quick but thorough search of the contraband storage facility. He recovered two weapons, a Browning Hi-Power pistol and a Mossberg twelve-gauge shotgun. Then he secured the woman and her son to assure their continued silence.

Cal hustled back to the casita, grabbed his duffel bag, and quietly drove from the winery. He headed east, along Ruta Nacional Seven, guiding the stolen Range Rover toward the little town of San Antonio de Areco.

Chapter 123

San Antonio de Areco, Argentina

IZZY RAN WITH fervor, arms pumping, legs churning, feet pounding. She was desperate, sprinting for her life—a hunted animal afraid to look back, a ball of frayed nerves and jangling senses that knew at any moment people would appear to take her.

It would be men, bad men, on horses, in jeeps, traveling in a pack, all wanting to earn the prize, each wanting to claim the distinction of catching the escapee. She had hurt the boss, and she knew he would act with violence.

Isabel focused on the running. She had always loved to run. There was a freedom, an exhilaration in the process that became Izzy's healthy obsession. She learned to alter her speed and distance and to offset difficult outings. This helped her to rarely skip more than one day per week. It cleared her head. It provided a discipline. Now, however, she ran in fear.

Izzy crossed the humid pampa of the foothills. Rolling pastures stretched in all directions, bordered on one side by several long livestock fences that stretched beside the horse trail, and on the other side by a thick, tree-lined clump of foliage that dipped toward the low ground. Tall grass and dozens of beef cattle dotted the pastures. She needed to hide. Izzy stopped and looked. It was a large ranch.

Isabel angled from the horse trail toward the barbed wire fence. She felt her feet stumble over unseen twigs and stones as she veered off the path. Izzy estimated that ten or eleven minutes of time and maybe three kilometers of distance had elapsed since she jumped through the cabin window. She needed to make the woodline on the far side of the pasture. She needed cover.

The fence stood five feet high, intersected by four strands of stretched barbed wire. Izzy stuck her hands through the two middle strands and dropped her shoes on the far side. Then she pulled the second strand up and pushed the third strand down, separating the wire and creating a wider space. She stuck her leg through the narrow gap and caught a barb. The blood started. Izzy pushed through, getting snagged, feeling the wire tear at her forearm, her shoulder, her silk dress. Trickles of blood gashed her skin. Tears of frustration welled in Izzy's eyes. The wounds stung, but she was losing precious time. She had to keep going.

Isabel turned and grabbed at her dress, tugging hard, losing a small piece of silk in the barb. Finally, she was free and on the far side of the livestock fence. She picked up her two shoes and began sprinting straight for the tree line. The wire strands shook one last time and settled back into place.

Two minutes later, Izzy stumbled on something sharp. She winced in pain and hobbled into the foliage. Isabel sat on her knees, catching her breath, and inspected the foot wound. A deep cut oozed blood.

For a minute Izzy rested, brushing back tears. She needed her brother. Cal would tell her to keep going.

Isabel stood and put on her high heels. She examined the barb cuts on her forearm, her thigh, and her shoulder. Izzy was a bit frayed, but she wouldn't permit herself to feel sorry. What was the alternative? The consequences would be severe. If caught, Izzy would be raped, brutalized, killed.

Suddenly Isabel saw three gauchos through the foliage, galloping on horseback along the trail, on the far side of the wire fence.

They moved fast, looking ahead, focusing on the rolling pastures in the distance. The gauchos passed the point in the fence where Izzy had crossed from the trail. She watched them disappear on the horizon. Then Isabel turned and started threading through the tree line, under cover of the thick foliage.

Chapter 124

Buenos Aires, Argentina

PATSY PUSHED SOFIA away and stood. He stormed into the bathroom and slammed the door.

The dancer sat up in bed, disheveled, half clothed, and in pain. She wasn't quite sure what had just happened. Her lover had returned from the hospital, his face bruised and puffy, one eye wrapped in heavy gauze and bandages, and attacked her.

Bellocco was in a foul mood. Something bad had happened to the 'ndrina boss, causing a grave injury, and he lashed out at Sofia.

It all happened so suddenly. Patsy entered the apartment, grabbed Sofia by the arm, and pushed her toward the bedroom. Sofia was familiar with Pasquale's passionate moods, but this was different. This was not lust; it was anger. Patsy tore at Sofia's clothes, throwing her down, gripping the dancer until she cried in pain. Then Bellocco penetrated Sofia and pumped wildly until he ejaculated. The whole session felt void of warmth or tenderness.

Sofia curled up on the bed. She tucked both knees under her chin, distraught. She felt cheap and used. She wanted to help, but didn't know how. Pasquale needed to let her in. Sofia heard glass shattering in the bathroom.

Bellocco walked into the bedroom and threw on a satin robe. Then, without saying a word, he flung open the door and stepped into the living room.

Sofia started to cry.

"Quintino," said Patsy's brother-in-law, standing near the television.

Bellocco crossed the room and spoke in a low growl. "Twenty thousand pesos to the man who finds that putana."

Ettore nodded. Patsy had used a vulgar Italian work to refer to Isabel.

"Not a hair on her head missing," said Bellocco emphatically. "I will do the work, comprende?"

"Sí, Pasquale."

"The doctor said I am going to lose the eye." Patsy grimaced. "I will make an example of her."

"I understand, Quintino."

The brother-in-law stood in silence, awaiting further instructions. Finally he spoke. "And the other one?"

"Move her from the estancia. Bring her here to Buenos Aires, to the Palermo prostibulo. Let the regulars take her. Then we'll move her to the Blue Boliche. She's pretty. She should fetch good money."

"Sí, Quintino," said Ettore. He started to turn, but Patsy grabbed his shoulder.

"Remember, I want the putana untouched. She's mine."

Chapter 125

San Antonio de Areco, Argentina

CALIXTO DROVE ALL night. Fortunately most of the journey from Mendoza followed major roads until he hit the outskirts of the small town just before dawn.

Cal had a precise address for the estancia just off Alberdi. What he needed was the opportunity to view the ranch from a hidden location to best decide on a course of action. The bodega's matriarch stressed that contraband product always shipped to a waterfront warehouse in Buenos Aires, with the exception of human cargo. Female prisoners always traveled by separate delivery to a cabin at the estancia in San Antonio de Areco. The 'ndrina boss personally inspected all new women destined for his prized bordellos. Most of the captives were tricked or kidnapped into the sex trade, and therefore, usually had to undergo a period of transition. The quintino used his tough ranch hands, the gauchos, to break the women.

Lozen pulled the Range Rover off the road a few hundred yards beyond the winding entrance to the estancia. He took a few minutes to camouflage the car in a ditch and changed his clothes. Cal donned hiking boots, jeans, a tight pullover, and a dark kerchief. Then he pulled on his shoulder satchel and selected his weapons: the pistol, the shotgun, and the carpenter's hatchet. Finally he set off using the cover of the woodline. It took Cal twenty minutes to angle into position to view the various structures of the sprawling ranch.

It was a clustered layout, complete with a large colonial manor house, a barn, a stable, and several open porches and equipment sheds. Four hundred meters to the right was a lone wood cabin separated by a horse trail, several animal pens, and a small lagoon. This matched the old woman's description of the captives' prison. Calixto studied the grounds, committing the various points to memory, and then continued to circle through the woodline toward the cabin.

Fifteen minutes later, Lozen crouched with his minibinoculars just as a shimmer of early morning sun broke through the mist. As Cal studied the cabin, the front door opened. Two rugged-looking men in floppy, wide-brimmed hats and baggy pants stepped out on to the porch. They each carried a long knife tucked under their sash at the small of their backs.

The first man stamped his heavy boots on the porch, causing his spurs to jingle as he lit a cigarette. The second man looked off toward the manor house in the distance as he sipped yerba mate from a gourd with a metal straw. They stood in silence for a minute, and then the first man motioned. The two gauchos started for the stable.

Cal watched the cabin from the far side for additional activity. Then he adjusted the shotgun sling on his right shoulder. The new position partially hid the twelve-gauge, yet allowed him to move freely and aim the weapon. Calixto crept closer to the cabin, staying hidden in the tree line. He calculated the distance from his position across the open pasture to the rear of the wooden structure.

For the most part, the cabin itself was a visual obstacle separating him from the activity of the manor house on the other side of the lagoon. Just as Cal prepared to sprint from the woodline to the back of the cabin, three gauchos trotted along the trail on horseback from the stable. The two ranch hands from the porch had been joined by a third cowboy.

The gauchos stopped on the trail near the side of the cabin. They began a conversation. The first man pointed at the window that Izzy had escaped from and then up and down the trail in both directions. The second man pointed at the tree line where Calixto hid. They continued to talk until the three nudged their horses and started trotting up the trail.

Cal held his breath. When the three ranch hands rode out of sight, he braced and then hustled across the pasture and sidled up to the rear of the cabin. The back window was shuttered. Cal listened, hugging the wall, circling the structure from back to front. He held the carpenter's hatchet at the ready. All seemed quiet.

At the porch, Lozen crouched in the corner. The cabin's door faced the main house. He would have to move fast. In an instant, Cal jumped the railing, twisted the Mossberg in its sling, and barged through the unlocked front door. The room was empty.

He stood in a combined living room-kitchen space. Several chairs surrounded a heavy table next to a stove, and leather furniture faced a large flat-screen television. Calixto paced down a long hallway and began a room-by-room search of the cabin. The first room was an empty bedroom, as was the second. In the third room, Cal noted the obvious difference. There were no windows or furniture, but instead, there were eight evenly spaced yoga mats positioned along the walls under a series of chains and shackles: the prisoner room. This was where they held the girls. Lozen grimaced.

Finally Cal checked the hall toilet and the final room off the hall. It had a large bed with a soiled mattress, shackles on both ends, a single chair in the corner, and a private toilet. It too was empty. A stain on the floor looked like dried blood.

Seconds later, Lozen peeked through the front door toward the manor house in the distance. Then he exited and crept to the far side of the porch. He looked over at the horse trail where the gauchos had their conversation. It was twenty meters from the side of the cabin. Any way he sliced the picture, Cal would be exposed and in the open if anyone were watching. He couldn't hide from view; therefore, it was best to appear natural.

Calixto adjusted the sling to hide the Mossberg along his far side and then calmly paced toward the trail as if he belonged. He studied the ground, walking a few steps in each direction. It was filled with hoof marks, but less obvious, Cal noticed several human footprints. They were recent tracks, and the person was barefoot.

Lozen's instincts honed. He studied the impressions—their length, depth, and width. Then he analyzed the spacing of the bones and the weight of the displacement. It was a woman, between five feet seven inches and five feet ten tall, maybe a hundred twenty-five pounds, moving in balance. She was *running*. Izzy.

Calixto stood from his crouch and looked back toward the main house. Then he started moving along the side of the trail. He kept one eye in the distance for the gauchos and one eye down at the barefoot tracks along the horse trail.

Chapter 126

San Antonio de Areco, Argentina

IZZY SHIVERED AWAKE. Her foot throbbed, and her throat, dry and parched, felt like a piece of sandpaper. She was miserable—cold, tired, and sore, but mostly she was afraid.

She shifted her hands, holding the thin silk dress between her legs as cover from the cold and the bugs. It was hardly sufficient protection from the elements even for the moderate temperatures. Isabel wondered where she was.

It had been a tough night, but Izzy had actually slept for a few hours out of sheer exhaustion. The whole ordeal, a spine-tingling emotional roller coaster of an escape, had sapped her energy. She didn't like the dark. It scared her. Too many creepy crawlies to sneak up and bite her. Yet Izzy had few alternatives. The thick foliage was her salvation. She couldn't outrun men on horses, and she couldn't hide in the open.

She fought back the tears as she pulled off her shoe to inspect the gash in her foot. It looked bad. The wound was deep and painful. It needed medical attention—sutures and antibiotics—to prevent infection. She tugged on the high heel and winced.

Izzy was famished. She hadn't eaten since the basement prison. Since then, she had been moved twice. For someone who ate regularly throughout the course of a day, this was tough. She needed sustenance for a clear head.

Izzy thought about her parents, her brother, and then about Sandy. She worried in retrospect what they might do to her friend. The escape would assure their wrath, yet also, it would place the focus on her, not her roommate.

Isabel's thoughts were muddled. Her only hope—their only hope, as she saw it—was escape to freedom, and then go back for Sandy.

Isabel knew that she needed to drink. Food was important, but water was essential. One learned that growing up in a desert community. For a brief moment, Izzy put away her anxieties and welcomed the morning sun. The tree line sloped away from the pampas. In the clarity of dawn, she saw a stream in the distance. She stood, brushed off her legs and her dress, and started to walk toward the body of water.

Chapter 127

San Antonio de Areco, Argentina

CALIXTO WAS AN expert tracker. His ability developed early, under Naiche's watchful eye. The father earned a reputation as one of the finest trackers in all of Arizona, used regularly by local police and sheriff's departments to rescue lost tourists.

Special Forces took Cal's skills a step further. They sent him to train with the SAS in Australia, and then to the Malaysian Man Tracking School. His experience widened by a huge margin.

Lozen followed the bare female footprints for a couple of kilometers along the horse trail. He was sensitive to being in the open and expected the gauchos to appear on the horizon at any moment. Yet he was sure this was Izzy, and therefore he needed to continue along the rolling hills of the pampas as far as the footprints continued. He refined a loose cover story in his head lest he was confronted.

Calixto noticed several toe digs in the dirt trail, and then, inexplicably, the signature track stopped. He turned and retraced his steps to see if the woman had backtracked. She hadn't. Cal stooped. He saw several pebbles compressed into the dirt and then widened his search pattern. The runner had halted and swiveled in place, moving her feet as she turned both left and right. The weight of her standing pattern caused a different impression. Cal mimicked her move. He tried to visualize what she saw. To the left, rolling pastures, and to the right, tall grass intersected by a boundary fence. Beyond the fence, several hundred meters farther, was a tree line with thick foliage.

What would Izzy do if she escaped, outnumbered by men with horses or in vehicles? She would run, and she would hide.

Cal crossed the pampas on an azimuth parallel to the end of her signature track. He noticed little things not readily obvious to the untrained eye: bruised vegetation, broken stems. There was a slight sway to the tall grass as a gentle path tilted toward the fence. It was barely noticeable, but for Cal it was a billboard. He followed the cutting signs right up to the wire fence. There were scuff marks and a dislodged twig under the lowest strand. A very distinct print of female toes squished the dirt.

Lozen checked the four wires that stretched in each direction toward opposite wooden posts. Several of the barbs were stained with blood. Then Calixto saw the clincher: a small piece of cloth snagged on a barb on one of the middle strands.

He studied the ground on the far side of the boundary fence and picked up new cutting signs. Izzy had crossed here, heading for the tree line. Suddenly, to his left, Cal heard the light gallop of horses up on the trail. He turned and saw the heads of several gauchos as they cleared the top of the rise. Lozen was exposed, highly visible in the middle of the open field. There was no retreat.

Calixto did his best to look over casually as they approached. Then with a nonchalant air, he turned his attention back toward the boundary fence. The three gauchos slowed to a trot and eyed him with wary suspicion. One saw his shotgun in a side sling and pulled a rifle from his saddle bag. The three men spread out, surrounding Cal with their horses, and stopped.

Chapter 128

Santiago, Chile

THE DIA SUPERVISOR stopped at David Shields's desk just as the intelligence officer stood.

"We've been summoned," said the supervisor.

"By who?"

"The big guy down the hall."

"The station chief?"

"Yup."

"I was just leaving on an appointment. I have a contact in thirty minutes."

"Reschedule."

"It's important," said Shields. "I'll spook my source."

"Reschedule," repeated the supervisor.

Shields grimaced but obeyed. He reached for his cell phone with a scowl on his face and made the call.

Two minutes later, the supervisor led Shields, a second DIA humint officer, and two analysts down the hall deeper into the intelligence wing. They entered a large, windowless, padded, soundproof conference room, known as a SCIF.

The CIA station chief entered, followed by two men and a woman. One of the men carried a portable tape recorder and a steno pad. The chief sat in the middle of the conference table facing the door. He pointed to his right and motioned. The tape recorder was turned on.

"Everyone here knows everyone else," said the station chief in a gruff tone. He was a dapper man, well groomed, midfifties, with glasses and a streak of silver hair. "Luke, fill in the names for the record."

The subordinate's eyes shifted from his steno pad to the people sitting around the table. He spoke clearly for the tape, reciting names and positions. When he finished, he looked back at the station chief.

"It has come to our attention," said the chief, who leaned forward and folded his hands, "that a covert operation is taking place here in Chile." The station chief looked directly at the DIA supervisor. David's boss looked surprised but unruffled. "This is disconcerting," he continued, "as everyone in Washington knows that the only organization authorized to conduct covert action in a foreign country is the Central Intelligence Agency."

He pointed, and the second CIA man handed him a thick multipage dossier. The station chief slid it across the table at David's boss. "This is a copy of Executive Order one, two, three, three, three, issued by President Ronald Reagan in nineteen eighty-four, granting *exclusive* responsibility for special operations to the CIA."

He pointed again and received a second document, which he also slid across the table to the DIA supervisor. "This is a copy of the Hughes-Ryan Amendment from nineteen ninety-one, further designating the CIA as *sole* authority to conduct covert action on behalf of the nation."

The subordinate gave the chief a third packet, which he quickly slid across the conference table as well. There was now a pile of documents in front of the DIA supervisor. "And this," said the station chief, "is Title Fifty of US Code Section four, one, three sub e, which mirrors the first two documents. It is quoted regularly by our congressional oversight committees—the Senate Select Committee on Intelligence and the House Permanent Select Committee on Intelligence—and it specifies that the CIA must report *all* covert activity on a quarterly basis."

The station chief stopped talking and leaned back in his chair before spreading his hands. "Perhaps," said the chief finally, "you need to read these?"

"I'm quite familiar with them," said the DIA supervisor.

The station chief leaned forward. "So maybe it's time for you to tell me what is going on in *my* station."

David's boss looked sideways at Shields and then at the second humint officer on his team. Both men looked surprised and shrugged.

"I'm not sure what you are referring to," said the supervisor. "These men are on rotation from DX Center. They are trying to develop additional sources of information in the Chilean armed forces."

"Cut the crap," replied the station chief. His anger was palpable. "There is some type of operation in play. It is targeting former members of the Chilean military, people whom, I might add, we have had an excellent working relationship with for many years."

The DIA supervisor was caught off guard, but he kept his cool. He then looked at his two analysts. Both men acted puzzled as well.

Finally, the woman who had been sitting quietly on the station chief's left side touched his wrist. Her name was Becky Reynolds. She was an experienced operations officer in the CIA's newly reorganized National Clandestine Service. She was sharp, early forties, and unassuming. This was her third posting to South America, and she had spent the last eighteen months in Santiago. The station chief let her speak. "We understand that this action is related to those two college kids that disappeared."

The DIA supervisor gave her a blank look, and she shifted her attention to Shields.

"David, you were in Special Forces prior to DIA, weren't you?"

"For ten years," said Shields.

"I understand it is a pretty close-knit unit."

David nodded.

"I also understand that one of the young ladies has a brother in Special Forces. Is that true?"

"I wouldn't know. I've been out of Group for a while," replied Shields.

The station chief leaned forward and fixed his attention first on Shields and then on the supervisor. "For the record, *no* covert action is authorized in Chile without my explicit permission and involvement. You are all on notice.

If you are aware of or suspect any such action, you must report it to my office immediately."

He pointed at the man controlling the tape recorder, and the subordinate turned off the machine. "And let me be clear," said the station chief in a whisper, "if any of you screw with my station, I'll hang you out to dry."

The chief stood and paced from the SCIF. The two male subordinates immediately followed. Becky Reynolds, however, hesitated. She sat for a moment looking across the table at Shields. Then without saying a word, she stood and exited the room.

Chapter 129

San Antonio de Areco, Argentina

"You are trespassing," said the gaucho in the middle.

The three men watched Cal.

"No, I'm not. I'm working," he said with a yawn. Cal spoke in unaccented Spanish. They didn't know what to make of him—his looks, his attire, but most of all, his attitude.

"Doing what?"

"My job," said Lozen. He didn't show the least bit of concern. Cal touched at the barbed wire.

The gaucho on the left leaned forward in his saddle, lifting the muzzle of his rifle a couple of inches off the ground. Cal noticed that it was an old Mauser bolt-action model. The gaucho spoke. "What's your job?"

"Finding your missing person," answered Calixto. He pointed at the grass under the fence. "She crossed here."

The three men eyed Lozen curiously. The gaucho in the middle spoke again. "How do you know about her?"

"My boss sent me."

"Who's your boss?"

"He's a friend of your boss. My boss is in Santiago."

"You're Chilean?"

"Yes."

"And you were sent to find the girl?"

"Yes."

"Tell me about her."

"I don't know anything, except what the tracks tell me," said Calixto.

Cal had deduced rather quickly that the gauchos were excellent horsemen, but they did all of their tracking from a saddle.

"What do they tell you now?" said the gaucho on the right.

"That she's young, early twenties, height, about one meter, eight…weight, fifty-seven kilos…she's barefoot and tired."

Lozen let the information settle.

"So you track people," said the gaucho with the rifle. "Why do you need a weapon?"

Cal looked at the ranch hand and stroked the muzzle of his shotgun without moving the sling. "Sometimes they don't want to be found."

A small silence ensued before the leader spoke again. "What about the reward?" asked the gaucho in the middle.

Cal shrugged. The comment surprised him, but he acted uninterested. "I've already been paid."

"We know this estancia better than anyone," said the gaucho to the right.

"We are coming with you," said the gaucho with the rifle.

"Suit yourself. But give me a wide berth. I don't want the horses trampling my tracks." Calixto realized that he was pulling the gauchos into his process, but the only way to protect Izzy was to keep them in sight.

As the two younger gauchos started back down the trail toward a gate in the boundary fence, Cal used the barrel of the shotgun to spread the third strand of wire open and carefully stepped through the gap in the fence. The gaucho in the middle watched him from the far side of the fence and then reached for his cell phone.

Chapter 130

San Antonio de Areco, Argentina

IZZY MOVED WITHIN the tree line for thirty minutes, stumbling, light-headed, and fearing dehydration. Finally she reached an opening and crossed over to the stream. Isabel took a moment to remove her shoes and wade up to her ankles in the gently flowing riverbed. It was cool and refreshing. She bent over and washed the cuts and the dried blood from the barbed wire fence before doing her best to clean the deep gash in her foot.

She felt the current as the stream flowed sideways. Izzy knew she needed to drink. The body needed fluids, but she feared the effects of nonpotable water. She hesitated, and then she reached over and raised a cupped handful of water to her lips. She smelled, then drank. It was a risk, but dehydration was no better.

Isabel grew up in Arizona, but unlike many residents, she was not an ardent outdoors person. She liked to hike, camp, and ride horses, but it wasn't a regular pastime. Izzy preferred the fresh air and a good run more than a nature walk. Most of her experience in the less-traveled foothills was taking a stroll with Cal. She enjoyed their talks as much as he liked to teach her about the land. It was one of their bonding rituals. It kept them close as their lives veered along different paths. Fortunately, some of her brother's lessons stuck. Water ran downhill, the sun moved east to west, and the constellations in the Southern Hemisphere were different.

Izzy put on her high heels and walked along the riverbed, following the stream. She checked the early morning sun and knew she was moving generally south. Isabel walked for another hour.

It was slow treading, but steady. The high heels offered little support, but she kept at it. Finally Isabel took another break along the stream. She removed her shoes and soaked her battered feet in the water. The wound was throbbing.

Izzy tested the water and took another drink. She sat on the side of the stream, letting the cool current splash ankle high over her blistered toes. She massaged her legs.

Suddenly, over her shoulder, a noise. Izzy looked up and saw a horse step into the open. A gaucho's face brightened in surprise. He saw her, and Isabel jumped up in terror. She grabbed her shoes and started to run along the stream-bed, away from the ranch hand. Her mind was racing. Not now, please…

In the distance, in front of Isabel, a second horseman trotted from the tree line. He blocked her path. She stopped, turned, and looked in both directions. Izzy started to panic. She was caught between them. Her eyes shifted left to right, searching for an escape route as the two gauchos nudged their horses forward, closing the gap.

Ahead, toward the right, Izzy saw a break in the woodline. She started to sprint for the opening. The gauchos stopped their horses and laughed. The second man motioned, and the first gaucho broke his horse into a trot as he reached for a boleadora. The bola was a primitive hunting tool of three wooden balls connected with braided leather cords. The balls were unevenly weighted. The gauchos used the tool to entangle running cattle or game by throwing the bola and tripping the animal's legs.

The first gaucho let Izzy get a head start. Then he gripped the bola by the nexus of the cords and started swinging the tool overhead in a wide horizontal arc, much like a lasso. The three balls picked up speed, and the bola started to hum. Then he spurred his horse into a gallop and took off down the path after Izzy.

Chapter 131

San Antonio de Areco, Argentina

CALIXTO EDGED HIS way through the rolling pampas into the thick foliage for over an hour. Izzy's prints were fresh. They were close.

Cal balanced the tracking with a cautious eye toward the gauchos. He sensed they had a plan for him. First, however, the gauchos needed Lozen's help to find Izzy. So he played it both ways as well.

The oldest gaucho lit another cigarette as his horse sauntered lazily behind Calixto. This man had made several cell calls since they began. Cal presumed at least one was a verification call regarding Lozen's involvement. They didn't trust him, and they wanted the reward to themselves. This in itself indicated an abrupt change once Izzy was located.

The two younger gauchos wandered off to either side of Calixto as he tracked through the woodline. He followed Izzy's signature trail, and they gave him ample room to work.

Naturally Cal kept the vital information to himself. He didn't let them know that Isabel was injured and slowing. He didn't advise them that she intersected the path back and forth along the riverbed. Izzy needed water. Calixto reached down and felt at some heel marks from her shoes, noting the indentations in the dirt and the compressed pebbles. He followed the track as it continued weaving between the tree line and the stream for another thirty minutes. Izzy was heading south, paralleling the river.

He smiled to himself. Cal's little sister was a courageous young woman. She had discipline and drive. Lozen thought of brawny men who broke under this pressure. Not Izzy; she demonstrated real moxie.

Off to his right, Cal heard some rustling in the foliage and then a shout. He looked over. One of the gauchos squealed in glee. The ranch hand spurred his horse into a light gallop, chasing a young woman in a short dress. Izzy?

Calixto turned and broke into a run. The closest gaucho laughed as he sped past Cal twirling a bola over his head. Lozen used one hand to tilt the shotgun sling away from his body, while he used the other to tug the carpenter's hatchet from its sheath. Cal knew the first kill had to be silent to preserve the opportunity for surprise.

The woman stumbled. It looked like Izzy from behind. The gaucho closed the distance as she regained her footing and scrambled forward, gasping, desperate, breaking into another run just as the gaucho loosed the bola. The three wooden balls flew through the air, hitting her in the legs, knee high, the force wrapping the leather cords around her limbs, and sent Izzy sprawling face-first into the ground. The gaucho halted his horse. He sat and laughed, pointing forty feet to his front at the dazed woman.

Calixto slowed and then stopped. He threw the carpenter's hatchet in a powerful overhead motion. For most folks, the hatchet was a reliable tool. In Cal's hands, the hatchet was a weapon of tribal pride. Naiche spent hours training his son on the proper use of a tomahawk. The forged steel blade spiraled end over end and struck the gaucho between his shoulder blades with a thud. The man buckled atop his horse, stunned by the impact, partially paralyzed by the hatchet imbedded two inches deep into his back.

The gaucho fell off the horse as Cal sped past him to the woman. Lozen turned her over, and she screamed, raising her hands defensively. He covered her mouth with his palm and held her chin up so she could look at his face. It *was* his sister. "Izzy, it's me," said Cal.

It took Isabel a moment to focus. Finally a look of disbelief flashed in her eyes. "Cal?"

"It's me," replied Calixto again. He hugged his sister. The other gauchos were approaching from down the path. "Stay here."

Cal moved back into the woodline and swiveled his shotgun sling. Izzy watched him fade into the foliage.

The young gaucho with the rifle drew the Mauser from his saddlebag. They trotted up to the riderless horse before noticing their partner lying on the ground with a hatchet stuck in his back. They looked around, nervously scanning the area, and the young gaucho dismounted with his rifle. The older gaucho reached for his cell phone.

Calixto stepped from the tree line and fired a broadside from the twelve-gauge into the ribs of the leader. The older gaucho cried out as Cal instantly pumped, aimed, and fired again. The second shotgun shell tore into the younger gaucho's chest, blowing open a huge hole and knocking him backward before he could fire the Mauser.

Cal raced back to his sister. Izzy tried to stand, a little shaky, and reached out to grab at Calixto. She pulled her brother close, burying her face into his neck, and started to cry. All the tears that Isabel had held in check, kept at bay for nearly two weeks, suddenly burst forth like from a break in the dike. She collapsed against Lozen, drained, her body shaking in a huge cathartic tremble of emotion.

"Can you move?" asked Cal.

She nodded into his neck, gripping him tight, needing the physical security of her brother's presence.

"Can you ride?"

"Yes, I think so. But don't leave me."

"I won't," said Cal, "but we've got to move, Iz. They made phone calls, and someone probably heard the gunshots." He gently pulled her head back. "We've got to go. Do you understand?"

Isabel half smiled, happy to turn the decisions over to her big brother as the tears continued to flow. "Yes."

Calixto picked Izzy up and carried her to the closest horse. Her shin was bruised where the wooden bola balls struck. Her feet were raw and blistered. She had multiple cuts and scrapes on her skin and a nasty gash on the bottom of her arch. Her dress was torn and filthy. Izzy slid her bare feet into the stirrups and took the reins.

Cal turned as Izzy grabbed at his free hand.

"I knew you would come for me," she said, looking down at her brother. "I knew it."

Lozen patted her hand and moved away. He checked the three gauchos on the ground, searched them, and smashed their cell phones. Then he retrieved his hatchet and the other two horses. He mounted one and took the other by the reins. "You okay?"

"Yes," answered Izzy, managing another smile. Her confidence increased with each moment.

Cal winked. "Stay close."

Chapter 132

Buenos Aires, Argentina

CALIXTO DROVE THE Range Rover southeast along the Ruta Nacional Eight toward Buenos Aires. He took his time, fighting the urge to move too fast. Drawing attention now would undermine all his previous efforts.

It had taken them forty minutes on horseback to circle back through the tree line and skirt the pampas toward the hidden vehicle. Izzy held up, dutifully obeying Cal's instructions. Fortunately the trek proceeded without incident, and they were able to secure the car and get away from the estancia.

Cal felt good—a little lucky, but satisfied. Lozen had found and rescued his sister, and though banged up, Isabel appeared in working order. He wondered what transpired during her captivity, but she would share that experience on her own schedule. Calixto pushed the worst fears from his mind.

For Izzy's part, she seemed relieved—a little jumpy, but overall, almost content. She refused his suggestion to lie down in the rear seat and nap. Instead, his sister curled up in the bucket seat to his right, where she could see Cal and hold his hand. She gripped it fiercely. Several times Lozen needed to pull the hand away to attend to driving, and Iz instantly sat up and opened her eyes. Calixto soon realized she needed the physical touch, the closeness, to feel secure. He would extend his hand; she would grip it and fall back to sleep by his side.

Lozen pulled out his cell as he drove and dialed David Shields.

"Hey, where are you?" asked the DIA officer. He sounded relieved.

"East."

"You okay?"

"We're okay," said Cal, smiling to himself at the play on words.

"Really?" asked Shields.

"Affirmative."

There was a pause, and then a slight exhalation over the phone before Shields spoke again. "Thank God. Both parties?"

"No, I'll need some help on that. Is there any way to bring us in?"

"Yes, but once we play that card, if we don't control both packages, the diplomatic channel will close. It's better to beg forgiveness than to ask for permission."

"Understood," said Calixto.

"Are you ambulatory?"

"Yes."

"And the first package?"

"Affirmative, but needs some attention."

"Okay…" Shields took a couple of minutes to think before continuing. "Can you hold up for a few hours?"

"I'll figure something out," said Cal.

"How far east are you?"

"Lots of folks, hide in plain sight." That told the DIA officer that Cal and his sister were near the population center of Buenos Aires.

"Good. It will be tricky, but I may have a contact."

"Double-screen your source; last time I had visitors."

"I know," said Shields. "How's the count progressing?"

"You don't want to know," said Cal, thinking of the dead Argentineans in his wake.

"Screw them," replied Shields in a sarcastic tone. "They picked the fight."

"You catching flak?"

"Nothing I can't handle. Same shit, different day."

"I'll await your call." Lozen clicked off his cell phone. He felt better. Cal needed to find a quiet place to lay up. Preferably one where Izzy could take a hot bath, and he could get her some food, rest, and attend to her wounds. Cal also needed to steal some Argentinean license plates for the Range Rover.

Calixto looked over at his little sister. Izzy breathed in short, shallow breaths, her eyes closed, her grip firm. His extended arm was falling asleep, but he dared not pull it away.

Chapter 133

Buenos Aires, Argentina

THE PHYSICIAN ENTERED the bedroom on the second floor of the gentlemen's club. His practice of medicine had changed over the years, no longer taking on the full range of patients, but rather catering to a few, very wealthy clients. One of the clients had special needs in that he employed many people. Often, these people in turn became the doctor's actual patients, but the compensation always came from the wealthy client.

In the beginning, the client manipulated the doctor's principles in small ways and offset any hesitancy with extra cash. However, it didn't take long for him to identify the physician's weakness. Soon the client corrupted the doctor with copious amounts of money and perquisites.

Sandy lay handcuffed to the bed, watching as the physician crossed the room. She was awake, wearing makeup, dressed in a short skirt, a plunging V-neck blouse, and glossy high heels. There was a wide gap of bare midriff exposed between the skirt and the blouse, and more bare skin showing from her naked legs.

"How are you doing, Sanchia?" asked the doctor as he sat on the edge of her bed.

"My name is Sandy."

He patted her arm reassuringly and then felt for a pulse before answering, "No, it is Sanchia. You must remember that. Things will go easier." He felt her forehead. "How are you feeling?"

"A little sick," said Sandy.

The doctor opened his medical bag and pulled out several items, lining them up on the side table: a glass vial filled with liquid ketamine hydrochloride, a syringe, and some alcohol swabs. "That's normal; the feeling in your stomach will pass." He started to prep her forearm for an injection, swabbing with alcohol, wrapping her bicep with a thin rubber hose.

Sandy pulled at the shackles as she looked at the physician, imploring him with her eyes. She spoke softly. "No, please, no more needles." She started to tremble.

"This will help you adjust," said the doctor.

"Please," said Sandy as her lips quivered, "I can't think, but I'll be good."

"I know you will," said the physician in a reassuring voice. He poked her arm with the syringe and injected the clear liquid. Sandy started to cry.

"Shh," said the doctor, "be strong. You have a special guest tonight. If you cry, you'll smudge your makeup."

The doctor stood, packed his medical bag, and exited the room.

Downstairs, the club was in full sexual overdrive. Scantily clad strippers served cocktails and flirted. Several naked women pole danced on stage, and well-dressed men sipped overpriced champagne. Pesos flew in every direction. The doctor approached the club manager and whispered in his ear. Then the manager smiled and wove his way to the rear of the club.

He approached a special VIP section on a raised dais, marked with a sign and a velvet rope. Several men sat on the heavy furniture, drinking expensive cognac and smoking large Cuban cigars. Two very attractive women in clingy dresses hovered nearby.

The club manager stooped beside a fifty-year-old man in a comfortable leather chair lazily rolling a Cohiba between his fingers. A shock of thick white hair and a full mustache set the man apart. He drew the attention of the crowd.

"Comisario," said the manager quietly, "tonight we have added something special to our inventory."

The mustached man raised an eye curiously at the manager. He didn't show the least concern about being addressed by his police inspector's rank. He flicked an ash from his cigar. "Special? I thought you told me they are all special, Cortez." He squinted an eye at the club manager in jest. Then he broke into a hearty laugh.

The manager grinned before continuing, "Sí, Comisario, something quite special, different. She is very pretty, with excellent breasts," he motioned with both hands, "and succulent thighs." He made a smacking sound with his lips.

The police inspector listened politely before asking, "Is she pliable?"

"Sí, Comisario. She is still a little headstrong," answered the manager, "but in a few days, we will transfer her to the Blue Boliche."

Mention of the very expensive club in the pricey Recoleta neighborhood intrigued the inspector. He brushed at his thick white hair. "They expect her to bring a hefty fee?"

"Sí, Comisario, but of course for you, there is no charge this evening."

The police inspector spread his bushy mustache in a wide grin. "I think I would like to try this special young inventory."

"It would be our pleasure," said the club manager. "Enjoy your cigar. I will make the arrangements."

Chapter 134

Villa Adelina, Argentina

Calixto located an inexpensive roadside hostel in Villa Adelina. It was a gritty, unremarkable town twelve kilometers outside of Buenos Aires that fit his needs: quiet, unassuming, and inexpensive.

They had put sixty miles between themselves and the estancia. He had stopped in Villa Adelina primarily because of its proximity to the big city and also because it was on no one's radar. Cal needed quiet time to regroup and allow David Shields to work his resources.

Izzy stepped from the bathroom and presented herself to Calixto. She had bathed, brushed her hair, and rummaged through Cal's duffel bag for some clean clothes.

Standing six feet tall and weighing in at one hundred eighty-five pounds, Lozen was lean but sinewy. Nonetheless, Isabel couldn't offset the difference of four inches and over fifty pounds in their frames. She selected tight spandex athletic shorts, a collared golf shirt, and a pair of shower shoes. Despite Izzy's best effort to nip, tuck, tie, and pin Cal's clothes to fit her torso, she looked discombobulated as she stood in front of the bed draped in excess material. "What do you think?" she asked, standing for inspection with a serious expression.

Lozen studied his sister for a moment in silence, but then Cal could hold back no longer and he broke into a spontaneous laugh. "You look ridiculous."

At first, Izzy acted embarrassed. Then she turned and gazed back at the bathroom mirror. Her expression became one of humor. She flopped unceremoniously on the edge of the bed and joined in his laughter. "I always wondered why Mom never gave me any of your hand-me-downs to wear," said Isabel.

Calixto sat in a chair across from the bed, facing his sister. He laid the shotgun across his lap. "She was afraid you would become a tomboy. Now we know you wouldn't have." Cal leaned forward. "Do you wish you had a big sister?" he asked.

Isabel's eyes twinkled as she considered the question. Then Izzy smiled her natural smile. It was both rare and arresting. "No," she said, "I think I lucked out in the sibling department."

A short silence ensued before Cal started verbally checking off their itinerary needs. "We need to treat that foot, get food and water, clothes for you, and then…"

"We have to go back for Sandy," said his sister.

"I know."

"That cabin was on a ranch?" asked Izzy.

"Yes. We are in Argentina, but Sandy's not at the cabin. I was there."

"Where is she?"

"I don't know. When did you see her last?" asked Lozen.

"Just before I escaped," replied Izzy. She gave her brother a solemn look. "They hurt her, Cal. They did bad things."

He nodded before asking, "Rape?"

"Yes, repeatedly. Who are these people?"

"Criminals. Mobsters."

"Mafia?"

"Yes, like that."

"What do they want with us?"

"Money. Forced prostitution. People pay to have sex with pretty women." She shivered before Cal asked, "Are you okay?"

Isabel considered the question, searching for Cal's meaning. It was the elephant in the room for her big brother. "Yes," she answered, "but I wasn't raped. I was lucky. In the beginning, there was lots of touching and intimidation. When we got to the cabin, it changed." Tears started to flow as Izzy recalled her interactions with Patsy Bellocco. "He wanted me," said Izzy. "The guy in charge, he blamed me for Sandy's rape. He said it was my fault. She begged me to stop them."

Isabel quivered as she relayed the events and the sexual abuse of her roommate. Cal sensed a touch of guilt, which of course made no sense. He stood, walked over to the bed, and sat beside Izzy. Lozen threw his arm over her shoulders. She poured out the story as Calixto pulled her close.

"I didn't know what to do," said Isabel, "I was confused. I was scared. He told Sandy that only I could make it stop, but I wasn't even there. I had to *want* him. He put ideas in her head, and they kept raping her. When they brought her back, Sandy was in a bad way. I knew I was next. I had to try something." Izzy buried her head into Cal's shoulder. Her despair was evident. "We have to find her, Cal. We can't leave without Sandy."

"We won't," replied Lozen, laying his sister back on the bed and covering Izzy with a blanket. "We'll find her. You rest."

Chapter 135

DAVID SHIELDS ENTERED the lobby of the Ritz-Carlton Hotel in Santiago and turned right toward the bar. He passed through the double doors into a very masculine décor: mahogany wood, leather chairs, indirect lighting around circular marble-top tables. He saw Becki Reynolds sitting on a divan in the corner. She waved.

Shields took a seat across the coffee table from his CIA counterpart. "I'm surprised you picked here," said David.

"When you called, I figured the least I could do would be to meet somewhere you felt comfortable."

"So you picked an earthy British décor where I could smoke a cigar?" said Shields with a smirk.

"Military types are very rugged. Special Forces especially so."

"You've got me all figured out," replied David.

"Not at all. I just wanted to set the mold, so that I could help you break it."

Shields leaned forward with a curious expression on his face. "Which is your way of saying?"

"Neither of us is necessarily what the other thinks," said Becki.

The two intelligence officers studied each other across the coffee table before ordering lunch. They made small talk and traded war stories until their food arrived. Then Shields watched in chagrin as Becki dug into a thick cheeseburger, French fries, and a Newcastle Brown Ale. The slim lady attacked the meal with gusto, appearing every bit a woman who hadn't eaten in a week.

"I take it you don't have a cholesterol problem," said David as he picked at his Caesar salad.

"Lucky. Good genes. Last physical, it was one fifty-two. The Agency physicians shake their heads."

"You eat a lot of red meat?"

"I lived in Argentina," said Reynolds, pausing to emphasize the country. "I ate steak every day."

David squinted through his beer glass before sipping at the pilsner. "You were posted to the Buenos Aires station?" asked Shields.

"Three years. Good duty. Fun city."

The DIA officer leaned back in his seat and replied, "It's starting to make sense."

"What's that?" asked Reynolds.

"The meeting."

"Lunch was your idea," said Becki.

"Yes, but you threw up a flag."

"I sensed a need."

"Would your boss approve?" asked David.

Becki sipped at her brown ale and shrugged. "Probably not. The chief's an old suit. He has thirty years at the Agency. This is his third posting to Santiago. His relationships go back many years. It's hard for him to be objective."

"Would help cause you a problem?"

"Only if it disrupted protocols. My responsibility ends at the border. The buzz I hear is that the issue moved east. Is that true?"

Shields hesitated.

"David," said the CIA officer, "I'm not playing you."

Shields bit his lip and spoke in a quiet voice. "I need a contact in-country and a reliable safe house."

"What's the current status?" asked Becki.

"He retrieved the sister. He needs help locating the roommate. We can't bring them in piecemeal. We need to play one card for everyone."

"Wow. That's news."

"Hot off the press," replied Shields.

"Your guy is pretty resourceful."

"Yes. Can you help?"

Becki gave David a poker face before answering. "I think so. I'll call you."

Shields reached for the lunch tab. Becki covered his hand. "It's on me, David. Langley's the senior service."

Shields stood and looked down at Reynolds. "Quick question?"

"Sure," said Becki.

"Why are you doing this?"

The CIA officer looked up at her defense department counterpart with a philosophical expression. "Well, as naïve as it sounds," said Reynolds, "some of us got into this line of work to do good. Let's just say that I have a thing about people who exploit women."

Chapter 136

Buenos Aires, Argentina

PATSY ENTERED THE rear of the antique shop in San Telmo. By design, he never kept a static headquarters for himself. Bellocco viewed all of the city, even the country and the continent, as his domain. However, over the years, he did find value in maintaining a quiet, protected location in the heart of the old neighborhood. For this reason, his brother-in-law spent a few days every week maintaining loose office hours in the back room of a legitimate business.

The 'ndrina boss stormed through the door and sat behind the desk. A black patch covered his left eye. His split lip was healing, and the facial sutures had been removed. Patsy was in a rage, unable to control his volcanic temper. This put everyone on edge, but as was typically the case, Bellocco only discussed important issues directly with his inner circle. In the world of the 'Ndrengheta, that meant blood relatives.

"What happened in Mendoza?" asked Patsy.

"Three dead," answered Ettore. "The old woman, her son, and one employee."

"Theft of our inventory?"

"No, Quintino. The employee was stabbed in the heart with a sharp instrument and found on the floor. The other two, however, were strapped into chairs."

"Torture?"

"Minimal. But it appears they were held captive and then executed."

"How?" asked Patsy. He sought a message in the methodology, as was customary in mob hits.

"Clean, efficient," said Ettore. "It happened very quickly: a sharp weapon driven down into the carotid, under the clavicle." The brother-in-law pointed at his own neck by way of explanation. "They bled out in seconds."

"They didn't suffer?"

"Very little. Our man in Mendoza said they would have gone into shock right away."

Bellocco considered the information in silence. Violence was part of Patsy's profession, but this was not typical of his experience. No theft of valuable goods. No torture. No atrocity to the victims. He was a little confused at the lack of a symbolic message.

"Did you contact Santiago?"

"Sí, Quintino. They said the shipment was delivered intact. They questioned their transport team. Apparently, everything proceeded on schedule."

"The transport team was the last to see the old woman and the men?"

"Sí, but the inventory is secured at the storage facility at the bodega. Nothing is missing."

"It doesn't make sense," said Patsy, more to himself than the other three men in the room. He leaned back in the chair. "What else?"

"Your estancia," said Beppe, speaking for the first time. "Three gauchos are dead."

"Dead?" The news surprised the 'ndrina boss.

"Sí, Quintino," said the nephew, continuing the explanation. "They didn't return at sunset. Their horses were found in the woodline, near the connecting road."

Bellocco's face tightened as he touched at the black eye patch. "What happened?"

"We're not sure," said Beppe. "Their bodies were discovered at the far end of the estancia, a large distance from their horses."

"Bodies?" repeated Patsy.

"Two were killed at close range with a shotgun. The third was killed with a sharp weapon to the back. One of our ranch hands said the wound resembled some type of axe blade."

It had been a long time since anyone had dared to challenge Bellocco. It incensed him. Someone actually killed *his* employees on *his* property.

"Also," said Beppe, "there was a phone call made by the senior gaucho. He said some type of tracker was sent from Santiago."

"A tracker?"

"Sí, Quintino. To search for the woman."

"The putana?"

"Sí," replied Beppe.

"How would anyone there know that she escaped?"

The nephew didn't have an answer.

Patsy stood and turned toward the wall. His thoughts wandered. "This makes no sense," said Bellocco. His back was to the other three men as he spoke. "But somehow it is related." Patsy whirled on his heels and pointed at Lino. "How many men do you have on the street?"

"At least a dozen," said the second nephew.

"You take charge of finding this putana. You go out to the estancia. Find out what happened. I want her. I have a score to settle."

"Sí, Quintino," said Lino.

Patsy pointed at Beppe and said, "You go out to Mendoza. Take some people. Check the inventory. Check the story."

"Sí, Pasquale," answered Beppe.

Bellocco touched his brother-in-law on the forearm. "You must call our associates in Santiago. Press them. Something does not add up. They know more than they are telling us."

Finally Patsy sat back down behind the desk. He was quiet for a moment, and then in a display of anger, he slammed his fist down on the wooden surface and swept his arm sideways in a horizontal motion. Everything on the desktop went tumbling to the floor. "I am going to hurt someone."

Chapter 137

CALIXTO PACED FIVE steps behind his sister, pretending to be strangers, as they approached the corner of Avenida Quintana. Every few meters she turned and glanced over her shoulder to assure her brother was still in sight.

It had taken David Shields a day and a half to get back to Cal with a point of contact. Calixto used the time well. Their bodies needed rest and decompression. Every couple of hours, Izzy would suddenly sit up and nervously twist in bed until she spotted Cal sitting in the chair facing the door. When their eyes met, Isabel would lie back down and fall asleep.

The next morning Cal redressed Izzy's foot wound and his thigh injury using the stolen first-aid kit from the farmhouse near Santiago. Then they ate a quick breakfast on the run and went clothes shopping for Izzy. To her credit, she followed his instructions: clean underwear, sensible walking shoes, a couple pairs of cotton or denim pants, and several pullover blouses. This was about function, not fashion. Toiletries and a makeup kit followed. When the DIA officer finally called, they were rested and refreshed. Izzy had started to get her bounce back.

At the corner, a huge, century-old ombu tree signaled the coffee shop. Isabel turned left and entered La Biela Café. It was a beautiful day, enticing many of the patrons to take advantage of the sidewalk tables overlooking the plaza and the Church of Nuestra Señora del Pilar. This left the inside tables only half full.

Isabel strolled through the large coffee shop, selecting an empty seat facing the rear. Cal walked straight past his sister and chose a table near the back facing the front door. They were separated by five tables, but had direct eye contact. Then Lozen tied a red kerchief to his left forearm, exactly at the elbow, and opened a local newspaper. He ordered a coffee.

Several patrons entered the coffee shop and selected seats in various locations. It was a popular café, drawing an eclectic crowd of artists, politicians, tourists, businessmen, and racing enthusiasts. Cal sized everyone up as they entered. After twenty minutes, a tall, elegantly dressed woman in her forties, with long blond hair and tasteful jewelry, appeared at the door. She hesitated and removed her sunglasses, making it a point to survey the room. The woman spotted Lozen in the back and whispered to the headwaiter. Then she walked the length of the coffee shop past several empty tables and stopped in front of Cal. Their eyes met, and Lozen folded his newspaper and set it atop his lap to hide the Belgium Hi-Power pistol.

"Is this seat taken?" she asked in formal Spanish.

"Not if you drink coffee," replied Cal.

"I prefer tea."

"So does Becki."

They had just exchanged bona fides. The open newspaper and the red kerchief tied specifically at the elbow were far-recognition signals. The folded newspaper was near-recognition, and the dialogue was challenge-password confirmation. She sat.

Everything about the woman was polished: her speech, her mannerisms, her attire. She folded her sunglasses and waited for her tea. It gave Calixto the opportunity to take a long, hard look.

"Not what you expected," said the woman.

Cal's face broke into an easy smile. "I never know what to expect."

"How do you know Becki?"

"I don't," said Lozen.

"But you need help."

"Yes."

"From what I understand, you've caused quite a stir. You've managed to irritate some very powerful people."

Cal gazed at the woman without expression. She was not attractive in the traditional sense, but every hair was in place. The woman was aware, perfectly coiffed, and under control. "It's personal," said Cal.

"Yes. I understand it's your sister and one other."

"That's correct. We need to find the friend."

"Easier said than done. The man that holds the friend is ruthless, and he has people everywhere."

Cal shrugged without comment.

"You don't scare easily?" she said.

"I don't have the luxury."

The elegant woman took a deep look into Calixto's eyes. Then, very slowly, she turned in her seat and scanned the other patrons in the café. When she spotted Isabel, she stopped. Their eyes met, and then Izzy looked down at the magazine she was pretending to read. The woman turned back to face Cal. "You brought your sister?"

Lozen realized there was no point in denial. The woman met the screens, and he needed help. "Yes, she refuses to be separated."

"I see. She looks nothing like you."

"Same mother, different father. How did you know?"

"She's beautiful. It's just the kind of young lady that your adversary would want."

There was a short lull in the conversation as the woman sipped her tea.

"Will you help?" asked Calixto.

"Of course. It will take some digging, but we'll find your sister's friend. Nothing in this city can be hidden for very long if one knows where to look." She took another sip of tea before asking, "Shall we get started?"

"Yes," said Cal. He laid several Argentine peso notes on the table and slipped his pistol between the folds of the newspaper.

The woman noticed the movement under the table but said nothing. She stood and spoke in a quiet voice. "I have a driver waiting. Meet me outside with your sister." Then she extended her hand to Calixto and said, "My name is Daniella Pedraza Lepes. My friends call me Dan."

Chapter 138

Santiago, Chile

THE TELEPHONE RANG once, and David Shields plucked the receiver from the cradle. "Shields."

"Meet me," said the familiar voice.

"When?"

"Now. I'll grab the joe."

David cradled his phone and stood. He thought for a moment and then nodded at his fellow intel officer. "I'll be back in ten."

Downstairs, sitting outside in a shaded portion of the embassy grounds, was the FBI legal attaché. The agent grinned and offered David the second cup of coffee. "We need to stop meeting like this," said the agent.

"It sounded important."

"It is." The FBI agent consulted his wristwatch. "Twenty-seven minutes ago, the CIA station chief charged into our wing followed by an entourage and proceeded to berate the DEA country supervisor on protocol."

"Protocol?" said Shields. "Regarding what?"

"Covert operations."

"Whoa." Shields leaned back and raised a hand. "He actually said that?"

"He did. Then he made it clear that the DEA would immediately cease and desist from any line of inquiry regarding the *Empresa*."

David lowered his voice. "He identified the organization by name?"

"Distinctly," replied the agent.

"How did that go over?"

"Like a bomb," said the agent. He paused to blow on his hot coffee.

Shields leaned forward. "What did the super say?"

"The super kept his cool and explained to the station chief that the DEA could not comment on current investigations."

"And then?" asked David.

"And then the station chief went berserk. He started screaming and pointing his finger, threatening, promising all manner of recriminations. He emphasized to the supervisor that this was a 'career decision.' Then he flat-out ordered the super to spike the investigation."

David could see a hint of mischief in the agent's eye. He was enjoying the retelling of the events. "And then what happened?"

"After listening to this tirade, the DEA super stood, glanced around the office, and then calmly told the station chief in a polite tone to fuck off."

Shields coughed in surprise while swallowing a sip of his coffee. They sat in silence for a moment. "I'm a bit thrown by the station chief casually using the term *Empresa*," said David.

"So am I," replied the FBI agent. He leaned forward. "But then again, maybe that was the point."

David squinted. "Give up a known to protect an unknown?"

The FBI agent shrugged. "In the big picture, we are all pawns."

"You think they'll go after my guy?" asked Shields.

"If they have something to hide," said the agent, "then anyone in the wrong place at the right time is expendable."

Chapter 139

December 14, 2006
Gladwyne, Pennsylvania

Peter Burdis rolled his wheelchair back to the picture window to enjoy the late afternoon sun. "As you get older," said their host, "you come to appreciate the little things."

Mike and John followed the mansion owner to the far side of the large study.

Burdis coughed and then continued the narrative as he gazed at his expansive, manicured lawn. "No one wanted to deal with the problem. They all had a reason to put their heads in the sand and hope it would go away."

"But it didn't," said Mike, taking a seat next to the cripple.

"No. Volunteers at the university created a website. The blogging was incessant. The disappearance of the two students became a cause célèbre, fueled by the energy and computer savvy of youth. Every one of the mother's recorded interviews was captured on YouTube."

"It spread to official circles," said John.

"They couldn't ignore it," replied Burdis. "Reporters from the mainline media focused on the more nefarious aspects of the story: the cover-ups, people with something to hide. A criminal organization called the Empresa and its ties to generals still in power; the connection to the School of the Americas, Italian mobsters, Mexican drug lords. The scoop had all the earmarks of a great international conspiracy, with the United States at the center of the vortex."

"The worst of all worlds," said Mike.

"And the brother was loose in Buenos Aires," replied Burdis.

"Was he their greatest fear?" asked John.

Burdis hesitated before responding, "No. The concern was that by exposing the Empresa, someone could make the connection back to the contingency fund."

"The Agency nest egg hidden from Congress?" asked Mike.

"The same," replied Burdis.

Chapter 140

Buenos Aires, Argentina

THEY SAT AROUND a kitchen table in the private living quarters of a boutique hotel in Monserrat. The small establishment was owned by Daniella Pedraza.

Cal and Izzy faced the elegant woman and one other man. He looked hard, like someone immersed in the seamier side of life. She identified him simply as Sebastian and said he had her confidence.

"Understand the nuance," said Daniella. "Prostitution itself is legal in Argentina. Nothing prohibits a woman from selling her own body. But the marketing of sex, coercion, or providing a place of prostitution is illegal."

"He hides it?" asked Calixto.

"Yes. Strip clubs are legal. He owns several. There are ways to work the system, and he has protection." She spoke in a matter-of-fact tone.

"Payoffs?"

"Of course. He uses the second floor of his club in Palermo to develop new talent."

"Develop?" said Cal, focusing on her choice of words.

"Not everyone is a willing participant. Some need to be broken."

Lozen looked at Daniella before asking, "How?"

"He medicates them. Then he offers their bodies to a regular group of guests for free."

"Rape," said Izzy in a quiet voice.

"Yes," answered Daniella. She looked at Calixto's sister, realizing what Isabel had been through, but also that she was the least worldly of the four adults sitting at the table. Nonetheless, she offered Izzy the same level of respect as the others. "We have it on good information that there is a very attractive new girl, named Sanchia, being developed for the Blue Boliche. She is an American."

"She's held captive in Palermo?" asked Cal.

"Sí, and guarded," replied Daniella. "She will not be in a clear mind. Will she recognize you?"

Lozen considered the question for a moment. "I've met her a couple of times. She would certainly know my name."

"Getting you up to the second floor will be a challenge in itself. Will she recognize you?" asked Daniella again, pressing the issue.

There was a brief silence before Isabel spoke. "She'll recognize me."

"No," said Cal with a wave of his hand.

"If she's drugged, you need me," said Izzy.

"It's too dangerous."

"You can't leave without me," replied Izzy.

Calixto realized that Isabel still feared their separation. Daniella hid them in a twin room overlooking the garden, with a private bath. Their meals arrived by room service, and a physician called to attend to their wounds. Izzy only relaxed if Cal was in the same room. Nonetheless, Lozen sensed a touch of guilt creep into his sister's decision. Isabel felt responsible for Sandy.

Daniella leaned back in her seat and spoke. "Your brother is right. Someone could recognize you."

"I don't know anyone in Buenos Aires."

"Who saw you at the estancia?"

"The guy in charge and two younger men. He spoke to them in a different language. It wasn't Spanish. It almost sounded Italian."

A knowing expression crossed Daniella's face. "It sounds like the nephews. They're a couple of hyenas off the boat from Calabria. They would know you?"

"Yes."

"You realize that you harmed him."

"I could tell," replied Izzy.

"The rumor is, he's blinded in one eye," replied Daniella.

The information caught Isabel by surprise, but Calixto was nonplussed. He said, "Which means that he's out for blood. It's too dangerous."

"You need me," said Izzy, "I'm the only one Sandy will definitely recognize."

Daniella threw up her hands and leaned back in her chair. "You two will have to work this out."

Sebastian spoke for the first time. "The police are no help. He has them in his pocket. We are operating alone."

There was a moment of silence before Izzy looked directly at Daniella and asked, "Why are you willing to help us?"

Calixto reached over and touched his sister's wrist. Daniella exchanged a curious look with Sebastian and then Calixto. They all looked surprised at the question. Then the woman focused on Isabel with a sincere expression.

"The man that threatened you, that is holding your friend, took something that was mine. I want it back."

Chapter 141

THE STRETCH LIMOUSINE pulled up to the front door of the Encantar Gentlemen's Club in Palermo. Calixto and Izzy stepped to the sidewalk dressed for the occasion. It had been well planned.

Daniella Pedraza knew all the angles. The crowd was pulsing, and they were expected. It was prime time; word had been passed and money flowed to ensure they gained entry. Isabel was a hot new model from Venezuela, in town with her manager, fresh off a major photo shoot in Rio de Janiero.

They looked the part, and more importantly, there was no way to disavow the story. It worked because the club manager, Cortez, saw all the signals and wanted to believe the spin. He wanted the notoriety.

Daniella dressed and coached them. Lozen stood in a smart Armani suit, a silk shirt, with dashes of gold bling and his hair swept back into a thick French part. The attire and Cal's natural ethnicity helped him pass for a trendy South American.

Isabel proved even more fun for the elegant woman to prepare. Izzy was already tall, slender, and beautiful. So Daniella accentuated Izzy's tight curves and shapely legs with a short, formfitting, backless, single-piece dress. She added spike heels, stage jewelry, and glossy makeup to darken her features and long hair. In many ways, Izzy didn't look like Izzy. She looked striking and glamorous, but different.

Sebastian led the way past the doorman as Cal escorted his sister. Cortez greeted the group and seated the three at a special table to the side. They could easily see the dancers onstage and, in turn, be seen by the club's other male patrons. Sebastian ordered Cristal champagne, and the three eased back into a private, whispered conversation. Two men in the employ of Sebastian repositioned themselves in the crowd. Both had arrived early to scope out the club and the procedures.

Daniella was an astute lady. She realized rather early in the process that Izzy was more focused than most women her age. The sister was quite mature for a student of twenty-one. However, she also displayed a layer of innocence. Pedraza needed to transform Isabel into a flashy, superficial, self-indulgent party girl. But Izzy was too self-conscious of her looks to pose. So Daniella pushed Isabel, drilled her, on how to prance like a model, fling her hair in a wavy gesture, and flash her pearly teeth when she turned her head.

Fifteen minutes elapsed, time that offered all the male patrons the chance to check out the three-person group huddled to the side. Gradually the eyes floated away from Izzy back to the stage.

Cal and Sebastian reviewed their plan. Lozen then compared the actual layout to the memorized sketch. Sebastian nudged Isabel to remind her to smile and laugh for effect. Izzy settled into her role in the operation. She was a stage prop and a major part of the plan.

Another two minutes elapsed before Sebastian stood and walked to the men's room in the rear. One of his two men followed from across the club. Ten minutes later, Sebastian returned to their table. He looked at his watch. It was almost midnight, and the club was full, following the late dinner habits preferred by most Argentineans.

"There is one man at the bottom of the stairs," said Sebastian. "Another is in the hallway on the second floor. The manager has taken two guests upstairs over the last hour. Neither man has returned. This is as good a chance as we will have."

Cal looked at Izzy and asked, "Are you ready?"

His sister swallowed and nodded. Then she stood, and with an irritated scowl, she snapped at Lozen in a brusque, fiery tone. Her voice carried to the crowd seated nearby. Izzy tossed her hair back and, with a sway to her hips and a pronounced attitude, strutted toward the rear of the club.

Chapter 142

Buenos Aires, Argentina

IZZY STARTED THE diversion. Buenos Aires effused a certain vibe in its sexually charged nightlife. Headstrong Latinos, if attractive, were granted a certain latitude. Daniella had convinced Calixto that his sister's presence was integral to the rescue plan. Just as important, the woman understood Izzy's need to be involved and to not be separated from her brother.

Cal gave his sister a five-step head start. Then he stood and followed.

Up ahead, at the bottom of the rear staircase, a bulky security guard in a suit with a headset protected access to the second floor. Izzy nodded as she approached; suddenly the man's hand shot out and blocked her route.

"What?" said Izzy in a frustrated tone.

"Esta prohibito," answered the man.

"I need to use the toilet."

The man motioned across the rear of the club to the other corner just as Calixto caught up to his sister.

"I need privacy," said Izzy to the guard. She pointed at Cal as she began to climb the stairs. "Keep him away."

With a deft motion Lozen stuffed a roll of pesos into the security man's hand and spoke in a low voice. "She's difficult—you know the type. We don't want trouble. She'll make a scene. Let me get her."

The guard noted that Izzy had already climbed halfway up the stairs. "Get her and bring her down. The toilets are that way." He pointed across the club. Then he called the security guard posted on the second floor to warn him.

Calixto reached the top step just as Izzy was confronted by the second security guard. The man grabbed Isabel's wrist, and she protested. Then Izzy pulled her arm away. Cal approached with a wide grin and a nonconfrontational demeanor. He apologized for Izzy's attitude. She started berating the guard and pointing her finger as Lozen slipped his right hand beneath his suit coat. Izzy snapped her fingers, whirled on her stiletto heels, and started strutting toward the far end of the hallway. It forced the guard to turn and shift his attention from Cal.

In a second, Calixto tugged the Browning Hi-Power from the small of his back and swung it sideways at the man's forehead. The barrel cracked the guard above his ear, he stumbled, and Cal hit him again. The man collapsed. Then Cal frisked the security guard, removed his firearm, and yanked off his radio headset.

Izzy froze, a bit stunned by the ferocity of the attack. Calixto pointed to the far end of the hallway. "Move," said Cal.

Chapter 143

Buenos Aires, Argentina

IZZY SPRINTED DOWN the corridor. The game was on, it was real, and people got hurt. Her heart thumped in her chest. Izzy feared many things: being recaptured, her brother getting injured, and not finding Sandy. She worried about doing something wrong. Thankfully, Cal had forced them to rehearse at the boutique hotel. Again and again, they walked through a mock-up of the club's second floor. There were six bedrooms upstairs, some with private baths. All were used at various times to detain captives and to entertain guests.

She opened the last door on the left. It was empty, except for a bed, several chairs, and a toilet. There were no people.

Across the hall, Cal thrust open the second door. Same thing. They worked their pattern in reverse, a long oriental runner covering their footsteps as they moved back toward the stairs.

The third door was locked. Izzy knocked, speaking in a loud, insistent voice. A minute passed, and then the door cracked open. The face of a short, fat man with a receding hairline, dressed in a bathrobe, peered at Izzy. His eyes opened wide.

Cal reached over his sister's shoulder with an open hand and pushed the man backward by his face. The man backpedaled in fear, and then he saw the gun.

"Not a word," said Lozen.

The fat man swallowed and nodded. Izzy moved to the side of the bed and looked down at a naked young girl in a drug-induced state. She shook her head. Cal motioned, and they exited.

The fourth door was unlocked and the room empty. As was the fifth door. They moved fast, having rehearsed the layout on the second floor of the club countless times. Speed was crucial.

Calixto checked the fallen security guard and then signaled to Izzy. The sixth door was locked. She knocked and spoke in a normal tone. A gruff voice told her to go away. Cal hid behind the wall as Isabel pounded hard and spoke in a loud, clear demand.

The door snapped open from inside and exposed a husky man with thick white hair and a matching mustache. "What?" replied the Comisario. He stood unabashed in a long bath towel, looking at Isabel. "You dare to disturb me?"

Izzy stepped sideways, and Cal snapped his free hand forward from the hip. He caught the police inspector's throat with a flat horizontal thrust. The man gagged, gripping at his neck as Cal pushed him backward into the room. Then Calixto waved the nine-millimeter in an ominous fashion.

"You fool," said the Comisario between labored breaths. "Do you know who I am?"

"Silencio," replied Cal. He motioned for Izzy to approach the bed, where a naked woman rolled her head from side to side.

The police inspector coughed and sputtered as he tried to speak. Isabel reached over and held up the head of the drugged woman. She looked at Cal with a grimace. "No."

"You're sure?"

"Yes," said Izzy.

Cal motioned to leave as the Comisario stepped forward, pointing at Izzy, threatening her. She whirled, and in an uncharacteristic moment, spit in his face. Lozen raised the muzzle of the pistol, and the police inspector stepped back.

"Let's go," said Calixto.

In the hall, they turned left just as the first security guard from the bottom of the stairs appeared with the club manager. The jig was up. Cal dropped into a balanced shooter's stance, aimed, and squeezed off two rounds. The Parabellum bullets hit the guard center mass, tearing a hole in his chest and knocking him backward. Cortez, the manager, turned and scrambled down the stairs, screaming over the music.

"Don't run," said Cal, "but stay close."

He gripped Izzy with his free hand while hiding the pistol behind his suit coat. They descended the stairs and acted like victims as Calixto angled toward the door.

"Someone up there has a gun," said Cal.

Izzy took his cue and spoke as they moved. "Gunfire," she said, pointing back at the rear staircase.

Lozen made eye contact with Sebastian. Apparently the fireworks upstairs had not penetrated the veil of music and noise downstairs. Cal motioned, and Sebastian started toward the door.

Cortez started yelling and pointing from across the club. The manager was in a frenzy. A huge security guard jumped in front of Izzy. Cal swiveled his pistol and fired three times. Now people heard the gunshots.

The club broke into chaos. Patrons started screaming and running in every direction. Cal raised the weapon over his head and squeezed off several more rounds. Mirrors shattered, and chandelier pieces crumbled. Breaking glass filled the air. Patrons panicked, rushing for the exits in a display of mob fear.

Cal and Izzy were propelled forward in a human wave. They saw Sebastian and his two men close ranks and create a perimeter around the brother and sister. At the door, a huge arm grabbed at Isabel just as she stepped to the sidewalk. It started to drag her back. Izzy clutched Cal's free hand and yelled. Suddenly, a knife from behind sliced at the arm, there was a screech, and the guard released Izzy.

Cal turned his sister to the left, and then Sebastian was at their side. He guided them to the waiting car.

Chapter 144

Buenos Aires, Argentina

PATSY BELLOCCO TOURED the Encantar Gentlemen's Club with Cortez, the manager, his brother-in-law, his two nephews, and a bodyguard. Patsy's shoes crunched the broken glass that littered the floor. He noted the bloodstains on the newly installed carpet, and the general disarray. The shootings, and the stampede that followed, created a swath of destruction to his prized, upscale strip lounge. Even worse, dancers were in fear, and wealthy customers went elsewhere.

Bellocco looked up at the ceiling mirrors. They were cracked and jagged, and spider lines of ruin flowed in several directions. His pricey Italian chandelier, imported from the Venetian island of Murano, lay in a crumpled heap on the floor.

Cortez spoke in an exaggerated, hypersensitive manner. He recalled the events of the evening and his own close brush with death. A mestizo-looking talent manager with his client model had shot up the club in a rage. He killed two security guards, put a third in the hospital, and terrorized two regular guests of the Encantar. One of the special guests was a powerful inspector with the federal police.

Patsy listened patiently. It was rare, even in his agitated state, to show concern. These were his people. He could display anger, but never distress. "Are you finished?" asked Bellocco.

The manager realized he was rambling, and he stopped talking.

"Good. Now clean it up. I want to reopen in twenty-four hours."

Cortez's jaw dropped. "Pasquale," he said with bulging eyes, "it is not possible."

The 'ndrina boss cut him off with a wave of his hand and replied, "I want dancers onstage. Bring in the best girls from our other clubs. Set up a free, one-hour service upstairs for the regulars."

Patsy turned toward Beppe. "I want five new security guards on duty. Make sure they dress and act appropriately."

He looked at Lino. "Push all of our suppliers. I want the best liquor and champagne. Add caviar and the finest steaks. At midnight we will offer a complimentary buffet for everyone."

Finally he circled back to Cortez. "Stop whining."

Patsy motioned to Ettore, and the two walked to the rear of the club and entered the manager's office. The bodyguard stopped outside and closed the door. "What do you think?" asked Bellocco, leaning on the desk.

"It doesn't play. A talent manager carrying a gun? A top new model that no one in Caracas has even heard of?"

"A ruse to gain entry."

"They were looking for someone," replied the brother-in-law.

A minute elapsed before Patsy spoke. "Any word on the putana?"

"No, Quintino," answered Ettore.

"Raise the reward to fifty thousand pesos."

"Pasquale..."

"I want her found," said Patsy. He touched his eye patch self-consciously. "She and I have some unfinished business."

"Sí," answered Ettore. He reflected for a moment before continuing, "This mestizo from upstairs feels wrong."

"How so?"

"Something our associates in Santiago said. They spoke of a mestizo that was giving them trouble."

"What kind of trouble?"

"They didn't say. But they called him El Lobo Gris."

Patsy's face contorted as he translated from Spanish. "The Gray Wolf?"

"It's some type of nickname," said Ettore.

"Pressure them for more information. Someone is making a move on our operation," said Patsy. "Just when we land a new distribution channel with the Mexicans."

"Do you think it's them?"

"Los Zetas?" replied Bellocco. "No, they have nothing to gain by disrupting the money tree."

"What about their competition in Mexico?"

Patsy considered the information. "Maybe, but Santiago is still holding back. Three dead at the bodega in Mendoza, three more at the ranch, and now someone is shooting up my best club in Buenos Aires."

"Someone thinks we've lost our edge."

"Sí," answered Patsy. "It will encourage others to take a shot." Bellocco stood before continuing, "I want to know everything about this *Lobo Gris*."

He flung open the door and reached out with an open hand to his bodyguard. "Give me your gun."

The man looked at the 'ndrina boss with apprehension, and then he handed Patsy his Beretta pistol. Bellocco nudged his brother-in-law to the side, chambered a round, and then faced the desk.

It was an antique Louis XIV hand-carved desk with inlaid walnut and rosewood marble. Cortez purchased the piece of furniture with his own money. It was the manager's pride and joy.

Patsy aimed and fired three times at point-blank range.

Everyone came running. Beppe and Lino approached from two different directions, and Cortez from the front of the club. When they all arrived, Patsy grabbed the manager by his shirt collar and pulled him through the open door. He pointed at the wood-splintered bullet holes and pushed Cortez's face closer. "Do you see that?"

The manager swallowed, fighting back his urge to vomit. "Sí."

"Those are bullets," said Patsy in the manager's ear. "They didn't hit you. But that can change. Fix my club."

Bellocco shoved Cortez aside and handed the pistol back to his bodyguard. Then he exited the office and strode from the Encantar.

Chapter 145

December 14, 2006
Gladwyne, Pennsylvania

Burdis swiveled in his wheelchair and spoke in a quiet voice. "They call it the Reservoir."

"An apt name," said John.

"Yes," replied Burdis. "The years ticked off, new administrations came and went, but the existence of a contingency fund, the Reservoir, stayed hidden."

"I suspect just the director and a few senior officers knew," said Mike.

Burdis scowled. "Never." He leaned forward in his wheelchair. "The director of the CIA is a presidential appointee. The career intelligence officers would never trust a politically connected insider with that kind of information."

"Who then?" asked John.

Burdis considered the question before answering, "A handful of founding members at the Empresa—all former military men from Operation Condor, and several covert types from the CIA's National Clandestine Service."

"The old DDO," said Mike.

"Precisely."

"No one from the analytical or admin sides at the Agency?"

"Desk jockeys," said Burdis with a hint of sarcasm. "No need to know."

"So the existence of the Reservoir became a nonstarter," replied John.

"Pretty much."

"Was it ever necessary to tap into the funds?" asked John.

"On occasion, but only when there was a particularly sensitive matter that needed attention. For the most part, the Reservoir stayed dark and dormant."

"Did it grow?" asked Mike.

"Oh yes," replied Burdis with a grin. "Exponentially."

Chapter 146

Buenos Aires, Argentina

Sofia stepped from the taxi at the corner of Medrano and Avenida Rivadavia in the Almagro Barrio. She entered a recently restored patisserie called Las Violetas. It boasted vaulted ceilings, huge French stained glass windows, ornate wood, and columns of Italian marble. The setting was uniquely feminine, down to the engraved bone china and pressed tablecloths. Flowers were everywhere.

The expensive confiteria offered a renowned tea service, with complimentary sweets, pastries, and finery. During the Dirty War, the grandmothers of the Plaza de Mayo would secretly gather at Las Violetas under the pretense of a birthday to discuss methods to recover their kidnapped grandchildren. They rarely succeeded.

Sofia turned to the right, weaving between patrons to an open but somewhat private table, positioned between two soaring columns. It provided an excellent view of both the entrance and the streets outside. Sitting alone was Daniella Pedraza.

The two women looked at each other, and Sofia sat. As always, Daniella exuded polish: dressed in a two-piece skirt suit, medium heels, sparse jewelry, and subtle makeup. Every hair was in place.

"You look great," said the dancer.

Pedraza smiled at the compliment before responding, "Thank you. Unfortunately, I can't say the same. You look stressed. You are tired and nervous."

Sofia managed a weak smile. "It's been difficult."

"I know," said Daniella. "Your willingness to meet me attests to that. It's become very bad, hasn't it?"

"Sí."

"Does he hit you?"

"No," said Sofia. "But he scares me. Something dramatic has happened, and he has turned very hostile."

Pedraza reached forward and signaled to the waiter. Then she turned her attention to a dulce de leche–soaked pastry that she had been nibbling. "It will only get worse. He is a very dangerous man. There are things you don't know."

"I realize that. When I try to talk, he shuts me down."

"And the intimacy, it's leaving you cold?"

Sofia stirred. She was a passionate woman, but hesitant to discuss one lover with another. "I've become his release," she said finally. "He leaves me feeling cheap and used."

Daniella sipped at her tea as the waiter brought Sofia's cappuccino. "Empty sex is unfulfilling. It lacks tenderness. Have you tried discussing it with him?"

"Sí. I even hinted that if he didn't want me anymore, then maybe I should leave."

Pedraza's eyes opened wide. "And what did he say?"

"He gave me a very threatening look. Then he whispered that *he* and only *he* would decide if I should leave." Tears crept down the tango dancer's cheeks. She blotted them with a napkin.

"He's been having trouble with his business. How is his eye?" asked Pedraza.

Sofia stared at Daniella in surprise. "You know about his injury?"

"Of course. I know everything," said Daniella. "It happened at the estancia."

"He said it was a horse-riding accident."

"Hardly. The man is a predator." They lapsed into a moment of silence before Pedraza spoke again. "I've missed you. I thought we had something special."

Sofia remained silent.

"Are you prepared to leave him?" asked Daniella.

The dancer looked down at the table before responding, "How? I am afraid of what he might do."

"It can be arranged. It will take some planning, but then I will have to hide you."

Sofia nodded.

"And I will need you to do something in return," said Pedraza. "He has a journal he keeps at the apartment in Recoleta. It is filled with names and numbers. No one else can get close. You must find it and bring it with you when you leave. Finally, you must be prepared to depart on a moment's notice," said Daniella. "Leave everything behind—just bring yourself and the journal. He *cannot* see it coming. Do you understand?"

"Sí," replied Sofia, the tears starting again. "I understand. Tell me what to do."

Pedraza tugged a thick envelope from her purse. It was stuffed with peso notes. "You'll need this." She slid the envelope across the table. "When you are safe, I will explain everything. In the meantime, locate the journal and be ready."

The dancer took the envelope.

"Wait for my call," said Daniella. "Then follow my instructions exactly. Can you do that?"

"Sí."

Pedraza leaned back in her chair. "You look thin. Let's order some lunch. There is much to catch up on."

Chapter 147

Buenos Aires, Argentina

THE FOUR SAT around the kitchen table in Daniella's boutique hotel in Monserrat. Cal faced their host, and Izzy and Sebastian sat to either side. A huge street map of Buenos Aires lay spread across the table.

"They have still not made a connection between the two of you," said Pedraza.

"Surprising," replied Cal.

"Not really. Their mind-set is different. They worry more about competitors moving in on their turf."

"They don't think of you as an American," said Sebastian. "Between your appearance and your Spanish, nothing stands out."

"I guess that's a good thing."

"Yes," said Daniella, "and it may give us options." She looked at Izzy. "We confirmed that your friend was moved from Palermo that morning. We just missed her."

"Where is she?" asked Izzy.

"We need to find out. She was scheduled for the Blue Boliche, a club in Recoleta."

"What does that mean for Sandy?"

"It means the medication has her under control," said Daniella. "Are you sure she will recognize you?"

"Yes," said Isabel with confidence.

"Good. Things got tense the other night. Are you still feeling up to this?"

"Yes," replied Isabel.

Daniella examined the look of determination in Izzy's face. It impressed the woman. She turned toward Calixto. "He is in a rage. He has increased the reward to fifty thousand pesos for her. Maybe we can somehow use that?"

"Reward?" asked Izzy.

Pedraza looked at Cal in surprise. "She doesn't know?"

Lozen looked at his sister and then back at Daniella. He shook his head. "I didn't tell her."

"What?" asked Izzy, nudging her brother. "Tell me what?"

"About a reward for your return," said Cal.

Isabel's expression changed. "A reward? You didn't think I should know that?"

"No," answered Cal. "I'm against you being involved to begin with. The more you have to think about, the less focused you will be on the plan. Things are complicated enough without giving you something else to worry about."

"When did you find out?"

"At the estancia. I learned from the gauchos."

Daniella remained silent, allowing the two siblings to work through their disagreement.

Isabel knew that Cal was being protective. Nevertheless, she wondered what else he wasn't sharing with her. Finally she spoke. "I had a right to know."

"Yes," said Calixto. "But things were moving fast. There didn't seem to be a good time to bring it up. I don't care if you're mad. I just need to get you home safe."

There was a moment of silence as Izzy digested the information. Then she looked at Daniella. "You said that maybe we could use this?"

"Yes," answered Pedraza. "You are something he wants. The man is head-strong and expects to get his way."

"Could I be used as bait?" asked Isabel.

Calixto threw up his hands before anyone else could answer. "No," he said emphatically.

Sebastian released some tension by pointing at the map and changing the subject. "The Blue Boliche is here, in Recoleta. I have some people reviewing the finer establishments owned by the quintino. They are quietly searching for a 'Sanchia.'"

Cal studied the map. He traced his fingers along the streets of the wealthy barrio. "If we can find Sandy, we need an escape route. It has to have car access. We also need contingency plans."

Sebastian looked at Daniella and asked, "What about the cemetery?"

A smile curled Pedraza's lips. "Yes," she said, "that could work."

Calixto looked at Daniella for an explanation.

"It is a huge labyrinth of stone monuments and tombs," said Pedraza. "It stretches over four city blocks. It is easy to get lost."

"Or lose someone that is following you?" asked Cal.

"As the case may be," said Daniella.

"I need to see it," said Cal.

Chapter 148

Buenos Aires, Argentina

Patsy was a night owl. He liked to be on the town, hitting clubs, having dinner, and taking the pulse of his many businesses.

His brother-in-law, by contrast, was a morning person. Ettore preferred the daytime, sunshine, and warm afternoons for a walk. In many ways, the brother-in-law tried to emulate the simple life left behind in Calabria. He enjoyed the small pleasures: a good meal, a glass of wine, and an evening with friends.

To this end, Ettore made it a habit twice each week to leave his unofficial office in San Telmo to enjoy a leisurely walk in Parque Las Heras. He followed this with a late lunch at the Alvear Palace Hotel. It kept the 'ndrina visible and assured their constituents that the family still ruled.

The brother-in-law entered the lavish lobby of the Alvear accompanied by his driver, who doubled as a bodyguard. The Palace was consistently recognized as the premier hotel in Buenos Aires and arguably all of South America. The décor was lavish, the service impeccable, and its food renowned. Most of all, it was very expensive. There was no greater legitimacy to their illegal activities than to see the underboss patronizing the finest establishments.

Ettore was greeted in the lobby by a floating concierge, who escorted him to the L'Orangerie Restaurant. The maître d' guided the brother-in-law past the tasteful mirrors, flowing drapes, and elegant furniture to his regular table at the midpoint of the dining room. Ettore sat alone, and his bodyguard slid off to a small side table. The waiter served a Campari and soda.

Four minutes later, Calixto walked into L'Orangerie with Sebastian and a third man.

"I see my friend is already here," said Cal as he brushed past the maître d'.

The man reached toward Cal until Sebastian pressed a fold of pesos into his hand and gave him a stern look. Then Sebastian took a table next to Ettore's bodyguard and made a point of facing him.

Calixto was dressed in the Armani suit again, with a new silk shirt and a borrowed Rolex watch. He stopped in front of the brother-in-law, who had observed the entire sequence unfold. "May I?" asked Lozen, referring to an empty chair at Ettore's table.

The brother-in-law regarded Cal with a wary eye, then he motioned. Cal sat.

"Gracias."

"Do I know you?" asked Ettore as he studied Calixto's face.

"You may have heard of me. More important, I know of you."

"You are the mestizo," said the brother-in-law in an agitated tone.

"Sí," answered Cal.

"They call you El Lobo Gris."

"Sí." Cal exhibited an air of arrogance to ruffle the brother-in-law.

"You have big cojones," said Ettore, using a slang term for a man's testicles.

"Sí," answered Cal a third time. "I know the quintino has a temper. I was hoping you could convey a business offer to him."

"I'm listening."

"I would like to arrange the recovery of something you have."

The brother-in-law's eyes narrowed as Cal produced a photograph of Sandy. He slid it across the table. "I was sent to find her."

"By who?" asked Ettore.

"It doesn't matter. She was taken in Santiago, and my employer wants her back."

Ettore glanced at the picture of an attractive, smiling Sandy. It made no impression on him. He had never seen the roommate. "What makes you think I know her?"

"Because," answered Cal, "she was taken with this girl." Calixto slid a second photograph across the table. It showed a radiant Isabel. "They are friends. They were abducted together in Santiago."

The brother-in-law gave a wave of his hand. He had never seen either of the girls. However, as he looked closer at Izzy's picture, a trickle of interest seemed to catch his demeanor. "I don't know her," said Ettore.

"No, but your boss does. In fact, he has offered a large reward for her. The quintino would recognize her, even with only one good eye."

The brother-in-law stirred. The sudden twitch caused his bodyguard several tables away to move. That set off a mini–chain reaction with Sebastian and his colleague. Ettore recovered and motioned for everyone to remain calm. "Is that the putana?"

Cal shrugged and slid a third photograph across the table. It showed Izzy reading a copy of *Clarin*, the largest newspaper in Buenos Aires. The date was clear on the newspaper. It was that morning.

Ettore picked up the two photographs of Izzy and took a long look. Then he leaned back. "What is it you want?"

"A trade," said Cal. "I get the one I want, plus the fifty thousand pesos reward for giving you the one you want."

The brother-in-law pointed at Sandy's picture. "Do you collect on her as well?"

"I have a separate arrangement on her."

Ettore sipped at his Campari before asking, "They were friends. Why would you give up one for the other?"

Lozen shrugged. "They are not *my* friends." He pointed at Izzy's photograph. "She is the one I found. I tracked her, hoping to find the one I want. You have her."

"Do you know who you are dealing with?" asked Ettore.

"Sí."

"You must be crazy."

"It's just business," said Cal. He motioned toward the photographs. "Keep those." Calixto slid a cell phone across the table and stood. "That's a burn phone, so it can't be traced. It has only one number recorded in its memory. Give it some thought. If your boss is interested, call me."

Lozen turned and walked from the restaurant.

Chapter 149

Buenos Aires, Argentina

IT WAS A stressful day and a half. Calixto sat with his sister in their room at the boutique hotel overlooking the garden. The anticipation was always the most difficult aspect of an operation. Lozen had presented an offer to the quintino. The ball was in Patsy's court.

It was a business arrangement in the criminal world, using people as products and negotiating profits as incentive. Cal had honed his pitch with the help of Daniella. There was a certain amount of posturing that was expected. The key was to appear credible. There were certain things that Bellocco would believe and others that he wouldn't. The gangster in him thought a certain way.

Lozen mentally replayed his conversation with Ettore. Then he recalled everything for Daniella. They both agreed that Cal's approach sounded plausible. Yet still, the call had not come.

The change in tactics came from their inability to locate Sandy. Sebastian's men combed the Barrio Recoleta to no avail. The noose was tightening. Daniella warned that the word on the street indicated Patsy was activating resources. He wanted the escaped Izzy. People talked, and the reward caught everyone's attention. Soon Daniella would lose her ability to hide and protect the siblings.

As the time elapsed, Isabel pushed the idea of using herself as bait to flush out Sandy's location. Cal was prepared to play his wild card and ship Izzy alone to the United States. Everyone understood that this action would condemn Sandy to a lost cause. In the end, Isabel was so determined to rescue her friend that Calixto realized sending her home alone would cripple Izzy with guilt. He would emotionally devastate the very person he sought to save.

Isabel stood and walked barefoot across the room. Her wound was healing; she was moving well. "Don't be angry," said Izzy.

Cal looked up from the map he was studying. "You can be stubborn, a real pain in the ass, just like Mom."

Isabel wrapped her arms around her big brother from behind and gave him a quick hug. "I know. I'm sorry. Do you understand?"

"Yeah," replied Cal.

Isabel circled Calixto and looked down from above. There were tears in her eyes. "I can't leave her behind."

"I get it," said Calixto. "But in the grand scheme of things, I don't agree with putting you back in jeopardy to rescue her."

Izzy knelt on the floor in front of her brother. "I'm scared, Cal. But we're running out of time. No one can find Sandy. We don't even know if she's in Recoleta."

"I know the arguments."

"You already need me to identify Sandy and to assure she connects. This is just taking the plan one step further."

"Hey," said Cal, with an extra bite in his voice, "it's a pretty big step."

Isabel stood and leaned over to kiss Calixto on the top of his head. He frowned. Then he handed her his map. "Just memorize your escape route and the different contingencies. We'll go out late this afternoon to walk the streets again."

Izzy relaxed a little and paced back toward her chair.

Ten seconds later, Calixto's disposable cell phone rang. It was a model identical to the cell phone he had given Ettore at the Alvear Palace Hotel. Patsy had made a decision.

Chapter 150

Santiago, Chile

DAVID SHIELDS WAS driving the embassy car along Las Talaveras approaching the Arauco Mall when his cell phone rang. He recognized the caller and pulled the vehicle to the side of the road.

"Hey," said the DIA officer, "are you okay?"

"Affirmative," answered Cal. "Just a preview: we're going to take another crack at recovery."

"You've located the second package?"

"We think so. It needs to be confirmed up close, but initial indications are positive."

"Good. Do you want me to prep the transfer loop?"

"Yes. If it is confirmed, we'll process both packages and me together. A sum total of three. Will that work?"

"Yes," replied Shields. "Just assure you're satisfied that everything is in working order. When we initiate the sequence, we'll only get the *one* shot. Do you understand?"

"Affirmative."

"Do you have a window?" asked David.

"Tomorrow, late morning. Anytime after eleven."

"Got it. I'll make the call."

"Hey," said Cal with a pause. "Thanks."

"Good luck."

The DIA officer disconnected the call and then immediately dialed the number for the FBI legal attaché at the embassy in Santiago.

Chapter 151

Buenos Aires, Argentina

PATSY SAT ALONE in the rear seat of his Lincoln Town Car as they circled the block for a second time. In the front seat next to the driver sat his nephew Beppe.

The 'ndrina boss had agreed to the exchange with the mysterious mestizo on a public street in broad daylight before lunch. Appropriately, the man was afraid of Bellocco. Of course, Patsy may have agreed, but he had no intention of honoring the deal. He refused to pay a reward to an outsider to return something that was rightfully his. In addition, this El Lobo Gris needed to be taught a lesson. No one messed with the quintino's operation. Everyone in Buenos Aires knew that. Once Patsy's "gift" was recovered, he would find this outsider from Santiago and extract a penalty for the disruption. "Is everyone in position?" asked Bellocco over his cell phone.

"Sí, Quintino," answered his brother-in-law. "Lino has the girl, and men are posted on every corner."

"Where are you now?"

"Standing outside the Alvear Palace," said Ettore.

"Good," said Patsy. "Stay alert; he may have brought some help."

"Sí, Pasquale."

The Lincoln eased down the hill from Avenida Callao and turned left on Posadas.

→⟫● ●⟪←

Calixto walked against the traffic along Alvear with his sister. Izzy held his arm. She was dressed in comfortable walking clothes and shoes. Isabel understood the plan and the risks. She was nervous but committed to recovering Sandy.

"Your foot feels okay?" asked Cal.

"A little pain, but it's feeling better."

"Remember, you can't enter a car for any reason."

"I understand," nodded Izzy.

"The faster you confirm Sandy, the better. Anything can happen."

"Yes," repeated Isabel.

"Sebastian has people posted along the escape route. You remember the rally point if we get separated?"

"Yes."

Izzy continued to look straight ahead on the sidewalk. She was already breathing a little fast as her adrenaline pumped. She gripped Calixto's arm tighter and spoke. "Cal?"

"Yes."

"Thank you."

"Yeah," said Lozen, his mind racing in thought.

"Love you."

Lozen squeezed his little sister's hand.

--->===) (===<---

Sebastian was a Spaniard by birth. He had killed a man in a bar brawl at the age of twenty-two. To avoid prison, he stole away on a freighter from Barcelona that sailed the Mediterranean. While onshore in Marseilles, Sebastian enlisted in the French Foreign Legion. The Légion étrangère gave him a new name and a new start. It changed his life.

Over the next five years, Sebastian learned many things—most of all, how to work with military precision. The Legion taught discipline and vigilance. It gave him new skills and a sense of fidelity. When his enlistment ended, Sebastian took his new identity and traveled to South America. Argentina felt comfortable. It had a Spanish culture and a low risk of apprehension being so far from home.

He met Daniella. The elegant Señora Pedraza Lepes was a fixer. She provided information and contacts to a host of foreign governments and corporations seeking to get things done in Buenos Aires. Often her methods were less than savory.

->=® ©=<-

Sebastian's cell phone rang. "Seb," said the caller, "two men, 'ndrina associates, are at the corner of Callao and Alvear. Another two are across the street from the hotel."

"Sí," answered Sebastian. "Where is Ettore?"

"Standing at the entrance to the Alvear Palace."

"Any sign of the quintino?"

"No."

"Okay. Check the route one more time."

->=® ©=<-

Daniella Pedraza received a voice call on her cell, listened for a few seconds, and then disconnected. She immediately texted a message to a different party on her BlackBerry. Finally, she picked up her cell phone and called Sofia.

"Hola," answered the dancer.

"This is Dan. It's time. Are you alone?"

"Sí," replied the dancer.

"Did you find the journal?"

"Yes," answered Sofia.

"Leave the apartment. Bring nothing but the journal. Walk straight down Parana against the traffic, and turn left on Arenales. You'll see the Bel Air Hotel."

"I know it," said Sofia. "The hotel has a baroque architecture."

"That's it. If anyone stops you, you are going shopping."

"I understand."

"There is a blue jaguar parked in front of the Bel Air. The driver is a woman. Her name is Tanima. Get in. Do you understand?"

"Yes."

"Good. Now go."

Daniella disconnected. Sofia picked up her pocketbook and the journal and exited Patsy's apartment.

Chapter 152

Buenos Aires, Argentina

CAL KNEW SOMETHING was wrong. He couldn't explain the feeling. It was the "wolf sense" that his dad, Naiche, believed in. Lozen did not trust the quintino, so he excused the anxiety as healthy paranoia.

Lozen had required that the meeting take place in public on a busy city street. The 'ndrina boss could muster too much muscle, and Calixto needed to protect Izzy. Bellocco agreed to the location. It seemed the quintino was fervent in his desire to reclaim Cal's sister.

"Something is wrong," said Calixto. They approached the impressive front entrance to the Alvear Palace Hotel. "If I say 'go,' you take off running. Use the escape route. Don't hesitate. Don't look back. Understand?"

"Yes," replied Isabel.

Cal noticed several of Patsy's men loitering along the sidewalk. That was the difference between professional thugs and Sebastian's men. Mobsters loved to intimidate. The persona worked, but they couldn't turn it off. They talked big and acted big—loud, crude, flashy, and often violent. They had no misgivings about shooting victims or breaking legs, but they found it difficult to blend into their surroundings.

Sebastian's men, by contrast, were cut from a different cloth. He only employed former Legionnaires. If a man had not earned the Kepi Blanc, the coveted white hat of the French Foreign Legion, he didn't work for Daniella's subordinate. It assured a certain level of discipline and tactical training. Cal was counting on that rigor now.

Calixto stopped with Izzy on the sidewalk in front of the hotel. Taxis pulled up, doormen jumped, and guests came and went. The Alvear Palace was buzzing with activity. He looked up to see Ettore standing on the top step in front of the lobby doors. The brother-in-law pointed inside.

Calixto shook his head and motioned at the sidewalk where they stood. Ettore frowned and stepped through the glass doors. He returned a moment later, followed by Lino and Sandy. Izzy saw her friend and gasped.

Lozen's head swiveled. He noticed Patsy's men on either side slide closer to the sidewalk. Cal gestured to the brother-in-law, who spoke in Calabrian. Both pairs of men halted.

The nephew descended the steps with Sandy and approached Cal and Izzy. Sandy looked sallow and drawn. She hesitated. Then Lino smirked at Isabel and gave her a lewd wink. He shoved Sandy forward for inspection.

Izzy studied her friend, staring into the glazed, unfocused eyes, and started to choke up.

"I know you," said the roommate.

"Yes, Sandy, it's me, Izzy."

A slow expression of recognition spread across Sandy's face as she looked at Isabel in wonder. "Izzy. You're my friend."

"Yes," said Isabel, nodding in agreement.

"That's it," said Lino, accepting the confirmation. He pushed Sandy toward Cal and reached out to grab Izzy's forearm.

"Wait," said Cal, raising an open hand as he moved Sandy to his side. "What about my money?"

Lino made a point of glancing at his men to the left and right. Each stood only a few steps away near the sidewalk. Then he smirked at Calixto and said, "Fuck you."

The nephew grabbed at Izzy's forearm; instantly Cal took a step forward and head-butted Lino in the face. "Go, Izzy, go," said Lozen.

Isabel turned and broke into a run, dodging traffic, and angled toward Ayacucho Street.

Sebastian's car screeched to a halt next to the sidewalk, and the rear door was flung open. Cal pushed Sandy onto the back seat and jumped in behind her as the car accelerated. One of Patsy's men reached for the open door as Lozen kicked at his hand.

"Rally point," said Cal, turning to look for Izzy. He saw her running across the avenue.

Patsy Bellocco jumped out of his Lincoln and yelled to his men. "Forget her," said the quintino, waving off Sandy's car. "Get *her*." He pointed back at Izzy. "Get the putana."

Two men across the street from the hotel fanned sideways, blocking Izzy's escape route. They were large bruisers, standing side by side with their arms spread wide to intercept the fleeing Isabel.

The original group from the sidewalk stormed across the avenue and joined the chase. They pressured Izzy toward the two men. She was being sandwiched.

Wheels from behind screeched, and a second car spun right onto Ayacucho. It sped past Isabel. Suddenly the vehicle veered at the corner and crashed sideways into both men. They went flying headlong into the street. Izzy slowed, altered her course around the collision, and accelerated again. Behind her, she heard the screech of more tires, yelling, and then gunshots. Cal had conditioned his sister to forget what was behind her, keep moving, and head for the rally point.

A hundred meters farther back, Patsy jumped into the Lincoln and yelled at his driver to follow Izzy.

Chapter 153

IZZY SPRINTED DOWN Ayacucho, keenly aware of the activity to her rear. She was being chased. Several men, bulky but determined, did their best to catch the fleeing Isabel. People watched and cars passed as Izzy turned right on Avenida Quintana and ran toward Plaza Francia.

Cal had selected the Alvear Palace for the exchange for several reasons. He knew the area and liked its proximity to the cemetery. He also wanted an escape route that felt familiar to Isabel. Finally, he reasoned that both Patsy and Ettore would accept the choice. Still, Lozen left nothing to chance. He walked the streets in disguise with his sister several times. Cal pointed out landmarks and visual images. He knew that under stress, the body reacted instinctively.

Izzy heard a car turn the corner behind her and accelerate. She saw La Biela up ahead. The café where they first met Daniella was on the corner. She picked up the pace. A man pushing a vendor's cart, loaded with handmade leather goods, paralleled Izzy from the sidewalk. As soon as she passed him on the street, he turned into the traffic and crashed the small wagon into the first car behind her. Souvenirs and bric-a-brac went flying in every direction, and the wooden cart broke apart.

Several cars in traffic screeched to a halt, and the driver of the first car stepped to the street, shaken, and started screaming at the vendor.

Up ahead, Izzy ran past the large rubber tree outside the café and onto the paved walkway that threaded through the green of Plaza Francia. She saw the impressive façade of the Nuestra Señora de Pilar and then to the left, the massive doric columns of Recoleta cemetery.

⋙ ⋘

Beppe jumped out of the Lincoln to survey the collision. They were two cars back, but the street was blocked and people were arguing. Horns honked, and the vehicle to the front refused to drive over the scattered merchandise that littered the street along with pieces of the wooden cart. The nephew ran up Avenida Quintana and saw Izzy as she crossed Ortiz Street by the café into the pedestrian zone. He ran back to the Lincoln. "She's heading toward the church," said the nephew to Patsy.

"The church? She thinks she'll be safe in a church?"

Bellocco slapped his driver on the back of the head and yelled, "Get past this. Run him over if you have to." Then Patsy pulled out his cell phone and made a call.

⋙ ⋘

Sebastian gunned the engine, and the car sped down Alvear for a block before taking a hard right on Calle Rodriguez Pena. They needed to get to the rally point for Izzy.

Cal turned toward Sandy, who had sat up in the rear seat. She appeared confused by the events. "Do you remember me?" asked Cal.

She looked at Lozen with a frustrated expression. Sandy thought she might know him, but her thoughts were murky. She couldn't place the face.

"I'm Cal, Izzy's brother."

"Izzy," said Sandy to herself. "Where did Izzy go?"

"We are going to get her. You and I met in Tucson. Do you remember?"

Sandy struggled to think through the fog. She bit her lower lip. "I used to live in Tucson."

"Yes," said Calixto, patting her hand. He realized this would be an uphill battle. "You are going to be okay, Sandy."

Cal returned his attention to the window as they took a right onto Vicente Lopez Street.

⤛▤ ▤⤜

Izzy slowed to a walk and joined the crowd of tourists that passed under the white neoclassical portico and into the peristyle entrance. The entire cemetery lay before her, a walled city within a city. The graveyard was a stone maze, sectioned into streets and alleyways, with ornate mausoleums stacked in rows shoulder to shoulder at right angles. The crypts themselves were as varied and unique as the family names on their vaults. It created a collage of monuments, stone architecture, statues, and stained glass.

Isabel caught up to a tour group and blended into their ranks. She used the opportunity to check over her shoulder. Izzy noticed two men moving her way. They resembled men she had seen on the street near the Alvear Palace Hotel.

Isabel drifted from the pack in a fast walk and entered the central square. She stood near the tomb of Guillermo Brown, paused, and then broke hard to the left. As Izzy started to run, the two men behind her gave chase.

The central square of the cemetery had several stone benches for contemplation and numerous plants, as well as eight different alleyways, each filled with mausoleums. The two men stopped in the square and looked in all directions. They realized she could have gone anywhere.

The first man threw up his arms in disgust, walking in circles to catch his breath, while the second pulled out a cell phone and called Patsy.

Chapter 154

Buenos Aires, Argentina

IZZY CHOSE THE alley that jutted off the central square at a forty-five-degree angle toward the tomb of Julio Roca. She passed several groups of tourists, who wandered without purpose and paused to take photographs of the various monuments. There were over five thousand vaults aboveground in the cemetery, each displaying impressive sculptures and unique carvings with identifying plaques. It was a visual blur, and precisely why Cal selected the cemetery.

Isabel looked to her rear. If they followed, they chose a different alley. Izzy turned again and moved at a quick walking pace toward the southern side of the cemetery. She strode past the crypts of presidents and admirals, authors and industrialists, each family name popping from the façade of the engraved mausoleum.

Finally, after a series of left and right turns, Izzy saw the crowd and the narrow passage that led to the Duarte Family crypt, the final resting place for Argentina's favorite daughter, Evita Peron.

-→═◉ ◉═◄-

Patsy disconnected his cell phone and spoke to his nephew in the front seat. "She's in the cemetery."

"It's filled with tourists," replied Beppe.

"I don't care. Bring everyone there; we'll cover the exits and flush her out."

Beppe directed the driver to Junin Street and then called Ettore on his cell.

→→■○ ○■←←

Sebastian slowed the car along the sidewalk on Vicente Lopez. He hugged the curb as he rolled beside the tall brick wall that bordered the southern boundary of the cemetery. The rally point selected by Cal was an old, seldom-used service entrance cut in the rear wall of the graveyard. It faced several unobtrusive neighborhood businesses.

"Sandy, stay here," said Cal in a soft voice. "I'm going to get Izzy."

She gave Lozen a tentative nod as he patted her hand.

In seconds, Cal was on the sidewalk, striding toward the old gate. A large Lincoln sped by, swerving, and then jumped the curb a hundred meters to his front. A young man sprang from the front seat and bounded through the narrow service gate. Then Patsy Bellocco stepped to the sidewalk and pulled out his cell phone.

Calixto turned left and crossed the street away from the wall, slowing his pace to window-shop.

→→■○ ○■←←

Early that morning as they prepared for the meeting with Bellocco's men, Cal insisted that Izzy carry only two articles: a wad of paper money and a cell phone. Each could easily be stuffed into a separate pocket, and neither would encumber Izzy's hands. The phone was disposable, loaded with plenty of minutes, and had Cal's own cell number programmed for autodial. The plan was that whoever got to the rally point first would call the other.

Izzy's phone vibrated against her thigh. "Yes," she answered, a little out of breath.

"You okay?" asked Cal.

"Yes."

"Where are you?"

"Evita's tomb, bunched in among about fifty people."

"Do *not* go to the rally point. They have it covered. Abort, understand?"

"Yes. They have people here, Cal, in the cemetery. They're searching for me."

Lozen hesitated for a few seconds before speaking. "Can you get to the backup point, the alternate?"

"I think so," said Izzy, squeezing her eyes together as she recalled the location. "It's a distance."

"It's on the west wall."

"I remember," said Izzy.

"I'm leaving now. I'm entering the cemetery through the alternate gate. Do you remember the LaValle Mausoleum?"

"Yes," replied Izzy. "It has statues of soldiers guarding the vault."

"That's it. Can you make it?"

Izzy worried about the distance and being intercepted. She worried about getting lost. She worried about letting her brother down. "I'll try," she blurted.

"Use the crowds. Go now."

Calixto disconnected and motioned toward Sebastian, parked next to the curb.

Chapter 155

Ettore sat in the rear seat of his Cadillac. The driver tapped on the steering wheel as Lino held a bunched handkerchief to his fractured nose. The nephew was covered in blood.

Everyone was angry. The exchange had not worked in their favor, and they were frustrated that they had been outmaneuvered by an outsider. The mestizo didn't even *want* the money. He was after the girls.

"Pull everyone in to the cemetery," said the brother-in-law, "the quintino's orders. The putana is inside, hiding with the tourists."

Lino grunted through his handkerchief, holding the cloth tight while he attempted to inhale through his nose.

"Women," said Ettore, more to himself than to the other two in the car, "they always bring out the worst in men."

⵮⵮

Isabel started moving again, staying to the major alleyways, trying to avoid being trapped in a dead end. On the third row, she saw the two men from the central square. At first, they didn't see her. Then one looked over and whispered. They broke into a run. Izzy took off sprinting.

Fifty meters to the front, Isabel angled to the west, in the direction of the alternate gate. At the crypt of Federico Leloir, she took a hard right and continued running. Suddenly to her front, a third man appeared. He saw Izzy and started coming toward her. She stopped, looked in both directions, and then cut left, aiming for an alley that paralleled the west wall.

A few steps farther, and Izzy saw the open well of an unlocked vault. On impulse, she squeezed through the wrought iron door and swung the barrier closed. Then she knelt in the stairwell below street level.

The two men strolled by, one speaking on his cell phone while the other panted heavily from the run. There were voices above, and then Izzy realized some tourists were also in the same alleyway. She took a chance and called Cal.

"Where are you?" asked Lozen.

"Near the west wall," said Izzy in a quiet voice. "I'm in the stairwell of a crypt, but I think I'm surrounded."

"I'm inside the cemetery. I just passed the tomb of Alsina," said Cal, consulting a cemetery map. "I'm near LaValle, the soldiers' statues."

"There's at least one other guy here looking for me," replied Isabel, whispering between gulps of air.

"Can you get to a main thoroughfare?"

"I don't know." Izzy bit her lip, analyzing the cemetery's layout in her head.

"You need to move as fast as you can back to the main alleyway," said Cal, "and make a run for it toward the LaValle crypt. I'll be coming toward you."

"Okay," answered Izzy as she inhaled several times, controlling her fear. She stood, climbed the few stairs, and squeezed past the wrought iron door.

Izzy moved in a fast walk, checking in both directions, heading back toward the wider alleyway. At the corner, she paused to look around the tomb. It seemed clear. She turned left and, in a brisk walk, started heading north.

Isabel paced herself, conserving her energy, yet watching in all directions as she walked past row after row of stone mausoleums. In the far distance, she saw Cal walking toward her. She started to feel better. Izzy gave her brother a short wave.

Passing another alley of tombs, Izzy didn't notice the lone pursuer from earlier. The man popped his head around the statue of an angel and watched. Then, sure of his mark, he broke into a run.

Suddenly Cal was jumping up and down and waving at his sister. He pointed in her direction, and then in a loud voice, she heard the one word: "Run."

Isabel turned just as the man grabbed for her shoulder. She dipped, dodged to the right, and broke into a startled sprint.

Chapter 156

Buenos Aires, Argentina

THIRTY METERS TO her front, Cal slowed and took aim with his Belgium Hi-Power. The lone man was fast and ran well. He bore down on Izzy. Lozen motioned with his free hand, and she shifted to the right side of the wide alley. Their distance closed.

The lone pursuer was so intent on catching his prey that he didn't realize until the last moment what was happening. Cal squeezed off a round, and the nine-millimeter bullet tore into the man's shoulder, twisting his torso and tumbling his fast-moving body to the stone walkway. Izzy flinched when the pistol fired, but she kept running.

Cal watched behind Izzy as a scene developed. Several tourists yelled, and cell phones were activated. She slowed abreast of her brother; Lozen grabbed Izzy's hand and led her to the west service gate.

-→⟩═◉ ◉═⟨←-

Patsy's Lincoln took a sharp corner on Vicente Lopez Street and sped down Azcuenaga. He saw Calixto and Isabel dash through the gate into the waiting car and then accelerate in a blur of screeching tires.

Sebastian's car leaped off the sidewalk into the heavy midday traffic. "Hang on," said the former Legionnaire. "We have company."

Cal reached into the back seat, and Izzy grabbed his hand. She said nothing, but her facial expression spoke volumes. Then she cradled Sandy on her shoulder and stroked her hair.

--»═◉ ◉═«--

Three cars back, the large Lincoln threaded aggressively as they turned on to Avenida Pueyrredon. "Where are they going?" asked Patsy in an agitated voice.

"It looks like Palermo," answered Beppe.

"Palermo? Why?"

The nephew shrugged. He didn't have an answer.

"Catch them," said Bellocco to the driver. Then he turned back toward Beppe. "Where is the Comisario?"

"He was en route to the cemetery."

"Tell him to go to Palermo."

"Sí, Pasquale," replied the nephew. Beppe picked up his cell phone.

--»═◉ ◉═«--

Sebastian wove the vehicle through the busy streets with a deft knowledge of the city. In minutes, they were out of Recoleta heading north. He heard the police sirens in the distance. Then they were on Alcorta and savoring the broad expanse of the Palermo Parks to all sides, with the distinctive Spanish monument to the left. He couldn't shake the large Lincoln. It hung on his tail with a determined tenacity as the sirens got louder.

--»═◉ ◉═«--

Beppe turned in his seat and spoke to Patsy. "The Comisario says he thinks they are heading for the embassy."

"The embassy?" replied Bellocco. "Which embassy?"

"The United States."

Patsy rubbed his black eye patch in an agitated fashion. "The mestizo is from Santiago."

"The girls are American," replied the nephew.

A strong look of frustration creased the quintino's face. "This is Argentina. The Comisario is federal police. He can stop them."

"He is setting up roadblocks," answered Beppe.

⇥ ◯═◁

Sebastian saw the flashing lights and the row of police cars as they started to stack end to end along Avenues Sarmiento and Libertador. They were being funneled to a safe spot away from heavy traffic.

In the distance he saw lines of helmeted riot police wearing body armor, forming lines along Avenida Colombia right in front of the high fenced compound to the Embassy of the United States. "Calixto…"

"Get as close as you can," said Lozen, seeing the same blockade. He stuffed the pistol under the front seat.

Sebastian swerved left and then right, forcing a break in the still-forming human barrier. He accelerated straight across the green, heading for the intersection of Kennedy and Colombia beside La Rural. The car leaped forward and screeched to a halt before ramming the line of police.

Lozen jumped from the car. Then he pulled Izzy and Sandy from the rear seat as a ring of police closed around them. They heard the heavy breaking of wheels, and Patsy climbed from the back of his Lincoln. A beefy Argentinian police comisario in full uniform with a shock of thick white hair and a matching mustache joined the fray. The police inspector took charge.

"Arrest them," said the comisario, stepping forward with two deputies.

The front gates to the embassy opened, and a contingent of marine guards dressed in full battle gear swarmed from the compound, carrying their assault rifles at port arms. They formed a double row and then marched in a deliberate, sure cadence toward the rear of the police line.

Patsy yelled at the comisario and pointed.

The police inspector yanked at Isabel's arm and motioned. "I said, arrest them."

Calixto grabbed at the inspector, and several police jumped forward to restrain Lozen.

"We are American citizens," said Izzy as the comisario held her arm.

Another deputy stepped forward to grab Sandy. They started to pull the three apart. Then, from behind the marine guards, a well-dressed man in a business suit stepped through the embassy gates. He held credentials over his head and bellowed in a loud voice. "I am the senior legal attaché for the United States in Argentina. You are on sovereign territory. These people are under our protection. Let them go immediately."

The comisario stepped forward in his full dress uniform to face the FBI agent. "I am a comisario inspector of the Federal Police in Buenos Aires. These people have broken the law. They are my prisoners."

"Not today, Inspector," said the FBI legate. "They are American citizens on US soil, with full rights and protections under the law. Our law."

"This is *not* US soil," replied the comisario. He pointed where they stood. The red in his cheeks contrasted with the deep white of his hair. "This is Argentina."

"Not here," said the FBI agent. "The Status of Mission Agreement clearly stipulates the boundaries of the US embassy to Argentina. You and your police are standing on US soil."

"That is ridiculous," said the inspector, pointing at the ground.

"No, Comisario. Our mission property extends another thirty meters to your rear." He lowered his voice and then motioned at the third-floor window of the beaux arts–looking embassy building. "See the open window up there?"

The comisario peered over the FBI agent's shoulder.

"We are being filmed and recorded. You have been warned. There will be a full legal and diplomatic investigation if anything should happen here. Everything will be exposed."

The comisario looked at the legate, then the window, and then at Calixto. He hesitated, threw his hands in the air, and pushed Izzy toward the marines. Then he barked at his deputies, and the line of riot police turned to the side. The FBI legal attaché raised his voice. "Gunnery Sergeant McCoy?"

"Sir," answered a sharp voice to the rear.

"Take charge of these people. Escort them inside the compound."

Calixto reached for his sister and Sandy and then whispered into the FBI agent's ear. The legate turned and saw Sebastian handcuffed and held prostate across the hood of his car.

"That man as well," said the FBI agent, pointing at the former Legionnaire.

"He's *not* American," said a police deputy in protest.

"He's trespassing on US soil," replied the FBI legate.

"We need to question him," said the deputy.

"Of course," answered the legate, "as soon as we are finished. Just file the necessary paperwork through your consular office."

The deputy looked at the comisario for guidance. The inspector waved in frustration. Then he turned from the crowd and started walking toward Patsy.

Two marines stepped forward and took control of Sebastian. Then several other marines formed a cordon around the four and escorted them toward the tall steel gates of the US embassy.

Izzy gripped her brother's hand on one side and draped her arm over Sandy's shoulder on the other. The roommate gazed at Isabel with a confused expression. "Izzy, I don't understand. What's happening?"

"It's okay, Sandy, we are going home."

Chapter 157

December 14, 2006
Gladwyne, Pennsylvania

PETER BURDIS LEANED back in his wheelchair and emitted a deep sigh.

"A long day," said Mike, leaning back in his chair. "How are you feeling?"

"Tired," replied their host. "Weary."

"That's understandable," said John, standing. "Can you excuse me for a second? I need to use the toilet again."

Their host gave a cursory wave toward the door. He took a look at Mike and then said, "Quite a story, isn't it?"

"Compelling. Like so many problems, it took on a life of its own."

"Yes," replied Burdis, stifling a cough. "The Agency was intent on putting distance between itself and the Empresa. They were prepared to throw those college kids into the fire."

"Yet they could have interceded at any time."

"Could have…but chose not to. They had a bigger concern. It was easier to disavow and step aside."

"And then," said Mike, "the brother somehow managed to save the girls."

"Yes, to everyone's dismay, he succeeded. This in turn made the Empresa the focal point of the story."

"A mysterious organization at the center of a dark web of secret activities," said Mike.

"It connected Operation Condor to the School of the Americas, the Italian mob, and vast sums of illegal drug money."

"Everyone got involved."

"Yes, the FBI, DEA, State, the Department of Defense…it was a circus."

"And yet," replied Mike, "no one mentioned the Reservoir."

"That's because there was intense pressure to flesh out the extent of the Empresa's influence, not locate hidden funds. It was information overload."

"It dead-ended."

"To the good fortune of the Agency," said Burdis as he guided his wheel-chair over to the far corner of the study. "Come."

Mike followed their host as John returned. Then they both watched as Burdis leaned over a large hand-painted globe of the world. The ornate sphere was bolted into a decorative mahogany base straddled by four sturdy legs. Burdis gave the globe a casual spin and then popped a hidden latch. It opened the top half of the sphere. Inside was a heavy metal combination safe. He spun the tumblers in a series of back-and-forth motions until the safe clicked open.

Burdis extracted a single brown envelope that contained a USB flash drive. "It's all here," said the cripple.

Mike took the flash drive with a nod. "I have to check it."

"Help yourself," replied Burdis, pointing to a desktop computer.

John took a seat next to their host as Mike signed on to the computer, in-serted the stick, and started to scan the information. "Are there any backups?" asked John.

"None," replied Burdis as he took a shot of oxygen. "As instructed, I kept everything off the grid. No one knows, and no one had access."

After ten minutes of scrolling through pages on the computer screen, Mike looked over and nodded to John.

"You've been a great help," said John. "Is there anything else that we've neglected to ask?"

"No," said Burdis, pausing for another gulp of air.

"Is there anyone else who would know how this worked?" asked Mike.

"No," answered Burdis with a shrug.

They sat in silence for a moment, and then Mike reached over, cov-ered Burdis's mouth with a handkerchief, and turned off his oxygen. Burdis struggled, surprised by the action. Then John pulled out a hypodermic needle and quickly injected the cripple in the cleft between his middle and ring fingers.

The agent was succinylcholine, a paralytic drug used to induce muscle relaxation and short-term paralysis. It was commonly used to euthanize horses. A seven-milligram dose in humans caused complete paralysis in thirty seconds and death in three minutes. It shut down all muscular functions, including the diaphragm. Although it did not directly attack the heart, it did resemble a heart attack.

Mike and John looked at each other while holding their host in place. Thirty seconds elapsed. Then Mike checked his wristwatch and nodded. John held a small mirror under Burdis's nose and mouth before he pulled out a stethoscope and listened to the old man's heart. He motioned.

The two men donned surgical gloves, turned on the oxygen, and started wiping down everything they may have touched during their visit: glasses, chairs, windowsills, and doorknobs. After twenty minutes of cross-checking, they exited the study.

"Place the call," said Mike.

John's cell call was directed through two scramblers and a special trunk line before it reached the STU-III telephone unit sitting on the conference table in the corner office on the seventh floor of CIA Headquarters. A deputy director answered.

"Yes?"

"M and J calling."

"Report."

"Problem solved. The architect is retired," said John. "All doors are closed."

"Very good," said the deputy director. "What was the final tally on the Reservoir?"

"Two point six billion."

"Excellent. Debrief on Thursday at the usual location."

The line clicked dead.

Epilogue

In December 2006, General Augusto Pinochet died in a military hospital in Santiago. He was ninety-one years old.

In the months leading up to his death, Chilean investigators discovered ten tons of gold, worth an estimated $160 million, in Pinochet's name in a Hong Kong bank.

US Senate investigators uncovered a network of 125 securities and deposit accounts at Riggs Bank in Washington used by Pinochet and his family to launder tens of millions of dollars through foreign bank accounts.

In February 2009, Italian prosecutor Nicola Gratteri publicly stated that the control of the distribution of cocaine from South America to Europe had effectively made the Calabrian 'Ndrangheta the most powerful criminal organization in the world.

Rave Reviews for VILE MEANS

"VILE MEANS is an incredible suspense thriller in the vein of Tom Clancy's beloved political and military thrillers."

—IndieReader Approved, 5 STARS

"VILE MEANS...this epic spy novel offers an appealingly unique combination of action and suspense."

—BlueInk Review

"Dimodica crafts an intricately plotted spy game in VILE MEANS...A smart, layered spy thriller."

—KIRKUS REVIEWS

"VILE MEANS...is perfect for readers fond of historical fiction, spy dramas, or political thrillers."

—Portland Book Review

"VILE MEANS...is extremely intense and fast-paced...Dimodica knows his stuff."

—San Francisco Book Review, 5 STARS